WITCH'S HONOR

ANYA J COSGROVE

" Ever tried. Ever failed. No matter. Try Again. Fail again. Fail better."
- Samuel Beckett

GLOSSARY OF THE SUPERNATURAL

*A*conite. Sometimes called wolfsbane, monkshood, or Queen of all Poison. Can be distilled to make a highly efficient poison and hinders the power of a variety of demons and half-breeds.

Angels. Angels are one of the most peculiar demons there are. They propagate like some sort of parasite through the passing of cursed blood to dying but willing hosts. Their taste for dying flesh makes them appear at humans' deathbeds, and their incredible physical appearances spawned many legends. Their caste system is a mystery to anyone who hasn't been initiated to their way of life.

Bounty Hunters. Human scum. They hunt the supernatural for money. Kill on sight.

Cerberuses. What they lack in brains, they make up for in brute strength. They live in packs and are highly loyal allies. Their sense of smell is unparalleled.

Demon compass. There are three types of crystals that can be bewitched to darken as they are held over a map, or if an actual demon is present near them. The most powerful of all was crafted in the 1800s by a very powerful warlock. He is believed to have made four. Made of diamonds and blue apatite, they can pinpoint the exact location of a demon using just a drop of blood. The other models are fairly common, and their strength depends on the witch who crafted them.

Demon snare. Device made from a precious stone, blood from an original demon, and aconite. It incapacitates any member of the demonus genus for about a minute, longer if the demon is wounded and bleeding.

Divination. Divination is the ability to see the future. Some druids are known for a highly accurate recounting of future events. Witches are also suspected to possess this ability through spells and potions. A famous random witch at the turn of the first millennium was sold to a sultan and described his death and the fall of his empire in detail decades before it happened.

Evil bone. Bone harvested from an original demon's skeleton. The few pieces that still exist were shaped into weapons or jewelry. Priceless. Kills all kinds of demons.

Exorcism. The process of banishing a demon from a third party's body.

Furias. Parasitic demon who takes control of its host by short-circuiting its nervous system. Humans and animals are perfect hosts. Weakened demons might also be susceptible.

Mind reading and telepathy. Most supernatural beings can communicate telepathically. Reading thoughts and the inception of fabricated thoughts into a healthy mind is a rare and unreliable skill. Inception is not to be mistaken for possession or the replacement of one's mind by another entity such as parasitic demons. See Furias.

Possession. Demons are known to mark lesser species. The rituals vary among breeds, and the effects differ. Can be avoided by consuming a specially brewed tea, though the recipe is unknown.

Randoms. Random witches are born out of non-magic parents. They activate anywhere from a couple months to seconds before midnight on their twentieth birthday. They are usually less powerful and dangerous than proper witches, but it might be because the latter are trained since birth. They are left to their own devices. Easy to identify as most do not know how to mask their flare and auras, they sell for a nifty price on the slave market.

Seers. Humans attuned to the supernatural. They can see auras and sense magical flares. The gift is genetic and passed down generation to generation. A few families have been associated with demons for centuries, and those without loyalties are for hire.

Shadow Walkers. Powerful half-demons excelling in trickery, mischief and deceit. Only males. They mingle sparingly with other demons and half-breeds. Obsessed with consuming witch blood since the late 1900s, they fight fiercely for every drop available on the dark trade. Can regenerate quickly from wounds, though are susceptible to aconite, killed by evil bones and neutralized by large quantities of iron. They share a mental link through what they call the Collective, though the details and the extent of the connection are unknown.

Shifters. Shifters are able to transform their entire being or a part of their body into a human or animal shape. The shape depends on the sub-species.

Silver. Silver is used as a powerful ingredient in healing potions. It's also the only metal known to harm shifters.

True-born Witches. Proper witches belong to covens. They hide within society, craft potions and cast powerful spells to remain hidden. They breed between themselves and train their children from infancy. Captured, they will kill themselves to protect the many. The ones that threaten their secrecy die. It is unknown how many members they have, or how many covens there are. Stay away.

Vampires. Vampires are the most common supernatural species in existence. Contrary to popular belief, they reproduce between themselves. They do feed their blood to humans on occasion for its healing and strengthening abilities, and the strongest CAN turn humans into a barren, pale version of themselves. The most powerful families operate under a system of absolute monarchy and that has been upheld for centuries. They aren't immortal but live long enough to appear as such. Beheading works best. Sunlight and holy water are myths though a stake to the heart could work.

Vandellas. Powerful and rare half-breed demons sometimes confused with the deadlier succubus. Highly sexual, they feed on the desire they incite in their prey. Highly social, they get along with many species and are sought-after mates.

They are born human. The change usually happens around puberty, a process that's as mysterious as the creatures themselves.

1

MR. BRIGHTSIDE

Liam

*W*hoever coined the phrase *only a kiss* hasn't been kissing the right girl. Things are worse than ever before. I thought I could move on. I thought I could forget.

I'm a proud jackass.

The air electrifies every time we come within a few feet of each other, and I know she feels it too. The rush of blood to her freckled cheeks whenever our gazes meet only enhances her maddening scent. What used to be denial and cover-up is now lying bare between us.

Pandora's box lies in shambles.

She knows I want her.

She kissed me back, and it changes everything. Faint touches are no longer innocent, stolen glances mean more than they used to, and witty quips are automatically construed as flirtation. So we scowl, avert, and take turns hiding behind Thom.

Now that I know they're together, their shared laughter and hushed conversations shouldn't irritate me as much. I should be grateful they are not flaunting their happiness in my face because I sure as hell don't want to catch them making out again.

Maybe I shouldn't relish the fact that Alana always rips her hand away from his when I come into a room or that she hasn't sneaked into his bed since we kissed. Maybe I shouldn't notice these things at all. Maybe I'm allowed to feel however the fuck I'm feeling without guilt crushing me down.

Maybe time heals even the most odious cases of jealousy.

I guess we'll find out.

2

HEART ATTACK

Alana

"Show me again," I demanded.

Liam passed a hand through his black, spiky hair, and the illusions around us disappeared. "Alana, we've been doing this for the past five hours. If your parents had left you a message, you would have seen it by now."

Liam had agreed, at last, to take me through a magical reconstruction of my parent's house in case I could figure out where they'd gone. I'd sifted through his memories for hours and found nothing, but I refused to give up. They must have left me a clue leading to their hiding spot, and I was just too distracted to see it.

I tapped the floor with my foot. "Are you sure you're doing it right? Maybe there's no message because *you* missed it."

The demon leaned on the back of the couch, his white knuckles sinking into the gray cushions. "I showed you an exact replica of what I saw. Down to the last thread sticking out of the carpet."

"You might have missed something."

"I didn't."

Patience was wearing thin on both sides, our tones becoming

sharper and drier with every sentence. Liam and I excelled at bickering.

Thom, Liam and I had moved a week ago into our temporary home in Mobile, Alabama, and the volatile emotions following our brush-up with Frank had somewhat settled.

But dust settles, too, and makes a mess. We were all in a weird place.

Spending time alone with Liam was nerve-wracking to say the least, and I couldn't concentrate. I felt both hot and cold and smacked myself mentally every two minutes for thinking about the damn kiss. Whenever Liam stepped closer, my stomach twisted up in knots, and I didn't know how to move or stand without betraying my flustered state. To make matters worse, his new haircut was really sexy.

If you check him out one more time, I'll kick your ass. My rational brain was furious about the whole Liam debacle.

I gritted my teeth and said, "Show me again. From the start."

Liam grumbled. "Suit yourself."

The world around me bled back into my childhood home. I'd managed to keep my cool until now, but frustration and fatigue weakened my defenses.

My throat tightened at the crooked stairs of the front porch, the comfy living room sofa where Mom and I had enjoyed countless movie marathons, and the bright yellow kitchen with the small breakfast nook where I had devoured many of Dad's pancakes—all so real but only here because of Liam's magic. My heart longed for the familiarity of it all, and a bittersweet ache settled deep into my bones.

Last April, I'd healed my father after a bad fall. Mercenaries had abducted me so that a demon could harvest my blood. Thom and Liam had rescued me and educated me on the supernatural world, but I still yearned for the uncomplicated happy life I'd left behind.

Until I found out where my parents had gone, the gaping hole in my soul would remain.

One thing I knew for sure: they had packed before going. A few key things were missing from the kitchen and living room. The swiss clock Mom had inherited from her grandmother had been taken. The photo albums were gone, too.

Nothing was out of place in my bedroom.

The ball of sorrow in my throat burned at the sight of the black and white polka dot wallpaper on my bedroom walls. Without thinking, I tried to grab my fuzzy, pink pillow, but my fingers glided right through it.

Damn illusions.

I balled my fist and punched the air. "Ugh! What if the message is beneath something? I need to go there for real."

The whole scene disappeared.

"You need a break," Liam said.

My temper flared. "I can't afford a break. I need to figure this out. You're not helping."

His jaw clenched, and he looked to the side. "Then *I* need a break."

I raised my brows. Liam was a Shadow Walker, a demon with superhero strength and speed coupled with the ability to craft life-like illusions. He could create entire landscapes that looked as real and vivid as the real world. Since when did it exhaust him to do so? "*This* is tiring you out?"

"*You* are tiring me out."

Without thinking, I smacked his shoulder and growled under my breath as our eyes met for yet another staring contest.

This was normal for us... except our fights would never feel normal again.

The heavy atmosphere thickened as we struggled to tear our gazes away. His silver eyes darkened, and sweat gathered on the nape of my neck, my body heaving with shallow breaths.

He was like an exposed wire. If I got too close, I'd catch on fire.

"Death by spontaneous combustion" is not something I wanted written on my tombstone. Nor did I fancy, "she had to know what the poisoned apple tasted like" or "the wolf looked friendly enough."

I forced myself to pivot and walk away before covering my heated cheeks with my hands. *Stop letting him rattle you like that. Get it together.*

Thom walked through the green front door and created a nice

distraction. "Any luck?" he asked as he kicked off his shoes. His blond curls were all in disarray, and his white shirt stuck to his skin in the humidity.

I gave him a thousand-yard stare and sighed. He walked over and stroked my arm.

Liam focused his gaze on the corner of the room like it was the most interesting thing he'd ever seen. We had this bizarre act-as-if-nothing-happened dance figured out.

Contrary to what Liam believed, Thom and I weren't an item. I hadn't pretended we were, but I hadn't denied any of Liam's assumptions either. Why bother? Demons and witches were mortal enemies, and Liam would go mad consuming one tiny drop of my blood. It's not as if we would stop fighting long enough to share more than a kiss anyway.

Thom was the only one without blame, and I felt responsible for how his eyes didn't quite light up when he smiled. My actions and words had led him to believe I wanted us to be a couple, and I'd pushed the envelope as far as sleeping in his bed to fend off my nightmares. And not in an over-the-cover, please-keep-your-distance kind of way. We'd snuggled. A lot.

I hadn't sneaked into his room since the showdown with Frank, since Liam and I had kissed. Guilt kept holding me back. I'd had a huge crush on Thom for ages, so kissing Liam had been completely out of line. One part of my brain kept insisting that it was just a kiss, a heat-of-the-moment slip. The other argued that I had to come clean. A tiny, inconsequential third voice kept asking why kissing Liam had felt so good if it'd been such a mistake. Clearly, I needed a breather on the romantic front.

Or a big slap in the face.

I swiped my sleeve across my forehead and headed to the kitchen to get a glass of water. In three short strides, I reached the fridge.

This rental house was much smaller than the one in Virginia. It was a one-story ranch with an open-concept kitchen and living room, three bedrooms, and one full bathroom, plenty of space for three adults but not quite as private as the Walker's mansion.

The close quarters undermined my efforts to keep my distance from my roommates. I always seemed to need to shower at the same time as Thom and had already caught both brothers walking back to their bedrooms with just a towel around their waists.

That had done nothing to calm my raging hormones.

After my shopping spree with Lilah in Washington, I'd retired all my unflattering undies, replacing them with hot, lacy, colorful ones, and my legs were freshly shaved. Sure, I liked to feel good and look pretty, but I found myself making bolder, sexier choices with each passing day, and I didn't know why.

A smoking gun for my crimes, really. Maybe I was subconsciously preparing for a bad spur-of-the-moment decision. I was attracted to both of them: two witty, headstrong, six-foot-three brothers with killer abs and broad shoulders.

Spontaneous combustion was a real concern.

I gulped down a few mouthfuls of water and turned back to Thom. "Where were you all afternoon?"

He'd left before lunch to get groceries, but he'd changed his plans because he'd come back empty handed.

"I found her. The next potential," he said, excitement gleaming in his blue eyes.

Liam grabbed a ham sandwich from the fridge and sat down at the kitchen table. "Nice work."

Leaning against the counter, I asked, "How?"

We had only known she was nineteen and living in Mobile, not much of a solid lead.

Thom sat down next to his brother. "I brought Liam's sketch to the university."

My face creased with confusion. "What sketch?"

Thom reached into his shoulder bag and handed me a drawing of the girl in question. I gaped at the quality of the black and white close-up.

My brows raised. "I didn't know you could draw."

Liam shrugged and bit into his dinner like it was no big deal to doodle a lifelike portrait.

Thom grinned. "I figured a girl like that wouldn't go unnoticed. Her name's Rachel. She's enrolled there. I copied her file from the student affairs office." He tossed a pile of photocopies on the table.

I sat with my leg folded beneath me and picked them up. Rachel Thompson. Economics major. Her grades were average, but her attendance record was perfect. A thrill shot through my spine. We'd found a new witch to save. A witch like me.

I'd finally get an opportunity to help someone the way Thom and Liam had helped me. A chance to do good. A chance to spare someone the horrible fate of being abducted by the seers that had almost killed me last spring. A way to stick it to the clan of demons I was on the run from for the rest of my life.

"How did you know what she looked like?" I asked Liam.

He averted my scrutiny by concentrating on his meal and mumbled, "I saw her." Liam was linked to others of his kind by a mental tether, but he didn't like to talk about the Collective of demons chatting inside his head.

My eyes narrowed. We'd spent the entire afternoon together. "Why didn't you mention it earlier?"

He shrugged. "You only wanted to stare at your parents' house."

I pinched the bridge of my nose and forced my attention back on Thom. "What else did you find out about her?

"Not much. I checked out her address, and she lives with her parents in Park Hill. Nobody was home. I think we should case the place tonight and see if something is off in the neighborhood." He sat down and took half of Liam's sandwich. "You. Any idea where Frank is?"

The mention of the maniacal demon brought icy goosebumps to my neck.

Liam engulfed the last chunk of bread and dusted off his hands. "Nah. The Collective is stale. We're lucky I got a whiff of Rachel. Frank's actively trying to keep me in the dark."

After days of vigilance, expecting another attack, we'd come to the conclusion that Frank was taking a break from us. But for how long?

"Let's hope he's not getting ready to pounce again," Thom noted with his mouth curled down.

Thom was rarely pessimistic, and I felt obligated to cheer him up. "Maybe he moved on."

Liam bit my head off for my efforts. "Be realistic. This ends when one of us is in the ground."

I bit the insides of my cheeks. "You think I don't know that? I'm not stupid, but I can't live in fear 24/7."

"You should be afraid," Liam said, his mouth and fists balled. "Frank's obsession with you will only grow now that he has tasted your blood."

My chest tightened. "Stop freaking me out."

Liam waved dismissively like I was being dramatic. "We offered to stay in Virginia for a few weeks. You said no."

"Damn right, I said no."

All the Frank Hales in the world wouldn't be enough to convince me to sit on my hands while another witch was being hunted.

Thom rolled his eyes. He'd developed a sharp and uncompromising distaste for our fights. "First things first. Let's find the seer assigned to this new witch. Discreetly."

Seers could see auras and recognized untrained witches at a glance. Most of them profited from their abilities by spying on potential witches for powerful demon clans like the Shadow Walkers. I could see auras, too, but most witches couldn't, and I still didn't know what it meant.

I gnawed on my thumb thinking about Thom's analysis. "Wouldn't it be easier to just tell her that she might become a witch? We have plenty of ways to prove magic exists. She could help us find the seer."

Thom shook his head. "Any suspicious behavior on her part might alert the seer to our presence here in Mobile, which will send Frank straight to us."

"Have you ever thought about bringing the potentials to Virginia before they turn?" I was curious. This spying life was complicated as hell, and Liam detested complications.

"We did, once." Thom averted his gaze. "It didn't go well, and the guy didn't turn. So few of them do that it's better not to wreck their lives if it can be avoided."

"The less Rachel knows, the safer we all are," Liam added.

I nodded. If Rachel could steer clear of our world altogether, she'd be better off.

Thom grabbed a soda can from the fridge. "Her seer will cross her path at least once a day, so we need to figure out her schedule in order to spot who else is watching her."

"When is her birthday?" I asked, stealing a sip of Diet Coke.

"In six weeks," Liam said.

If she hadn't turned by then, she'd be safe, and we'd move on. Six weeks in Mobile... I'd better not get too comfortable. I was a nomad, now. For better or worse. I got up and retrieved my phone so I could mark the exact date on my calendar.

Liam grabbed his leather jacket and car keys. "The chances of her turning increase exponentially until the night of, so the sooner we find the seer, the better. I'll go for a quick recon. See if she's home. Text me the address."

Thom grabbed his phone. "You should take Alana with you."

I cocked my hip to the side and crossed my arms. "I don't need a babysitter anymore." I sucked at magic, but concealing my aura, though exhausting, had become second nature in the span of a few days. I didn't need to follow Liam around anymore.

When my life hinges on something, I'm somewhat capable. When success means that Liam has to stop bossing me around, I'm a paragon of accomplishment.

Besides, we'd already spent the day together. Playing spy at night in the car separated only by the stick shift would be awkward as hell, so I faked a yawn. "I'm pretty beat."

Thom gulped down his drink. "You want to help with surveillance, right?" He leaned closer, and his gaze bore into mine like he was appraising my reaction.

"Y—yes." It felt like a trick question because he knew the answer. As a potential witch on the Collective's radar, Rachel was priority number one.

"That's what I thought. Liam can explain how we operate and get you up to speed on the seers' usual M.O."

Liam worked hard to hide that he didn't want me to come, and I did my best to cover up that I didn't want to go. We ended up saying, "Okay, good idea," at the exact same time, and the words came out insincere on both sides. To my guilty ears, our distaste at being alone together was blatant and suspicious.

Thom scratched his neck, looking at us sideways. Whatever theory he had hoped to test with his sneaky suggestion, Liam and I had failed miserably.

Thom: 1 The guilty kissing party: 0.

3

WICKED GAME

Alana

*R*achel's house was a classic two-story colonial with light blue shutters and a white picket fence surrounding the freshly cut lawn. The cherry on the classic suburban sundae.

I craned my neck around to look at the other houses on the street. "We'll need to check her neighbors thoroughly."

My seer had been a neighbor of my parents, and the thought of him brought a bitter tang to my mouth. Liam handed me a leather bag.

I rummaged through the contents. "Night vision goggles?"

"*Military grade* night vision goggles. They're Thom's. I can see perfectly well in the dark."

"I bet you can." Nerves added to my usual snarkiness.

Since I no longer needed a bodyguard, I should have insisted that Thom be the one to teach me the ropes of seer hunting.

Liam's fingers drummed on his blue jeans, a gesture that betrayed his growing impatience. "You're extra bitchy tonight."

Ignoring the jab, I looked through the binoculars. "This is too creepy. My plan would be way more efficient."

I'd worked it all out. I would get to know Rachel and activate my aura. Anyone watching her would come for me instead, and voila! A seer on a silver platter.

Liam huffed. "You mean the part where we dangle you as bait? It might work. Or it might spook the seer and cause him to call for backup. If I was watching a potential witch and she suddenly turned up with a witch friend, I'd go to ground and figure my shit out. At best, it smells like a trap. At worst, it smells like a coven."

"Oh." I hadn't thought about that.

The surviving witches' covens were deemed incredibly powerful. Since Liam was adamant that both my parents were witches, logic dictated they belonged to one. I 'd been adopted as a baby but had never searched for my roots.

Maybe they were still alive. Maybe they had meant to protect me from the other coven members, especially if covens were as terrible as their reputation implied. We'd moved to Alabama to help Rachel, but I also wanted to find answers about my lineage. Covens were rumored to be particularly active in the South.

Liam was determined to never cross paths with one, but I hoped for the opposite. I'd seen enough demons. I wanted to meet other true-born witches like me.

When Liam had consumed my blood to spruce up his powers in order to save my life, he'd discovered my special pedigree. It weirded me out that Liam had tasted me. Not only my blood, but my soul, my essence. Like humans distinguished between different spices in a spaghetti sauce, he'd tasted that I was a true-born witch.

That bit of information had been totally new and amazing to me, but Liam had paid a big price for learning it. The small piece of knowledge had cost him dearly. He'd spent months barricaded in the basement, clawing his way back from his addiction to witch blood. There would be no further tasting of my blood to find out more about my origins. Not if I didn't want to end up dead.

A shiver tickled its way up my spine as I shot a glance to the demon on my left. *He almost devoured you that night.* "When you drank my blood, did it—"

"I'm not chatting with you about how your blood tastes." Liam's voice was breathless.

"Why not?"

His shadowy aura thrashed around him, and he leered at my neck for a fraction of a second too long for it to go unnoticed. "Because."

A hot flash blazed from my shoulder to my breasts. *He could still drink you now. He certainly wants to...* The desired fear-response refused to RSVP to my mental musings, and I rubbed my sweaty palms on my thighs.

"Why did you decide to come with us?" Liam said before adding fast, "besides the obvious, I mean."

The obvious being Thom.

"I want to help. What you guys do, it's worth doing. You saved me. Now, it's my turn." My eyes darted to the shadows dancing over his skin as they slithered in my direction. "Why do *you* do it?" I never got the sense Liam loved this hide-and-seek life.

He rubbed his jaw and looked out the window. "Because it's what my dad wanted."

Oh... He'd never talked about his dad. My chest tightened, and I had to fist my hand not to reach for his. Thom and Liam's parents had been killed years ago by a demon named Marcus Black.

I inched closer to Liam's seat. "I think my parents would want me to do this too, wherever they are."

"I think you're right," he breathed so low I barely heard it.

I bit my bottom lip and scanned the row of houses with the high-tech binoculars to see if anyone else was spying on Rachel, but all the curtains were drawn. The lights in Rachel's room ignited, and I zoomed in on her window. She was tall and thin, with long blond hair. Holding her cell to her ear with her shoulder, she spoke animatedly.

She set the phone down on her bed, probably on speaker because her lips were still moving, and shrugged off her jacket. She stripped down to her underwear, not bothering to close the curtains.

Uneasiness spread to the pit of my stomach. I pursed my lips and peeked at Liam from beneath my lashes. Was he enjoying the peep show? "Did you spy on me like that?"

The hand holding the steering-wheel twitched. "Aren't you glad I did?"

It annoyed me to no end how sensible he sounded when admitting to a misdeed. I clicked my tongue and flipped my hair behind my shoulder. No matter how reasonable he made it sound, the knowledge that I'd once been on the other end of this espionage operation crept me out. When Liam and I had met, he'd known every little detail about my life. Thom too.

I grimaced at the thought.

Liam shifted in his seat. "If you're wondering if Thom spied on you while you changed, you should ask him. I wouldn't expect the answer to soothe you, because he was utterly obsessed with you."

"You have no respect for privacy. Thom does," I snapped.

He stared ahead, not breathing. Not even blinking.

I flattened myself against my seat. "And I doubt he was utterly obsessed with me."

Liam snickered. "Yeah, sure. And I'm the worst. Got it."

My eyes narrowed. "May I remind you that you sneaked into my bed and watched me sleep? That's stalker 101."

His knuckles blanched.

Emboldened by his reaction, I added, "God knows what else you did while I couldn't see through your powers." I was mostly pushing his buttons. I'd searched many nook and crannies inside his head, and he'd done terrible things but not in the way I was implying.

Liam's breath hitched, his hand now clutching the wheel. "I'm not the only one keeping secrets. Frank let you get away unscathed. I was impaled to the wall, and Thom was locked away. You were at his mercy, but he vanished. You never told the truth about what happened in that room."

I bit the inside of my cheeks hard. "Nothing happened. I don't know why he left."

The falsehood heated my face. The memory of what I'd done that day haunted me. I'd killed a demon with one touch, and the rush had been incredible. My so-called powers weren't restricted to healing, but I didn't know what this new power meant, and, honestly, I wasn't ready to know.

The more time that went by, the heavier the secret got. I was afraid of Thom's and Liam's reactions if I confessed. Thom would have a theory or two, and Liam would add some doomsday hypothesis about my lineage to the mix. No, telling the boys wouldn't get me any answers, just trouble.

I had to concentrate on the only solid lead I had.

We'd found a photograph of our dads embracing each other in an old family album. The picture was our only clue to uncover the possible link between my adoptive father, Robert Mitchell, and Thom's and Liam's father, Daniel Walker.

I tugged on a rebellious curl. "About that picture. Any developments you forgot to mention?"

Liam passed a hand over his face. "We already discussed this. I have no clue how they knew each other and no way to find out." His tone was dry. He clearly hated the idea of his Dad keeping secrets from him.

I rapped a random pattern on my lap. "I want to take a look at it again."

"Be my guest." The lights in Rachel's bedroom flickered off, and Liam put the car in gear. "We'll work out a schedule to keep an eye on her. Break off the day in shifts."

I nodded. It was a very *Liam* way to announce that we wouldn't play spies together again anytime soon.

FRESH OUT of the shower the next morning, I tied a robe around my frame and knocked on Thom's door.

"Come in," he said, his voice gruff.

He had a major case of bed hair and rubbed his eyes, his sleepy gaze roaming over me from head to toe.

Wet hair, pink fuzzy robe, and naked legs. The lingering glance he gave the sash holding the robe in place made me gulp. I blushed, reconsidering the dress code for the next time I thundered into his room.

"Hey, I was wondering. Where did you put the picture of our dads?" I said too quickly.

"I have it here." He grabbed a book on the nightstand.

Wow. We'd both gone to bed thinking about this, which comforted me in my instinct that we were two peas in the what-are-you-waiting-for pod.

With my hands tucked deep in my pockets, I sat next to him.

The haze of sleep lifted from his face. "I found something last night while you were gone. There was another picture stuck behind the ones we looked at in the album. Check it out."

He handed me two photos. The first one was the one I'd already seen: three adolescents embracing each other and captioned *Rob, Dan and John, Summer 1972.* The second was new. Dad posed with Daniel in front of a huge oak tree. Long strands of Spanish moss hung from the branches, and the silhouette of a large building towered in the background. I flipped it around. *Rob and Dan, Fall 1973.*

"Lana, do you notice anything in the picture?" The spark in his eyes told me he was unto something.

"Not really. I'm still stunned that they knew each other."

He pointed to my dad's body. Gosh. They were wearing identical uniforms. Green vests and ties with red and silver stripes. My dad was wearing a black blazer, and Thom's dad had his propped over his arm.

My shoulders itched, and I met Thom's excited gaze. "They were classmates!"

Thom nodded. "Yep. They went to Bellegrave Academy in New Orleans. My dad and all my uncles graduated from there. It was a fancy live-in high school and tuition cost an arm and a leg."

A fancy school? Snobbish. Expensive. The anti-thesis of Dad. I grabbed my forehead, trying to wrap my mind around this. "Dad never told me he went to boarding school."

The photo was tangible proof he'd lived in Louisiana, at least for a time. The only hint at his life before he'd met my mother. "My paternal grandparents died long ago, and my dad was an only child, so I know next to nothing about his family. I never found it strange until now that I've never met other Mitchells."

If I could find someone who knew him then... How did Thom's dad fit into the picture?

"They were friends. Now that we know where they likely met, we can investigate."

My brows furrowed. "Did your dad's job have anything to do with adoption?"

He shifted on the bed. "My dad was an accountant until Liam was taken. Why? Do you think he had something to do with your dad adopting you?"

"It's too coincidental that they were friends."

His voice grew quiet. "I guess."

A disturbing and unwanted hypothesis latched on my brain. "And you're sure he never talked about me or my dad?"

"Liam would remember," he said with a decisive shake of the head.

There weren't many reasons why a man would call up an old friend to adopt a newborn baby girl and not tell anyone in his family. I bit my lips and psyched myself up to brush the delicate subject, my knuckles turning white against the edge of the bed. "You don't think he could have tried to cover-up... you know... a mistake?"

I couldn't believe I was implying that Thom, Liam, and I actually could be half-brothers and sister. Ick.

Thom's wide eyes shot up to meet mine, and he grimaced. "No. I'm positive. My dad had a vasectomy right after he had me. He always joked about how he'd closed down the baby factory." There was an obvious edge to his voice, but the question had to be asked.

As appalling and disturbing and completely terrifying as the possibility was, I had to know the truth. Before I kissed one of them again... even if there was a million to one chance.

I carefully worded my next question and paired it with a calm, pleading voice. "Would you mind terribly if we made sure? Your father must have been a lovely man, but I need to know 100%. Don't you?"

Thom's arms fell flat on his sides as his demeanor softened. "Is that why—" He stopped mid-sentence.

I raised a curious brow. "Is that why what?"

"Never mind." A smile tugged at the corner of his mouth, and his eyes glowed brighter. He entwined our fingers and gave my hand a gentle squeeze, something he hadn't done since our aborted kiss.

Did he think this was the reason why I didn't want to date him? I'd only thought of it now, but it made for a great explanation. Better than admitting I'd rejected him because I'd made out with his brother a couple of days before. Thom and I were great together. We laughed. We rarely fought. There was zero chance he'd kill me. After this was settled, I'd be Team Thom. 100%.

His new optimism gave me enough courage to look up DNA testing on my phone. "We only need a mouth swab, and we should have the results back in two to three weeks. They also test for first cousins, but the result isn't as accurate."

With a gentle nod, he said, "Okay."

I ordered the kit on-line, and it got delivered two days later. Thom came to my room with the package. We followed the instructions and packed everything back up.

As Thom stepped out in the hallway with the box under his arm, he paused and turned back to me. "Don't tell Liam, okay?"

I'd had no intentions of doing so, but I was curious as to why. "Why not?"

"I was four when you were born, but Liam was nine. He'll find the idea utterly ridiculous. Dad and Liam were crazy close, especially after... after everything. Mom was too emotional when we first got Liam back. He was violent and mean, in withdrawal from witch blood, as you know. Dad stayed by Liam's side day and night for months, practically willed Liam back to sanity. My brother will never believe Dad could have kept something so huge from him, and he'll resent us for taking the test," Thom explained, his face pained.

"I won't say a word," I promised.

Another secret. Great.

4

DO I WANNA KNOW?

Alana

$\mathcal{A}$ lengthy Google search of Bellegrave Academy revealed that it had burned down a while back, but a new school stood on its old grounds. I'd start there. Alone.

I needed to do something on my own. Thom was less commanding than Liam, but he was still used to doing things the Walker way. Efficient but uncompromising. It was hard to take the lead on anything without resistance.

As I neared the door and grabbed the keys to the brand-new blue Yaris Liam had stolen for me, I hesitated. There was another set of keys in the bowl. Liam's Vanquish was sitting in the driveway, and a grin slowly spread on my lips. It would be a thrill to drive the sleek sports car instead of suffering Liam's maniacal racing from the passenger seat.

Why not?

Without second-guessing myself, I pranced over to the driver's seat and started the powerful engine.

Every little push on the accelerator made the motor roar to life, and I finally understood what that damn flashy car was all about. It was about adrenaline, yes, but also about freedom. I could go anywhere and do anything, and that was priceless.

After spending months cooped up inside the Walker's residence, I appreciated little things, like driving alone, to a whole new degree.

The newfound independence was exhilarating, and all my senses were heightened. I lowered the windows and let the wind fly through my long strawberry-blond waves.

The road, the trees, even the air was different in the South. Especially in December, while the nature up in Massachusetts slept and waited for spring. Here, it soldiered on.

A few heads turned as I parked the car and climbed out.

The contemporary building contrasted with the older, Victorian houses and stores in the area. The teenagers chatting in the school yard were in uniform, a sight both bizarre and charming. I didn't think a school like this still existed.

As I waited in the hallway for the principal to see me, I looked at the pictures hanging on the wall. None of them showcased classes older than 1990.

The headmaster was an old, bald man with a serious face but warm eyes. "How can I help you Miss—"

We shook hands. "Winters. Nina Winters." The fake name vexed my tongue, and I hid my discomfort with a cough.

It was my first false identity, but it wouldn't be the last. A witch needs a lot of false papers to elude the long arm of the law.

I showed him the photo of my dad in front of the old school. "I was looking for any information you might have on Bellegrave Academy."

He scratched his beard. "It was an old-fashioned boarding school, and it burned down barely a year after this picture was taken."

I nodded. "Is there a record of students and teachers during that time?"

He shook his head. "I'm afraid that was lost in the fire. Why are you so interested in Bellegrave, if you don't mind my asking?"

I pointed to my dad. "This is my father. I'm adopted, and all I have is this photograph," I lied.

His gaze softened. "Newgrave was built three years later, to be bigger and less exclusive. Many teachers had found other jobs by then, but a few came back. Mrs. Adeline Lecompte taught for over 30 years and retired a few years ago. I can give you her address."

"That'd be great, thank you."

He perused through his desk for an old ledger, flipped through the pages, and scribbled an address on a small piece of paper. "Here it is. I hope you find what you're looking for."

I left the school grounds and walked the nearby streets, hoping to find the exact spot where the picture had been taken. A park captured my attention. I compared the trees in the picture, and, though they were bigger, it looked right. I searched and recognized the oldest tree. It was a southern live oak, thick with Spanish moss. Its canopy offered plenty of shade, the sturdy S-shaped trunk extending into gnarly branches. There was no mistaking it. My dad had been standing in this exact spot, thirty plus years ago. I sat on a nearby bench, and my fingers ran over my dad's teenage face.

Where are you? Why did you disappear? Have you always known what I was? If so, why didn't you tell me?

When I'd learned that demons were after me for my blood, I'd made the hardest decision of my life—to stay away from my loving parents. Their absence had carved a deep gash into my heart, but I'd kept my distance to keep them safe. I'd thought that they were innocents in all this and that they had no idea witches existed, let alone that their precious adopted daughter was one.

All my decisions had hinged on the belief that they were home safe, but they hadn't been. I'd been so sure they had no idea the supernatural existed that I hadn't asked Thom or Liam to confirm they were home. ASSumptions, as they say.

I used to picture my old life and imagine what it would be like to go back. I'd spent hours rehearsing believable explanations for my disappearance. My parents would hug me, and we'd cry. In a matter of seconds, everything would be normal and safe again.

That possibility no longer existed. No one was waiting for me back home.

A tangled mess of emotions consumed me. Even faced with proof that my father knew Thom's, I couldn't quite believe he'd known about all the otherworld stuff. Demons. Witches. Maybe he knew very little or was warned to watch for weird occurrences happening around his adopted daughter. Maybe he'd been advised to go into hiding if I disappeared. Maybe they'd packed and left under duress...

Conflicting hypotheses kept popping into my brain and prevented me from concentrating on solutions. I hated the unknown. Surprises equaled a lack of control.

I sat in the park long enough for the bright sun to reach its height in the powdery blue sky. My chest was tight, my muscles sore. I allowed myself to wallow, but not before I vowed to sweep the record clean and start fresh the next day.

My parents were out there, alive, and I would find them. There was no other option.

I entered the teacher's address in my phone and sighed. She lived all the way across town, and the fastest route would take about twenty minutes, not counting potential traffic, parking, and finding the right door. It would have made more sense to visit her that day, but my energy had fizzled out. If this teacher turned out to be a dead end, I'd simply be trampled by sadness. I was in no shape to continue, so I returned to the car and headed for Mobile.

I'd come back another time.

With music blasting from the speakers, I drove fast, eager to erase the bite of failure. When red and blue lights and a siren went off behind me, I cursed under my breath and pulled over.

I wasn't worried.

This was as good a time as any to test my fake I.D. I hadn't been reported missing, and my driver's license looked like the real deal. Speeding tickets were one thing I didn't have to worry about anymore, but my heart flip-flopped as the policeman walked towards me. The teenage girl inside me cringed in shame.

"Going a little fast, Miss," the policeman said as he stared at me through dark sunglasses.

I tilted my head to the side and bit my bottom lip. "Sorry, officer." I handed him my driver's license.

"Title and registration."

Without thinking, I reached over to the glove compartment, and my eyes widened as I realized my mistake. This was Liam's car. A leather pouch rolled down to the carpet, followed by a bunch of knives.

My eyes flew from the weapons to the officer's face.

His breathing hiked, and his brows knitted together. "Step out of the car, Miss."

Shit. Shit. Shit.

I obeyed. His eyes roved over me to check for possible threats, but I had no jacket on and wore form-fitting clothes. He seemed satisfied I wasn't hiding anything and pointed for me to wait a few feet away from the car. I checked his name tag. *Louis.*

He circled the vehicle. The knife tucked in my boot burned against my calf. I had put it there every morning since Frank, and I'd be in a world of trouble if Louis found it.

I remained poised and tried to look as contrite as I could. The clear blue sky had turned into the pinkish orange of dusk, and I wrapped my arms around my frame to keep from shivering.

When Louis opened the trunk, his eyes spelled trouble. His whole demeanor transformed, and he got a pair of cuffs from his belt. "Miss Winters, I'm going to take you down to the station."

He cuffed and escorted me to the back of the police car, keeping one hand on his gun. I cursed myself for not thinking this through. If I hadn't borrowed Liam's car, this kerfuffle would have been avoided.

I forced a deep breath into my lungs as he drove off.

When we arrived at the station, one of his colleagues met us out front.

"What have we here?" The younger policeman asked, his eyes roaming over me like I was a stick of candy.

"I don't know, Greg. I don't know," Louis answered.

A metal detector hung from the newcomer's belt, and I made a quick decision. "I have a knife tucked in my right boot."

The men exchanged a solemn glance, and Greg knelt down in front of me. I shifted my weight to the other foot, and he removed the small, sheathed dirk from my boot, his fingers lingering on my skin. *Ugh.*

Louis coughed. "I'll put her in a room for now. You can go."

Thank you, Louis.

He placed me in an interrogation room and passed the metal detector over me once more before he removed the handcuffs.

"Can I have my phone call?" I asked politely.

"Just sit tight."

My fingers rapped on the table in front of me as I considered the cameras blinking from the corners of the room. It was one thing to be stopped by a policeman. Being filmed and interrogated at the station was another. Demons had eyes everywhere, especially in law enforcement, and I was a sitting duck. Sweat gathered at the nape of my neck, the stuffy atmosphere of the room pressing down like a thundercloud on my shoulders. What if Frank was close and learned that Liam's car had been impounded? He'd be here within minutes.

My heart quickened, and I smacked myself for driving a car so recognizable that I might as well have been shooting fireworks from its sunroof.

THEY LET me stew in there for close to an hour before Louis and another policeman came back inside. Louis set a file in front of me while his colleague sipped his cup of coffee and stood in the back.

"Why would a twenty-year-old girl with no priors drive around with such an arsenal?" Louis asked.

"Arsenal?" I didn't mean to play coy since I genuinely had no idea what they had found beside the knives. Knowing Liam, it must have been some pretty twisted and unexplainable demonic trinkets.

Louis stared at a list in front of him. "Two hand guns, two sniper rifles, five grenades, surveillance equipment, three medieval swords, eighteen knives, throwing stars, a bone wrapped in leather, and a few items we could neither recognize or identify. You carry some nasty stuff around, Miss Winters. Never mind the fact that this flashy car of yours isn't registered anywhere. Now, I might be able to help you, but I have to know what's going on."

"The car isn't mine," I admitted on a sigh.

"I thought so." He tugged at the end of his mustache, happy with himself. "Whose is it?"

I opened my mouth to answer, my first instinct to obey law enforcement, but thought better of it. *Whatever I tell him won't make a difference, and the longer I'm in here the more I attract attention.*

If they hadn't already, they would photograph and inventory Liam's supernatural armory, and that'd be bad. I pressed my lips together. "I want my phone call."

Both officers clicked their tongues and exchanged a knowing glance. The one drinking coffee set his cup on the table and handed me a cell phone. "Here."

Luckily, I had memorized Thom's, Liam's, and Lilah's numbers. I didn't want to have to depend on my phone in an emergency. Thanks to my lengthy kidnapping experience, I knew how fast someone could take it away.

Fingers on the screen, I hesitated, but dialed Thom's number.

He answered on the second ring.

"Hey, it's me." My greeting came out rough.

I pictured Thom's jaw clenching on the other end of the line because his voice was rushed and dripped with worry as he asked, "Where are you?"

"I'm at the Mobile County Sheriff's office."

"Thank God— I mean why? Sorry, I thought Frank…"

"No, I'm okay. I got arrested for speeding. And there was stuff in the car." I whispered that last part, and Louis raised a brow, probably thinking I was talking to my accomplice.

"I'm on it."

"Thank you." I shot both men a severe gaze. "My lawyer is coming. I won't be answering any questions without him."

My goal to shut the interrogation down succeeded. Both men got out of the room, and I was left to my mix of worry and boredom for another hour. My nails were in pieces by the time the door to the interrogation room opened again.

To my surprise and dismay, it wasn't Thom, but Liam who'd come to the rescue.

Greg, the perv, held the door open and then walked in behind him. Liam had used his powers to project a glamor that made him look like he was wearing a uniform rather than his leather jacket. I could see through the crafted illusions but played along with the glamor instead. I'd never seen Liam in a suit.

Louis whizzed inside the interrogation room and placed himself in front of Liam. "What's going on here?"

Liam gave me a hard look and handed a stack of fake papers to Louis. "Thank you, officer. This car thief has been a real problem for us."

Car thief? What the hell is he saying?

Liam showed a make-believe ID to Louis who raised a suspicious eyebrow. "The FBI deals with stolen cars, now?"

"She has stolen a vehicle related to a series of murders in Georgia and Florida. We want to make sure she isn't involved," Liam said, a smile threatening to show on his lips.

"But her record showed no trace of this?" Louis asked, unconvinced.

"It's a federal matter, sir, but we do appreciate your vigilance."

Greg gave his colleague a nod. "He's legit, Louis, I checked him out."

Louis scratched his neck but stepped aside.

Liam came to stand next to me, no trace of humor left in his demeanor. "Stand up and face the desk, Miss. Palms on the table."

I frowned at the ridiculous demand but obeyed anyway.

A rush of heat washed over my body as Liam fucking frisked me in front of the policemen. He patted my arms, waist, and legs. I swallowed hard when his fingers trailed the inside of my thighs, his touch lingering well beyond police standards.

"What are you doing?" I asked telepathically.

It was frighteningly easy to communicate with Liam this way. A lot like thinking to myself but louder.

"I'm cuffing you," he answered.

Cuffing didn't seem to cover the amount of touching involved. *"Why?"*

"I want to make it believable."

"You could make them think you're cuffing me." The cold metal of a pair of cuffs glided against my wrist.

"What would be fun about that?" Mischief perspired through every word.

Liam manhandled me to the Vanquish. He had used a glamor to make it look like a typical black sedan. He opened the back passenger door and motioned for me to sit. "Watch the head."

I scowled. "This is ridiculous. Uncuff me."

"Nope."

"Can I at least sit in the front?" He knew I struggled with motion sickness.

"Nope."

I huffed. The obnoxious invasion of privacy had frazzled me. Things were simply not the same. My skin tingled everywhere his hands had roamed, and I felt breathless.

He slammed the door behind me and climbed into the driver's seat.

As we sped off, I frowned. "You went to get the car before you got me?"

Liam met my gaze in the rear-view mirror. "Of course."

I stuck my tongue out. "Do you have any leads on Rachel's seer?"

"I spied on a few students while Thom followed her, but they all checked out." He hiked his sleeves up. "You disappeared all day."

I held his suspicious glare. "I needed air."

His head tilted to the side like he was measuring the truth in my words. "Frank's out there. Watch yourself."

I nodded, cold tingles scurrying across my shoulders. "Aren't you going to tell me to stay home?"

The corners of his mouth curved upwards. "I know better than to give you rules."

I found myself grinning, too.

Once home, Liam opened the door so I could get out of the car.

I jiggled the cuffs. "When are you going to remove these?"

He tucked his chin up and crossed his arms. "When you apologize for stealing my car."

I rolled my eyes. "I'm sorry."

His brows raised. "I don't think you meant that." The light chuckle coloring his words bordered on snicker territory.

I summoned the best cajoling tone I could muster. "Sorry, oh bright and powerful one."

His thumb rested against my left wrist for half a second before he withdrew. "On second thought, Thom can help you with them. He's the one you called, after all." The humor lifted from his voice at that last part, and he walked away.

I frowned. "What about Rachel? It's my turn to watch her."

"I'll do it." He dropped my purse on the step, got back into his precious car, and drove off.

I had to contort myself to reach the doorknob, but it was locked, so I knocked.

Thom opened the door a minute later. "Why are you outside? Didn't Liam get your keys back?"

"He did, but as you can see, my hands are tied behind my back." I wet my lips. "Liam wanted to teach me a lesson."

A huge grin spread on Thom's face as I showed him my predicament.

"Don't laugh. Don't encourage him," I said.

Thom covered his mouth with his hand. "You stole his car."

I glowered. "How is it *his* car? Everything we own has been stolen."

He sobered up. "Okay, okay. Come with me. There must be something strong enough in the garage to cut these."

Thom found a huge pair of metal scissors and cut the chain holding the two cuffs together. "Better wait for the key to get rid of the actual cuff.

I nodded in agreement.

Since Liam had taken over "Rachel Watch", I helped Thom make dinner, but I couldn't help thinking about Liam's hands on my body as we cooked.

Around ten, I heard the demon return home and knocked on his bedroom door three times before he opened it. He braced his lower-arm on the doorframe, and his eyes traveled to my wrists. A wry grin tugged at the corner of his mouth. "Nice bracelets."

My death glare only widened his smirk. "Where's the key?" I asked, a sharp edge to my voice.

He shrugged. "No clue."

My jaw clenched. "I hope you're kidding because I'm not sleeping with these on."

"You might like it…"

He was saying crap to annoy me, and it was working. But bondage would never be something I'd be interested in. Not after Frank.

I still had marks from that night. I hadn't been able to heal them.

"Stop messing with me, Liam," I growled.

"Relax. Here." His fingers brushed my skin as he tore the cuffs away like paper. A frown darkened his features as he touched the purple blemishes on my wrists. I guess he'd been too keen to cuff me earlier to notice them.

"You didn't heal them," he said quietly.

I scratched the carpet with the tip of my toe. "I can't, okay. I tried."

"But you can do everything else."

"I know."

He grabbed my lower arm and turned it over to examine the bruises. "That's not normal."

"I figured."

His eyes flicked up to meet mine. "You could have said something."

The heat of his hands radiated up my arms, and my lips pressed together. "Like you're Mister Openness."

His shadows caressed my skin as he grazed my pulse point, and a line of ants climbed up my spine. *Does he always have to be so intense?*

To my extreme displeasure, I noticed things about him I'd never noticed before like how his aura darkened when he was mad. And he didn't shave everyday. The shadow of a stubble was visible one day out of two, and I wondered if it was rough to the touch.

It's an infatuation. That's all.

Liam was Walker-tall, scary-but-sexy-dark, and handsome like the devil. His broody quality enhanced the mysterious bad boy factor, and clearly his silver stare had gone to my head.

A crush. Nothing more. The luster of Liam would fade, in time, and I would go back to thinking of him as an annoying roommate.

He let go of me, and I breathed deep.

"Try to heal them again." His voice cracked and spelled out how shaken he was to see these marks on me. Beyond the black and blue, they symbolized Frank's hold on our lives.

Instead of taking offense at Liam's command, I nodded. His haunted expression warranted a bit of slack. "I will."

He stepped closer, scrutinizing me. "I mean now. I might be able to figure out why it's not working. Try."

The heat of his body dizzied me, and I strained to keep my breathing steady. My nerves and imagination went into overdrive.

There was no chance he'd kiss me again. Not here, outside his room, where Thom might see. *God. What happened to being Team Thom?*

As I avoided Liam's hypnotic stare, a searing warmth blazed through my body. I wet my lips at how his black shirt hugged his torso and wondered how his muscles would feel underneath my fingers. Regret pinched my chest for not finding out when I'd had the chance, but this fleeting notion got quickly smothered by my cautious nature. I couldn't afford to feed this crush. It would ruin me. *He's childish, impatient, uncompromising and not human. Stop looking at his lips, for God's sake.*

Blood rose to my cheeks, my mind too far in the gutter to entertain witchcraft, but I pushed the restless energy forward. Static electricity arched from my fingertips to the purple marks, but they remained.

I let go of my wrist and brushed my hair back, forcing my thick mane behind my ears. I expected to meet Liam's patronizing glare, but he was distracted too, focused on a stranded curl that licked my tattooed breast. Its loopy end barely touched the head of the snake.

Liam swallowed as he stared at the tattoo. His hand twitched, raising slightly before he returned it to his side and curled it into a fist. The flash of hunger in his eyes rattled me to my core.

He dragged his attention back to my bruises, and I let out a shaky breath.

I'd had the tattoos since Liam had carved a piece of his soul into me. According to him, the intimate bond created by the ritual was stronger than he'd anticipated and allowed him to track me wherever I was. I'd never had an inkling that he paid attention to them until now.

To demons, these marks equated to ownership, a concept that disgusted me, but it wasn't disgust that twisted my stomach at the moment.

I did my best to sound unaffected as I said, "It's not working. I better go to bed and try again in the morning."

Liam cleared his throat. "Yes. You'll be more focused if you're rested."

We were both lying. I cursed myself inwardly and tightened the long-sleeved romper around my frame. The tension hung in the air as we both waited a bit too long before heading to our rooms.

Once my bedroom door closed behind me, I tapped my forehead against it and groaned.

Will things get better? Or will it get progressively more awkward until we can't stand to be in the same room together?

My tiny, derisive inner critic added, *or until you end up naked in his bed.*

5

HUMAN

Alana

Sunglasses and ear buds on, I followed a few steps behind Rachel as she made her way to school the next afternoon. Her perfectly aura-less figure glided along the sidewalk, confirming that she hadn't turned. The plan was to get a rundown of her routine, but in addition, I also watched the people crossing our paths. If I got lucky, I might catch her assigned seer.

I was so busy scanning the faces around us for someone who looked too familiar or too out of place that I unconsciously increased the pace and bumped into her. *Shit.*

"Sorry." I tucked my shoulders in and walked past her with long strides. Thank God, a hood was covering my hair. My sight zeroed-in on the nearest building, and I hurried inside. Adrenaline fisting my stomach, I rested my head against the nearest wall and inhaled, eyes to the ceiling.

You suck. I blew hair slowly out of my mouth.

It was only a matter of time before she would notice me. Long fiery hair isn't exactly nondescript, and all the ponytails, hoodies, and sunglasses in the world wouldn't make up for my total ineptitude at shadowing.

I cut my shift short and returned home.

"What are you doing here so early? Did something happen?" Thom asked as I pried off my shoes.

My shoulders sagged. "I bumped into her."

Liam snorted from the couch and stretched his arms over his head.

I threw him a nasty look. "I need a new approach. I want to audit one of her classes until the end of the semester and spark a friendship. We'll have better access to her schedule, and it'll be more interesting than trailing ten steps behind her."

"Well, maybe—" Thom started.

"This is such a bad idea I can't even—" Liam said at the exact same time.

I interrupted them. "Thom became my friend, and nothing bad happened."

Liam jumped to his feet. "And this is exactly why I was against it. Just because it didn't blow up in our faces that one time doesn't mean it's a good idea."

I could only imagine how annoyed he'd been at Thom for giving me his real name and spending time with me. "Still, it helped that I already knew him. It made for an easier transition."

Liam rolled his eyes. "Are you hoping Rachel will crush on you?"

I clicked my tongue, my mouth set in a pout. "No."

"Then it's not the same thing at all."

I lunged at him and put myself in his face, invading his personal space, about ready to wrap my hands around his neck. "Oh, you just love to disagree with me no matter what I say." Liam's nostrils flared, the corner of his mouth tensed, and his eyes widened like he was warning me off, but I ignored him. "If you'd come up with the idea, you'd expect us to fall in line and follow you blindly. Two words: God Complex."

His teeth gritted together. "I'd never come up with such a *ridiculous* idea."

"You're full of ridiculous ideas."

"And you're full of—" he stopped.

"Say it!"

His body inched towards mine before he retreated all the way to the wall and shoved his hands into his pockets.

Thom stepped into my peripheral vision and threw his arms in the air. "ENOUGH. Lana can give it a try." Liam opened his mouth, but Thom added, "and your inflexible opinion is noted."

As the tie-breaker, Thom was often put in the middle, but it was the first time he sided with me on a supernatural matter. I cocked my hip to the side and threw Liam a sassy smile.

EQUIPPED with a school bag and a cute notebook, I showed up to Rachel's afternoon class, eager to graduate from stalker to undercover agent.

The classroom allowed for about fifty students, and I couldn't believe my luck when I saw the seat next to Rachel was one of the last spots available. I gave her a polite smile as I sat next to her. Her stunning beauty was even more intense up close, her golden skin glowing.

My red waves came with freckles, and my alabaster skin had the tendency to roast in the sun, not to mention its quasi-continuous blush-a-thon.

Thinking it'd be a nice ice breaker, I unpacked everything but a pen, feigned to fumble around in my bag, and winced as I came up empty-handed. "Hi. Sorry to bother you. Can I borrow a pen?"

"Sure." She reached in her fancy shoulder bag and passed me one. Her perfect French-manicure made me consider my gnawed fingers, and I vowed to stop biting my nails.

"Thanks."

"No problem. Where are you from?"

My accent was so different from everyone around, no wonder she'd asked that question. "Boston. I'm Nina." I wondered whether I should extend my hand but settled for a smile and a tilt of the head.

"Rachel."

"Nice to meet you."

The lecture started, interrupting our conversation. Some students slouched over their desks to nap, a few whispered quietly to each other, others typed on their phones, and the rest listened or at least pretended to take notes.

The insane familiarity of the scene slammed into me like a twelve-foot wave.

I'd opened a window into the past, into the normalcy I'd left behind all those months ago. With it came a cold aftertaste of grief at losing my parents, my friends, and all the preconceptions I'd had about my life after college. A home, a nice job, good friends, a husband and 2.5 kids down the road. My traditional, safe, and perfectly boring but acceptable plan had been blown into pieces.

A dark intuition spiraled in my bones, telling me I would never stay in one place long enough to graduate college. Thom, Liam and I were in survival mode, and there was no guarantee we'd last the coming year, let alone live long enough to have children. Saving Rachel and finding my parents encompassed my entire long-term plans, and I didn't dare jinx myself by thinking about a less immediate future. The implicit faith that life would work out had deserted me.

I chatted up Rachel again during the break.

"This class is hard to follow," I said, hoping she wouldn't want to talk about the lecture since I hadn't listened to a word.

"The teacher loves the sound of his voice." She let out a soft feminine chuckle. "So, Boston, huh? I would kill to live on the East Coast."

"Yeah, it's great." Nostalgia tainted my voice.

Rachel features softened. "You just moved?"

"Yeah."

"Give me your phone." She entered her number in my contacts and sent herself a text. "Here. Call if you feel like getting a cup of coffee, and I'll show you all the great places around campus."

Yes! I put my hand over my mouth to cover a big smile. I was in. *Nina* was a good spy, and this idea didn't suck as much as Liam had implied. "Thanks. I'll hold you to that."

"I expect you to. Must be hard to move here when you're used to Boston."

Pride swelled in my chest. If I hung out with her a lot, I'd be able to find the seer much quicker. "There's not many new students around..." I trailed off. I was checking to see if a stranger had introduced himself to her recently.

She wrinkled her nose. "This town is boring. You've been warned."

"Boring isn't so bad."

A hint of curiosity sparked in her eyes. "Why did you move?"

My shoulders sagged. "It's complicated."

She immediately leaned closer, letting me know that my evasiveness intrigued her. I decided to play up the mystery card to keep her interest.

Rachel tied her hair up into a bun. "Do you live on campus?"

"No. I live with family not too far from here."

"I live with my parents, and I can't wait to move out. It's time, you know? I'm almost twenty."

The teacher started up again.

I peeked into her planner as she scribbled the week's assignment into it. Her handwriting was meticulous and elegant, but I was more interested in her schedule for tonight and tomorrow.

Liam's voice suddenly thundered in my head. *"Everything good in there?"* He asked.

Rachel stifled a yawn as I answered, *"Yeah."*

"Seen anyone suspicious?"

Between the anxiety and the over-thinking, I'd stopped looking for people who appeared out of place or glanced too often in Rachel's direction. *"Not really."*

"What's on your mind?"

Our mental conversations had one big drawback. They had a flavor to them that had nothing to do with tone of word choice. I was either not skilled enough in telepathy, or it was impossible to mask the emotions lacing the words like with real speech.

"Nothing."

"Liar."

I pinched the bridge of my nose.

. . .

AFTER CLASS, I met up with Liam to gloat over my success.

Perched on a bench outside the building with his ear-buds on, he surveyed the people scurrying out of class. His eyes jumped from one student to the next, but he found no one suspicious enough to retain his attention, because he stood up as I drew near. A gush of wind made me shiver, and I rubbed my cold arms.

He rolled his headphone cord around his case and tucked it in his leather jacket. "You talked to her."

"Yes. She offered to take me out for coffee, so I daresay it went well enough." I raised my brows, challenging him to say otherwise.

He looked to the sky. "I'll take the next shift."

The sound of footsteps drawing near distracted me, and I craned my neck around.

Rachel was hurrying in our direction. "Nina, you forgot your phone."

I took it from her hands. "Thanks."

Her gaze jumped from me to Liam, and a smidgen of heat appeared on her cheeks. "Hi, I'm Rachel."

"Mike."

I arched an eyebrow at him. He could have chosen to be invisible, so his decision to introduce himself threw me for a loop.

Rachel smiled. "Are you Nina's boyfriend?"

We both answered too quickly, "No!"

"He's err—my cousin," I lied.

"Your cousin?" Liam's amused voice resonated in my head.

Rachel's lips curled up, and she tucked a strand of hair behind her ear. "You study here?"

Liam shook his head. "No, I'm here to pick Nina up."

"That's nice. You moved here recently, too?" She was flirting with him, her southern accent slightly emphasized.

"Nah. I've been here for a year. I live in College Park."

Rachel's eyes almost sparkled when he mentioned the neighborhood, and she played with her necklace, bringing attention to her chest. "I live in Park Hill."

"We're practically neighbors." Liam's congenial tone was devoid of his usual snark, and I gawked at him. Why was he so friendly?

Rachel tilted her head to the side, her long hair blowing in the wind, and looked him up and down. "I have to go, but maybe I'll see you around?"

"You bet."

"Nina, call me for coffee like we talked about, okay?" she added before walking away.

"Sure."

She turned to give Liam one last glance before heading back inside.

I played with the hem of my shirt. "She's into you."

He shrugged. "It was your idea to infiltrate her life."

"I guess."

"Then what's the problem? You're giving me your disapproving face."

Why are you encouraging her to flirt with you? "I have a disapproving face?"

"Yes. You get two little creases between your brows, and your lips curve downward in a half-grimace."

My tongue pressed against the roof of my mouth. "Thanks. Now, I'm not only depressed, but I also feel hideous."

There was a long pause before Liam asked, "What's gotten into you?"

Since when was Liam insightful? Couldn't he be taciturn and distant like every other day?

I scoffed and buried my hands in my pockets. "I'll see you later." I left Liam to his "Rachel Watch" and stomped off to the parking lot.

Maybe he shouldn't bother to make himself invisible. I'm sure she wouldn't mind if he followed her home.

I opened the car's door wide, and it closed behind me with a loud bang.

I needed a long workout to blow off steam.

We'd rearranged the basement to continue my sparring lessons, and I practiced my katana moves almost every day. My technique had improved loads, but unfortunately my weapon of choice was not travel-sized, so I also played around with the dagger.

Today though, I opted for boxing instead of my usual routine. The punches started out as rhythmic, calculated thuds, but it wasn't long before they escalated into brute force attacks punctuated by grunts.

He criticizes my idea to introduce myself to her and then does the same.

Him and his double standards.

He can shove them up his sullen, pessimistic ass.

The shocks to my joints and ligaments radiated outward into my entire body, and the dull, repetitive pain weakened the day's frustrations, one punch at a time. Thankfully, I'd taken the time to correctly wrap my hands.

After I worked up a good sweat, I showered and met Thom in the living room. He'd unpacked a week's worth of groceries and looked desperate for a break from the household chores.

"Want to watch a movie?" I asked as he crashed down on the sofa.

"Sure."

I skipped to the kitchen to pop a bag of popcorn while he shouted movie titles. The microwave beeped, and my mouth watered at the smell. Returning to the living room, I sat crossed legged on the plush gray sofa next to him and tackled the arduous task of untangling my wet waves.

Thom settled the bowl in his lap. "Yum." His fingers dug with enthusiasm into the buttered, inflated corn. It was about the only thing I could cook properly. "Are you in the mood for a classic or a new release?"

"I don't care as long as it's funny."

He smiled. "I like your attitude."

He browsed through Netflix for a light comedy, and my brain disconnected as I nibbled on the popcorn and watched the screen.

These movie nights had become a tradition in the last few months, and my entire body relaxed. It was so easy, so effortless, so fluid.

I unfolded my legs from beneath me and sprawled them out on the ottoman. Thom put the bowl down and draped an arm over my shoulders. Out of habit, I snuggled up against his side and reached for the wool throw to cover our bodies, but my hand clenched around the fabric instead.

Were movie-night cuddles off-limits, too?

I almost straightened up but didn't. If Thom noticed my hesitation, he didn't say. His eyes were glued on the screen as he drew slow circles on my shoulder with his thumb.

The comfort Thom offered so naturally was addictive. It was easy. Normal.

Uncomplicated.

I never sensed that his actions had strings attached. The constant, judgy voice pestering me these days was mine, not his. A distorted version of mine. Shrill. Pessimistic. I struggled to draw the line between what I thought was proper and my actual emotions. Besides, snuggling was more normal for us than not. If I was going to succeed in rewiring my rebellious heart strings, I had to encourage such behavior.

I still lacked the courage to come clean about kissing Liam but felt it was a necessary step. If Thom found out while we were dating, it'd ring like a betrayal, and with all the supernatural shit going on, no secret was 100% safe. God, I was so NOT ready for that conversation...

Letting my head rest against Thom's chest, I closed my eyes, enjoying the heat of his body and the calm his arms offered me. I'd get my feelings in line and start fresh.

Soon, but not tonight. Tonight, I just wanted to watch a movie with this great guy I liked. The insubordinate, self-destructive part of me that was crushing on his brother could go to hell.

6

EVERYTHING AT ONCE

Alana

A string of feel-good rock songs blared from the speakers as I drove to the heart of New Orleans the next day. Avoiding another brush with law enforcement was imperative, so I took great care not to speed.

Mrs. Lecompte lived in the famous French Quarter, and I parked as close to the river as I could, eager to visit the area. The neighborhood was guarded by the Mississippi, and a paved sidewalk allowed for a nice stroll right by the edge of the water.

The long drive from Mobile had eaten away most of the afternoon, so the gentle winter sun was already going down in the sky. I walked across the wooden ramp traversing the three rows of train tracks and admired the view. A young couple was sitting by the water, holding hands and whispering in each other's ears without a care in the world. For a second, I envied them. In another life, it would have been me and Thom.

With a voluptuous chocolate-hazelnut coffee from a local bakery in-hand, I explored Jackson Square, admiring the southern vegetation. The lampposts were adorned with big red bows for the coming holidays, and yet most trees still flaunted their green leaves. The Northerner in me would never get used to it.

In the back of Saint-Louis Cathedral, the statue of Christ, arms raised to the sky, greeted me. The ominous effigy cast an enormous shadow on the white church, and a large clock at the top reminded me of the clock tower from *Back to the Future* where Doc catches the lightning strike.

The impressive buildings surrounding the church took up entire blocks, their brick exterior switching from red to sand-colored with no clear pattern.

On Saint-Peter Street, most first-floor real estate displayed a wide variety of shops and restaurants. Because the condos and apartments were located on the second and third floors, I struggled to find the right address, unfamiliar with the maze of back alleys. Balconies towered above me, wrapping around the whole block. White wooden windows were set at regular intervals, the tight buildings blending into one another with no space to spare. After I found the right door, I double-checked the teacher's address on my phone and rang the bell.

A good minute passed before an old woman answered. "Yes?"

"Sorry to bother you. Are you Mrs. Adeline Lecompte?"

She nodded. "Yes."

I approximated her age to be around 70, the deep wrinkles and sun-battered skin not tarnishing the intelligence that shone through her sharp, brown eyes.

"I was told you used to teach at the Bellegrave Academy?" I asked, hope quickening my speech.

"Yes."

"I wanted to ask you a few questions if you don't mind. I think you taught my father in the 70s."

"That's very possible." She reached around her neck for her glasses and used one crooked finger to prop them up on her nose. As she took my appearance in, she drew in a small breath, and the steady hand grasping her cane wavered.

Her gaze roamed over me from head to toe and lingered on my hair before she opened her door wide. "Come in, child."

I followed her inside, her peculiar reaction sparking a flurry of questions in my suspicious mind.

Did she recognize me? It sure seemed like she had, but my mind was drawing a blank.

We went up a daunting flight of narrow stairs that opened into a quaint kitchen. The flowery wallpaper had paled over the years, and the appliances looked like they had been there since the late 1980s. Lacy curtains that used to be white wafted in the early evening breeze.

Mrs. Lecompte motioned for me to sit. The antique metal chairs surrounding the matching kitchen table looked like they would crumble under my weight.

Her small hands shook as she put an old-fashioned kettle on the stove. "What's your name?"

"Nina. Nina Winters."

She mumbled to herself and got a few scones from a tin box while I pried the picture of my dad from my purse and laid it on the table.

"Do you by any chance recognize those boys? My dad is the one on the left." I searched her face for signs of recognition.

Still standing, she grabbed the picture and pursed her lips. "Mmm, I don't recognize him. He must have transferred out before senior year." She tapped lightly on the face of Thom's dad. "Him I recognize. Daniel Walker was a timid, lovely boy. His father was an atrocious man."

She handed the photo back to me and served two cups of tea. I wasn't thirsty since I'd just finished a large coffee, but I sipped from the delicate flowery teacup all the same.

Mrs. Lecompte grabbed a tissue and cleaned her small glasses. "How did you get my address?"

"The headmaster of the Newgrave Boarding School gave it to me," I explained, hoping she wasn't offended.

"I hope for your sake you didn't come on his behalf." The congenial tone was gone, replaced by a pained but confident drawl.

My forehead crunched in confusion.

What was she talking about? "On whose behalf? My father's?"

"Your demon, child."

48

"My w—" I stopped mid-sentence. My vision blurred as if a glassy fog had perspired through the walls, and I grabbed my suddenly feverish forehead. An unstoppable need to sleep overwhelmed my senses, my legs like solid lead below me, and I rested my head on the table. A pasty jasmine aftertaste clogged my tongue.

"Sleep now."

The last thing I saw before everything went black was her frail hand tightening around an old-fashioned, corded telephone.

A HUMONGOUS HEADACHE radiated outward as I regained consciousness and made me want to bust my skull open with a hammer. My wrists were bound together behind my back. *Hell, not again.* A poignant fear that Frank had taken me prisoner escalated my sluggish heartbeat into a furious fanfare.

Before I opened my eyes, voices reached my ears. "Thanks for calling me first, Adeline." The assertive feminine voice didn't ring a bell.

"I was torn, Faye, I'll admit it. She wears the devil's marks, but she looks so much like Jane."

"That she does."

The memories from my meeting with the old Adeline stumbled back into place. She'd drugged me, but why? And she'd grabbed the phone to call this other woman?

I forced my eyes to remain shut as I listened to the hushed conversation between the two women, hoping to shed some light on my predicament.

"It makes no sense. You checked for the usual, right?" Faye said.

"Of course. She has no glamor and no active enchantments. She wasn't carrying anything beside the picture I showed you and her purse. I went through it and found car keys, lipstick, ibuprofen, and a tampon. Nothing noteworthy."

Despite my best efforts not to move, I squinted, surprised at the mention of glamors and enchantments.

"Shh. She's conscious."

I opened one groggy eye then the other, and two faces came into focus.

From one side, the wrinkled Adeline was assessing me through thin lips. On the other, a tall woman in her thirties paced the cramped room. She had short, spiky, black hair, but the light shade of her crunched eyebrows hinted it wasn't her natural color. A long cotton tank top flowed to her mid-thighs, hiding the top part of her gray leggings. The running shoes laced to her feet combined with the sporty outfit and the wet armpits seemed to indicate that she'd jogged here or had been running when Adeline had called her.

I was sitting in the same spot as before my impromptu nap, but now, both my feet were tied to the legs of the chair. A sudden burst of frustration unfurled as I tested the strength of the ropes.

The young woman, Faye, towered over me with her hands on her hips and asked, "Who are you?"

It couldn't hurt to disclose things I'd already discussed with Adeline. "I'm Robert Mitchell's daughter."

"Adopted daughter," Adeline added.

Faye tapped her foot. "Why are you here? Who are your real parents?"

I rolled my eyes. "I came here to find out. Obviously, I wouldn't be knocking on strangers' doors to ask questions if I already had an answer."

Faye's brows disappeared into her bangs. "You have a lot of cheek for a tied-up girl."

I wiggled my wrists to loosen the knot, but they didn't budge. "I've had a bad year. Believe it or not, this is not my worst kidnapping experience."

Faye's eyes bounced to my tattoos. "You mean the devil's marks? Don't fret. Your master won't find you here."

I scoffed. "I don't have a master."

"Even if I was blind, I could smell him on you. You reek of demon," she said, her voice rich with hate.

I *reeked* of demon? I scrunched my face in both aggravation and self-consciousness. "The tattoos are there to protect me."

A dry chuckle grated Faye's throat. "Is that what he told you?"

My shoulders sagged. I didn't feel like arguing with a stranger whilst tied-up about whether or not I was a demon slave. I'd read about demons marking their followers and what it usually meant. Demon worshiper. Demon slut. She had no reason to believe I was the one exception to the rule. The mental image of me kissing Liam's feet made me cringe. "Let's forget the marks for now. Who are you?"

"You go first," she said, fingers drumming against her arm.

We were at an impasse, and the advantage rested with her. "I'm a witch."

"I already knew that."

"How can you tell?" Had she seen my aura while I was unconscious? Or was it something else?

Faye huffed. "Don't be ridiculous. You know we recognize our own kind."

Excitement bubbled in my stomach. "I don't know anything. I only discovered I was a witch last April."

Her firm posture wavered. "You're untrained?"

The way she spat the word made me feel dirty. "I'm a newbie."

"What's your power?" she asked.

"Tell me something about you first or untie me." She had to give me some wiggle room, or I'd clam up and not say another word.

She assessed me with a serious, threatening stare, and I stared back with the same zeal. Her arms fell at her sides. "Alright. I'm a witch too, and I can tell when someone is lying."

Was she bluffing? It seemed awfully convenient, given the circumstances.

Faye tilted her chin up. "What's your real name?"

I didn't bat an eyelash as I lied. "Nina."

An impatient grin curled her lips. "You're smart to test me, but I despise liars."

"Alana."

The snark vanished from her features, and her eyes widened as if I'd punched her in the gut. Her voice shook as she asked, "How old are you?"

"I turned twenty in April."

Thick tears glazed over her green eyes, and her face paled. She stormed out of the room with Adeline hurrying after her.

I stretched my shoulders and neck as far as I could, but I couldn't see or hear anything. I fought against the ropes. What the hell had just happened? My name and age had never brought someone to tears before... besides maybe my mother when I'd turned eighteen.

They stayed out of view and earshot for about ten minutes before Faye came back alone. Her lips were pursed tight. "Okay."

"Okay what?"

"Okay, I'll untie you. But only if you promise not to bolt."

"I promise." Was she crazy? I didn't want to run. I was on the verge of answers.

She cut the ropes. "Why did you come here?"

"I told you. I'm looking for information. My parents disappeared. I found a picture of my dad in boarding school. He'd never told me he went to boarding school, so I found that odd." I left Thom's dad out of it, hoping that omitting facts wouldn't trigger her truth-power.

"How did you survive this long if you're untrained?"

"I almost didn't, but I was rescued by a demon and kept out of reach until I learned to hide my aura."

Faye's forced laughter sounded more like a cry. "Gosh, you think you're telling the truth. Girl, the demon didn't rescue you. He tainted you."

The flagrant disgust rolling off her tongue irked me. My tattoos looked fine, why was she acting so grim? "He didn't. He saved me. Can't you tell I'm not lying?"

"Yes, but the fact that you would defend him is just more frightening."

I clicked my tongue. "I'm not saying he's Mr. Perfect, but can you believe that I wouldn't be alive without him?"

She bit her bottom lip. "That, I can."

"So, what's the deal here? Why did you run off when I told you my name?" My curiosity was begging to be quenched.

She hid her face behind a trembling hand. "My sister Jane always gushed that she'd name her daughter Alana. And you're the spitting image of her."

Wait.

Is she saying...

Could it be?

A burst of emotion cracked my tough exterior. "Are you saying you're my aunt?"

She shook her head violently, and her voice raised. "No. It's impossible."

I squeaked, "You wouldn't be telling me all this if you were sure."

"Alright, I'm not. I was barely twelve twenty years ago."

"Call and ask her." *Preferably right this instant.*

Faye's breath hitched. "She's dead."

The simmering elation that had been building up my chest fell flat, and I forgot to breathe. *No. My biological mother... Dead? But I didn't even... I won't be able to...*

The sting of grief was both unexpected and suffocating. I felt like I'd been robbed, like there wasn't enough *time.* Tears spilled down my cheeks, and I swallowed back a bitter wave of disappointment. I'd discovered my birth mother's identity only to learn she didn't exist anymore. She was a stranger, and yet... not. My lips quivered. "I guess we'll never know."

Adeline returned, holding a large wooden bowl in both hands. "Oh, we'll know soon enough."

Faye crossed her arms. "Blood magic? It's barbaric!"

Adeline set the bowl on the kitchen table. "It might be out of style, but it's reliable." The old woman passed a shiny pocket knife to Faye, who begrudgingly uncrossed her arms and grabbed the blade.

She cut the tip of her finger and let a few drops of blood fall into the bowl.

Adeline reached into the cupboards behind her and sprinkled a pinch of a flour-like substance over the red drops. As it came in contact with Faye's blood, the powdery white material turned a flamboyant shade of red. Adeline added a few herbs to the mix and vigorously stirred the ingredients with a tiny silver spoon.

Adeline's every movement absorbed my attention as I tried to control my jittery feet. My witchcraft education consisted only of meditations, telepathy, and dealing with my aura. My so-called powers acted on their own, and I hadn't read or even heard about how to cast a real spell besides what was shown on *Sabrina the Teenage Witch* reruns.

When Adeline walked away from the mixture, Faye struck a match ablaze and threw it inside. The contents ignited, and a beautiful, blood-red flame rose from the bowl.

Both witches turned to me, and nervousness latched onto my stomach. They looked at me expectantly, so I picked up the pocket knife and raised my brows.

They nodded in unison, and I almost giggled at how every significant moment of my life required a self-inflicted wound. My hand trembled over the flames, but there wasn't any heat coming from them. Surprise distracted me from my goal, and I tentatively let the fire lick my fingers. The absence of pain wasn't the only remarkable effect.

A drop of my blood fell into the mix. The flames responded to my skin, caressing it as if they were alive, the rich burgundy hues showing hints of orange and yellow as they climbed like little ants on my hands and melted into my skin.

"The blood has spoken. She's a Garret witch," Adeline declared with awe.

Faye exhaled loudly.

The glass tabletop and the ingredients danced and sparkled in front of me, my vision veiled with tears.

Garret. Alana Garret. How weird.

The revelation plunged the three of us into a weird melancholy. Faye seemed about to burst, and Adeline looked older than ever. A part of me was ecstatic to have found other witches, especially since one of them was my actual aunt. Another part was grieving. My biological mother was dead. I might not have spent my life yearning to know her, but I hated the emptiness that came with the knowledge that I would never meet her. Never talk to her. Never see her smile. Never really know why she'd given me away.

Adeline passed her open palm over the bowl, and the flames fizzled out. Her solemn expression flew from Faye to me, and she bowed her head. "Oh boy! We're going to need something stronger than tea to drown those sorrows." She put aside the ingredients she'd used to cast the spell, walked out for a minute, and returned with a glass bottle in her hand.

She set three shot glasses in front of us and filled them to the brim before sitting down.

I eyed the amber liquid with suspicion.

A light chuckle rasped her throat. "Don't worry, child, the time for sleeping potions has passed. After all, we're family."

I shot her a confused look. Was she saying we were related?

She nodded. "Faye here is your aunt, and I am Faye's. That makes me your great aunt."

I slid into the chair in front of me, letting that information sink in, and searched their faces for familial traits. Between Faye's dyed hair and Adeline's gray, I couldn't tell if they were redheads too, but freckles peppered their noses. And we kind of had the same chin and small ears. "Do you have a picture of her?"

Adeline made a quick trip to the back of the apartment. "Here."

I sucked in an audible breath. My mother had her arms wrapped around a young, blond Faye. She had my hair, my smile, and though she had a leaner face and clear blue eyes, I was indeed the spitting image of her. No wonder Adeline had recognized me. Trivial questions popped into my brain. What was her favorite color? Did she like to read? Was she stubborn, like me?

My breath caught in my throat. "Was she dating somebody? Or married? Who's my father?"

"No idea. Jane never talked about boys, and the investigation following her murder didn't reveal she was involved with anyone," Adeline said.

Murder. This confirmed my hunch that my witch mother hadn't

died from natural causes. "But there had to be someone. What about a good warlock friend?"

Adeline shook her head. "There's no one I can think of."

My nails scratched the lace table runner. "What else can you tell me about her?"

"What do you want to know?"

"What was she like?" The question came straight from the heart.

Adeline smiled. "Jane was a natural. One of the most powerful and generous young witches the coven ever nurtured."

"When did she die?" My voice cracked.

The fancy teacup Adeline was holding shook a little. "In March. Almost twenty years ago."

A year after I was born. "How?"

"Like we said. She was murdered." Faye's voice was filled with rage.

"By who? A demon?" It would explain Faye's apparent hatred of demons.

The young witch grimaced. "It was Jonathan Hale."

Hale!? My eyes opened up like saucers at the mention of Frank's surname. "Who's Jonathan Hale?"

Adeline shook her head in disapproval. "Faye's just guessing. She doesn't know for sure who killed your mother."

Faye hit the table with a closed fist. "I know what I saw."

"You were twelve. You saw him meet with Jane on the day she died. Anything beyond that is pure speculation."

"It was him. I know it."

"Or an unfortunate coincidence."

Faye snorted. "Coincidence my ass. He's a Hale. They're monsters."

The subject seemed to be a sore wound between them, and I thought it best not to press on, though I tended to agree with Faye. I almost asked how this Jonathan might be related to Frank but remembered my resolution to share only what was strictly necessary.

"You belong to a coven, right?" I asked.

The question snapped Faye out of her frazzled state, and she stood. "What do you know about covens?"

"Not much beside the fact that they make demons very nervous."

A genuine smile lit up her face. "Is that what your master told you?"

I rolled my eyes. We were going in circles.

She leaned against the kitchen counter. "Look, this is uncharted territory for me. I should really bring you to my people so they can assess you."

Assess? That did not sound friendly. "But you won't?"

"They won't care that you're Jane's daughter. We have strict rules about strangers, especially witches with demon marks." The somber tone of her voice indicated that those strict rules might lead me to a swift death.

"Why do you hide? Why don't you help other witches?" I'd wondered for some time now why random witches were left to their own devices with virtually no chance at survival.

"Untrained witches are a liability."

My tone hiked up a few octaves. "And for that, they should die?"

"They are not our problem. You, on the other hand, are. You should have been here with me. I should have been the one to raise you, to train you. Jane clearly thought she'd go back for you. Otherwise, she wouldn't have left you with normals. You need to tell me everything about your life. I want to know what happened to her and how she hid something this big from me." The more Faye talked, the more agitated and breathless she became. My arrival had stirred too much grief, and I empathized. I understood exactly what it felt like to have your world turned upside down in a matter of minutes.

Adeline put her hand over her niece's and patted it down. "We should leave that for tomorrow."

"But—" Faye started.

Adeline interrupted her. "You are in shock, dear. The heart blinds the mind when it is sore."

Tomorrow? I peeked at the oven clock and realized how late it was. I had a long drive ahead to return home. "Wait. I can't stay here until tomorrow. I'm already late as it is."

Adeline shook her head. "You should stay, Alana. We can protect you, and we have much to discuss."

For a second, I was tempted to stay. Wouldn't it be better to spend the night and get the answers I so desperately craved? My impatience threatened to overwhelm my common sense, but I reined it in. Even if they were in fact my flesh and blood, I needed a plan. I couldn't forget my mother had thought it best to hide me from them.

With a few days to think, I might be able to figure out why. It would also confirm whether or not they trusted me enough to allow me to make my own decisions. I bit my bottom lip.

"Your master awaits?"

The judgment in Faye's tone made my blood boil. "No, it's not about *my* demon at all. I need time to digest, too."

Adeline nodded. "Perhaps it's best not to rush into anything. We all need time to understand what this means for the future." I interpreted her agreement both as a way to build trust and as an opportunity to discuss things further with Faye before they revealed anything more.

Both hands clasped around her glass, Faye met my gaze head-on. "We are breaking the rules by letting you go, so don't you dare breathe a word of what transpired here to your demon. If you tell him, we will not break the rules for you again."

The bitter warning inflated the unease rumbling through my stomach.

Adeline stepped in before I could answer and said, "We'll meet here in three days' time and talk."

Her calm voice soothed my fears and extinguished my anger, and I wondered if she might be an empath, like Lilah. I didn't ask, not wanting to reveal Lilah's existence to them, but noted that I should be cautious of my emotions around Adeline.

A breath of relief escaped me as I walked out of the apartment. The wind gusted through the narrow alley, seemingly coming for nowhere and everywhere. My eyes darted up to the balcony where dangling glass birds chimed into the night.

The tinkling noise sounded both like a goodbye and a hello.

7

WALKING IN MY SHOES

Alana

The touristy streets swarmed with people admiring the shiny New Orleans lights as they stumbled half-drunk out of the neighboring restaurants.

My mind ran laps, processing all that had happened, and the bad headache resurfaced.

I hadn't been as scared as when I'd first woken up in the Walkers' house or when Frank had abducted me, but a small, less-daunted part of my brain was acutely aware I'd almost been taken prisoner for a third time.

Thoughts tumbled like clothes in a dryer.

They drugged me.

They tied me up.

They let me go.

I'm related to them.

I'm going to see them again in three days.

A treacherous mix of nausea and elation hopped from my belly to the back of my throat. I climbed into my car and checked my phone.

One missed call from Thom. I composed myself before hitting the call-back button.

It rang once before he answered, "Lana?"

I did my best to sound aloof. "You called?"

"Where are you? Are you okay? I was worried."

"I'm fine. I went to New Orleans to ask questions about that boarding school and lost track of time."

"You went where?" He sounded shocked.

"To that school in the picture."

He paused. "Alone? It's a three-hour drive."

"I know. I was itching to do something useful."

"You sound breathless." His tone hardened. "What's our safe word?"

"Edelweiss. Don't worry, it's me. I jogged a few miles. I'll be home in a few hours."

"Okay, see you then."

We hung up.

I got home way past midnight.

Thom and Liam were in the driveway playing basketball. They'd installed a hoop, and a bright spotlight on the garage's roof formed a halo over the asphalt.

They both glanced in my direction as I parked on the street in front of the house. I rarely got to see them so relaxed, and it made me think of the first time I'd seen them play. Back then, I'd been scared of Liam and only noticed Thom's sculpted arms and mouth-watering abs.

Simpler days.

Now, their muscular bodies and chiseled jaws followed me everywhere and taunted me for being an indecisive moron. The sight of Liam's snake tattoo slithering across his naked shoulder blades made me scratch the identical one on my breast.

My demon sure looked good in black shorts.

Thom passed Liam the ball and ran over to me. "Had a nice drive?"

"Well, I didn't end up in prison, so it's an improvement." A forced chuckle dissipated the heat that had spread to my chest.

"Did your research go well?"

Faye's warning that I shouldn't breathe a word of our meeting was fresh in my mind. "Only a few snippets about how our fathers were in school, but nothing interesting."

Liam pretended to be engrossed in his practice shots, but I knew he was listening in. My hunch was confirmed when he spoke to the mental tether between our minds. *"You're lying again."* It wasn't a question or an accusation but a flat fact.

My jaw tightened. *"You're eavesdropping again."*

Liam never reported his day-to-day affairs to me, so I didn't owe him anything. If I wanted to learn more about my origins, I had to keep this secret close. But it annoyed me all the same that my improved lying skills hadn't fooled him. What gave me away?

Liam couldn't read minds, but he sure had his way of getting in my head.

I AWOKE the next morning with the headache gone, but my heart still tied up in knots. The warmer weather of the last few days had been blown away by a chilly wind, so I closed my window and put on a pair of dark, skinny jeans coupled with a long-sleeved, red, scoop-neck sweater. I braided the front section of my hair into a headband and let the rest of the curls roam free after I tamed them with my styling mousse.

First, I had to decide if I'd abide by Faye's rule not to breathe a word of our encounter. My instincts told me to stay quiet since I believed her motivations came from a hatred of demons and not a fear that Thom or Liam would warn me against her. But how could I go to New Orleans again without sparking Thom's curiosity? Or lie without being outed by Liam? The demon seemed awfully intuitive these days.

Around nine, the front door opened and closed, and I waited a minute to see which brother had gone.

If Thom had stayed behind, he'd turn on the TV and scrub the dishes. Liam would shower, change, and quickly slip out of the house.

The happy chirp of the morning cartoons gave me my answer.

After applying a hint of eye shadow and mascara, I joined Thom in the kitchen. A lonely and cold bacon strip remained on the table, so I gobbed it in one bite. "Morning."

"Morning." He poured my coffee and set the mug at my usual spot around the table. "So, you said you got to hear a few tidbits about our dads yesterday?"

I blew on the hot beverage and took a tentative sip. *Yum.* "Yes. Mostly unimportant stuff. The teacher talked about your grandfather, though. She called him atrocious."

Thom scratched his stubble and nodded. "She knew what she was talking about."

"He must have been a real prick for her to remember him after so many years, but I guess a family of seven boys doesn't come around that often."

Thom motioned to the window. "Want to go for a run?"

"Sure."

I changed and met him outside. Goosebumps branded my entire body, but I knew I'd be sweating bullets in minutes, so I didn't get a coat.

Thom's large shoulders, emphasized by his blue and white striped shirt, made my chest pang with longing.

Why couldn't I get my heart on board to spill my secrets and date Thom, a man who knew how to support me and make me laugh?

Why couldn't I forget about a kiss that should have never happened? Why did I lust after a man who would never love me? A man who might still devour me if he went off the rails.

A man who wasn't a man at all.

My phone vibrated in my pocket, stopping my inner ramblings, and Rachel's name appeared over the new text message.

Hi Nina. It's Rachel. Wanna grab a cup of coffee later?

"Oh. It's Rachel." I angled the screen towards Thom to show him the message.

"Good. It means your plan is working."

I nodded and typed back,

Sure.

Great. Meet me at the Satori Coffee House near campus at 4-ish.

RACHEL WAS PUNCTUAL, and I barely waited outside the coffee house for a minute before she turned the corner. Rain started to pour, so we hurried into the shop and ordered at the counter.

"Do you want to sit here?" I pointed to a table near the window.

Rachel nodded, and we sat down with our steaming cups of coffee and our snacks.

"Did you have class today?" I asked, but I knew she didn't.

"No, but I was at the library studying. My finals start this week, and they're a bitch. But I couldn't read another sentence without my brain exploding, and I thought you might be free."

I bit off the gingerbread man's head. "Bored out of my mind. I thought auditing a few classes would help me get used to the rhythm of the teachers for next semester. But most lectures are exam-oriented, and it's hard to care when you don't have to take the exam." I was lying through my teeth. I hadn't gone to any other classes.

"Don't complain. You'll be properly enrolled soon enough."

I wiped the crumbs from my mouth. "I should relish in my boring life while I can."

"At least, you don't live alone." The remark hung in the air, and she folded her napkin as she added, "Your cousin's nice."

I really hoped she hadn't offered to get coffee so she could grill me about my hot cousin. "Yeah."

She sipped her coffee. Was she waiting for me to elaborate? In any case, I didn't take the bait. I had no desire to discuss Liam's love life, even a hypothetical one. *If she presses on, I'll tell her he's married.*

She finally broke the awkward silence with a more innocuous question. "Are you staying in Mobile for the holidays?"

I nodded.

"Cool. My whole family is celebrating at my grandmother's. We have something planned almost every night. It's a real drag because I have to take care of all the youngsters, and they fight like little devils."

I sympathized with her predicament, and our conversation went from family to school and circled back until we landed on relationships.

"Did you leave a boyfriend behind in Boston?" She asked.

"No. No boyfriend." *No boyfriend but plenty of boy trouble.*

I was afraid she'd bring Liam up again, but she sectioned her chocolate bar and asked, "Have you ever been in love? And I don't mean high school crushes."

"No." I understood what she meant. Sure, I'd had all the expected butterflies for my first high school boyfriend, but the break up hadn't torn me apart. I was a stranger to the kind of love depicted in movies and romance novels; I blamed my too-cautious nature for that. Falling in love looked daunting to me, especially in my circumstances, though I felt dangerously close to a breakthrough…

"Me neither. My parents are super religious. They expect me to go to college, meet a nice man, preferably a doctor or a lawyer, and get married. Be a housewife like my mom. They think I'm a virgin. I'm not cut out for this life. I want to travel. I want excitement. I want to fall in love for real."

Excitement. I wondered if she'd feel the same if she became a witch and had to abandon everything. "You could try and talk to them?"

She snorted. "Yeah, that'll go well." She tied her long blond hair into a bun and tapped on the table with her fingers. "What are your parents like?"

"They're great." It took everything I had for my voice not to break at the end of the sentence.

"Then why did you move?"

I went with the script I had prepared. "I was being harassed back home by a colleague. I needed a change."

She leaned in a bit closer. "What did he do?"

I planned to say he was following me around, taking pictures and whatnot, but I said, "He tried to rape me."

I closed my eyes as Frank's demented eyes hovering over me came back to mind.

Rachel paled, and her smile disappeared. "Oh my God! That's awful. I'm so sorry."

"It's okay. He failed."

"Still…" she bit her bottom lip.

I hadn't really talked about Frank to anyone. Lilah had asked all the right questions in exactly the right way, and Thom had offered a sympathetic ear, but I hadn't opened up to them about it. I didn't want them to pity me.

Rachel was different. She would most likely not be in my life for very long. Spilling your heart out to a stranger is freeing. It's safe. You don't have to deal with their questions if you don't want to. You don't have to see sadness or judgment in their eyes every day.

"Sometimes, I walk in the streets, and I feel like someone's watching me… Do you ever get that feeling?" I said, fishing for a lead on her seer.

"After what happened to you, it's perfectly normal to be scared."

"Yeah." I didn't want any awkwardness to linger, so I changed the subject. "Are you dating anyone?"

"No. I'd rather not put down roots here, and I'm too picky for my own good. My last boyfriend called me a princess, and I'm afraid he was right."

My lips curved up. "Liam calls me that, too."

"Who's Liam?"

Whoops. "He's a friend from back home." I straightened my shoulders and refocused my attention entirely on Rachel. I couldn't get too comfortable and lose sight of my mission. No new friend or boyfriend. No weird stalker. No job. No suspicious neighbor. The seer had to be crossing her path here on campus.

8

SAY IT AIN'T SO

Alana

The drive to New Orleans lasted for ages, my fingers drumming nervously on the wheel as I rehashed everything I wanted to ask and the facts I preferred to steer clear of.

Church bells were ringing midday when I stood stock-still in front of Adeline's door. I knocked a little louder than I'd intended to, and the door swung open a short second later. We hadn't set a particular time to meet, but the tension on Faye's face told me she'd been waiting.

"Come in," she said, her jaw set in a hard line.

I started climbing the narrow staircase. Faye looked up and down the street before she slammed the door shut and ran after me. "Wait a second." She blocked my path with her arm. "Does anyone know that you met with or are meeting with other witches today?"

I clicked my tongue. "No."

"Did you tell anyone where you were going?"

"No." I'd hidden Adeline's address on my nightstand, tucked in the novel I was reading. An innocuous breadcrumb and a great safety net if, for whatever reason, I didn't come home that night.

"Did your *demon* follow you?" Her face wrinkled.

"No."

"Do you have any weapon or enchantment on you?"

"Only a dagger in my boot."

Her gaze jerked to my feet. "Why? Do you plan to attack us?"

"No. I always keep it close."

She held her hand out. "Smart. Get it out and give it to me."

So much for establishing trust. I leaned down to retrieve the short dagger and handed it to her. She scrutinized it from all angles like she was checking for a secret mechanism. Her calculated movements and tightly-phrased questions flowed, like she'd been in the exact same situation many times before. What past experiences had rendered her so paranoid? So abrupt?

Relief engulfed me when she handed it back, turned on her heels and stomped upstairs. I inhaled deep and followed.

Adeline walked into the kitchen with a beige, wool robe wrapped around her frail frame. "Nice to see you again, Alana. Are you hungry?"

I shook my head, way too anxious to eat. The stark contrast between Faye's suspicious nature and Adeline's calming presence made me appreciate the old witch even more. She served us all some tea and invited both Faye and I to sit down. "I think we should start with you, Alana. How are you feeling?"

The open question put me at ease, and I suspected once again Adeline's powers allowed her to mold my emotions. I shrugged off my jacket and laid it on the back of my chair. "I'm anxious. I have so many questions. I don't know where to start."

Faye's knees bounced up and down under the table.

Adeline smiled. "It's okay. Take your time."

The encouragement gave me confidence. "What's your power?"

"Faye and I have very similar abilities. We can both distinguish between lies and truth, but while she relies on the elusive spoken words, mine sees the truth of the heart."

I leaned towards her, my suspicions confirmed. "You're an empath."

"Yes."

"And my mother?" Figuring out why my mother had left me with adoptive parents instead of the coven topped my priority list, but I had to tread lightly.

"Your mother also saw truth. Truth of the past, present, and future," Adeline said.

My jaw flopped open. "She could see the future?"

"Sometimes." Adeline tilted her head and observed me like her glasses were microscopes. "You've seen the future, too."

I averted my gaze. "Once. I misinterpreted it. And when I healed my dad, I saw stuff, too."

"That is the danger of such a gift. The healing is more straightforward and speaks of your generous nature. Magic has a knack for reflecting both the witches' qualities and desires."

I didn't quite grasp how my healing powers correlated with my ability to disintegrate a demon with my bare touch, but I wasn't ready to share that secret with them.

Adeline stirred her tea, deep wrinkles forming on her forehead. "I thought more about who your father might be. Jane taught math and science for three years at Newgrave, spying for us. A powerful demon clan used to send their young boys to school there. The Walkers were involved, somehow. Daniel Walker could be the father, but he wasn't around when Jane started teaching at the school."

I exhaled loudly. My worst fear was that I was a Walker, somehow, but if Daniel hadn't been around, it boded well.

A cringe bared Faye's teeth. "Jane would not have dated a Walker."

My knuckles tensed, and my shoulders hitched at the venom in Faye's voice.

Adeline chuckled. "Your sister was more of a rebel than you remember. She was headstrong and fearless."

"It still doesn't explain why a nobody ended up with Alana. Why a human when Jane could have left her with us? Why wouldn't she keep her? It makes no sense."

"You were young, Faye. You don't know everything that transpired while Jane was being groomed to become high priestess."

My heart quickened.

"Are you saying my sister hid her child because of ambition?" Faye said scornfully.

"Not at all. I'm saying other witches were deeply jealous of her. Most didn't agree with Rina's choice of a successor. Jane was always looking over her shoulder. Maybe she thought Alana would be safer with humans."

Faye chuckled darkly again, but the serious line of her mouth told me she was considering Adeline's hypothesis. "Your demon, what is he? A Fae?"

Shit. I couldn't lie here, and I couldn't feign ignorance either. "A Shadow Walker."

Faye's eyes widened.

The corners of Adeline mouth twitched. "A Walker, I bet."

I stared at my knees in embarrassment, knowing they would most likely be angry I hadn't mentioned it until now. "Yes."

"Aha. Faye, you might have to eat your words. This demon intended to save Alana. Is it James? Not Adam, surely. Maybe Fredrick?"

My finger picked at a loose strand of fabric on my shirt. "Liam. Liam Walker."

Adeline and Faye exchanged a glance.

"Impossible. Liam Walker is dead," Faye said.

My breath quickened. *Liam* and *dead* didn't go together, and my jaw clenched. "I'm not lying."

"I know."

"Maybe he didn't give her his real name," Adeline said.

"Why are you so sure he's dead?" I asked, and Faye grimaced. "You still spy on them."

Faye's neck was stiff and her face red. "If you're right, it doesn't help your case. Liam Walker was one of the worse ones."

"He left. He didn't want to kill anymore witches. He's a lone demon now." I was careful to add the word *demon* so it was strictly the truth. Thom was human.

Faye groaned. "He drinks your blood, doesn't he?"

"No!"

She crossed her arms. "He *never* tasted you?"

My teeth gritted together.

"I thought so. He's not the first demon to keep his snack around. Of course, a real witch would never allow that."

I grimaced. "I don't remember any *real* witches lining up to save me that night. He was my only option to live. Why is that?"

"Witches do not have the luxury to follow the ethics of the human world. In the last few centuries, we have been hunted by demons, betrayed by our allies, and burned at the stake by the same normals you expect us to help. We've all taken a sacred oath to protect each other and kill our enemies," Faye said.

"But surely random witches aren't your enemy?" I sucked on my bottom lip and bit down on it until I drew blood.

"I told you before. They aren't our problem."

Their logic pissed me off. *God.* "But—"

Adeline placed a gentle hand on my arm. "Alana, stop. I understand this is a sensitive matter, but you will not change our minds. The rules of the coven have been upheld for centuries. Outsiders aren't viewed well, and change only comes from the inside out, not the opposite." The sentence was carefully worded. She wasn't saying change was impossible. She refilled her tea and dropped in a sugar cube. "If your demon is in fact a Walker, we can do another spell to see if you're related to him at all."

I huffed. "I can't get blood from him if that's what you're suggesting." But I was curious. If a spell could confirm I wasn't a Walker, it would make my day.

Adeline waived dismissively. "No need for that. You shared his blood. A part of him lives inside you."

My pulse spiked, and they escorted me to the living room.

Faye got an imposing roll of thick parchment paper from a vintage chest. "Now, this is a bit more complicated than what we did the other day."

I held her stare and tucked my chin up. "I'm up for anything."

She untangled the leather thread keeping the roll tight and

stretched the parchment at our feet. It depicted a huge family tree going back at least 20 generations. The names were arranged in the form of an actual tree branching off from a large trunk and were written in red ink, most likely blood, in an old-fashioned and minuscule calligraphy. At the top, the word Walker towered above the rest. I leaned closer, fascinated.

My eyes quickly scanned the document for Thom's and Liam's names. I found them on the top left, their names crossed out, a small black dragon drawn next to Liam's name. I read downward, finding Daniel and his six brothers, which were followed by Thom's grandfather, the man everyone thought so horrible. I raised my eyebrows as I discovered his mother had been the one to bear the Walker surname, not his father. I ran my fingers along the inked lines to Thomas Walker, the one whose journal had captivated me last spring. His brother James and sister Emily were on the document, but their daughter Clara wasn't. The same dragon appeared next to James' name.

I arched a brow and put a hand over my mouth. How much of what they thought they knew about the Walkers was true, and how much was conjecture?

The tree was larger than expected, and other branches also bore demon pictographs. Names I didn't recognize. Fredrick. Damien. Arthur. Their names were not crossed out, and yet their births dated as far back as 1759. The oldest name that hadn't been crossed out had a gold dragon next to it. Adam.

"Who's Adam Walker?" I asked.

Faye sneered. "The head of the snake."

I put my hands on my hips. "How does the spell work?"

"First, we have to make sure your demon is in fact a Walker." She handed me a knife.

I groaned. "Why does it always have to be blood?"

Her lips quirked up. "I need more than the other day."

"Fantastic."

She motioned for me to step forward. "On the paper. Don't stain the carpet."

I cut my arm deeply and waited for the blood to splash down on the parchment.

"Now, smudge your hands in it and press the paper."

As I did what she asked, the red liquid became hot under my palms. It glimmered and formed thin lines that scurried all over the page. They swirled until the letters thickened and lengthened, the names now easier to read.

Faye nodded at the results. "Okay. He's a Walker. Now, for the tricky part of the spell. Since your blood is tainted, we have to use this." She passed me a small black vial. "Drink it in one gulp. I am warning you, it's nasty."

I trusted her advice. My eyes stung as if I'd squirted a fresh lemon into them, and my tongue burned like I'd chewed a hot pepper. I gasped for air and hunched on all fours over the family tree. Sweat poured out of every single pore. My underarms were wet, my thighs, even the soles of my feet. A fit of coughing shook me, my ribcage on fire from the effort. Finally, I heaved a thick, black mucus over the paper. Through hooded eyes, I saw a tremor ripple through the parchment, almost like a sigh, and the mucus disintegrated into nothingness.

"Does that mean I'm not a Walker?"

Adeline puckered her lips in surprise. "Yes."

Alleluia. I rolled onto my back to catch my breath. *Relief* is not strong enough a word to describe the elation that ran up my spine. A big smile threatened to split my mouth at the seams.

Faye clicked her tongue. "You're happy."

"I'm relieved."

"Because you want to bang him, you mean?"

I glared and braced my hand over the cut, noticing it was still spurting blood. "Do you have a first aid kit?"

"Why would you need to wrap it? Heal it."

Faye's expectant look tightened my stomach. If I tried and failed, I might get an explanation as to why I sucked at witchcraft. Faye was a real witch and might be able to help. But what if she couldn't explain why it didn't work? What if the problem was me, and it *couldn't* work?

My incompetence would only strengthen their beliefs that newbies weren't worth the effort.

"What's the matter?" Faye asked with a frown.

Drawing a deep breath, I put my hand over the bloody mess and closed my eyes, expecting it to fail 100%.

To my stupefaction, I found myself in the almost familiar labyrinth of strings. *It worked.* Why? Why now when I'd stacked failure after failure by myself? I wracked my brain to find an explanation. This was no life and death situation like the other times. Why was magic so unpredictable?

The spider webs hung all around me, and I studied their intricate patterns before raising my hand towards a particularly thick one. My breathing hitched as I noticed I could see myself doing the movement as if I was standing in a hall of mirrors. I stretched my arm out to touch my reflection. The hundreds of other Alana's shimmering both in front and behind me did the same. Just as my extended finger was about to reach the surface of the mirror, the reflected arm jerked back.

The Alana in the mirror, the one closest to me, smirked and wagged no with her index finger. She winked and disappeared as the mirror cracked. *What the hell?*

My mouth hung open as I returned to the present and dragged my fingertips across my healed arm.

"You had a vision," Adeline said.

I combed my hair away from my face. "Yes. I get them whenever I use my powers."

"What did you see?"

"Myself. A hundred reflections of myself," I sighed.

Adeline cleaned her glasses. "A hundred different futures. Go on."

"I tried to touch one, but she vanished."

"The future runs away."

Was the future running away, or was I? And from what? "Should I even try to make sense of it? I could interpret it wrong."

"As with any vision, the way we interpret it tells us more about ourselves than the vision itself. What do you think it meant?"

"I don't know..." I searched Faye's gaze. "Could you teach me? Witchcraft. I want to learn. I want to control my magic better." Unreliable healing powers weren't quite as useful as one hoped.

Faye chewed on her bottom lip. "It takes years to master."

"But could you?"

Her eyes narrowed. "Yes."

The similarities between us stuck out to me in this moment. The way she bit her lips and stared defiantly ahead. The way she gnawed on her thumb when she was nervous. What else did we have in common?

Adeline patted the back of my hand. "That brings us to a delicate truth. To be one of us, you must get rid of *him*. Completely."

I tore my hand away. If they thought I'd ever agree to get rid of Liam, they were sorely mistaken. "I won't kill him." This was non-negotiable, and the sharp edge of my voice spelled it out.

Adeline and Faye exchanged a look. "There is another way. You can dissolve the bond if you wish, but it'll be painful," Faye said.

I had no trouble believing that, but pain wasn't at the root of my hesitation. The tattoos protected me from Frank, and, beyond that, they were an indelible link between Liam and me. I was conflicted about what it meant and how it might have jumpstarted my crush on him, but I'd grown fond of them. They were kinda bad-ass.

Adeline rose to her feet, rummaged through a few books and hesitated before returning her attention to me. "You're uncertain. Your loyalty speaks highly of you, but a marked witch is as good as dead in our world. Faye and I will be out of town for the holidays. We'll talk again after that."

The abrupt dismissal startled me. There were so many other things to discuss. So many questions still unanswered. "Wait. Do I have other relatives?"

"That's not something we'll discuss for now." Faye tidied up the room while I paced back and forth from the kitchen.

They had a funny look on their faces as if an important idea had just struck them, but they remained eerily silent. I bit my thumb. "One last thing. About auras."

Thom had revealed before we'd left Virginia that witches couldn't see auras, and I could see auras. The *other*world was filled with exceptions, so I'd rationalized it was a glitch in the Walker's knowledge of witches. They had never dealt with a true born witch before, only randoms, so maybe they were wrong. Maybe every true born witch saw them.

I tucked a strand of hair behind my ear. "I struggled to conceal it in the beginning, and it sucks that I can't see it." It was true enough. The only aura I couldn't see was my own.

"Not even demons see their own auras," Faye said, fumbling around in her purse.

"What about other people's auras? Can witches learn to see them?" *Please don't ask why I asked.*

Faye unscrewed her lip balm and applied a thin film with her pinkie. "No. Sorry. Auras are a demon thing."

Not as sorry as me. "What about seers? Are seers demons?"

She cocked her head to the side. "I misspoke. Auras are just not in our range, I guess. Like working with demons." She raised a brow, her gaze burning holes in my tattoos. She handed me a piece of paper. "You can reach me at this number. It's perfectly untraceable. We can make plans to meet after the holidays... if you make the right decision."

I snatched the number from her hand and jammed it in my pocket. This was basically an ultimatum. Either I agreed to get rid of the tattoos, or I'd never earn their trust. But I had to know more. About them. About my mother. About witches.

I couldn't pass up this chance.

9

BEHIND BLUE EYES

Liam

*I*nvisibility is a drag when you're not living a life of crime.

Bored out of my mind after a three-hour lecture on the repercussions of World War II, I ache for a release. The halls of the university bustle with nervous students whispering about exams and their plans for Christmas break. I wade through the sea of bodies, careful not to bump into anyone while invisible. Most humans feel something isn't right and swerve away without knowing why, so it's not that hard.

Rachel struts a few feet in front of me, chatting with another girl about their homework. "I'll summarize pages 1 to 49."

"And I'll do the rest plus the newspaper article." The girl gets her phone from her bag, and I peek over her shoulder. "Friday night deadline." She enters the assignment into her calendar and glimpses at her Facebook in the process, so she doesn't raise any red flags. But I steal her phone anyway as she tucks it into her back pocket.

"Perfect. See you next week," Rachel says before walking away.

I hope not.

If I have to sit through one more of these mind-numbing lectures, I'll quit.

Rachel crosses the courtyard to the library, and I sigh. The library means studying, and as she unpacks her whole bag on one of the quietest tables, I figure we'll spend the whole afternoon cooped up inside. I search the phone that I stole, checking texts messages and emails, but nothing is out of the ordinary. Just another college girl trying to have fun without failing classes. I glamor myself to look like a student and give it to the librarian. I'm projecting Sheldon Cooper, but the lady doesn't blink. She doesn't watch enough TV, or maybe she needs a nudge...

"Bazinga."

Her brows pull together. "Beg your pardon?"

I point to book she has in hands. "This book is amazing."

Her face clears. "Yes. Quite right."

I walk around the library and search everyone's phones as well. Better than doing nothing. Seer hunting has never been more boring. I swear he or she has been warned to be discrete.

When I run out of suspects, I lean against the stack of books and close my eyes. I haven't done college. A month before my twentieth birthday, I was ankle-deep in a rice-field hunting a shape-shifter that had swindled my handler, Marcus. The corners of my mouth curl up. A fun hunt, that one.

The chatter of demons inside my head is stale. Frank often takes advantage of the Collective to spy on me. Turning the tables on him is overdue, so I coax a memory gently into the Collective, lowering the fish hook into the water. The reek of ginkgo fruits left to rot beneath the yellow trees is so memorable I can still taste it on my tongue. I wait for Frank to hijack my train of thought. I hope to lure him into a conversation and discover his location.

Japan was a blast, and Frank loves to reminisce.

Remember? Marcus ditched us for two months. We tested the limits of our strength bouldering the Kita alps and met exceedingly kinky Geminis.

There's my big secret. Before witch blood consumed every part of me but the monster, I enjoyed being a demon. I belonged. My abilities were praised instead of feared. I had a clear purpose, a sense of self-worth. A psychotic boss I loved to hate. *A partner in crime with a poetic taste for death that rivaled my own.*

Despite my rare admission, Frank doesn't take the bait, obstinate to hide his essence amongst the swarm. I glide down to the carpet, back propped against the stack next to Rachel, and stare at the ceiling.

Why anyone would prefer to spend their youth fighting with a tiny, rusted locker instead of traveling the world is beyond me. I yearn for a change of pace, a change of scenery.

With Frank out to get me, I can't afford to drop my guard. After I kill him, nail him to a cross, and FedEx him to his oh-so-Catholic mother, I'll take a break from saving witches. Go back to Asia for a while. My old buddy Wang is always looking for help catching polter-geists. That will be violent and bloody enough to drill some sense back into me.

Thom won't mind.

Three's a crowd when the third wheel wants to fuck your girl.

The first few witches and warlocks we helped before Alana went off to live their lives. Thom checks on them from time to time, but they want nothing to do with us. Lilah helps the witches we bring home, but she doesn't want to live on the road with us while we look for them. Alana dove into our lifestyle without hesitation or fear for her own safety. Sure, I told her she belonged in my world, but I didn't expect her to listen. I hoped she'd lure Thom out of the supernatural world and away from danger, not deeper into it.

Now, she's looking for her parents, and we're all in deep. Her quest will only stir danger and with low chances of success. They are either dead or far out of reach.

I can't wrap my brain around my dad's possible involvement.

Dad was the one to suggest we should save witches from my kind. I'd assumed he'd wanted me to atone for the ones I'd killed, but maybe he'd been looking for one witch in particular. Alana.

Everything revolves around that damn witch, like the Earth's axis shifted the day we brought her in. I hate her for it, and her lies are getting under my skin.

The Alana I know detests long drives, and yet, she's driven to New Orleans three times in the last two weeks. She has no idea I know, but her clothes and hair betray the aromas of the Crescent City mixed with the pungent earthiness of the swampy bayous. Nothing a human could have picked up, but my demon sense of smell is unequivocal.

She's met someone there, someone she wants to keep secret. The witch lacks some basic survival instincts, and I'm not about to beg for her trust. She can get killed for all I care.

I call bullshit on my own bluff. If something happens to her, I'll hate myself, but I still can't tell Thom about Alana's covert trips. I want her to spill her secrets to *me*.

Rachel gathers her books.

Finally. I do a last sweep of the room while she goes to pee—I draw the stalking line at toilets. The librarian has been working for the university for 30 years, so she can't be the seer, and the students coming in don't ring a bell.

We head out the building, and a guy approaches her. "Hey, Rach."

"Hi, Kevin."

Kevin's large, buff frame screams football player. The square glasses that give him a slightly intellectual look are non-prescription. *Nice trick.* I make a mental note to check if *Kevin* has any skeletons in his closet.

He smiles too politely for my taste as he flirts with Rachel and comes across as fake. "Want a ride home?"

Rachel's lips thin. "Nah, thanks."

"Sure?"

"Yep." She grins as she walks away, no doubt used to dealing with a lot of male attention.

I don't know why, but I step out of the shadows. I keep a brisk pace as if I'm coming from the main building and cross her path.

Recognition paints her features, and she bites her bottom lips before calling out to me. "Hey, Mike."

Not only did she recognize me, but she remembered my name. "Hi…" I let a fake uncertainty float in the air and wait for her help.

"Rachel."

"Rachel, right. Hi."

She points to the end of the block. "I'm heading to the coffee shop. Want to come along?" Despite the make-up, her cheeks betray a smidgen of heat, and her pupils are dilated.

Physical attraction is easy to read, except on infuriating five-foot-eight redheads.

Rachel's expectant smile makes me pause. "I have to go back to work."

She shrugs. "I have this boring test next week, and I'm looking for reasons to put studying off."

"Good luck with that."

"Thanks." She turns to leave.

I summon my warm-funny-guy persona, giving her my best Thom-inspired performance. "Err— Rachel? You'll need that cup of coffee. I'm parked next to the shop. Walk you there?"

"Sure." She bites back a satisfied smile. "Your boss lets you drive your cousin to class in the middle of the day?"

"I'm self-employed. I can do what I want, but I have a contract with the university."

"What do you do?" She runs a hand through her hair.

"Web security."

"Cool."

I bury my hands in my jeans' pockets. "Yeah, it's pretty boring."

A delighted chuckle escapes her.

I open the door to the café and order a drink too, making sure to pay for both. We chat about unimportant things as we exit the building.

Nice coincidence. I actually parked next to the café, and she can't mask the awe on her face when I stop next to my Vanquish. Good Charlotte said it best: "Girls don't like boys. Girls like cars and money."

I open the driver's side door. "Are you heading back to the library?"

"The bus stop, actually. I'm going home."

"Want a ride?"

She tucks her hair behind her ears. "Sure. Thanks."

What can I say? I'm harder to turn down than Kevin.

I take great care to drive at human-speed and circle personal questions back to her. She laughs at my jokes and brushes my arm multiple times, fishing for a date. No matter how hollow the exercise is, I enjoy every moment of it. It's a nice distraction. I need to feel something besides the bitter disappointment and continuous anger spiraling in my veins.

But finding solace in a fling with Rachel isn't smart. If she turns, I'll have to go to Virginia to train her. Sleeping with her beforehand might annihilate my chances of building a working relationship with her in the future, so I have to tread carefully. Thom will be upset if I jeopardize our plan and Alana...

Alana wouldn't like it.

She might even hate it...

I'm sick of the annoyingly perfect way her red waves frame her face. Sick of her smiles that make me want to behave. Sick of the damn spring in her step when she's excited about something. I can't stand how her expressive, green eyes always question me. Most of all, I loathe how much I want to kiss her pout away when we argue. She's a disease, and I'm infected.

Stop. Alana's off-limits. Thom loves her; you'll break her. He waited for months for her to trust him and accept this supernatural world before making a move. You can't swoop in now and steal her away. She drives you crazy. She's self-righteous and stubborn. She brings out the worst in you.

This mantra got me through the last few months, but its power was eroded by the lingering glances and "accidental" grazes. Kissing her blew my carefully crafted defenses to smithereens. Her gravity is irresistible. We're picking up speed circling down a drain that will inevitably lead us to disaster, but I'm not sure I can stop it. I'm even less sure that I want to stop it. She's gotten into my bloodstream... it'd be incredible to give in.

"This is my house," Rachel says, clawing me back to reality. "Thanks for the ride."

"No problem."

She grabs her stuff slowly. I should put her out of her misery.

I graze her arm and smile. "I'd love to take you out for a real coffee sometime." I remind myself Thom did the exact same thing with Alana. I'm really watching out for Rachel, not trying to make anyone jealous.

Rachel beams and grabs a pen from her bag. Her eyes dart up to meet mine, and she tugs my sleeve up to scribble her number on my arm. French manicured nails scrape my skin as she holds it in place, my hand dangerously close to her cleavage. Nice move.

The girl's got game.

MR. GRINCH

Alana

*N*o matter how much I wanted to put it off, Christmas crept up on us. My first Christmas away from home.

On Christmas Eve, Thom went shopping early in the morning and came home with a Christmas tree, lights, decorations, and a compassionate smile. I humored him, even though my chest was tight, and we worked hard to set a merry mood in our makeshift home. I almost choked when "I'll Be Home For Christmas" played on the radio, and Thom swiftly changed the channel, but it was no use. Every station played holiday music, and every song was like a poison dart aimed at my heart.

I eclipsed a few tears with a discreet swipe of the hand as we shaped cookie dough into gingerbread men. After sliding a full tray in the oven, I glanced down at my flour-tainted pants and sighed. "How can we even hope to have a Merry Little Christmas?"

Thom wrapped his arm around my shoulders. "We'll have to muddle through, somehow."

An unconvinced chuckle rasped my throat, and Thom pecked my forehead. "Can I do anything to make this easier on you?"

I sank into his warm embrace. "You already are."

With his free hand, Thom set the timer for the cookies. "Damn. It's already midday. I can call Liam and ask him to stay with Rachel for a few more hours. He won't mind."

"No. You should go. I'll be fine."

"You sure?"

I hid my face in his shoulder, scolding myself for being such a big baby. "Yeah. Sorry I'm such a bother."

"I'll go change. Just remove the tray when it dings." He looked distracted as he pulled away, a far-off look on his face, and I wondered if he'd listened to that last bit.

"Okay." I walked around the island and grabbed a rag to tidy the kitchen.

Thom disappeared into his room for a few minutes, and I started scrubbing the dishes.

He paused as he walked past me on his way out. "Lana?"

Concentrating on a rebel stain, I said, "Hmm?"

He grazed my arm from my shoulder to the back of my hand. I stopped my jerky movements against the ceramic plate and looked up at him.

His green sweater was brand new and made his blue eyes even bluer. "You're never a bother to me."

My lips curled up, and I almost tilted my head up so he'd kiss me, but I didn't, and he drew back with a thin smile. The front door closed behind him a few seconds later.

The loud bang sent a shiver up my spine.

If I got my heart in line, I might get everything I ever wanted in a boyfriend. It'd be sweet for the coming holidays to mean something more than being stranded from my family. If I stopped smothering this seed of affection between us, it might grow into love.

I yanked off the yellow rubber gloves and stomped to my room, pissed at myself.

Why did I have to be so fucking careful all the time?

What was I so afraid of? So what if Thom and I dated, and it didn't work out? What did it matter?

But it mattered to my inner voice of perpetual doubt. Dating Thom would be intense. We lived together. We worked together. Casual wasn't possible for us. The stakes would be high right from the start. I'd have to drop my guard completely and bare my heart to him. The good, the bad, and the ugly.

If things went south, I'd lose him.

AFTER A QUICK SHOWER, I wrapped my hair in a towel and caught a glimpse of my reflection. The sight of my glassy eyes was enough to start another fit of cries. I balled the used tissues and threw them into the waste basket by my bed.

All the hair on my body rose to attention at the sound of the door closing. Liam never came home right after his watch. Had Thom decided to come back? "Thom?"

No answer.

I listened intently and grabbed the dagger on my nightstand. A floorboard creaked, and my grip stiffened on the hilt of the blade. As I inched to the doorway, a tall, dark shape obscured it.

"Hey."

Liam. God.

I promptly hid the dagger behind my back, embarrassed.

His gaze traveled from my wet, tangled hair to my bloodshot eyes, and he scratched his neck. "Nice tree."

"It's festive," I croaked. Didn't we have a silent agreement to avoid alone time together? *I look like a wet rat with red eyes.*

Liam raised a brow. "I don't plan to attack you so you can put that dagger aside."

I chucked out a laugh and put the blade down on my dresser. "You didn't answer me when you came in."

"My bad."

He frowned as he sniffed the air. "I'm sorry to say... I think you killed a family of gingerbread men."

Shit! The cookies! I'd completely forgotten. My arms fell at my sides, and I hurried to the kitchen. The smell of burnt flour was still faint, but smoke wisped into the air as I opened the oven. The homemade treats were far too black to be edible, and my throat constricted. I looked down to the floor. "I wreck everything." *Can't even bake a batch of cookies correctly.*

"Hey, it's no big deal..." Liam said softly.

I swallowed hard, sinking my nails into my neck, my back stiff and my heart heavy. "It's a big deal to me. It took us an hour to—Thom counted on me."

"He'll understand. We can buy some. I'm going Christmas shopping—"

"You mean Christmas *stealing.*"

He breathed deep. "Yes. I'm going to *steal* some gifts for Thom and Lilah, and I figured you'd like to come."

My eyes narrowed. How nice of him. Had Thom warned him of my blue mood? "I—I don't know."

"You want to come. I can tell." If I hadn't known any better, I would have qualified the way each word rolled off his tongue as seductive.

"You're awfully jolly," I said with caution.

He rolled his eyes and walked away.

"Alright. Alright. I'm coming. Let me just... fix this." I waved in the general direction of my head.

"Don't bother. I can glamor you to look like a movie star if you'd like. Or Santa. Or invisible. You choose."

My bottom lip tucked between my teeth, I thought about his offer.

He would still see the wet rat.

I shook my head. "Just a minute."

WE PERUSED the department store's aisles in awkward silence. I debated whether to get him something but found it a bit silly since he was here and could take whatever he wanted. Maybe he'd pushed for me to come along so he could get a gift for Thom and Lilah without having to *steal* me one.

Lilah was driving down today. Flying was risky, and Lilah never took any chances with her new identity. She planned to stay overnight in a hotel to cut the trip in half, so she'd be here tomorrow for Christmas morning.

I spied as Liam got her a lovely, pink crystal watch and selected a new geeky phone case for Thom. He didn't ask for my opinion, so he hadn't invited me for advice. I chose tear-drop earrings for Lilah and trailed my fingers along a windbreaker, thinking it would suit Thom. It got chilly sometimes on our morning run. I raised the hanger towards Liam. "Thom wears large, right?"

He nodded in agreement, and I hauled the big jacket over my shoulders.

I grabbed wrapping paper and scotch tape and crammed every-thing in a cute wicker basket before entering the women's clothing aisle.

From the center of the display, a gorgeous green dress beckoned.

The extremities of the wide sleeves were lace, and a cute bow rested against the shoulder-blades of the mannequin. The length was on the short side, but I picked up my size on the rack anyway.

It was either that or fuzzy PJ pants.

"Ready to go?" I asked Liam who'd been lurking on the outskirts of the female-centric section.

He nodded, and we headed for the exit.

As I left the store, a loud shout came from behind and froze me in place.

"Hey! What are you doing?" A tall, middle-aged woman scurried in my direction.

Her screams alerted the shoppers.

All eyes zeroed-in on me.

A man gave me a reproachful sneer, and a woman hurried past me with her little girl in tow.

I craned my neck around. Liam was nowhere to be found.

"Don't move. I'm calling the police." The employee said.

Shame pooled in my cheeks as the word "thief" echoed through the crowd.

"Liam!" I squinted at the scene and felt a tingling behind my eyes.

He appeared out of thin air and extended his veil of invisibility to me. "You should see your face."

Liberated from the reproachful stares, I smacked his shoulder hard with my free hand and stomped off, leaving the bewildered employee and the confused passersby behind.

Liam was on my heels. "Don't be like that. It was funny."

"You always have fun at *my* expense. Can't you tell it's hard for me today?"

Liam's hand stopped my stride. "Oh, come on. I'm sorry," he said as he squeezed my shoulder.

My eyes searched for the familiar tug-of-war, and my thoughts got tangled up in his meek, apologetic smile. A cottony warmth spread down my thighs, reminding me why I'd vowed to avoid him. My hair fell around my flustered face as I looked down and barked, "You're not forgiven."

LATE IN THE AFTERNOON, I was in the kitchen securing Lilah's earrings with a piece of tape when Thom returned with grocery bags in tow. Ready-to-eat turkey, mashed potatoes, cranberry sauce, fruit cake, the whole shebang. He set them down next to my gift-wrapping station and shrugged off his coat.

I grabbed one bag and started unloading it. "I burned the cookies." My shoulders sagged, and a sob almost choked me. "I'm so sorry."

"Hey, it's okay. We can always make more."

"But I let you down." The words rang so true I wasn't sure what I was talking about anymore.

"Don't fret. There's still a bunch of stuff for you to burn today," he said with a bright smile, and I couldn't help but laugh.

We drank eggnog and cooked together.

Every task made me ache in its abnormal familiarity.

Turkey but no secret stuffing mix.

Yams but no lumps.

Cranberry sauce but not the exact shade I was used to.

While Thom heated the turkey, I retreated to my room to change. I contemplated my new dress and stripped to my underwear before sliding it over my shoulders.

The deep green looked amazing against my fair skin. I met my gaze head-on in the mirror, and the boulder resting in my stomach throbbed. My fingers fumbled with the hem of the dress, and I forced my eyes shut.

I couldn't wear this. Looking good wouldn't erase how wretched I felt.

Fuzzy PJ pants it is.

The smooth fabric pooled around my ankles.

I put on my red pajamas and matching slippers and topped the outfit off with a bland, white cotton shirt.

The sweet smell of onions and gravy floating through the house should have made my stomach grumble in anticipation, but I'd never felt less hungry in my entire life.

The cheery holiday music faded away as my thoughts drifted back to my parents, and I stared out the living room window. Green trees at Christmas and no snow. It wasn't right.

A twinkle of light caught my eye.

Wait. Was that... a snowflake?

The bare lawn was replaced by a blanket of snow. A snowman stood out front and looked in dire need of a warm hug. A northern cardinal was perched on its crooked nose. Nice touch.

The door closed behind Liam. He kicked his shoes off before walking over to me and bracing his hands against the sill of the window alcove. *"No green dress?"*

I shook my head and leaned towards the glass.

The attention to detail in the make-believe scenery blew me away, from the pines heavy with snow to the icy winding path leading up to a neighboring house. A red sleigh rested by the snowman, and a pair of skis leaned against the shed.

"Your house in Vermont?" I asked telepathically.

"Yes." Raw sadness cradled the silent word.

Liam never showed grief through real speech, and my heart swelled. I regretted my harsh tone from earlier. Sure, I was upset to be separated from my parents for Christmas, but I could hope to celebrate the holidays with them again.

Liam's parents were dead.

I stretched my pinkie out and brushed his, fully expecting him to rip his hand away. My cheeks heated up as he covered my cold fingers with his warm hand.

"Dinner's ready." Thom's voice thundered into our bubble.

Before I could blink, Liam had moved a few feet back.

Thom pointed to his brother with the wooden spoon he had in hand. "How come you always show up exactly when the food is ready but never early enough to help?"

Liam pranced over and took the spoon. "It's called good timing."

"I should learn that."

Liam patted Thom's shoulder in a condescending manner. "It's not something you learn, Junior." He plunged the spoon into the yams and brought it to his mouth.

Thom confiscated the utensil and swatted his brother's hand away from the food. "Neither is patience, apparently."

A soft melodic voice interrupted the brotherly banter. "Surprise!"

Lilah. She was early.

I jumped into her open arms and crushed her into a hug.

She giggled at my enthusiasm. "I left last night." Her blond hair was pulled back into a high ponytail, and her slender frame was wrapped in a bright red pashmina. Lilah always looked like she'd just hopped off the cover of a fashion magazine, an annoying movie star quality she shared with Liam.

I pulled away. "I'm so happy you came. It's a long trip."

"Are you nuts? I wasn't going to spend Christmas alone."

Liam swept her off her tiny feet.

"I missed you too, Liam," she laughed.

Thom kissed her on the cheek.

Her arrival soothed the previously heavy atmosphere. If we were a family, then Lilah was our heart.

Two delicious servings of turkey later, we gathered around the tree to open gifts. Thom looked handsome in his new jacket, and Lilah raved about her watch and her earrings.

"Wait until you see what I made for you," she said with a grin. She opened her luggage and threw each of us matching, cheesy Christmas sweaters.

Mine had a big snowman on it, and static electricity crackled as I pulled it over my head.

Liam contemplated the red and green glittery reindeer like it might lunge from the wool to eat him.

Thom unbuttoned his long-sleeved shirt. "Come on bro, be nice."

Liam grimaced. "It's not really my style."

Thom was trying hard not to laugh as he put on his Santa.

A hint of mischief sparkled in Lilah's bright blue eyes. "It was a lot of work. It won't kill you to try it on."

Liam scowled. "You did this on purpose."

She grinned from ear to ear. "You still owe me one."

Liam gave in, and Lilah set her camera on a tripod. I scooted closer to Thom who was already sitting next to his brother.

Lilah rummaged through her bag and pried out four sets of reindeer antlers mounted on headbands.

She put hers on before handing one to Thom and I.

Liam raised his hand in denial. "Over my dead body."

She snickered, set the camera time delay, hurried back to us and wrapped her arms around Liam's neck from behind the sofa.

The flash went off a few times.

She sat on the floor at our feet and checked the pictures from her phone.

Her mouth opened wide. "You, cheater." She smacked Liam's leg playfully a bunch of times.

Thom and I peeked over her shoulder. Liam had used his powers to project illusions for the camera so we were all wearing black satanic robes and holding up scythes.

"Can you believe Liam's favorite cartoon is the Grinch?" Thom's infectious laughter rumbled through the three of us.

Lilah stood back up. "Let's take a real one this time, and you," she pointed her finger at Liam, "I'm warning you. No cheating."

After the do-over, I served dessert and doubled-back to the kitchen for a water bottle. As I closed the door of the refrigerator, Thom was standing behind it, a huge grin on his face.

I arched a brow. "What's up?"

"Liam got the mail."

"The mail?"

His hand cupped my cheeks, and he angled my face to him.

The kiss was slow, almost chaste, and I found myself in no hurry to back away. He reached for his pocket and unfolded a piece of paper. "We're not related. Not even cousins."

"You opened the letter without me?" I said with mock outrage. Inside, I was relieved. One less secret to worry about.

Thom combed my hair behind my ears, and I got lost in those big, warm blue eyes of his. He lowered his mouth down to mine again, and this time, the kiss was anything but chaste.

I grabbed his neck and pulled him closer, planning to melt into his embrace and forget everything. To just *be* for a while. We were great together. We laughed, we talked, we were always there to support one another. We made sense. Why fight it?

His hands closed around my waist, and I stumbled backwards, my ass bumping the counter. A spoon clanked against the ceramic.

Unpredictable as a tornado and mighty as a hurricane, a lump of sorrow knocked the wind out of me. Tears exploded across my closed lids.

Thom froze, as surprised as I was by this sudden and awful development.

I avoided his bewildered gaze and covered a grimace with my hands. "I'm sorry. I can't. I shouldn't have. It's all my fault."

"I didn't mean to push things. I'm an idiot. You made yourself very clear the other day. Nothing is your fault."

My voice shook as I said, "But it is."

It's all my fault. Liam, Faye, the mess with Frank. The bucket of lies had festered.

"Alana, it's not—"

"Stop talking and listen." This was my chance. I had to tell him everything. I formed sentences in my head to explain my trips to New Orleans, my meetings with Faye, my weird dusting power, and my attraction to Liam, but they all sounded wrong and terrifying. Especially the Liam thing.

I had to parcel the secrets out in small, manageable bits. One today. Another tomorrow. But I couldn't. If I talked now, too much would come out.

Paralyzed at the prospect of seeing the hurt in Thom's eyes, terrified he would see me differently, I bolted without an explanation.

I was the mean one who'd stolen Christmas.

JESSIE'S GIRL

Alana

"Merry Christmas," I said tentatively as Thom joined me in the kitchen early the next day. I nibbled on toast, my outburst from the night before replaying behind my eyes. I grabbed my forehead in remorse. My swift exit had been simply inexcusable, especially on Christmas Eve.

"Merry Christmas."

We opened and closed our mouths without making a sound.

"This isn't awkward at all," he said, smacking his lips together.

I tilted my head in contrition. "I'm sorry I bolted."

Nodding, he grabbed two slices of bread and dropped them in the toaster.

"What did you say to Lilah and Liam?" I sipped on my mug.

"I told them you'd choked on mistletoe."

Hot coffee spurted out of my nose.

Thom's mischievous grin as he leaned against the kitchen counter confirmed he was messing with me. I threw my head back and laughed in earnest. Thom joined in, and our chuckles echoed through the house, the tension in my muscles melting away with each giggle.

Thom's sense of humor never ceased to amaze me, and I was incredibly grateful for it.

After catching his breath, Thom reached for his pocket. "I got this for you, but after my blunder, I figured it could wait until morning."

The small jewelry box glared at me from the table. I felt unworthy of whatever was inside. My stomach spooled in a knot, and my fingers grazed the velvet case before I found the courage to open it.

A silver four-leaf clover pendant came into view. It was identical to the one I'd had as a kid. Ages ago, I'd mentioned to Thom in passing that I'd lost this necklace on my first day of college, but he'd never seen it.

With trembling fingers, I traced the silver chain with my index. "How?"

"I found a picture of you wearing it in the album. Had it made special." He handed me a glassy photograph. A close-up of me at around fourteen in which the necklace was clearly visible.

An incredibly thoughtful gift. "Thank you." I opened the clasp and secured it around my neck over the Christmas-y one I was already wearing.

He met my stare head-on. "I pushed you yesterday, and I'm sorry."

"There's no need to apologize."

"I thought the DNA matter was the reason you were holding back."

I grabbed my head with both hands. "It was, and it wasn't..."

He held his hands up in surrender. "I get it. You know where I stand. You're not in the same place. I won't push you again."

"I'm sorry. I'm sending mixed signals. You see..." I couldn't form a proper explanation in my head, let alone speak one.

He shrugged. "It's okay. No need to explain. If you find yourself in that place, let me know. Otherwise, I'll know that this isn't meant to happen." He was letting me off the hook without assigning blame and reprimanding me for leading him on.

I loved him more in that moment than ever. "Thank you." My mind reeled at my own admission. I loved Thom. Without a doubt. Yet, this love wasn't exactly what I wanted it to be. What I needed it to be. And I didn't know how to fix that.

Bursting into tears while we kissed was definitely not the answer.

He buttered his toast but didn't sit down with me at the table, choosing to eat where he stood instead. I supposed my answer had rubbed him the wrong way. He'd expected more. He'd deserved more.

I cleared my throat. "Where's Lilah?"

"I went to bed right after you. I assume she slept in Liam's room."

Those two were always thick as thieves. It bugged me. Never mind the fact that he was supposed to be struggling with his addiction to witch blood.

As if on cue, Liam appeared, wearing dark blue jeans and a black t-shirt, his hair wet. "Lilah's in bed. She's under the weather."

Had he heard our entire conversation with his demon hearing? I searched his face for an answer, but it was simply unreadable.

"Merry Christmas." I gave him a small smile.

He made a weird sound at the back of his throat, halfway between a cynical grunt and an acknowledgment, and sat down across from me with a bowl of cereal. He glared down at the flakes of wheat like meeting my gaze over them would turn him to stone.

I wiped my mouth with a napkin.

Lilah crashing in Liam's bed offered an unprecedented opportunity to visit the only room in the house that was off-limits to me. I faked a yawn before getting up and heading towards his bedroom.

Making as little noise as possible, I entered and waved to Lilah who was sitting with her back propped against pillows. I folded my left leg under me and sat at the edge of the bed. "Merry Christmas. Sorry I disappeared last night. Couldn't cope with the blues."

"It's okay. The first one is the worst." She sneezed loudly. "I'm sick though not surprised. The Mouse King was blowing his nose all over me during the show."

My curious gaze roamed the room.

Same washed-down wallpaper.

Same crappy light fixtures.

Totally different feel.

There wasn't a smidgen of dust visible, like he'd spent hours vacuuming the fluffy carpet. His all-black laundry was neatly folded in the basket at the foot of the bed. The door of the closet was cracked opened, and I glimpsed the black leather bag he used as an armory.

Lilah's words only then registered in my brain. Mouse. King. Blowing. Nose. I crunched my face in confusion and turned to her. "What?"

"The Christmas Show. Nutcracker. It was two days ago."

Lilah was a ballet instructor. "Right. Your show. How did it go?"

"Great actually. The parents were pleased, and the students were so cute in their costumes."

"Wish I could've seen it."

A pile of books on the nightstand caught my attention. Liam was an avid reader, a fact that had both surprised and intrigued me. Except for playing video games with Thom, he rarely sat in the living room without a book in hand. He always hid behind one cover or another and used it as a shield to thwart my attempts at conversation.

Lilah coughed into her elbow. "Can you get me another box of tissues? There's one right there." She pointed to the dresser, and I circled the bed to grab it.

A burst of red caught my eye.

Tucked in the narrow space between the dresser and the corner of the room was a katana. Instead of the black one I was used to, this one had a fiery red wrap handle. A small orange thread intertwined with the crimson cord created a beautiful contrast. The golden dragon on its scabbard had detailed and delicate wings.

I picked it up and unsheathed it. The carbon steel blade was engraved with gold Japanese lettering.

"Wow. It's beautiful," Lilah said.

"Yeah." It was also lighter than the one I trained with. I passed it from one hand to the other with ease. The grip was much more comfortable.

"It looks like it was made for you," she breathed.

As my brain came up with a hypothesis as to why Liam would have such a feminine piece of weaponry hidden in a corner, my fingers ran along the shiny blade.

When I turned around to finally hand Lilah her tissues, Liam was leaning against the door frame, arms crossed over his chest. "It's rude to snoop through other people's room on Christmas."

My complexion quickly matched the katana. "I wasn't snoo—" My throat dried up.

He raised a sarcastic brow.

I shrugged and cocked my head to the side.

He shrugged right back. "Now that you've seen it, keep it."

The weird phrasing hung into the air. Was he implying he hadn't planned on giving it to me? "Really?"

He held his hand out. "You don't like it. No big deal."

My grip tightened around the sheath as I drew the sword closer to my body. "No. I love it." I searched his gaze, but it was slippery as hell. "But did you want me to have it?"

"You're the only one around here who trains daily with one."

Liam mastered in the art of not answering a direct question. I pressed on, "So you did get it for me?"

"Jesus." He raised his arms to the sky and walked out.

I turned to Lilah for commiseration. "Why is he upset?"

She groaned and pressed on her closed eyelids. "Ow. You guys just gave me a headache."

That settled it: I was a moron for not getting Liam anything.

CHRISTMAS DAY WAS SPENT in a haze of leftover turkey and classic movies. The next day, Thom crashed into bed with a fever, too.

I played nurse and cooked a huge pot of chicken soup (the one you have to mix with four cups of boiling water and let sit for five minutes, nothing fancier than that). Liam stocked the medicine cabinet with every flu medicine known to man.

By the middle of the week, Thom and Lilah were miserable. We spent the day huddled up on the couch watching movies. Liam joined us after dinner.

As the credits rolled, I served my two patients tea and Tylenol.

"Want to watch another?" Lilah asked the room.

Thom sipped on his tea like it was the Holy Grail. "Not me. I think the fever's back again."

I ran my hand from the back of Thom's hand to his shoulder and squeezed. "I wish I could heal you guys." I'd tried a few times without a whiff of success.

He scooted away. "We have no idea if your powers even work on viruses. Be careful, or you'll end up like us."

I hadn't been sick in years, so I hadn't thought twice about spending the day with them. "My dad had this amazing tea for strengthening the immune system. I'll get the ingredients tomorrow and make some."

Liam huffed from the lounge chair, his face obscured by his latest novel. "Don't tell me you believe your dad's homemade tea is the long-awaited cure for influenza."

I clicked my tongue. "Don't be a jerk. It really works."

A dry snicker twisted his mouth. "I bet it does."

"Laugh all you want, but I've never caught a cold. Anyway, you're not the one who has to drink it."

Liam was immune to human diseases, another perk of demon-ism. He lowered his book on his thighs. "You're exaggerating."

"I'm not."

"You're telling me you've never had a cold in your entire life?"

"I've got the immune system of a crocodile because of Dad's herb. He grows it in his garden every year. It's a family secret, you see—" Three pairs of eyes zeroed in on me, and the rest of my boastful outburst about my perfect immune system got stuck in my throat. "What?"

Thom coughed. "What kind of herbs?"

"White dead nettle."

Thom shot a glance at Liam who said, "Never heard of it."

Thom disappeared into his room for a minute and came back with a small green book. "Here. White dead nettle." He scanned the text and flicked the page with the back of his hand. "Here. Your dad fed you Archangels. To advert danger, to protect, to *conceal*." He tilted his head to the side and shot me a sympathetic gaze. "He knew what you were."

"Wait a second," I breathed the words, trying to slow things down.

The carpet had been pulled from under me, again. For weeks, I had suspected my dad knew I was a witch, but the little girl inside me had refused to believe it. Stunned, I hunched down on a chair. "Dad knew. He knew, and he didn't tell me."

"Maybe he had a good reason," Lilah said.

What reason could there be for hiding such a secret? His lies had almost gotten me killed.

All the resentment and anger I'd been working so hard to smash down reared their ugly heads.

Where were they? Had Mom known or only Dad?

Mom was the worst secret keeper in the world, so I figured she knew nothing. How had Dad explained my disappearance to her? How had he convinced her to pack up and leave? Was she mad at him for keeping the secret? How had she reacted when he'd told her?

Had there been a plan in motion for the three of us to go somewhere safe together? Dad certainly hadn't gone to my mother's coven for help since Faye and Adeline didn't even know I existed. Maybe my biological father held the answers?

Lilah's brows bowed down. "Do you want to talk, sweetie?"

"No." If I emptied my heart to Lilah, I'd spill the beans on everything. "Excuse me." I had to talk to Faye, so I retreated to my room, closed the door and typed a hurried text, hoping for a swift response.

Need to speak. Are you guys back from wherever?

The phone buzzed back almost instantly.

Yes.

I'll be there early tomorrow morning.

There was a soft knock on my door, so I tucked my phone into my jeans, bewildered to find Liam on the other side.

Hands in his pockets, he swayed back and forth on his feet. "You okay?"

Liam had never asked me how I was feeling. Not ever. He made a point not to meet my eyes, glancing around like he was super interested in my wallpaper.

Arms braced around my chest, I lied, "Sure."

"Okay." He turned his back to me.

My chest deflated. "I'm pissed actually."

He spun around at the first syllable and entered the room.

The crack in my defenses got wider. "He should have told me."

"I bet he's beating himself up for not telling you."

"But why did he lie?"

Liam picked up the book on my nightstand and looked at the back cover before putting it back. "He probably thought he was keeping it a secret to protect you or out of loyalty to someone else."

Loyalty to someone else... What was he implying? My arms fell at my sides. "It didn't protect me in the end. He should have told me the truth."

"The truth is scary sometimes."

My phone vibrated against my butt-cheek, and I gnawed on my thumb, anxious to see what Faye had written. My eyes widened when Liam noiselessly closed the door.

The shadows around him thickened, and the energy in the room shifted. "We all keep secrets." His voice was quiet, intimate. He wasn't talking about my dad anymore. "We lie to protect ourselves and others." Liam searched my gaze. The graveness highlighting his silver irises blew all notion of Faye out of my mind. He reached for my hand, guiding it away from my face. Skin brushed against skin. "I'm tired of secrets."

The hushed words echoed through my soul. "Me too."

"Like what happened with Frank... or the mysterious person you were texting just now."

I jerked away.

God. For a second there I thought...

Humiliation and disappointment seared my face.

"You're all red," he said.

I re-crossed my arms over my chest and retreated to the back of the room. The foot of the bed created a nice barrier between us, and the distance cleared the fog that had taken hold of my brain. Is that why he'd acted so compassionate? To manipulate me into spilling my secrets? Knowing Liam, it made perfect sense.

My voice strengthened as I said, "Stop accusing me of lying about Frank. Is that why you came to my room? To accuse me of lying?"

"I came into your room to cheer you up."

"Well, stop! You suck at it."

"You're angry with me." He squinted like he was zooming in on my face, like he could read my thoughts through my skin and taste the emotions on my breath.

I straightened my button-down blouse, playing with the edges. "I'm not angry. I'd like to be alone, that's all."

"Oh." A strangled snicker twisted his mouth. He disappeared and materialized next to me, moving too fast for me to see. I cowered in surprise, my arms behind me, palms flat against the wall. He advanced all the way into my bubble, and the pull of his damn beautiful eyes became impossible to resist. "You thought I was talking about the *other* secret." The heat of his words caressed my chin.

Every hair on the nape of my neck stood up, and anticipation foamed inside my bones.

His index finger and thumb reached for the delicate silver pendant resting between my breasts, and heat spread from the pit of my belly to the tip of my toes.

"Are you feeling lucky tonight, Alana?" The low baritone of his voice dripped with sexual innuendo.

My nails dug into the wall at my back and my hips tilted forward, swallowed by his gravity. "Err—What?" *TeamThomTeamThom-TeamThom.*

"Your necklace. It's supposed to bring you luck."

Why are we talking about my necklace?

He flipped the four-leaf clover between his fingers. "It suits you. And you love it."

"I—I guess."

The pendant fell back into place as his fingertips grazed my skin all the way to the hollow of my neck. He hooked the choker I'd forgotten to take off. "The other one is no good in comparison. It's flashy, but it won't last." With a quick sleight of hand, he cut the fashion necklace in half and dangled it in front of my eyes. "Be careful. Wearing two at the same time ruins the look."

Holy shit.

A quiet gasp parted my lips as he jolted back about a foot, the brazen curl of his mouth telegraphing how satisfied he was with his carefully chosen words.

The double meaning of our conversation crashed into me like a high-speed train.

My hand clasped his to keep him from walking away. "Wait."

He jerked his arm out of reach. "Don't do that."

"Why not?"

Palms up in warning, he whispered, "You know why."

Thom's unmentioned name simmered in the distance between us.

1 2

REFLECTIONS

Alana

*A*long, long night followed my conversation with Liam, and sleep remained a stranger. I denied the impulse to release the sexual energy that had built up and disarmed me, and that choice increased my restlessness. Embarrassment still coursed through my veins.

Hell, I'd stuttered. Stuttered! I couldn't believe he'd acknowledged, even in metaphor, the attraction between us. His words replayed in my mind. *It's flashy, but it won't last.*

On Christmas Eve, he'd held my hand with no quibble. Why had he acted like it was totally inappropriate for me to do the same?

Unless... unless he'd heard Thom and I kissing.

I got up at the crack of dawn and sneaked out of the house. I had a long drive ahead of me.

No doubt Liam would notice my absence, and half-hashed lies wouldn't fly anymore. The second he ratted me out to Thom, I'd have not one but two suspicious roommates out to crack me open.

. . .

WHEN I ARRIVED at my destination, Faye answered the door and climbed the stairs, a lot more relaxed than the other day. She sat in front of a half-eaten omelet. "Did you come here alone?"

"Yes."

"Did you tell him about us?"

"No."

She nodded and put a forkful of eggs in her mouth.

Adeline's gaze rose from the pot she was stirring. "Why did you want to meet so urgently?"

"My dad... Robert..." my voice broke, a ball of sorrow choking me.

Adeline's arms fell at her sides "He knew you were a witch."

"Yes." I squinted. "Why aren't you surprised?"

"It makes sense."

My face crunched.

"Your father orbited around the Walker family, one fifth of the oldest half-demon species in existence. He's no white lamb," Faye mumbled.

"One fifth?"

Adeline nodded. "Shadow Walkers are divided into five bloodlines. The Walkers are the oldest but not the most prolific. The Hales have that honor with sixteen Shadow Walkers alive at this very moment. Then there's the Nolans, the Olsens, and the hopefully extinguished Blacks."

"There are about a zillion demon species. Why do you care so much about Shadow Walkers?"

The old woman sat next to Faye. "The legend says the first Shadow Walker came from Loki, a demon better known as the Norse God of illusion, trickery, and mischief, impregnating a witch. That's why the Shadow Walkers have such an affinity for witch's blood. Blood of the mother. They used to be pretty benign, grabbing randoms to restock on blood from time to time, using it sparsely. It all changed after the industrial revolution when the hunt became very methodical until they harvested and killed all the unsuspecting randoms they could find. It got even worse about 40 years ago. They don't attack *our* witches, though."

Faye interrupted. "Not yet."

My lips pressed together as I tried to compute all the information. "Why are they so desperate to get more? Are there more demons now?" I asked. If there were more, it'd make sense for them to need more blood.

Adeline cleaned her glasses. "Quite the contrary. Their numbers have dwindled."

"Their appetite is insatiable," Faye said.

Adeline shook her head. "There must be an explanation, but we have no idea. We've spied on the Walkers and the other clans for decades, hoping to figure it out."

"They need to be snuffed out for good. All of them." Faye shot me a dark glare. "Even yours."

I tensed and leaned back on the chair, arms tied around my frame. "Liam's not like them."

"He's a beast. They all are. You have this ridiculous notion that your demon is good. If he's indeed Liam Walker, which I still doubt, he spent a couple years tearing witches, demons, and humans apart with such brutality that his own family had to intervene."

To my dismay, Faye's information about Liam's past matched Frank's assessment of his violent murder sprees. I cringed at the thought that Frank had told the truth. "He saves witches. He saved me."

The venom in Faye's eyes melted into a mix of shock and fear. "Did you sleep with him?"

"No!"

Her arms relaxed, and she sank into her chair. Then, her lips formed a thin line. She leaned towards me over the table. "Did you want to?"

"Of course not."

She snorted. "That's a lie if I ever heard one."

My cheeks heated, and I looked to the side to avoid the judgment coming off of her.

"Janey blushed like that, too," Adeline said with a gentle smile. "Alana, we just met, and I can't pretend to know you, but you're family. You can't afford to fall for a demon. You'd condemn yourself to a life of exile, a life on the run. Plus, you'd never get to have kids. That might not seem important as you're still very young but trust me. The time will come."

I played with the end of my braid. "I know all that." I knew why I shouldn't be attracted to Liam. The cons column would have put Santa's naughty list to shame, but it didn't help me.

Adeline went on, "You don't want to chase after a doomed romance. Never mind the kids. He'll age differently than you. He'll always be connected to them. It's a tragedy in the making."

Faye rolled her eyes. "Who cares about age? He'll kill her before she ages."

I nibbled on my thumb. "Is there a way to get rid of it?"

Faye raised an interested brow. "Your demon? Sure."

My jaw clenched. "I mean my *feelings*."

"A few empaths can alter feelings permanently, but I'm afraid I never had that power," Adeline said.

My thoughts drifted to Lilah. Liam had once said she was incredibly powerful. I might have had the answer to all my problems under my nose all this time.

"The best way to get rid of him would be to accept our help to cleanse you," Faye said. "After, we'll tell you everything you wish to know. You'll be one of us. It's a benign ritual. Takes about 20 minutes."

Her offer enticed me more than I'd expected it to. Saving randoms was important, but wouldn't I be better equipped for the job if I understood my own powers, if I could study the world I should have been born into? It didn't have to be forever.

My answer surprised me, "I'll think about it."

PONDERING ways to get my feelings in line, I drove back to Mobile. The rip-the-band-aid-with-magic approach appealed to me the most.

I pulled in next to Lilah's Toyota, the Vanquish and Thom's pick-up truck nowhere in sight.

The house was silent. I cracked open Liam's bedroom door. Lilah was sprawled out on the bed wearing a robe, her hair tied in a towel like she'd crashed after taking a shower.

"Where's Thom?"

She peeled her back off the sheets. "He's on the mend. He insisted on taking his shift with Rachel."

I sat next to her. "What about you? Are you feeling better?"

"Much."

My eyes darted around the room, giving myself time to build up the nerve to ask about her powers.

She played with the corner of the duvet. "Nice weather outside," she said.

I nodded. "Sunny and warm."

Empty weather talk? Did she sense my hesitation? Was she waiting for me to speak?

I stole a glance from beneath my lashes. Bottom lip firmly tucked between her teeth, she crossed and uncrossed her arms. She wasn't giving me space and time to open up. She had the same look as I did, like she wanted to broach a sensitive subject.

She spoke first. "Where were you this morning?"

The apparently innocuous question surprised me considering the amount of time it had taken for her to get the words out. Why would she be so nervous to ask me about my morning?

Unless...

I unfolded my legs and stood back up. "Liam put you up to this."

She winced, pressing the heel of her hand to her forehead. "He's worried about you."

"I bet." I punctuated the disbelief in my voice with a forced chuckle.

"Is it true? Did you meet someone this morning?"

Eyes cast down, I held my tongue.

"Because if you need help, sweetie, I'm here for you." Her soothing offer was hard to deny.

"I do want your help." I sat back next to her and rapped my fingers on my thigh, not daring to meet her calm gaze. "Can you help me *not* feel something?"

"What do you mean?"

I bit the inside of my cheek. "I want to get rid of... an infatuation."

Her brows scrunched in confusion. "You met a guy?"

I shook my head no.

"But—" She looked down at her lap. "Oh."

I picked at the hem of my shirt. "You really didn't know?" I'd assumed Lilah was being sensitive by not mentioning my absurd attraction to Liam. She'd sensed my crush on Thom the minute we'd met, so it didn't make sense that she wouldn't have picked up on this, too.

"You resisted me so much, I figured I'd butt out."

My nose wrinkled. "Sorry."

She got up and fumbled around in her bag. "Give yourself some credit. It's not easy to block my powers."

The silence stretched on. She grabbed her brush on the dresser and untangled her hair. Lilah always knew exactly what to say. There had never been so much awkwardness between us, and it threw me for a loop. Had I opened a can of worms?

"I'm horrible, I know."

She pried a wet towel from a plastic bag and ran it across her face. "No. It's just... weird."

"We don't have to—"

"I'm not getting involved. It would be unfair to you, to Thom, to Liam... But I'll say this, I've never been in a situation where living a lie ends well."

"You think I should be honest with Thom?"

She patted foundation onto her skin. "You should find a way to be honest with yourself and not be ashamed of your feelings. Whatever they are, you need to embrace them. Shutting down emotions is like putting a longer fuse on a bomb. It'll always go off, and you might not get to choose when."

"How can I not be ashamed? I'm attracted to two brothers for God's sake. It's icky."

Finally, she stopped fidgeting and browsing her make-up long enough to meet my gaze. "Feelings are never wrong or right. How we act on them can be, but the feelings themselves are what they are. Pure."

I braced a hand over my breast. "It's doesn't feel pure to me. It's a weight that gets heavier and heavier as the weeks go on. It needs to stop."

She sat next to me and hugged a pillow. "Trying to control romantic feelings... It never works. Trust me. At the risk of sounding cliché... we love who we love."

I thought back to Rachel's unabashed question about love. I didn't know much about Lilah's past. She had a talent for returning my questions before she answered them, but she did so with enough finesse that I never called her out on it. She would have made a great shrink. "Have you ever been in love?"

Lilah exhaled like I'd punched her in the guts and closed her eyes. "Yes. My parents didn't approve. Her name was Sophie, but that was before the witch thing. I still think of her sometimes." She bowed her head, and tears glistened in her eyes. "I'm not ashamed, but I never talk about it because it hurts too much. You see, my parents were mighty conservative, but I loved them to death. When I told them I was gay, they flipped out and threatened to send me to some program to rewire my brain. They wanted to fix me. I cried my heart out. I wanted them to love me no matter what, not look at me as if I was sick, and I told them how disgusting their offer was."

My eyes fogged up.

She stifled a cry. "When I woke up the next morning, they were totally okay with it. Mom kissed my forehead and said everything I'd wanted to hear the night before. My dad offered to invite Sophie over for dinner. I was confused, but, most of all, I was happy and relieved. I thought the initial shock had relented. It was surreal. I'd barely made it three steps outside the house before Liam grabbed me."

I squeezed her arm, trying to convey despite my stunned silence how much I wished she'd have been spared this horrible ordeal.

"That's how I became a witch," she sniffled.

Magic had flared up when she'd needed it the most, similar to how I'd healed my dad, but in an incredibly heartbreaking way.

A mask of anguish covered her usual warmth. "Turns out, I re-wired *their* brains without even realizing it. It will never happen again. You think you shouldn't be attracted to Liam, and maybe you're right, but there's no quick fix for that. And if there was, you shouldn't pursue it."

"Of course. I'm sorry I even—"

"Please don't ask again. I'll never change my mind."

"I won't." I hid my face in my hands. "I'm so sorry, I had no idea."

"I know." She grabbed fresh clothes and headed for the bathroom. "If you really want my opinion... Yes, I think you should be honest with Thom. He deserves it."

Not once since I'd known her had Lilah been anything but compassionate and understanding. The smidgen of disappointment and annoyance I'd detected in her voice chafed me raw.

Shaken, I went out to the patio. Lilah was right. So right, and yet...

The wind blew unevenly against the wooden fence. Trees had grown beyond it and snuggled in from all sides, but the yard itself had fallen victim to the suburban way of life. I sat on the top step and rested my chin on my knees.

Living at the mercy of a gusty and changeable wind is not ideal, so despite Lilah's well-made argument, I still wished I could better control my emotions. Have them be a bit more like that lawn. Predictable and neat. Too many things *happened* to me. I wanted to happen to things if that made any sense.

I longed for control.

The urge to be strong and smart trampled the rest. Against the chaos in my life, I had to be steady. I had to stop crying long enough to get my shit together.

But there was also this voice in my head. As little as it was, it chanted for me to let go of the reins I held so tightly and see where that might lead. That voice always got particularly loud when Liam was around. I didn't trust that voice. It always got me into trouble.

The yard was angled to the west, and the late afternoon sun warmed me up faster than any positive thought could have. I hiked my black leggings up to my knees and leaned back, my hunched arms holding me half-up. I relaxed my neck and breathed deep. The silent beauty of twilight unfastened the knot in my throat. One loves the sunset when one's sad, or so a little prince told me.

Liam's voice boomed from behind me, "Want to break in your new sword before it gets dark?"

I craned my neck around, but he was already towering above me, his large frame contrasting against the pinkish sky.

"Okay." I tied my hair up in a messy ponytail and sprung to my feet.

Nerves squeezed my belly as I went inside to get my red katana.

The serendipity of his offer empowered the little voice inside. We hadn't trained since we'd kissed. He wanted to act as though nothing happened, and yet, he sought me out so we could get sweaty and breathless together?

Why?

Had he forgotten his speech from the day before? Was he also finding it hard to resist *that* voice? Did he struggle to sleep at night knowing I laid right across the hall? Was he itching to burn down these walls we'd built between us?

It cost me to admit I wanted the answer to those questions to be yes.

Some evidence supported my foolish musings. The corner of his mouth often twitched when I said something funny. His eyes had softened the other day when he'd caught me crying, and the fact that I could always get a rise out of him had to count for something.

Yet, he never let his guard down. Not really.

Our fights were loud and showy. Anything else was hush-hush and could not be mentioned without sparking a new argument. He embraced the violence and spit out all the rest.

It drove me crazy.

We exchanged a few practice strikes, the half-hearted cuts easy to parry. Ten minutes passed before the warm-up gained in intensity as we added foot-work and attitude to our routine.

No matter how stern our sparring sessions strove to be, they always ended up feeling like foreplay, and I was almost ready to acknowledge that fact out loud.

After I nearly got his left knee, he made the sword spin around his wrist a few times.

I called him out, "Show off."

"Let's make it interesting." He passed his T-shirt over his head and tossed it aside. "A bet. If you can't draw blood, you have to tell me whom you met in New Orleans. No super-speed."

I paused, trying hard not to gawk. Typical of him to bank on winning a battle to get me to talk. "How can I tell if you cheat?"

The corner of his mouth stretched into a playful smile. "You can't."

"That's no good for me."

He dug his foot into the ground and shot me a feral look that would have sizzled the Antarctic. "Oh, come on. You know you want to play."

Oh boy did I want to play. "What if I win?"

"I won't bring it up again."

I tucked my chin up, daring him to sweeten the deal.

"And I'll owe you a favor. Anything."

My audacity surprised even me as I stripped out of my long-sleeved shirt. My brand-new red sports bra looked a-mazing. Mind games go both ways, and I did an inward victory dance as he undeniably gawked.

I had to *embrace my feelings*, as Lilah had advised. Well, right now my feelings were yelling at me to make him bleed. And kiss him senseless.

Copying his stance, I raised my weapon. We circled each other. Our blades met, our eyes locking over them as I winced, trying hard not to cave under his strength. Knowing I wouldn't win without catching him off guard, I retreated, and we circled each other again.

When Liam whipped his head in the direction of the trees, I took a shot at his thigh. He pirouetted around my attack and wrapped me up from behind, immobilizing me in a bear hug.

The surprise made me drop my sword.

He'd caught me unprepared, though nothing could have prepared me for the feel of his bare chest against my almost naked back.

"I heard something." His voice was all business.

My eyelids fluttered.

His breath tickled my ear. "Shh."

"I didn't say anything." The words came out as a hot pant, and blood rushed to my belly.

"Your heart is beating like a drum."

"This is serious cardio," I lied.

I repositioned my shoulders, my moist skin rubbing against his, the friction making me shudder.

Liam seemed to forget all about the intruding noise, and his sight dropped to the red katana lying in the grass at our feet. "I win. Time to fess up."

I squirmed to free myself. "I never agreed to it, and I'm pretty sure you cheated."

He turned me to face him, his hands hot against my upper arms. "Bullshit. A bet is a bet."

Here was my chance to let go. It went up in smoke faster than a falling star. "I have nothing to say."

His eyes were dark and dangerous. "We'll see." He pushed away from me and stomped back inside without looking back, his fury palpable.

I sucked in a breath, aware I'd almost surrendered my secrets. *All* of them, including the one I could barely admit to myself.

I walked to the front of the house and barreled down the street. I had to clear my head before going back in there. After I turned the corner, a tingling sensation behind my skull told me I was being followed. Picking up the pace, I veered left, taking advantage of a thick line of bushes to lean and grab my dagger.

The sight of Faye stopped me dead in my tracks. I cocked my head to the side. "You followed me here?"

"I had to see it for myself. I had to see him. See the reason you're throwing your life away." She gripped my lower arm. "Alana, you can't go back there. You have to leave with me. Now."

The panic in her voice made my heart race. "Why are you so freaked out?"

"He's wickedly handsome. It's Liam Walker alright. I don't care what he told you, or what he did for you. He's a monster, and he's onto us. What do you think he'll do when he learns about me?"

"I won't say anything."

"Oh please, I saw you guys fight. You were bewitched."

Hugging my chest, I averted her gaze. "I was not, and Liam's not a monster."

"Killing witches was a sport to him, until it became an art form."

I shivered at the truth in her words. "He quit witch blood eight years ago."

Faye punched the air between us. "Don't be naive. Demons are never far from their next drinking binge. He's playing with his food. Don't stay on the menu. You have to toughen up to survive. You can't win here. You're outnumbered. I thought Thomas Walker was dead, too, but clearly he's still kicking, ready to spawn the next devil."

I shook my head vehemently. "You have no idea what you're talking about. They're my friends. My family."

"You have a family. You have me and your adoptive parents. I can help you find them. Come with me. You have to re-learn everything you think you know." She reached for me again.

I jerked away. "I can't forsake them."

Her eyes hardened. "If you refuse, you'll never see me again. Or Adeline"

"Don't make me choose." No matter how thrilling meeting other witches and learning about spells sounded, I'd never choose her over them.

She stumbled backwards. "You're a fool. We gave you a chance. I should have brought you in."

I shook my head. "You're the one forcing the issue."

"He'll tire of you. You're just too stubborn to admit I'm right."

My chest tightened. "Clearly, being pig-headed is in our genes."

She threw her hands up. "Can't you see I'm worried about you? I loved Jane. When she died, it took me years to recover. I can't tolerate the thought that you'll throw your life away for a *demon*."

Faye had always been collected, if not hostile. The only crack in her armor dated to when she'd heard my name and realized I was her sister's daughter. The torrent of emotions rushing off her froze me in place. "I can't. I'm sorry."

"Not as sorry as you're going to be when he kills you." Her seething voice resonated like a bad prophecy inside my skull.

She marched away and didn't look back. If she had, I would have run after her and begged her to reconsider. My heart sank, but I held strong. Leaving Thom and Liam for a few days, fine. Forever...

That was a hard no.

13

MORE THAN GRAVITY

Alana

"I want to search my old email account," I said to Thom near the end of our morning run.

Faye's ultimatum three nights ago had wrecked my chances to find answers, and I kicked myself for not convincing her to give me more time. I'd texted her a few times, begging her to reconsider, but I'd gotten no response.

I couldn't count on her changing her mind, so I needed a new lead.

Since Dad had known about my magical condition, I was convinced he'd left me a message. If not at home, then maybe via text or email. My old phone was long gone, but I'd rocked the same email address, AMGarfield@gmail.com since I was a tween. It was the perfect way to contact me discreetly.

"Okay," Thom said.

I slowed down. "I expected you to fight me to the nail on this."

"It's an unexplored lead. It's worth a shot."

"But?"

He rubbed the arch of his brow. "I advised you not to log in because your parents might be used as hostages, but that wasn't the only reason."

Advised was a soft word considering he hadn't let me use a phone or computer for months. "No?"

"I knew that if you read an email that pleaded for you to come home, you'd be miserable. It would have torn you apart not to write back."

A younger, naïver Alana would have been upset that he'd hidden the entire truth from me. He'd implied an army of tech-savvy demons were ready to trace my computer if I so much as logged into one of my accounts, but I understood.

I'd been in bad shape for a few weeks. Lost. Grieving. Confused. Reading how heartbroken my parents were over my disappearance would not have helped.

"Are you saying we could do it at home?" I asked.

"No. Let's be careful. We drive an hour out of town and use a public computer."

"Okay."

We turned the corner and sprinted the last few blocks. Once we reached the driveway, I leaned with my hands on my thighs to catch my breath. "Can we go now?"

"I need a shower first." He used the front of his white shirt to wipe his forehead. The movement bared his abdomen, and I gulped at the sight of his perfect abs. Heat swarmed in my chest, but I blinked and looked away before he let the fabric fall.

Oblivious, he ran his fingers through his hair and cringed. "And a haircut."

Thom's curls had the tendency to spiral out of control the minute they got too long, but it wasn't bad yet. The unruly look was actually pretty sexy. "Already? They barely stick out behind your ears." I tugged on a handful to illustrate my point.

He chuckled. "You always stand up for my curls."

I swung my ponytail around. "Curls are the best."

He shook his head. "Not when you're a guy."

"Well, I love them." I grinned up at him.

His smile fell. Eyes cast down, he scratched the back of his neck. "I'll shower first, and we can meet back here in an hour. I'll drive."

"Okay." I watched him walk away and sighed, dropping my head back in discouragement. My cheeks heated up. *I shouldn't have said that.* Shouldn't have used the word *love*. I'd have to be more careful.

THE STRAINED VIBE hadn't relented by the time he picked me up after said haircut, and I hurried through a short, minimal compliment about it. I couldn't help but contemplate the fact that last-week Thom would not have cut his hair if I claimed to love it.

I'd drawn a line in the sand, and I bet the no-snuggling rule he'd instated under the guise of being sick wouldn't be forgotten now that he felt better.

I guessed it was fair, but I didn't have to be happy about it. Was he punishing me for rejecting him, or was he protecting himself? Sure, we were attracted to each other, but I never got the sense he was about to confess his undying love. We'd spent months cooped up together, and he hadn't been in a hurry to make a move.

I straightened in my seat and wrapped my hands together. "Thanks for doing this with me."

"I'm glad you asked."

I peeked at him from behind my hair. "I wasn't sure you wanted to come."

He frowned and shot me a quick glance. "Why not?"

I smacked my lips together. "I don't know. It got weird earlier."

A long sigh was all I got in response.

We drove north to a small Internet cafe that still provided computers, chatting about anything but the new distance between us.

Once there, I chose the computer in the far back to get as much privacy as the small, low-budget cubicles offered. I felt hot and cold and excited and nauseous and worried. My fingers shook on the keyboard as I entered my user name and password. "How long do you figure we have?"

"Once you log in, if anyone's watching your account, I'd say two hours max. One if we want to be really safe." He sat a few feet away, giving me space.

My mouth formed an O as I exhaled and pressed Enter.

The unread emails went up to several thousand. Damn spam. I did a quick search for Mom's address. Then Dad's. The results showed old messages, but nothing since my abduction.

I sighed, knowing I had to sweep through all of them one by one.

Before I started, I entered Kelly's name in the search bar. Kelly had been my best friend since early childhood and the only person who regularly emailed me. Several unread messages popped up, and I read them in chronological order.

Mon, 11 Apr 16:45:15
You missed our lunch date. I texted you all day. Did you break your phone or something? Are we still on for tomorrow?

Wed, 13 Apr 20:35:23
Lana write back. I'm freaking out. I called your Mom four times and there was no answer. Mrs. Baker said an ambulance came to your house on Sunday night?

Thu, 14 Apr 00:18:46
I just came from your house. You parents aren't there. What the hell is going on?!!

My heart hammered at this unexpected confirmation that my parents had left quickly after my abduction.

Sun, 17 Apr 18:12:46
You parents haven't been home all weekend. I called the police, and they were huge assholes. I don't care who died. Just tell me so I can relax. Please.

Wed, 19 Apr 17:17:33
Your apartment's been ransacked. The policeman gave me his card and said to call if I heard from you. He was a super-creep, so I went to the precinct,

and they said he didn't work there. I can't eat. I can't sleep. Your Facebook is gone, your Twitter erased. Your mom's email bounces. It's like you dropped down the face of the Earth??????????????

I shot Thom an alarmed glance and tapped on the screen for him to come closer and read.

He leaned over me, one hand on the chair at my back. "They swept through your things."

I glanced up at him. "Do they usually do that?"

"Yes, but not the social media thing. That's weird."

My feverish fingers clicked for the next message to appear.

Sun, 08 May 18:12:46
You've been evicted. Your landlord let me pack up your stuff so he didn't have to do it himself. Lana, where are you?

Mon, 09 May 03:23:58
I'm going crazy thinking you're dead. Tell me you're not. God, Lana. Are you dead?

My eyes watered. Thom's hand squeezed my shoulder, and I rested my cheek against it.

Thu, 20 May 10:47:04
Screw that. You're not dead. I can feel it in my bones. I'll find you.

Sat, 29 May 3:51:39
My computer's been stolen. Every single one of my posts with your picture has been deleted. I'm scared Lana.

"Who would do that? Steal her computer?" I asked.

"Someone who didn't want your picture to go around too much."

My brows raised. "Sounds like it helps me stay hidden."

"Yes."

Had to be someone who wanted to keep me safe. If it was my parents, I might be able to reach them.

Tue, 11 Oct 00:01:41
Remember when we said we'd do something cool when we turned 21? Well, I'm in Spain, but it sucks without you. Wish you were here.
I miss you, Garfield.

A lonely tear fell down to my lap. God. All this time she'd been thinking about me and wondering if I was dead. How horrible. I'd spent so much time worrying about what my parents were going through that I'd almost forgotten about Kelly. I'd been so preoccupied with my own shit, I hadn't put myself in her shoes. If she'd disappeared like that... I would have gone to bed everyday thinking of her and woken up every morning with a sense of loss.

Thom handed me a tissue. "Are you going to write back?"

I sniffled. "No. I want to see her. She doesn't deserve to have this big question mark haunt her for the rest of her life."

Thom scratched his neck. "Are you sure? What can you tell her?"

"I don't know. I'll figure it out on the way."

He tilted his head to the side. "Wait. You want to go now?"

"Not *now*. I still need to sweep through all the messages."

"It's a hell of a long drive."

I shook my head. "Drive? Uh-uh. Too long."

"You want to fly there?"

"Why not?" I asked with a shrug.

Thom's forehead creased. "You'd need to get Liam on board."

I returned my attention to the screen. "I'll ask him."

"He'll say no."

Thom's conviction that Liam would deny my request clashed against my certainty that he wouldn't. I stared hard at the screen. Liam was the most stubborn and self-assured person I'd ever known, yet I was confident I could convince him to do something that would drive him nuts. Oh, he'd give me grief the whole way, but I had no doubt he'd do it.

Why is that? The sneaky little voice in my mind asked.

There was a time when Liam wouldn't have given me the time of day or bothered to answer any of my questions. Then, he would have met my demand for an impulsive, unplanned, and unreasonable trip to my hometown with nothing but a sneer.

"You'll help me convince him," I breathed to Thom, but the ace up my sleeve wasn't his assist. Not anymore.

Liam wouldn't say no because, as much as he'd hate the idea, he'd hate the idea of me going alone more. He cared about me, a thought I rarely allowed my brain to form.

I'd explored Liam's mind long enough to know he was attracted to me but didn't *love* me. In fact, he was utterly convinced he could never love anyone nor deserved to be loved after all he'd done.

Yet...

Liam and I, we had this connection. Magical or otherwise. While nurturing it was a horrible idea, I wasn't quite ready to snuff it out. It didn't make sense. It was volatile and ill-advised and scary as hell, but he felt it, too. I pressed my hand to my mouth, a smile threatening to twist my treacherous lips. *Concentrate on the emails. Time is of the essence.*

The long, fastidious search led nowhere. Thom and I grabbed lunch at McDonald's after.

As he passed me my food, he said, "It got awkward this morning because I don't know how to act around you anymore."

That was quite the ambush by ketchup. "Why?" I asked, winning the prize for stupid question of the year. I grabbed my forehead and groaned.

"I'm afraid to say or do the wrong thing." The soft and sad shape of his lips made my heart squirm.

I thought about his answer. We'd had a rough couple of months. I'd avoided him after kissing Liam, kissed him hard then rejected him, lied my ass off to cover my tracks, and exploded into tears for no apparent reason while we made out. No wonder he walked on eggshells around me. "I'm acting crazy, aren't I?"

"You? Never," he joked.

Fast food had never tasted so complicated. Happy Meal, my ass.

He opened the door for me on our way out, and I looked up at him. "I wish it would go back to the way it used to be." It was silly and selfish, but it was the cold hard truth. And I owed him more honesty, if nothing else.

To my surprise, his lips pressed together like he was considering my plea. "I don't know if I can do that. Maybe..."

My heart ran. Was he saying we could go back to a simpler time? *It might be just what I need to return to my senses.*

I snaked an arm around his back. "But you see, it would be a waste of a great snuggle buddy."

"Great? I'd say you're adequate," he said in jest.

I raised my hand to smack him, but he caught it and wrapped me up in a hug, laughing.

And it felt great, so I went with it. "Adequate," I grumbled against his chest, but I was thrilled, really.

Maybe we didn't have to be *less* or *more*. Maybe we could just be *us*. Maybe we didn't all have to fit into one of society's neat boxes. I needed to believe that we could beat the odds.

14

HOMETOWN GLORY

Alana

"No," Liam said after I asked him to come with me to my hometown.

A gleeful grin stretched across my lips, the smile of a girl who knew she had already won. "Yes."

He ruffled his hair. "You've already decided this. You're infuriating."

I nodded gravely. "It's time. I want to talk to Kelly, and I need to see for myself if my parents left me a message. I'm going home, and you're coming with me." I tugged on his sleeve and tilted my head to the side.

He opened his mouth and closed it again before raising his index finger and poking my chest with it. "But I'm in charge. If there's a whiff of trouble, you will do what I say."

I extended my hand. "Deal."

WE LEFT EARLY the next day. I didn't bother to pack a bag. If we hurried, we'd easily catch a return flight before dinner. There was no reason to drag the trip overnight, and spending a night with Liam in a hotel, alone, was not a good idea.

We landed before noon, and I took the wheel of our rental car. Liam didn't know these streets like I did.

The cold, the snow, the dead trees. Everything blurred behind fresh tears. I opened my eyes wide so they wouldn't spill over. "Let's go to my house first."

"Park at least five blocks away."

As we walked the rest of the way on foot, just before my house was about to come into view, Liam grabbed my arm. "Wait." He canvassed the street again.

"Is there something wrong?"

"Bear with me. My instincts are begging me not to let you inside that house. Last time I entered that house I almost—"

"You almost what?"

He shook his head. "Nothing."

"Almost what?"

He looked to the sky and growled.

The last time he'd entered that house, he'd left me handcuffed to a headboard, and I'd been kidnapped by an egotistical maniac who'd almost flayed and raped me. If anyone had the right to be upset about that day, it was me, not Liam.

My stomach flew down past my feet as we turned the corner. I couldn't breathe. I couldn't think. This house was the living, breathing proof of a life that didn't exist anymore and probably never would again. It stood there like an unshakable poltergeist, so familiar and yet so different. Had it always been so small? Had the roof always been that steep?

I held my breath as Liam opened the door. He shadowed me as I went from room to room, finding nothing but painful memories. I choked on a sob as I entered my bedroom.

His weight shifted from one foot to the other. "We should hurry…"

"Is compassion completely out of your range?" I cried out.

The corners of his mouth curled down, and he made a fist. "It's dangerous to stay. We've already been in here too long."

"Let me just get a few things."

Liam tugged on my curtains and glanced at the street. I hurried to my closet and pried out my childhood stuffed bunny and the old, creased copy of *The Little Prince* my dad read to me when I had nightmares.

Hugging my treasure to my chest, I headed back downstairs, Liam quick on my heels, and exited the house. I gazed back as I stepped on the curb, my insides in knots. Would I ever come back here? What if this was the last time I laid eyes on this house?

My chest expanded with a heavy breath.

Once in the car, I opened the precious book and gasped as a note fell out of it. My hands shook as I unfolded the paper.

Garfield, if you're reading this, it means you're alive, and for that, I'm eternally grateful. It also means I haven't found you, yet. Get out. Leave this house. Put at least forty miles between you and this forsaken place before reading any further. They are watching.
Call this number at exactly 10:38 pm, and I'll answer.
If I ask you for your location, don't give it to me. Even if it's my voice. It would mean I'm compromised. If I don't answer... never come back here. You need to put your safety above all else. If I'm alive, I'll find you and contact you when it's safe.
I love you, honey.
Dad

A lump was stuck in my throat, and I pressed a hand to my breast. Blood whooshed at my temples fast enough to dizzy me.

Liam leaned in, reading over my shoulder. "Your father is paranoid as fuck. I like him already."

I smacked his shoulder, about to burst. "It's not a joke."

"I know." He steadied my hand, his long, warm fingers molded against mine. "You're shaking."

"Well, duh!" I was shaking indeed. The note had sent goosebumps, shivers, tremors and a whole buttload of teeth-clanking, heart-hammering adrenaline through my body.

He pried my fingers away from the letter gently. "Careful, or you'll rip it in two."

Our eyes locked, and he let go of my hand. "We should go."

I exhaled and gripped the steering wheel.

Liam shifted in his seat. "That note's probably very old."

My throat tightened. What if it was so old that they wouldn't answer? I wiped the tears off with my sleeves and put the car in gear.

A ball of nerves popping around my chest, I drove to Kelly's mother's house, knowing she'd be there for the holidays. They might not get along great, but they only had each other. Her car was parked in the driveway. I was breathless and unsure of where to start.

What would I say? Nothing about magic. "I'm a witch and demons want me dead" is not a valid way to explain your sudden disappearance to your childhood BFF. Maybe the mobsters theory would work. After all, I'd believed it.

Liam's knuckles clenched as I opened the car door.

I paused. "You disapprove."

He looked out the window. "It's a mistake."

"Why?"

"No matter what you say, it won't be the truth."

"But she'll know I'm okay," I said with an indecisive sigh.

He leaned towards me. "You want to see her. I get it, really I do, but you're only putting her in danger. Love is a luxury you can't afford. A liability. The more you love her, the more likely she is to be used against you. She's sad she lost you, but she's still untouched by all our shit. Don't ruin that for her."

I inclined my head away from him and closed my eyes. His advice was devoid of snark and condescension. He believed every word, and I was touched by the rawness in them. It was a rare thing to witness.

No deception would ease Kelly's pain, only the truth, but the truth was unbelievable and dangerous. Lies had poisoned enough of my relationships. Was I willing to paint her last memory of me black?

I slammed the door shut and turned the engine back on. Not allowing myself the time to reconsider, I drove straight to the airport.

As we returned the borrowed car to valet parking, Liam shot me a sideways glance. "Well—"

Afraid to burst into tears if he said something harsh, I cut him off. "Don't be mean."

He sped past me.

I tucked my shoulders in and followed in his stride, unable to summon the apology he deserved. Angry and taciturn Liam was easier to handle. The brutal honesty he'd served me earlier scared me.

Fear ruled my tongue when it came to him. Fear of asking why, if he was so upset at me for lying, did he let me get away with it. Fear that my imagination was getting the best of me. Fear that, if I allowed myself to think these thoughts I refused to formulate, I'd head down a path that would put my heart in jeopardy.

Anger is my instinctual response to fear, and I'm a fierce protector of my heart. Too bad I agreed with him. Love was a liability I couldn't afford.

DAD DIDN'T ANSWER at 10:38 pm that night. Nor the night after that. I feared the worse, but maybe Liam was right, and the note was just too old. This field trip had crushed my hopes instead of lifting them.

Rachel invited me downtown for dinner on New Year's Eve, and I accepted. I couldn't spend the rest of my life staring at that damn phone number. Wearing my new skinny jeans, I zipped my black, knee-high boots up and made sure my dagger was tucked in safely at the top and hidden from view.

The boys' voices reached my ears as I grabbed my keys in the bowl.

"I won. You know I did," Thom said.

"No way," Liam scowled.

"Want to settle that with a little sparring session? Alana can be the judge."

"No. Lilah. Alana's biased."

Thom scoffed. "Yeah. Like Lilah isn't."

"It's not the same. Lilah's not my girlfriend."

I expected Thom to set Liam straight, but he didn't. All the same to me. I had no desire to judge a fight between them. I opened the door and crossed their path. Liam walked right past like I was invisible. We hadn't talked since the plane.

Thom scratched his neck. "You look great."

I blushed. "Thanks. Rachel suggested we grabbed a late dinner. I already ate, but it's best to keep an eye on her."

These days she spent most of her time at her parents' or grandma's house, and nobody weird had come around. Christmas was most likely a busy time for evil men, too.

"Want me to drop you off?" Thom offered.

I was going to drive but finding a good parking spot would be a nightmare. "Sure. "

THE STREETS WERE full of taxis and happy drunks as Thom dropped me in front of the restaurant.

"Call me if you need me to pick you up," he said.

"Okay. Thanks."

"Have fun."

I grumbled an acknowledgment and considered the bright yellow and orange neon sign spelling "Zazz". No doubt I was at the right place, but it looked more like a bar than a restaurant, and it was packed. Pajamas and a movie with Thom sounded so much better.

Inside, the restaurant was loud in both sound and style. Hot pink. Bright yellow. Deep purple. A rainbow had puked on the walls, and a cheetah had died on the seats. Animal print was back in style. The excited clientele, mainly under 25, giggled their way through cocktails.

I loosened my shoulders and took a deep breath. I'd have fun tonight if it killed me.

"Nina! Here!" Rachel waved me over to her booth, and I sighed in relief.

We ordered while she gossiped about the semester coming up. Teachers I should change my schedule to avoid. Courses that were essential. Opportunities we couldn't miss like the long-awaited spring break trip to California.

I soldiered through the conversation, knowing very well I wouldn't be around for any such trip, and, with a stroke of bad luck, neither would she.

"I can't wait for classes to start again." She sipped on her diet coke.

"Really?" I was surprised. My college Christmas breaks were never long enough.

"I can't wait for this semester to end. I have an internship lined up in New York for the summer."

"That's cool."

"What about you? Aren't you excited to start?"

I combed a hand through my curls. "I'm nervous. I still don't know many people."

"I'll introduce you to my friends." Her eyes lighted up. "Oh! I know the perfect guy for you. He has a great sense of humor, and he's a real gentleman. I've known him since I was five. I'll set it up."

"Thanks, but I'm not looking for a boyfriend."

Her shoulders slumped. "Too bad. I'll introduce you anyway. You might change your mind. He's a sweetheart."

It annoyed me when girlfriends spoke in such high terms of guys they deemed not good enough to go out with themselves. "Why don't you date him?"

"Like I said, I've known him forever. It'd be like dating my brother."

Brother my ass. If he looked like a young Johny Depp, she would have dated him anyway.

She propped a long, blond strand of hair behind her ears. "Speaking of family, I ran into Mike the other day."

My nose wrinkled. "You did?" I was flabbergasted by the news. Like… a lot.

Rachel leaned closer in a conspiratorial manner. "He gave me a ride home."

My mouth was dry.

"How old is he?"

"29."

"Wow. He looks younger."

Liam's voice boomed into my mind. *"It's the blood of the witches I tortured and killed. The miracle anti-aging cream."* A cringe overpowered my face as my shoulders rose in surprise, and before I could stop myself, I craned my neck around to search for him.

He was almost at our table, and my jaw went slack at the sight of his candy-red, button-down shirt. And I thought *I* looked good in red. On him, the color was glorious. I hid my heated cheeks in my hands.

He greeted Rachel with a carefree smile. "Hello."

Rachel's eyes were wide. "Hi, Mike. Nina didn't tell me you would stop by."

"My dinner plans fell through." He sat down on the bench next to me and stole a fry from my plate. Our thighs rested against one another, and I promptly scooted away.

"What are you doing here?" I asked through thought-speech.

"I was bored."

"Bored? Right!" I drew my bottom lip between my teeth. *"For a guy who didn't want us to speak to her at all, you're awfully chummy."*

He only had eyes for Rachel as he asked, "Busy holidays?"

"The whole family is in town. I needed to get away."

"I know what that's like."

"You guys have a big family?" She batted her eyelashes.

Liam relaxed against the cushioned seat. "Huge. The perks of a blended family."

Her shoulders straightened. "Blended...You guys aren't actually related, then? You look nothing alike."

"She's right, Nina. We look nothing alike." He chewed on another fry.

I played with my chicken with my fork. "I take after my mother."

"Are you an only child?" Liam asked.

Rachel beamed. "I have one older brother. He's an accountant in New York."

"New York's overrated." The way Liam said the words left no doubt he spoke from experience.

She leaned in. "You've been?"

"I lived there for a year. Paris is a million times better."

What. the. hell.

"You must travel a lot."

"As much as possible." A longing sad followed his words.

"How did you end up *here?*" The way Rachel's pitch increased at the end of the question spelled out her dislike for Mobile.

He winked—winked!—before saying, "A lucrative contract."

What was this? His mysterious billionaire persona? I took a sip of water to mask a wince. *"She's totally into you. If only she knew..."*

"If only she knew that I'm a monster?"

I gritted my teeth together. *"You said it, not me."*

Rachel folded her napkin. "I'm going to a party at my friend's house after this. Would you two like to come?"

I raised a cynical brow. Funny how she hadn't invited me before. I opened my mouth to refuse.

"Sounds great," Liam said.

My lips formed a thin line. "Sure."

"Great. Excuse me for a sec. I need to go to the bathroom." Rachel strutted to the back.

I shot Liam a glare, but he was too busy drooling at the tight skirt accentuating Rachel's ass. I swallowed hard because, up to this point, I'd been about 90% positive he'd crash this dinner to aggravate me. Now, I wasn't so sure. *Hell.*

I smacked his arm once Rachel was out of view. "A date? Really?"

"It's not a date. You're invited too."

"Stop playing with semantics and admit it; you're flirting with her." I mimicked his sugary tone, "Paris is better," I scoffed. "God."

"Fine. I'm flirting with her. Nothing wrong with flirting with a beautiful, single woman who's interested."

Double hell. He was serious. "Right."

"Good."

I wanted to disappear into a hole. "Great."

"Shh. She's coming back." His gaze jumped from Rachel to a 30-something man elbowing his way outside, all his cockiness gone in an instant. *"It's him."*

I craned my neck around. *"The seer?"*

"I've seen him before. I'll look into it."

He used his powers to make Rachel think his phone was ringing and cleared his throat. "It's a client. I have to go."

Rachel's face fell.

He turned on his heels and marched out. I'd never been more grateful for the impromptu appearance of an enemy before.

15

RUNNING UP THAT HILL

Liam

$\mathcal{A}$s soon as the door of the restaurant closes behind me, I shimmer into the shadows.

The short but large man crosses the street at a brisk pace, and I follow. I smell his trail. He looks human, but I'm not positive. He peeks over his shoulder, and my muscles tense, my legs getting traction on the asphalt. I'm more than ready to pursue him if he runs.

He doesn't.

Fingers grab my shoulder. Acting on instinct, I twist the intruder's wrist and snake my arm around his neck, ready to snap it off if needed. Alana's scent barrels into me quicker than my eyes recognize her form.

The recoil of my aborted choke-hold has her hanging a few inches from the ground for a second. "Ow. Let me go."

"Don't sneak up on me." I deposit her back on her feet.

"I wasn't aware that I could."

"I was focused on someone else for a change."

Both hands on her hips, she says, "I'm coming with you."

"I hunt alone."

Her nostrils twitch. "I'm coming. Deal with it."

I swallow back my next protest. Even I can see she's no longer the terrified and unexperienced tag-along she used to be. She inspects her bruised wrist, and I congratulate myself for the split-second decision not to smash it to bits. "What did you tell Rachel?"

"Nothing."

I press my lips together to erase the smile that surfaces at her answer. "You bolted without an explanation?"

"I'll explain— Why are you grinning?"

"I'm not."

I recognize easily the verdant shade of jealousy because I've been wearing the obnoxious color for months. The unwelcome giddiness is promptly snuffed out by my go-to scowl.

"I don't need your *help*." I punctuate the word help with air quotes to piss her off.

She pokes my collarbone. "I don't want to *help*. I want to do this. On my own."

No way in hell I'm letting her tail a seer without back-up. "No."

"You're coming with me, but don't make me invisible. I need to know if I could do this without you."

I growl. "You don't need to do this without me."

Alana jolts into a run. "Quick, he's turning the corner."

I look to the sky and groan, giving her a head start.

By the time the man disappears into a worn-out bungalow cramped between two equally derelict houses, Alana's cheeks are flushed, and her chest heaves with excitement. She points to the steel fence circling the lot. "Let's take a look around the back."

I humor her and let her take the lead. Cloaked in shadows, I walk right up to the house and check for surveillance while she crouches towards the backyard like she's Link in stealth mode. A glance inside the house confirms that the man is alone and too preoccupied with his phone to check outside.

Alana sticks out like a sore thumb against the overgrown yard.

"It's taking too long," I shout. The loud advice startles her, and I point to the roof. "What if he had cameras up? You'd already be staring at the barrel of his gun. They're not a bunch of incompetent newbies." Not all of them, anyway.

She curses under her breath and takes cover behind the large shed. "That's what I am, an incompetent newbie?"

I jog next to her at super-speed. "You said it, not me." I use my powers to shield us from our surroundings, the conversation getting a little too loud.

She tries to poke me again, but I step aside. She stomps to the nearest window. "Looks normal enough. Cozy. I'm going in."

I block her path. "You're no ninja. You need a gun for this type of job."

She pats her pockets. "I must have left mine at home."

The idea of Alana carrying a gun is ludicrous. She clearly prefers hand-to-hand weapons, and has a natural talent, too. "It's not as if you'd know how to use it."

"Another word, and I'll punch you in the face."

"I'd like to see you try."

Her spirited eyes find mine, and immediately the air's charged with the exhilarating energy our fights always conjure. I can map every speckle of color in those green eyes of hers, and somehow, I still can't resist their pull.

She chews on the inside of her cheeks. "Fine. Lead the way."

I whiz to the back door and break the lock with a swift twist of the wrist. We enter directly into the kitchen. Empty pizza boxes and open food cans litter the counter.

Alana purses her lips in disgust. "He's a slob."

In the living room, the man is zapping through channels in front of a plasma-screen TV. The microwave rumbles with the rhythmic popping and buttery smell of popcorn.

After making sure he's 100% captive in the illusion of normalcy I crafted for him, I bee-line for the bedroom.

A large table holds three laptops. Two are stacked in the corner while the third is hooked up to a printer and mouse. I press the power button, but the light doesn't turn on. The power cord on the wall is loose, so I push it back into the outlet. While the machine boots, I watch Alana go through the drawers.

She moves with ease, not disturbing anything as she sifts through layers of clothing. "Nothing here."

I swear this girl was a cat-burglar in another life. Despite my efforts to the contrary, it turns me on.

I open the closet. It's empty, so I turn back to the computer. The screen asks for a password, and I grumble. Technology is absolutely annoying. I can't hoodwink a piece of metal, and I'm no hacker. This search is proving to be a complete waste of time.

The printer roars to life. A picture of Alana and Rachel spurts out. Bingo.

The second picture makes me frown. Alana. Alone.

The third picture depicts Thom holding laundry detergent.

Adrenaline spikes in my veins. "He's not spying on Rachel. He's spying on us."

Alana walks over to me. "Maybe your people know we're here and put more than one seer on Rachel?"

I cram the picture of Thom at the grocery store in her hands. "No. That's not it."

"He's working for Frank, maybe?"

"It's not like him."

Her lips blanch.

I dash to the next room and wrap my hand around the unsuspecting man's neck, pinning him down to the lounger he's sitting in. He chokes on a terrified squeal.

"Who do you work for? Why are you following us?" I ease my steel grip on his throat by an inch.

His voice crackles from the trauma to his larynx. "I don't know what—"

I hold both hands behind his back and drag him to the computers. "You're busted, but you're not dead. Not yet." The tattoo on his neck looks familiar, and I grip his collar to see the whole thing.

It's a cross and a scythe. Brotherhood of the dead. Hitmen scum. Amateurs. Frank would never work with them. No Shadow Walker would give them the time of day. Somehow, this is about something else. I wrack my brain for a clue, but I've never had any run-ins with them. Not directly. Nothing that would warrant this type of surveillance.

He starts babbling, "I'm sorry. Sorry. Please. I was hired to follow the redhead. Somebody else tails the guy."

"Who do you report to?" I ask.

"I just know he's a demon. I don't even know his name."

I click my tongue. "What does he look like?"

"Young. Tall. Thick Irish accent. Brown hair. Built like a truck. Please let me go. I don't know anything else."

"I believe you." I don't know who he works for, and this surveillance is atypical to say the least, but he knows our faces. He has to die.

Alana grabs my lower arm like she read my mind. "Liam, wait."

I make sure our prisoner can't hear our conversation and say, "He's a hitman. Believe me. He might look helpless, but if we let him go, we'll have to leave Mobile."

"I understand." She bites her bottom lip. "I—I want to do it."

Her demand kicks me into next week. "To be clear, *you* want to be the one to *kill* him."

"Yes."

Whoa. My eye sockets hurt. The grief she gave me the last time we hunted down a human together is fresh in my memory. "*You* want to kill a man."

She grits her teeth. "That's what we're here for."

"You don't have to be the one to do it."

"It'd be hypocritical of me to look the other way when it's time to carry out the deed. I have to toughen up."

Toughen up? Sure, Alana has a taste for violence. It's something I like about her, but she's only ever killed a ghoul. This sudden need to try her hand at cold-blooded murder leaves me speechless.

The man squirms against my inescapable hold. I don't know what to do, and that doesn't happen to me often.

Alana raises her dagger. Beads of sweat accumulate on her neck.

139

Her bottom lip trembles, and her arm starts shaking before she lets it fall by her side.

Half-disappointed and half-relieved, I swiftly snap the neck of the man and discard his empty shell to the carpet.

Without warning, Alana spins around and hides her face in my chest. Her delicate fingers dig into my shirt, causing my stomach to tighten, and I force my body to stay totally still.

I'm not Thom.

I don't cuddle.

Not ever.

After a few seconds, I summon enough common sense to pat her on the back.

She huffs. "I froze. This man would have killed us given the chance."

"Killing is not easy."

"It is for you." It doesn't sound like a reproach, but the truthful words cut all the same.

I press my lips together and close my eyes, the scent of her coconut shampoo doing all sorts of twisted things to my guts. "It wasn't always. You shouldn't get a taste for it."

Oh, the irony. We're all but standing on top of my latest kill, and the brutal need to leave and take a hot shower imposes itself.

While most kills blur together, I remember my first like it was yesterday. Jeremy Holbrook. Marcus insisted I bring him the head of the boy who had annoyed me the most as a human. I refused. He flayed me to the bone and waited for me to heal before doing it all over again. I reconsidered quickly.

I learned a few valuable lessons that day.

Whips are a bitch.

Eyes don't close on their own after death.

Wearing white to a decapitation is a bad idea.

A car parks in the driveway, jerking me out of my reminiscing.

I hear the voices before Alana knows something is wrong and push her closer to the wall, away from the windows. "We have company."

"Let's slip out the back."

I click my tongue. "It's too late."

"Then what? You kill them too?"

"No. They're angels. I can smell them from here." My eyes search for a good hiding spot. "Here. Quick."

She swallows back a yelp as I manhandle her into the closet.

I point to the attic's hatch, boost her up through the opening above our heads, and jump up after her.

The uninhabitable loft space below the roof is littered with blown-in insulation. The yellowish gray of the fiberglass balls is dull to the eyes, and the stale air dries up my throat in an instant. The hatch is reinforced on all sides by large wood beams, the height clearance barely enough for me to stand.

"Did you say angel?"

I roll my eyes at the sharp interest in her mental squeal. *"Don't get excited. They're demons too. They can teleport and love to feed on dying men. Hence the nickname."*

"Gross. And you can't kill them?"

"They can teleport. That makes them dangerous as fuck in a fight." Especially with her in the mix. Thankfully, they have no super sense of smell or hearing. I make sure the trap is correctly closed behind us. Voices rise from the kitchen.

"The incompetent fool. He was seen. The Shadow Walker killed him." The voice is low and undeniably British, so either the guy from before didn't know shit about accents, or this isn't the leader.

"What? When?" A second, American voice says.

"It's pretty fresh."

"We need to call the boss."

"What if he's still here? Don't move. I'll check the rest of the house."

Alana bites her bottom lip and crosses her arms. She twists her body to face away and bumps into me. I grab her waist to steady her before she reveals our presence. *"Careful. Step only on the beams, or you'll go through the ceiling."*

She rectifies her position, our bodies grazing.

Goosebumps tighten her skin. The stuffy atmosphere of the empty attic is probably not to blame. I let my arms fall at my sides and flatten my body snug against the vertical thrust at my back to avoid pressing against her. She stares ahead as if she's mesmerized by the almost pitch-black space in front of her.

Despite my encumbered brain, I listen for the steps of our enemies a story below. One angel leaves the house, and an engine starts. The other one is still in the kitchen. In a few minutes, we'll be able to leave, but with no leads on the identity of their employer. That worries me.

Alana shifts from one foot to the other and coaxes her hair to the front of her left shoulder. *"I can barely see my feet."* The silent words are heavy and breathless.

Too bad I can see her perfectly.

The black top hanging around her frame dips way too far down her back and offers a sinful view of her spine, right to the hem of her jeans. Her red, lacy bra clashes against her skin. The freckles running up her right shoulder blade form a distracting constellation, and I fist my hands to resist the urge to reach up and graze them.

I remind myself she didn't expect to end up here with me. I didn't intend to guide her into a dark corner.

Well... maybe I did.

She whispers her next question, probably aware that our thought-speech is tainted by a dangerously intimate undertone. "Do you think they'll check the attic?"

I can't even remember why we're here. "No."

"We'll wait for them to leave?"

"Yes."

She clicks her tongue and shakes her head, probably aggravated by my curt answers. "What are we going to do after?"

I have one or two ideas...

The angel inspects the bedroom beneath our feet, and Alana holds her breath when he opens the closet. I tilt my weight to the tip of my toes and lean ever so slightly into her. She backs ever so slightly into me. It's an intoxicating dance, and I'm instantly hard.

The demon beneath our feet follows his associate outside, leaving us utterly alone, but I choke on the "all clear" as her ass grazes my erection. The crazy notion that she knows exactly what she's doing sinks its teeth deep into my brain. She's seen into my soul. She has to know I could never huddle up against her without lust scraping at my every ounce of sanity. Without temptation trampling reason. Without her heat melting me into a puddle of need.

There's no denying the magnetic force beckoning me to reach for her, and I trace a path from her spine to the edge of her shirt with the tips of my fingers. The soft skin feels delicious. My palm travels up, and I stroke the nape of her neck with my thumb, waiting for her to ask what the fuck I'm doing.

She whimpers instead. The sound unravels me.

She twists around, and the opportunity is impossible to resist. I bury my hands into her alluring copper locks and dip my head down to swallow her gasp.

My cells scream in triumph. She tastes like sin and coconut, and I want to consume her. To mark her. To sear her flesh with a damning kiss.

When her fingers dig into my stomach, I take it as a sign of protest and pull back. Disappointment nicks my ribs. With lips slightly parted, she's fighting for breath, her beauty terrible to withstand. The longing written across her flustered face blows me away.

A small hand sneaks under my shirt, trembling fingers trailing up my stomach.

Half-mad, I pick her up. Her legs spread to each side of my midriff, and her arms wrap around my neck. Our tongues greet each other like old friends.

Fuck yes. I bump my head against a beam. Pressing her hard against me with one arm, I kick open the damn latch and jump down.

"What about—"

No talking! We suck at conversation.

I silence her with my mouth and don't let her breathe until she tugs on my hair. Her lips, her scent, her waist, her thighs... I'm shaking.

The blood rushing to her chest gives her skin a stunning glow as I kiss my way down the slope of her neck.

She hums. I growl. Desire blazes through every nerve ending as I pin her against the wall and hike her shirt up. I graze the tender flesh of her sides all the way up to the lace of her bra and trace the curve of the underwire with my thumb.

Her stomach tightens. She adjusts her weight and ends up flush against my erection. A low hiss escapes me. Instead of cowering away, she grinds her hips harder into it. My fingers dig into her back, my body hungry for her, frantic for her.

Our gazes lock, my bottomless lust reflected in her eyes. The arguments, the fights, the lies. They don't matter.

She wants me.

No weird, magical, out-of-body phenomenon to blame this time around. No easy excuse, no misunderstanding, no other explanation. Nothing to hide behind. No one around to interrupt.

I'll tear the clothes off her sweet, sweet skin and take her right here against the wall, and nothing will stop me.

Not even Thom.

The intrusive thought turns my blood to ice and my muscles to stone.

Thom.

Fuck.

A torrent of guilt and self-loathing floods me. The darkness fractures my defenses, and a familiar pressure wraps around my brain. Filled with horror and utterly unable to stop it, I feel the vicious strain of my unshakable disease snake around my synapses.

The Collective rides hard into me, Frank heading the charge. The world around me freezes, and I'm left standing a few feet beside myself.

It's only an illusion, but I can see the scene from the outside. I can see it all. My hands are gripping Alana's waist as I pull her close, her arms are wrapped around my neck, her back is arched...

Frank's form appears beside the frozen image and points to us, his jaw dislocated in mocked awe. *"K-I-S-S-I-N-G... Oh boy, you're a real sucker for punishment. Didn't you hear her make-out with Thom on Christmas Eve?"* He counts to seven on his fingers. *"That was what? Seven nights ago? Bet you gave her the sword after all."*

He eyes Alana up and down, his sight lingering on her bare stomach.

A territorial growl tears my throat.

"Let's take a look at what's next." Frank snaps his fingers. *"Sex. Hushed conversations. More denial. A fight. A love scene."* A string of images flanks his words, acting as visual aid to his predictions. *"You and Lana ridden by guilt but not enough to stop. Yada-yada-yada... And we arrive at— Ah, yes. My favorite part."*

I'm standing between Alana's legs, my jeans pooled at my feet. She's sitting at the edge of the kitchen counter as I push into her. The rapture on both our faces is eclipsed by Thom's horrified grimace as he walks in on us.

"When Thom catches you two sneaking around behind his back, who do you think he'll blame? His perfect little witch or the untrustworthy beast he used to call his brother?" Frank pauses, leaving me to my shame for a few seconds as I contemplate a future I can practically taste.

He cracks a smile before continuing, *"The best part is, Junior will forgive you. It's not like he expects better of you."*

I cringe at the truth in Frank's words but stay silent. He obviously wants me to attack him, but I won't give him the satisfaction of sending me into a debilitating mania. The assault has to be nearing its end.

"They might have been happy, you know? Without you." Frank zooms in on a picture of Alana wearing a clean, white dress. She's leaning against Thom. There are flowers and rings involved.

The happiness on their faces is simply pornographic. I squeeze my eyes shut, hoping to erase the image from my memory.

Frank snaps his fingers again. We return to the present moment. He grabs my chin and angles it towards her. *"The little minx has you wrapped around her fingers. She loves to play with fire. How long do you think it'll last? It's not like you will ever give her up. Thom will make a good husband, but you'll be the better lover. Demon stamina and all. Do you think she'll call you up the night before the wedding for a last tryst? Or will she keep you around to ease the boredom of domesticity? Will you fuck her until she's old and wrinkly?"*

Frank leans toward my ear, his voice but a murmur, *"Wouldn't it be better to kill her now? Fuck her first, of course."* He takes a pregnant pause and grazes her hair.

Unable to stop myself, I swat his hand away.

He lets out a soft breath, *"Fuck her all night; then kill her. Blame it on me. Don't let her ruin the rest of your life. We both know that's what you're really into... Blood and death. Am I right, brother?"*

His body blurs as he tries to plant a vicious kiss on my lips, and I ram what's left of his throat up against the wall with my arm.

"Liam!" Alana's mental yell barely registers against the snickers of the Collective.

I've been too weak to withstand the assault, and I hurt her. Again. I quake in shame. My entire existence can be boiled down to a string of broken promises amounting to weakness and disloyalty.

I let him win. Let him taunt my demon out to play. I'm stronger than this. I'm more than the lust-driven lunatic she reduces me to. If things keep escalating, I might do more than bruise her. The beast is a part of me that I can't cut out. Blood and death... I don't want that for her. It has to stop. Now.

Before I lose my grip and end up doing exactly what Frank suggested.

16

THIS KISS

Alana

*L*iam was gone. The Collective had ripped through him mid-kiss, his eyes unfocused like he was seeing them and not me.

It wasn't the first time the Collective overtook his mind during a crucial moment, but this timing sucked the most. I cradled the sides of his face and extended my mind towards him, trying to find a way in.

Eyes closed, I heard an echo, and the sound of Frank's voice curdled my blood. *"Fuck her all night; then kill her. Blame it on me. Don't let her ruin the rest of your life."* I flinched back in disgust.

Frank had a way of twisting everything. His speeches had affected me for weeks, and I didn't even know him. He'd totally ruin the mood. On the tip of my toes, I planted a kiss on Liam's lips to shake him out of his episode.

Wrong move.

His arm slammed my throat against the wall and stretched my neck almost to breaking. "Liam. Liam stop."

I couldn't breathe. I couldn't speak. Black spots danced in front of my eyes.

All my strength went into a mental yell. *"Liam!"*

One second he was killing me, the next he was pure stillness like he'd pressed the pause button on his entire being, his bloodstream probably hanging in stasis.

The statue reminded me how fragile I was.

Being fragile sucks.

I extricated myself from his frozen grasp and massaged my bruised neck. He looked as though he was far away, locked into a deep corner of his mind. Despite the pain, I roved my eyes over his face. It was a rare opportunity to observe him up close without words getting in the way. His skin was smooth, freshly shaved, and most of his red shirt's buttons were undone. I'd been keen to explore the hard muscles underneath.

I blushed. "Hey, can you hear me?"

Long seconds passed before his pupils contracted and focused back on me. I expected him to be shaken and apologetic, so the hatred burning in his eyes threw me for a loop.

"You're still here," he growled.

"Ugh?"

"I came this close to crushing your neck. Run, for fuck's sakes. Don't you have a smidgen of self-respect?"

Arms crossed, I stepped back. "Self-respect?"

"You kissed me."

I huffed. "I remember it differently."

"I'm a demon. It's not enough to *kiss* you. I want to *inhale* you. I want to chop you off into little pieces and snack on you until the end of time. It's not romantic. It's a sickness."

The words created a hard band in my stomach. "I'm not some love-struck teenager. I don't find it romantic when you almost strangle me to death."

"Then stop kissing me."

"Again, I think you're the one that—"

His nostrils flared. "Jesus! Are you twelve? It doesn't matter who kissed who first."

"*You* did. Twice."

"Fine."

Fine was Liam's equivalent of *piss off*, but this time, I wouldn't let him act as though nothing happened. This wasn't an out-of-the-blue make-out session. The entire week had been leading up to this, and no amount of denial would convince me otherwise. "Don't pretend the blood is the only reason you're attracted to me."

A muscle in his jaw twitched. He turned away. When he turned back, his eyes were cold. So cold. He looked me up and down. "What else is there?"

With both hands, I shoved his stomach. Hard. "Go to hell!" I stormed out wishing I'd sucker punched his throat instead. He deserved it, though I doubted any blow from me could ever hurt him. Boy, did I want to bring him pain.

He had to be lying, but I didn't know for sure, and the uncertainty stung. If he wasn't lying…

I marched into the night and slammed the door behind me hard enough to make the walls shake. If he wasn't lying, I was the most pathetic loser on the planet. Fairy tales had messed with my head so bad I thought he might have feelings for me. *Feelings.*

God. I AM twelve.

What else is there? That asshole.

Letting this infatuation sprout had been a huge mistake. My current course tasted like a biblical cautionary tale minced with a dash of doom. Adeline was right. Liam and I were a tragedy. I'd known this would happen. I'd known how dangerous it was to let him under my defenses. I was done chasing shadows. *If I were smart, I'd cross them both off my heart.*

I checked my phone. It was a quarter past midnight.

Happy Fucking New Year.

Time for a resolution. No more wavering. No more foolishness. No more Liam.

I called a cab first, then Rachel. My behavior from earlier made no sense to me now. Why hadn't I stayed with her? Her safety was supposed to be my priority.

"Nina? What the hell, girl? You totally ditched me." The anger in her voice was rich and unapologetic. Rachel wasn't the kind of woman that allowed anyone to dump her twice.

"I'm so sorry."

"Well? What happened?"

If I didn't think fast, she'd hang up on me. "He was there."

"Who?"

"My stalker. Mike saw him first and made up an excuse to follow him outside. I should have stayed put and let him handle it, but I couldn't. I reacted." Webbing lies had become a second skin.

There was a pause before she breathed, "Wow. I'm sorry for the guilt-trip. I totally understand. What happened next?"

The excitement in her voice bugged me. Not only was she eating my fake story up, she wanted seconds. Did she think her life so boring that she wished for a dangerous stalker? I suspected the bulk of her interest in me derived from the stalker story. That and *Mike*, of course.

"We called the police. I have a restraining order. He's in jail as we speak."

"Phew. Did you want to come to the party?" she offered.

"No, I'm heading home. I'll pay you back for the meal."

"Don't worry about that. Happy New Year. I'll text you tomorrow."

"You too. Bye."

My cab pulled up, and I thanked the heavens I had cash in my pockets.

Desperate to avoid Thom and Lilah and not willing to take the gamble that they were already sleeping, I entered my bedroom through the open window.

MY NECK HURT like a bitch in the morning.

I met my gaze in the mirror. *Look at this mess. Nothing romantic about it.* I stroked the inflamed skin. With some luck, I'd heal it and forget all about last night. All of it. Especially the kiss. *But not my resolution to stay away from him.*

Eyes closed, I tried to access my magic. Long minutes passed without a whiff of success, and I finally gave up. Why didn't it work all the time? What secret ingredient was I missing?

A major make-up emergency followed. I shook out my travel kit over my bed in search of concealer. I had no desire to explain the black and blue marks to Thom or Lilah. The cream was cool and smooth as I patted it onto my skin, and I let the first coat dry before repeating the process a second time. A touch-up of white powder dusted into the air, and I threw the only turtleneck I possessed over my head. It hurt too much to do my usual morning training, so I went looking for Thom. He was boxing downstairs.

I tousled my hair so it'd fall around my neck as an extra precaution and greeted him, "Hey. Happy New Year."

"Happy New Year." He hugged me and grabbed his water-bottle. "How did it go last night?"

"It's a hell of a long story."

I told him about the possible seer, the computers, the pictures of us, and the arrival of the angels. His eyebrows furrowed as I talked. Hypotheses about the identity of our stalkers passed in his eyes.

"We hid in the attic until they left." My voice trembled over the word *attic*, and I looked out the window.

A dark shroud landed over Thom's previously warm features. "How come no one woke me up?"

I gritted my teeth together. There came the lies. "I thought Liam did. I crashed into bed."

Thom's frown stayed in place. "Where is he?"

"I don't know."

Lilah startled me from the stairs. "He didn't spend the night here, that's for sure. What time did you get back?" She squinted at me a little too hard.

I strengthened my hold on my emotions to fool her powers. "Late. I was wiped out."

Her stare drilled holes into my skin.

Thom huffed. "He's probably hunting for answers alone. I don't care what his excuse is this time. I'm fucking tired of being left in the dark. I'll find him." He flew up the stairs and disappeared.

Lilah tightened her cardigan around her frame, eyes fixed on me from her elevated position halfway up the staircase.

After the front door closed loudly, she asked, "Did you guys hook up?"

My jaw fell to the floor. "No. Why on Earth would you think that?" Yes, I'd admitted my attraction to Liam, but I'd also asked her to help me get rid of it. Her question would have offended me if she hadn't been so on point.

"Your feelings are all over the place. When Thom asked where Liam was, the energy around you thrashed so hard I thought he might be in your bed."

My ears, my heart, and every shred of my wounded ego bled at her words. "Well he's not. And he's never going to be." I swallowed hard, the motion sending a sharp pain to my neck.

Lilah finally descended all the way into the basement. "I wasn't super helpful the other day. You caught me off-guard. But I'm here now. We can talk about it if you want."

I secured my arms around my frame. I didn't want to be put under a microscope. Lilah's abilities were starting to get on my nerves. "There's nothing to talk about. It was temporary insanity. It's over now."

"You had a fight," she sighed.

"You can say that."

"That's what you guys do. You'll make up."

I traced my brow and shook my head. "Not this time."

The tilt of her head pleaded with me to be reasonable. "You're exaggerating."

I let the curtain covering my emotions fall. "Am I?"

"Shit." She raised her hand to her neck. "He hurt you."

"He hurt me."

She opened her arms, but I recoiled and looked away, my jaw open just enough to allow a painful breath inside my lungs. "I can't." Empathy wasn't what I needed. No matter how great of a listener Lilah was, she would always be team Liam.

I walked around her to leave and ran up to my bedroom.

A claustrophobic ache shrank my chest. Everyone had an opinion on what my feelings and actions ought to be, and I disappointed everybody. Lilah. Thom. Liam. Faye.

Myself.

I was no closer to finding my parents. No closer to controlling my powers. No closer to doing good. On top of it all, we had this new angel threat to worry about, and we had no clue if it was related to any of the other stuff.

The rented house had never felt less like home. My anxiety had ramped up. I was free falling and actually missed the easy, uncomplicated days I'd spent in Virginia. A languid ache invaded my body. I had no control over what the future had in store and no clear way forward.

My phone rang, and I jumped. The "Walking on Sunshine" ring tone was such an insult to my mood that I answered without giving it a second thought. Before I said hello, my eyes widened at the No Caller ID sign. Everyone who called me was in my contacts. I brought the phone to my ear, expecting the worse.

"It's Faye. I'm outside."

I followed her instructions and met her a few blocks away. She was the lifeline I hadn't had time to pray for, and I didn't think twice about jumping into her car. She drove off as soon as the door closed behind me, a gun clenched on her lap.

We cleared the city in record time, her knuckles white around the wheel like she expected Liam to jump on her windshield at any moment.

When she finally slowed down and parked on the side of the highway, she was breathless. She opened her mouth, closed it, then met my gaze like she couldn't find the words, or that they cost her too much. "I'm sorry."

I exhaled.

"I'm a hot head. I freaked out when I saw him. I should not have forced the issue. Not so soon."

God, I wanted to hug her, squeeze her in my arms and never let go. My lips trembled.

"I'm willing to meet with you. Here in Mobile. Twice a week. We can do what you want." Her lips twisted in a half grimace.

My anxiety crashed down into a glimmer of hope. Maybe I hadn't messed up everything.

A big frown twisted her face, her eyes falling a few inches down. "Alana. What is that?" She leaned in to get a better view of my neck.

"Nothing." I brought my hand around to cover the black and blue. Those damn bruises would annihilate her goodwill.

Swatting my hand away, she breathed, "He did this to you."

I averted her gaze. "He didn't mean to."

She gently cupped my cheek. To my astonishment, there was no anger in her voice, just pain. "Oh, Laney. You have to stop making excuses for him." She straightened in her seat. "Why don't you heal them? They must sting like hell."

"I can't. I don't fully control my powers. They wouldn't work this morning." Would she change her mind about teaching me if she knew I sucked?

Her shoulders hitched. "Magic takes years to master." The news didn't faze her at all, and I breathed a little easier. "Listen. I know you're not ready to hear me say you shouldn't go back, so I'll say this instead: want to spend the day with me?"

"Yes, please."

WE PARKED downtown in front of a recently renovated residential building, and Faye tucked the gun against her back in the waistband of her jeans. Steep stairs lead to the second floor, and she struggled with the lock of one of four doors in a narrow hallway. The smell of fresh paint assaulted my nostrils. Eclectic furniture that didn't quite fit together greeted us from the open living room and kitchen. A big round wood table with wicker chairs, two large flowery sofas, and a brown Barcalounger completed the look.

"Where are we?" I asked.

"My place."

"Since when?"

She threw her purse on the kitchen table and opened the blinds. A thin film of dust rose into the air. "This morning."

"You rented a place just to meet with me?"

She shrugged. "Yeah. Meeting at Adeline's was getting too dangerous."

I pursed my lips together. "Because you don't trust me."

"No, because Adeline's place is close to another witch's apartment, and she's a real snitch."

"Oh."

She sat on one of the sofas with her elbows braced on her knees. "Now, about those nasty bruises... try to heal them again."

I tried and failed before slumping on the seat across from her.

"Walk me through this. What happens when you succeed?"

I recounted in detail all the times my powers had worked versus the times they hadn't.

Faye rapped her fingers against her lips. "You've got to find your trigger."

"Trigger?"

"Some witches have triggers. It's usually an emotion. Anger. Joy. Fear.

My nose crunched. "Well, I can rule out joy."

A snort escaped her, and she crossed her legs at the ankle on the coffee table.

I shifted in my seat. "What else can you teach me?"

"You sure you're up for it? We can talk. Or not even that if you prefer."

"I need the distraction."

"Okay." She stood up. "I brought a few things with me. I know you want to learn spells, but I'm more of a brewer myself. I figured I'd show you potions first."

She opened a large trunk between us on the table. The inside looked like a tea shop had married a chemistry set. There were glass vials in all shapes and sizes tightly strapped individually to one side, and a throng of little clear plastic bags holding herbs and such on the other. They were all labeled with printed stickers.

"Fell in love with a P-touch labeler?" I teased.

Faye stuck out her tongue. "I'm organized."

A few flasks contained liquids, gels, and creamy, colorful substances. She unzipped a small pouch and passed me a teardrop-shaped vial. My mind flashed back to the night Frank had used a pink substance to force me to kiss him back, and my heartbeat quickened. "What kind of potions can we make?"

"*Brew*. The correct verb is *brew*. Sleep potions, like the one Adeline used on you. Love potions, though the effects are fleeting and unpredictable." She snickered. "Truth serums, but that's useless to me. Healing tonics are my favorite. They'll cure a cold in no time. They don't have the same effects as your powers, though, since they can only help with infections and such.

Maybe Dad had fed me this type of potion along with the one that concealed my powers.

She continued, "There's endurance or strength boosters. The sky's the limit if the brewer's skilled."

My grip tightened around the clear bottle. "Is there some sort of mind control potion?"

"Yes. But those are volatile. I don't brew anything that dangerous." She glanced at me sideways. "Why do you ask?""

"Remember when I said I'd been kidnapped before?" She nodded. "Well, the demon that abducted me used a pinkish liquid to control me."

She flinched in horror. "That's *punicea animus*. It's one of the strongest potions in existence. Who used it on you?"

"Frank. Frank Hale." Anyone else would have found her power annoying, but I enjoyed not being able to lie to her. It simplified things.

Both fists on her hips, she said, "Weird how you forgot to mention him when I spoke about Jonathan Hale."

I looked down. "Sorry."

"Aren't he and your demon best buds?"

"Not anymore." I didn't give her the opportunity to express her disbelief and added, "So, how did he have that? Can demons brew potions?"

"No. Only witches can. Think of it as pouring your essence into a vial. It takes time and energy to brew potent potions, and you have to recharge after."

"Where did he find it, then?"

"I'd like to say all witches are good people, but that's not the case."

I pursed my lips to the side. "I didn't drink it. He poured it on me. Is that how some potions work?"

"Potions can be absorbed in many different ways. Don't think of it as a human medicine. Whether you inject it, drink it, or pour it over an open wound, it enters the bloodstream."

She demonstrated how to make a sleep tonic, the potion that had knocked me out on our first meeting and gave me a crash course in witchcraft brewing ware. I listened intently and took notes. My blood raced at the whole new world of knowledge that was opening to me, and a genuine smile stuck on my lips for most of the afternoon.

After potions, we returned to the couch and chatted a bit about ourselves. Our favorite TV shows. Our childhoods.

Jane's death had catapulted Faye into adult life, their parents—my grandparents—had died when she was very young, and Adeline had raised both girls in New Orleans even though they were born in California.

When my phone rang for the second time in five minutes, I stood up. Thom would begin to worry if I didn't answer. "Thank you for this."

Her lips formed a thin line. "You could spend the night."

"No, thanks."

"Is there anything I can say to persuade you not to go back?"

I pressed my lips together. "No, but I'm really grateful. Can we meet again soon?"

"Wednesday at noon?"

Wednesday was five days away. It seemed like an eternity. "Great."

She passed me a small book torn at the edges. "Read that. Next time, you can brew an easy one."

"Okay. Oh, and by the way, you better not come around our house again. We've been followed, so the boys are suspicious of anyone who passes in the street."

Faye cringed. "You speak of them like they're your roommates."

"They are my roommates."

She threw her head back and blew air through her mouth.

BANG, BANG

Alana

*L*ate on Saturday afternoon, Lilah entered the living room and sat right next to me on the couch. With a sigh, she set her packed bag on the floor. "I don't want to leave with you mad at me."

I didn't want her to leave like that either. I combed my hair back. "I'm not mad at you."

She gave me a small, unconvinced smile.

"I shouldn't be." There was nothing to be mad about. Her being friends with Liam didn't negate her friendship with me, and if someone had enough heart to go around and love everyone, it was her.

I clasped her hand. "You told me something really important, and I let my own stuff get in the way."

"No, *you* told me something important, and *I* let my stuff get in the way."

The spark in her eyes met the smile curling up my lips, and we giggled.

"Agree to disagree?" I grinned.

She chuckled. "Sure."

We hugged goodbye. Our friendship had survived the first hurdle and was stronger for it.

"Call me whenever you want," she said.

"I will."

Thom walked over to us. "What are you two giggling about?"

"Nothing," we answered in unison before laughing again.

I retreated to the kitchen and waved when Lilah stepped out. After she left, Thom asked, "What do you want to do?"

"What about some brainless TV, huh?"

He smiled. "Sounds good to me."

I laid over a pillow in his lap, and he played with my curls, lulling me into a comatose state as we watched yet another episode of *Pawn Stars*.

I tapped my index finger against the back of the hand that rested against my stomach. "It's going to sound weird, but I want you to teach me how to shoot."

He brushed my hair away from my face. "A gun, you mean?"

"Yes."

He nodded like it made sense. "We'll go to a shooting range tomorrow."

THE RANGE WAS TUCKED between a laundromat and a bowling alley. It was the middle of a work day, so Thom and I were pretty much alone, but I felt more uncomfortable in there than out in the streets hunting for demons.

Thom caught my uneasiness quickly. "Spread your legs a little. Relax your arms. You're too tense. Here." He grabbed my hands and shook them out. "It's no different than a sword, just louder."

I didn't know if it was the noise canceling headphones, the security glasses, or the nervousness, but I broke into a fit of laughter. My gun-control militant mother would freak if she knew where I was.

Thom waited for me to sober up. "Safety first. Keep the gun pointed that way." He motioned to the target. "The magazine's empty for now. You want to have a firm grip. Hold it as high as possible to mitigate the recoil." He passed the gun to me. It felt awkward. Too big and too heavy, though it was small and barely weighed anything. I'd never been a gun person, but I didn't want my tombstone to spell that either. My palms were sweaty as hell, but Thom was happy with my grip. "The support hand is going to go thumb against thumb. Like this."

He showed me how to load it. "Stance, grip, and trigger control. The first thing you need to learn is how to pull the trigger without jerking the gun. Aiming is meaningless if you move while you pull the trigger. For now, concentrate on two things, holding the gun tight and pulling the trigger. Try it."

I struggled to keep my eyes open as I shot the target and missed the mark big time. The strength of the recoil surprised me, too. Each following shot made me shiver, and I grimaced.

"You'll get the hang of it. No one's good the first time. I certainly wasn't." He shot his target with his own gun, each bullet dead in the center.

He displayed such ease, control, and accuracy that I became curious. "When did you learn to shoot?"

"I was thirteen. We'd just moved to Virginia. Dad and I practiced every day in the backyard, and we learned to shoot every type of gun Dad could get his hands on. It drove Mom crazy." A sweet smile lit his face, but a shadow eclipsed it almost immediately. "Dad knew we'd need to know how to defend ourselves."

He rarely talked about his parents. I knew a demon named Marcus Black had killed them to get back at Liam for defecting, but not much else.

"Thirteen. Wow." So young to be afraid for his life.

"But I didn't get to shoot at anything real before I was seventeen. After Liam got better, he was restless. He needed to hunt. If not witches, anything. Dad, Liam and I started hunting local demons. Dad had a lot of hate to work through, so he overdid it. Years later, we hunted the wrong one, and it got my parents killed."

I wrapped an arm around him. "That's how Marcus found them?"

His eyes widened. "You know about Marcus?"

"I saw him in Liam's mind when I healed him."

All of the sudden, Thom was more somber than Liam on a gloomy day. "What do you know about him?"

"I know he was Liam's handler. I know Liam hated him. I know he killed your parents," I breathed the last part.

"What else?" Curiosity and pain mingled on his breath.

Gosh. He was actually asking. Had Liam refused to talk about Marcus all these years?

Thom looked at me expectantly. I knew how infuriating it was to ask Liam questions and hit a brick wall. "The images blurred together. Marcus gave Liam his first shot of witch blood. Sort of forced him to take it."

"Wow. Nothing else?"

I looked to the side. "Frank was there."

His fists curled. "Liam never talks about Marcus. The bastard tortured him for years."

My mouth hung agape. "Liam told you that?" I was surprised I hadn't seen it in his mind, but Liam's memory of the man did possess an aftertaste of fear and servility. When Marcus had come into view in the memory, his whole body had quivered.

"Not in details, but he flinched away so fast and with such disgust from a whip once that I filled in the blanks."

THE MARCUS TALK shook something loose inside me. The crisp mental image of a young Liam pulling his shirt over his head before being whipped to shreds floated behind my lids. The picture was so detailed and lifelike, I was pretty sure it did not come from my imagination. The part of me that dealt with dreamlike visions and strange, sleepwalking bouts had awakened again.

Since we'd left the Walker mansion, I hadn't been cursed with those vivid dreams, and wondered why, after all this time, they would come back.

I was strong enough during the day to keep the ghosts at bay.

Nights were different. Dreams are sneaky as shit, especially when you can't distinguish what's real and what's fantasy. My brain was playing tricks on me.

The next three nights, I had the exact same dream.

I was in an underground cave. Obscure. Humid. Warm. There was a squishy bed of moss under my feet. And blood. So much blood. It reeked of death.

Screams of pain hammered at my eardrums. The voice might have been mine, the pain in it so thick I couldn't tell if it was male or female or even human. I had a feeling I was supposed to die in that cave, like so many had before me, but was it me, Alana, or someone else?

As I stood up, my vision cleared slowly. A tangle of black linen, arranged more like a nest than a bed, darkened the corner. Voices echoed behind me, but they were unintelligible.

Then, the cave melted away, and I braced myself for the next part.

Liam's naked body lay on top of mine. Smooth. Hard. Powerful.

I protested and wiggled to get back to the cave, but he kissed me, and I forgot all about it. Our tongues competed for dominance, my skin singing under his rough hands.

Every night I'd beg for more as he kissed every inch of my skin—and I do mean every inch.

Every night I'd moan, and he'd laugh.

Every night I'd wake up exactly as he entered me.

My eyes snapped open, and I groaned in frustration. There I was again, shuddering with need, my heart chafed from the agony of waking up alone in an empty bed.

I forced a deep breath in and out. Inhale and exhale. I was sweaty and confused and so, so wet. My body was screaming for release, but I refused to give in. Dreams I had no control over, but this I could control, and I could not, would not, would-rather-die-than touch myself thinking of *him*. But this was the third messy morning in a row, and my will was wavering. A cold shower was my last resort, and I leaped out of bed.

Thankfully, Liam didn't hang out at the house these days. He was supposedly busy tracking down information about our angelic stalkers. Bumping into him at breakfast would have been too awkward.

Why couldn't I stay in that cave long enough to make sense of the voices?

It was like my subconscious was too horny to bother with the premonition any longer. That closeted make-out session was still too fresh. If Frank hadn't showed up... well... Liam would have taken me against that wall. And I would have let him. Hell, I would have ripped his shirt off and cheered him on.

It infuriated me that I had Frank to thank for keeping me from the biggest mistake of my life.

Only the slightest and littlest part of me felt robbed, and the sexy dreams had to be the manifestation of that smallest, minimal part. They would fizzle out in time.

Besides, only imaginary sex could be that good.

WEDNESDAY FINALLY ARRIVED. Faye gave me an ingredient list with simple steps and asked me to concoct an endurance potion. Potions required patience and precision, two things I lacked. Missing a beat in the recipe could make it explode in my face.

Witchcraft is a lot like chemistry, if chemistry involved waiting for a certain moon to do an experiment or required locks of hair and blood to work.

My third attempt bubbled and turned yellow, a sulfuric smell assaulting my nostrils. "I suck at potions."

She peeked over my shoulders. "Yeah, you really do."

I bared my teeth and growled.

She made a funny scared face. "Didn't you ever make a cake?"

"I hate cooking."

"You don't say." She reined in her chuckles. "Let's move on from this disaster. What are you good at?"

My chest deflated. What was I good at? "I killed a ghoul once."

"How?"

"With a katana."

Her jaw dropped. "You fought a ghoul with a hand-to-hand weapon? Was it stunned?"

"No. My technique is decent, actually."

Her laughter doubled. "You're even crazier than I thought."

I repressed a pout. "*My* demon had my back." The brazen comment made her cough, and I bit back a smile.

She hated to be reminded of Liam, but I was done walking on eggshells. Having a demon in my corner was a major advantage, and she might never acknowledge it, but I wouldn't let her forget it.

With a scowl, she handed me one of the small red vials. "Drink that around lunch time tomorrow and meet me back here at six."

"What is it?"

"A little something to make us stronger and stealthier. Tomorrow night, I'll show you how a witch hunts for a demon."

I SHOWED up to the meeting fifteen minutes early, wearing black leggings, black sneakers, and a black jacket. Liam would have been proud. I'd tied my hair in a tight bun and removed all jewelry. I didn't want to drop anything at the scene of a murder.

Faye huffed when she met me by her car. "You brought your sword?"

"Of course." She hadn't given me a clue as to what our evening might look like, so I'd come prepared. With my katana on my back and my dagger in my boot, I was ready.

So was she. Her straight black hair framed her face perfectly and complimented her dark and form-fitting clothes. Underneath all the bravado and judgment, there was a beautiful woman. I'd be lucky to look that young at 32.

"You hunt demons often?" I asked.

"Someone has to keep our streets safe. The bright ones don't set foot in New Orleans anymore, but we should find loads around here."

I couldn't believe my aunt was a demon-hunter. It was like my instincts had known this was my path, my destiny. Saving lives while embracing the magic running through my blood. Evening the playing field between humans and demons. It felt so right. "How do you find them?"

"Demons can be summoned, but it takes serious mojo to do it. Otherwise, we use a demonic compass to locate ghouls' nests or Fae hideouts." She got an orb from her jacket. It was made of white glass and as big as an orange. "Here." The surface of the glass was smooth and transparent. She unfolded a regular tourist map of Mobile against the dash of the car and clicked on the overhead light. I leaned in.

She glided the glass against the paper slowly. "The blacker it becomes, the more demons are in an area." A black fog clouded the pendant as it ran over the streets. She stopped when it turned black as ink and entered the address on her phone. "That's an abandoned lot." A Google Earth satellite image showed a bunch of old, rusty containers laying around piles of scrap metal. "There must be a nest there, but that's no good for us. It's your first time. We need a crowded area and a lone wolf. She repeated the process until the glass fogged again but this time not enough to turn the whole compass black. "There. A nightclub. I'm sure we can find one demon there to kill." She folded her map and put the compass back into her pocket.

Faye had her own version of the bestiary in English. It had less pages than the one we had, and it was entirely devoted to how to defeat the creatures on the pages. Witches clearly didn't care about anything else. I flipped through it while she drove. The potion manual was a dictionary compared to this one. Decapitation was basically highlighted on every page.

"That book is the secret to a successful demon-hunt. That and this." She got an amber sphere from her purse and put it in my lap. "It's basically a grenade made of aconite. It neutralizes most demonic powers for a few seconds, and then I shoot them with iron bullets before administering the *coup de grace*. Beheading works best for most species. Except hydras, obviously."

"Those snake-like creatures in Hercules that keep sprouting heads?"

Her brows created a perfect line. "I keep forgetting your frame of reference for this is TV."

"Not TV. Disney. You know: Hercules, Meg, Pegasus, the little horned man. I won't say I'm in love…"

I didn't know if she looked aggravated or downright scared to be hunting demons with the likes of me as she said, "Oh boy."

"So… hydras?"

"They're demons capable of regenerating any severed part. Including the head."

I raised a brow. "Same difference. Disney was right on the money."

We parked a few blocks from the nightclub. "Keep the grenade but lose the sword. It's too big." She opened her coat. There was a long, narrow knife tucked into a sheath sewn beneath her arm. Very clever.

My palms were sweaty. "Am I supposed to feel the effects of that potion, yet?"

"It works best coupled with adrenaline. Don't worry. If we get to fight, you'll know the difference."

The acrid odor of pot and cigarette smoke dried up my mouth as we elbowed our way inside, and I winced at the atrocious music blaring from the speakers. Faye gripped the steel banister that ran all around the mezzanine.

"What now?"

"Look down." She motioned to the dance floor beneath us. "Breathe. Concentrate. You told me you could see through glamors. This is the same thing. *Feel* the energy surrounding them. Humans give off a very linear and steady vibe. Demons ooze power. The air around them vibrates."

My eyes roamed the crowd and zeroed in on a girl sitting at the bar. She had long dark hair flowing down to her butt.

I had no clue what the energy around her felt like, but her neon-pink aura almost blinded me. "The black-haired girl at the bar."

Faye looked at me funny.

"Am I wrong?"

She squinted at the girl in question, then at me. "No. You're right, but you did it so fast… Faster than me. You've done this before."

"Never."

Her features darkened. "Say it again."

Was she fine-tuning her lie-detector? I crossed my arms at her lack of trust. "I've never done this before."

She pinched her mouth to the side, considering my answer. Finally, she shrugged. "Beginner's luck."

"What is she?"

"The hair. The slutty outfit. The middle range vibe. She's a Gorgon."

"Like Medusa?"

"Well... she won't turn anyone to stone, but yeah, like Medusa."

"What does she do?"

"She's a demon. She feeds when she's hungry and kills for fun when she's not. Let's get her." Faye leaped forward.

I grabbed her arm. "Wait. Shouldn't we wait for her to do something—I don't know—evil?"

Faye straightened her coat. "Okay. I'll humor you since I'm convinced the man she's dragging outside is her next meal."

The woman did have murder in her eyes, but if a demon's predatory gaze meant they were about to kill, I wouldn't be alive. Everyone deserved the benefit of the doubt.

We hurried after the couple to the back alley. The neon-pink aura had become almost red as the man pinned the gorgon to the wall. Kissing was not strong enough a verb to describe the voraciousness of their make-out session.

Faye blocked my path with an arm as we drew closer. "Feel the guy's energy to confirm he's human. I hate surprises."

The sound of a fly being opened brought a hot flash to my chest, and I stared at the ground.

Faye marched forward. "He's human. Let's go."

"But they're having sex."

"Even better. She's distracted." The eagerness in Faye's voice was a bit disturbing.

A low grunt turned into a gasp, and I couldn't help but peek. The girl had just sunk long, totally inhuman teeth into the man's neck.

"Should we wait for her to kill him to see if she's evil?" Faye mocked me as she threw the grenade with the strength and accuracy of a baseball pro.

The couple staggered, and the gorgon hissed. Faye shot her in the head. It only bought us time, though, as the bullet spurted back out quickly.

Faye pushed the unconscious man into my arms. "Hold him."

I was surprised to find that I could hold him up with ease. That potion was no joke.

Faye never missed a beat as she pried the long blade out of her coat and beheaded the gorgon. She looked so powerful, so in control.

I wanted that. I wanted to be like her and do good on my own. "That potion is amazing. You must drink it every day."

"No. It's potent because I use it sparsely. If you drink it every day your body becomes accustomed to it."

"Too bad."

She inspected the guy's neck. "Well, he's in rough shape. Good thing we have a healer here."

My head shook before I could process her words. "I can't."

She tilted her head to the side and gave me an encouraging smile. "You can." She got a flask from her jacket and poured it on the man's wound. "Sleeping potion. I don't want him to ask questions if he comes to."

She pointed to a dumpster. "But first things first. Let's get rid of her."

I groaned. "Really?"

"We can't leave her body here."

"It'd be great if their bodies could go poof like on TV."

"Amen. FYI, vampire bodies do go poof. Talk about a self-cleaning hunt."

The thought of a body disappearing into thin air reminded me of my mysterious power, and I played with a loose curl. "I did that once."

"Huh?"

"I made a body explode. Turned it to dust."

She looked at me with interest, the cogs of her brain visible in her eyes. "Show me."

I buried my hands in my pockets. "Like I said, I don't control it."

"You never will if you never try."

"I thought you wanted me to heal him? I don't have enough energy for both." Last time I'd done both, I'd spent hours in a daze.

"Ah, he'll live. We'll call an ambulance. I'm way more interested in that dusting thing." She motioned for me to set him down against the wall, so I did.

I crouched next to the corpse and put the tip of my fingers on the dead gorgon's arm. Her head was still attached by a sliver of flesh, and I prayed that if I managed to do this, it would go poof with the rest of her. I closed my eyes and inhaled.

Nothing happened.

Faye shackled my wrist with her hand and pushed my palm down on the demon's bloody torso. "Come on. Don't be a wuss. You have to mean it."

I bit my cheeks and tried again. This time, the wicked place behind my skull rose to the challenge, and the body disintegrated under my touch.

Faye whistled. "I thought you were exaggerating, but you're the real deal, kid."

I wanted to share in the elation, but my fears were unchanged. "Aren't I supposed to have only one power?"

"Says who?"

I shrugged.

She shook her head. "I told you. They don't know shit about witches." Her bottom lip tucked between her teeth, she tilted her head. "But aren't they the same power, though? Your healing is really about mending cells and bringing the flesh back together. Pulling flesh apart is the continuation of that same ability, no?"

A bright smile burst at the seams of my mouth. I wasn't a freak, just an inexperienced witch that happened to be powerful. Cool. "Do I get bonus points because we don't have to get rid of the body?"

Faye hooked her arm around mine. "I'm never hunting without you again. Come on. I'm buying you dinner."

I beamed, my chest all warm. We called 9-1-1 and skipped out.

"What do you do when you're seen?" I asked.

She put a hand over her heart. "Kid, I'm no amateur. I'm never seen."

I stuck my tongue out.

"Careful. Your face will stay like that," she teased.

I threw my head back and laughed.

We ate delicious steaks and fries. As we were about to go our separate ways, Faye fumbled around in her huge purse. "Here. Keep one."

"A grenade?"

She closed my fingers around it. "Just in case."

"This isn't necessary. He won't try to kill me."

She signed the check and put it aside. "I'll feel better if you keep it. Think of it as demon pepper spray. It could come in handy."

I handed it back to her. "No thanks. If I get caught with this, I'll have to tell them about you."

She stood up and swung her coat over her shoulders. "You wouldn't."

I rested my chin in my hand and drummed my fingers over my mouth. "I would. And then, you might have to learn to get along."

She pursed her lips in disgust at the idea.

A big smirk glazed my lips as I hopped to my feet. "Careful, your face will stay like that."

A loud chuckle popped out of her mouth. "You got me, kid."

I fluffed my hair over my jacket and followed in her wake. "Oh, and what's with the 'kid'? I'm not a child. I'm almost twenty-one."

Her eyes sparkled with humor. "Which means I have 20 years of teasing to make up for, so get used to it, *kid*."

18

9 CRIMES

Alana

On Friday afternoon, Rachel called to invite me and *Mike* to a Back-to-School party. Liam overheard me talking with her on the phone and shouted "yes" from behind me, erasing my chances to get out of it.

On a normal day, crowds irritate me.

On any day, I'd rather be swallowed by a black hole than go to a frat party.

On that day, the sheer idea of dressing up to stand around drunken strangers with Rachel and *Mike* made me want to hurl.

I almost called to cancel a dozen times, but Rachel offered for us to meet at her house beforehand, and curiosity won me over. There was only a week left before her birthday, so if she didn't turn by then, we'd move on. How badly could one evening go?

Rachel gave me a quick tour of the house before showing me to her bedroom. The décor was a mix of old-world money and contemporary chic, the pink, white and gold accents to die for. A mountain of clothes and accessories lay on her king-sized bed. Many dresses still had tags on them.

"I went a little crazy and bought a bunch of new stuff," she said as she kicked a pair of heels off.

She disappeared into the bathroom for a minute and emerged wearing a sleek, gray dress. "What about this one? Is it too much?" The plunging neckline dipped low between her breasts. Granted, she had smaller breasts and could get away with not wearing a bra, but I'd never dare to wear that in a million years.

I couldn't lie though... it fit her like a glove. "It looks great on you."

Bet Liam would think the same.

I glanced down at my jeans. "I'm under-dressed." I hadn't even done my hair. Me.

"Want to borrow one of mine? This one would look gorgeous on you." Hanger in hand, she aligned a strapless navy dress with my body.

"I don't think it'll fit." My curves would stretch thin anything she owned.

"Nonsense." She waved for me to try it on anyway, and I relented.

A few inches were missing in the ass area, and I caught Rachel making a wrinkly face in the mirror. I grumbled. "Told you so."

Despite my efforts not to care, it undermined my confidence, and I started going through scenarios that would cut this outing short. Headaches and periods cramps are overused, so I'd go with an unexpected allergic reaction to the dog I'd briefly petted downstairs. I sneezed once for good measure.

Rachel bit her bottom lip and fumbled around in her closet. "Now, this one will fit for sure, and it'll look great with your boots. Love them by the way."

She passed me another hanger. I made a last-ditch effort to salvage the night and pulled it over my head.

The above-the-knee flowy skirt allowed for my wider hips, and the top was tight but not *too* tight. The laced-up front wasn't see-through and held everything in place. My hot pink bra straps were mismatched, but I hid them under the spaghetti straps.

Looking in the mirror, I cocked my hip to the side. *Not bad at all.*

The sexy outfit boosted my enthusiasm, and I abandoned the dog-allergy scenario. I grabbed the hair straightener on her dresser and started untangling my curls. Straight hair would be a nice change for one night.

Rachel whistled when I was done. "You look freaking amazing. Guys are going to be all over you."

I clicked my tongue. "No boyfriend, remember?"

"Why not?"

"A relationship would be far too complicated right now."

"Who said anything about a relationship? Aim for a fling. Have fun."

I averted my gaze. "I've never been a fling person."

She pouted like I was being unreasonable. "Then become one. You just moved. You get a fresh start. You can be whoever you want without the stigma of who you were as a teenager."

She had her parents, her friends, a good education. What more did she want?

Both hands on my hips, I let my annoyance show. "Starting over is hard. What's so bad about your life?"

"What's so good about it? I don't mean to sound like a spoiled brat, but there should be more to life. Life should be an adventure, not a rerun of your parent's best-ofs."

Part of me agreed. Most of me was angry at her aloofness. She didn't appreciate her tranquil life because she had no idea how quickly it could be ripped away.

"I get what you mean," I said, knowing it wasn't fair to pick a fight with her about things she had no way of understanding.

"Speaking of adventure. Mike likes me, right?" Her voice rose at the end, full of barely contained excitement.

I didn't know how to answer that, so I picked on my cuticles. "You should know he's not a relationship kind of guy."

Oh, and he's an entirely different species than you. You don't mind, right?

My warning didn't deter her at all. "Why settle down when you look like that? Girls must be all over him."

Present company *not* excluded.

A familiar tingling at the base of my neck alerted me that I was being watched, so I peeked outside. Speak of the devil. Liam was waiting for us, perched on the hood of his damn car.

Magnet to magnet, his eyes rose to meet mine. My pulse quickened, and I bit my bottom lip. God. It was hard to deal with him before, but now it was next to impossible… especially when he looked like that with his hair gelled and his body dressed to impress.

It's hard to stay cool and collected around someone you have mind-blowing dream sex with every damn night.

"Mike's outside." The fake name brought bile to my mouth.

Rachel applied mascara and winked from the mirror. "Let's make him wait a little."

WE MET Liam by the car 15 minutes later. I watched him closely as he raised his gaze from his phone. It darted from me to Rachel after a millisecond.

He eyed her up and down and up again. "Wow. You look…" He trailed off approvingly. He didn't even glance my way as he added, "Hey, Nina."

I stomped to the back seat and sat down, arms crossed over my chest. Rachel's happy glow practically blinded me as he opened the passenger door for her.

"How come I feel like I'm the chaperon here?" I asked Liam through thought-speech, not caring if it made me sound petty.

"Cheer up. This is how I feel every day." The words tasted like just desserts, and it was so unfair.

I never batted my eyelashes at Thom or purred my words like Rachel did. And Thom never undressed me with his eyes like I was a piece of meat.

We parked outside a big white house.

"Lead the way," Liam said to Rachel. His smile surrendered the full top row of his teeth.

I could count on one hand the times he'd smiled at me like that but reminded myself he was playing a character. It was fake as hell, but the fact that he upheld the Oscar-worthy performance for more than a few minutes baffled me.

Once inside, Rachel introduced us to a few of her friends. When we got to a tall boy with brown hair and a dazzling smile, she wiggled her eyebrows behind his back to indicate he was the one she'd been telling me about.

I made an effort to remember his name. Brayden. He was cute, I'd give her that.

A guy arrived with a plate of tequila shots complete with the lime and salt. I hated tequila, so I emptied the glass in one quick gulp.

The walls seemed to creep up on me as more and more people entered the house. I kept an eye out for a suspicious face, but they quickly blurred together, the individual features lost in a sea of red lipstick and over-gelled hair.

What if Rachel turned?

If Rachel became a witch, Thom, Liam and I would move with her to Virginia. She'd have to leave her world behind. She'd feel betrayed if she learned Liam was faking an interest in her. Except... was he faking his interest?

He had to be.

I gulped down another shot to avoid contemplating that question.

The alcohol kicked in a few minutes later, uncoiling the unease in my throat. Who cared if Liam was into Rachel? Not me.

"Is your cousin even human?" A girl with short brown hair shouted over the music.

I choked on my first sip of beer. "What?"

"He moves like the commando-type guys in spy movies. Was he in the army or something?"

"No."

"Rachel's crazy about him." A big guy bumped in to her, and she shoved him off.

My brows pulled together. "Why is she into him? He's not even nice."

The girl chuckled. "I know he's your cousin, but you have eyes, right?"

"I do have eyes. That's the problem." The loud music saved me.

The brunette leaned towards me with one ear out. "What?"

"Nothing."

She was bubbly and talkative, and I ended up chatting with her for a while.

Many shots later, Rachel pulled me aside. "I hadn't noticed how clear his eyes were before. I swear they're almost silver. He's wearing contacts, right?

"No. I mean... I don't know." My chest shrank.

She took a step back and appraised me. "You're drunk."

I nodded emphatically. "Yeah. Isn't that the point?"

She giggled. "Listen, Margery's the designated driver tonight, and she agreed to take you home if I spirit Mike away."

"Uh?" Who the hell was Margery?

Rachel's head tilted to the side. "Margery's the girl you talked to earlier? Are you sure you're okay?"

"Yep, but I need to pee." I pushed past her.

On my way back from the restroom, I saw Liam and Rachel in the hallway. Rachel leaned against the wall, Liam's arm propped over her head, almost pinning her in place. They were talking in turns in each other's ear.

Was he really going to bring her home, have sex with her?

My stomach churned. I shouldn't have drunk so much. I tucked my chin in and walked around them quickly.

Dazed and dizzy, I stumbled across the dance floor back to Rachel's friends, but the flock had moved, and I couldn't find Margery.

Brayden approached me. "Hey, you okay?"

I rested my hands on his chest to find my balance again. "Yeah. Sorry." The room was spinning. He helped me get out of the way of the dancers, and I leaned against the wall for support.

The air electrified around me, and shivers branded my body. I twisted around to face Liam as he closed in on us, and all of the sudden there was no music. He'd silenced it, and from the way the world blurred, he was probably broadcasting a different image to the people around us. I was way too intoxicated to see through any illusion.

Eyebrows knit together, he clicked his tongue. "How much did you drink?"

I giggled. "A lot."

He scowled.

My lips formed a perfect heart-shaped pout. "Can't I have fun for one night without you raining on my parade?"

"Your aura was visible a moment ago. Are you trying to get killed?"

"Shit." In my drunkenness, I'd forgotten to rein it.

"I caught it immediately, but we need to go. Come on. Let's get you home to your *boyfriend*," he growled under his breath.

The music resumed. Rachel was standing next to us.

"I'm going to take Nina home. Rain check?" Liam said.

"Okay." Her nose creased in disappointment despite her understanding tone.

Liam kept a hand on my bare shoulder as he guided me outside. I staggered, acting tipsier than I was, hoping… *Yes!* He swooped me up into his arms. Heat slope-styled to my throat and landed in my knees. I hid my face in his chest and inhaled.

Citrus bound to a hint of leather and sweat. Masculine. My gut squeezed.

He deposited me back on my feet, but instead of getting into the car, I leaned against him. My hands trailed the planes of his chest to his neck, his muscles hard and strong beneath my fingers, and I stood on my tiptoes to plant a kiss on his lips.

He became the marble statue.

He didn't respond.

"Alana, what the fuck are you doing?"

Flustered, I squeaked, "I don't know."

A stern, disapproving frown hardened his traits as he opened the door for me. "Get in."

We drove in silence. The hem of my dress absorbed all my attention as he shot me the most resentful glare. He was fuming. I was vexed.

Not only vexed, I was crushed. I bit my tongue not to let him know.

I climbed out the car and waited for Liam to follow. He didn't. Bending down to look at him through the opened window, I asked, "Aren't you coming in?"

"Not a chance. Sober up, princess." He turned the corner at full speed.

The thought that he might be going back to her choked me, and I dragged myself to my room. I was too drunk to use the window, but Thom had already gone to bed. My room was pitch black, and I didn't bother turning on the lights.

Using the wall for support, I pried off my boots. They were sexy, weren't they? I guess not.

Where was Liam's lust now? Gone. Latched onto the next pretty girl that came along. If she turned, she'd check all his boxes, and he'd forget I existed.

The stiffness of his arms had betrayed nothing but his iron clad resolve to rebuff my advances. No hesitation. No hidden desire to kiss me back. Nothing but distance and judgment.

Judgment because he thought Thom and I were dating even though we were not. Judgment because I lacked the self-respect—his word, not mine—to stay away from him.

A sob dribbled through my lips. *Let's get you home to your boyfriend,* he'd said. Well the joke was on me.

I'd never felt more alone or foolish in my entire life.

While my irises adjusted to the obscurity, I patted my way to the bed and crashed into the sheets. My head spun. I couldn't go to sleep now. I'd dream if I slept. If I dreamed of him tonight, it'd kill me.

The door cracked open, and a sliver of light made me squint. "Lana?" Thom whispered.

I squeaked.

There he was, my non-boyfriend. The sweetest and most affectionate guy in the world, and I'd rejected him, refused the happiness that was staring me in the face in favor of a dark and barely formed hope. An absurd desire to gamble my life away.

Well, I'd lost, and like a bad dice throw, the loss felt quick and empty.

Thom sat next to me on the bed. I hid my face in his chest and draped an arm around him. What sane person would sack a bright future for nothing more than a few shadows on the wall?

"You okay?" He stroked my hair. "Where's Liam? How did it go?"

I drew back and met his eyes. So open, so warm, so tolerant of my whims. In that moment, I saw him as he was: the most beautiful man I'd ever known. I couldn't form a sentence, so I crushed my lips to his.

He kissed me back, and his hot tongue was a salve to my wounded soul. My stupid heart could go to hell. The little voice could drown itself in the sea of my humiliation.

I pushed him back to the pillows and straddled him. He kissed me harder, and my lips were raw by the time I came up for air. I nuzzled his neck to taste his skin, and a hint of mint and chocolate lingered on my tongue.

No doubt could hold me down. A thousand resolutions would never be enough. This would push me over the edge. Make it a done deal, a tipping point. Choosing Thom had been the right call all along, I'd just lacked the strength to slam the door to the alternative.

We worked. End of story. This should have happened months ago.

I grabbed the hem of his shirt and pulled it over his head. His hands ran up and down my naked thighs, each migration creeping higher until he reached my underwear. I pushed my hips into his, satisfied to find him hard and ready.

He froze. "Fuck, Lana. Slow down."

"For months, we have slowed down. Now, we're going backwards. What's here," I motioned back and forth between the two of us, "it's good." My speech was slurred.

He extricated himself from my drunken grasp and stood next to the bed.

No. No. No.

Disappointment dripped from his tongue as he said, "You're drunk, Lana."

"So?"

"It's not right."

Right. I was so sick of that word. Nothing was right in my life, nothing. Why couldn't I enjoy one wrong thing. Why? My derisive inner voice snickered. *You waited too long and now he doesn't want you anymore. Neither of them do.*

My naked legs dangled at the edge of the bed. "You don't want me." I stared at the floor.

"Lana, if you weren't drunk, I'd already be inside you."

I looked back up. *Yes, please.* I liked this dark shade on him. It turned me on. I should have reflected on that a little more. "It's not taking advantage. I want this."

"Then, you'll still want it in the morning."

"What if you don't?" I hid my face in my hands.

He knelt down in front of me and pried them away to meet my gaze. "I'll always want you."

Thom knew how to talk to a drunk girl, and my chagrined frown melted. I tugged on his arm. "Come to bed. We can just *cuddle*," I said the word cuddle like it was *broccoli*.

He chuckled darkly, "Give a man a minute," and exited the room, muttering to himself.

The water turned on in the bathroom a few seconds later, and I considered crashing his shower. Thom is a gentleman, but he's no saint. I'm pretty sure it would have worked, but I wasn't drunk enough to try. In fact, to my extreme displeasure, my throat itched with a blinding thirst. I was starting to sober up. I grabbed a water bottle from the fridge and emptied it in one gulp.

Back in my room, I stripped out of my dress, put on my pajamas, and crashed back into bed. Thom returned shortly after, and I snuggled into him. His skin was cold. I nestled my head in the crook of his neck and closed my eyes.

I woke delighted to find I'd had a dreamless night, stretched gingerly, and hugged a pillow. My head pulsed. My tongue was drier than dry and my lips cracked. Last night replayed behind my eyes.

Rachel. Liam. Tequila. Beer. Rachel. Tequila? Liam. Botched kiss. Thom. Not-so-botched kiss.

Oh God.

My mind buzzed with hideous reflections.

Self-absorbed. Insensitive. Two-timing.

Liar.

Bitch.

19

LOVE THE WAY YOU LIE

Liam

"Sober up, princess." I crush the accelerator down.

Before I change my mind about returning that kiss. Before I slam open my door and run up to her. Before I bend her down on the hood of my car to check if her underwear matches the pink of her damn bra.

I almost lost my mind seeing her strut out of Rachel's house in that dress. Carrying her destroyed any chances I had of sleeping tonight. That drunken kiss ruined me, especially since she spent the whole day giggling in Thom's arms.

I need to exorcise her from my guts. I need an out for all that pent-up rage.

Without making a conscious decision, I drive back to the party. My fingers rap against the steering wheel as I consider going inside. I shouldn't be here. It could get messy. Before I make up my mind, Rachel taps on my window, and I lower it.

She gives me a thousand-megawatt smile. "You came back."

"I came back."

"Is she okay?"

"She's fine."

Turning to her friends, she says, "You guys go ahead." She hurries around the car, climbs inside, and slams the door. "Drive."

I zoom through the streets. The exhilaration on her face increases with each burst of speed.

I meet my gaze in the mirror. *You're going to do this. It's no big deal. One-night-stands used to be your specialty. You'll feel better after. Alana's not the only girl in the world.*

But she kissed me. For the first time, I might add.

She was drunk out of her mind. It doesn't count. You're free to do whatever you want.

The prospect of having sex with a willing, beautiful woman has never required such a pep talk in the history of mankind. I haven't had sex in months and try not to dwell on the reason. Jesus. I'm a lost cause.

Rachel's lips form a disappointed pout as she realizes where we're headed. "You're driving me home."

"Yes."

"Why?"

"Because I'm trouble. The kind you don't want," I sigh as I stop in front of her house.

"What if I don't care?" She leans in, capturing my lips.

I kiss her back. It's nice. It's easy. As her tongue tries to coax me out of my indecision, I break an oath I'd sworn to myself.

It starts innocently enough.

Tweaking the light catching Rachel's hair so her blond locks look a shade warmer.

Ignoring her scent as I kiss her neck.

Changing the pitch of her voice when she moans.

Adjusting the size of her hands as she tugs on my pants.

Disgusted with myself, I catch her wrists as she's about to unzip my jeans.

Stop. Remove the glamor. Now.

Rachel's sexy as hell, and I force myself to look at her.

Shiny blond hair.

Deep blue eyes.

Tanned skin.

Slim, with legs that go on forever.

Not what I want.

In 14 years, I've only let my own illusions fool me one time, and it was to see my parents and Thom. Marcus tortured me for a week for being homesick. I haven't done it since. Illusions are hollow. Guys like me get what they want. Demons even more so.

I grab the side of Rachel's neck and pull her in for a slow, mind-numbing kiss. A part of me breaks, and I close my eyes. As I draw back, I feast my eyes on the body of the woman who derailed my life.

Green eyes.

Long red waves.

Pink, heart-shaped lips.

A constellation of freckles.

Perfect.

She gasps as I use super-speed to usher her onto my lap, her nails digging into my back. My body shakes, my stomach cramping in a mix of disgust and need. A sweet, sweet, disaster. The wave of nausea threatens to choke me, but I shove it down.

In a minute, I'll tell her to go inside. If I'm going mad, I might as well enjoy it for one more minute. Demons don't go to hell because of one fake, twisted kiss. They go to hell for all the rest. *No one has to know.*

"Except me."

"Shut up, Frank."

A BITING sourness sits heavy on my shoulders as I come home the next morning. Last night left me empty and driving around hasn't eased the knot in my throat. It's a huge wake-up call. Hunger I can handle, lust I could deal with, but *this*… this is fucking annoying.

How can I be in so deep? When did it start? How did I not see it?

I cross Thom's path in the driveway. He's got his hoodie draped over his head and his ear-buds in. He removes them as he sees me. "I hate this weather." He frowns as he notices my clothes. "You spent the night out?"

"Yeah. I looked into a possible seer, but he turned out okay," I lie. I can't say I spent the night wracking my brain for a way to make this insane fantasy happen. Me. Alana. My bed... or hers. Any surface will do. She might whisper her secrets in my ear while we revel in—

Thom whisks me out of my daydream. "Did something happen to Lana last night?"

The last thing I want to do is talk about her. I'm... unsteady right now. He'll see right through me. "She drank too much. I drove her home and went back to the party." I don't let him ask another question. "I'm going to shower and head right back out. Want to grab breakfast somewhere?" We haven't spent nearly enough time together the last few weeks, and that hasn't helped.

His gaze is unfocused like he doesn't quite hear my voice. "Nah. I have something to do here."

I raised a brow.

He bounces from one foot the other. "I'm waiting for Lana to wake up."

"You okay?"

I don't know exactly what it is, but something is off. He's... shifty.

"Yeah, I just have something on my mind."

"Something like..." I trail off.

The strangest smile glazes over his lips, and he chuckles as he shakes his head. "It's nothing." His hood falls down, and I can't think.

There are three, big, fat hickeys on his neck.

Look at them closely. Get it into your god-damned head. She's poison.

I force myself to nod at whatever Thom's saying, wave goodbye, and walk inside. The light breathing sound coming from her bed echoes like thunder in my ears.

She kissed me and came home to him.

It drives me mad. My mind's full of her smiles and her lips and her scent, and I want to die.

I double back and don't stop until I'm miles and miles away. I march into an empty house and shower there. I steal a black shirt and jeans and roam the fridge. The guy who lives here has good taste. Maybe I should move. I pour some cereal.

Before I can understand what's happening, I fling the bowl at the wall so violently I dent the counter with my hand. The force of the blow shatters the ceramic.

I shake. I burn. I think I scream. I destroy everything in sight. I have to bleed not to cry.

Rage stings. Jealousy suffocates.

A pressure at the base of my skull makes my eyes roll inward.

"Knock, knock."

"Not now, Frank."

"Who's there? Not Alana. She's too busy doing your brother." He breaks into a fit of giggles.

I concentrate hard on ejecting him out of my mind, but he holds on like a leech.

"Wait. Wait. What's the difference between Alana and a weather man?"

I groan. *This. This is what's going to kill me.*

"They're both lying their asses off, but Alana's the only one who's always wet."

My whole face crunches in disgust. *"Are you done?"*

"Yes."

Since I can't get rid of him, I push back into his mind and peek at his surroundings.

He's deep underground, armed to the teeth, crouched inside a sewer pipe. His all-silver arsenal spells shape-shifter. Shape-shifter plus underground tunnels means New York or Los Angeles. The frost on his breath indicates New York, and for a moment, I'm jealous. *"You stopped in the middle of a hunt to tell knock knock jokes?"*

"I prioritize well."

"Your sense of humor has gone downhill. Remember those five years we didn't talk?"

Five years of blissful silence.

There's a long pause before he breathes, *"Vividly."*

"Let's go back to that."

187

"I missed you too much."

Frank has served five years for a crime we perpetrated together. We killed our psychotic handler, Marcus Black, the last member of the Black bloodline. Killing one of our own is against our most sanctified law. We fully expected to be executed, but the Council left it to our families to punish us as they saw fit. The Hales are big on torture and solitary confinement.

I got a slap on the wrist.

It probably helped that there hasn't been a new Shadow Walker in my family in a century. Numbers are key to power and leverage, and our numbers are dwindling.

Five families. Five Council members. With Marcus gone and no one to fill his shoes, there was a tie. They elected a leader. After centuries of dirty democracy, power plays and back-stabbing, there was a crown to vie for. The Hales had the numbers on their side, so the Nolans and Olsens refused to give them any more power. The Hales were pissed at them for it and refused to support them in return. Adam Walker won by default.

That's how I became demon royalty. That's why I can get away with defying the powers that be. They'll need me when shit hits the fan.

That's also why Frank and I haven't killed each other yet. We kill each other, we spark a revolution. I'm willing to go there, but for what?

For a girl. A girl that kisses one guy and screws another in the same night—scratch that—same hour.

I could have had her that night in the attic if Frank hadn't showed up, but that wouldn't have helped. Fucking her once wouldn't be enough. I'm an addict. I tend to fall hard for things that are bad for me. Losing myself in her would be far too easy. She's sex, drug, and violence disguised as one pretty, pretty warrior princess, and God knows I have a Buttercup and Xena fetish.

Life's too short to pine over one girl.

Nobody's worth that much trouble.

I've had enough.

Frank senses the shift. *"Are you finally growing some common sense?"*

"Yes."

"Good for you." He leaves.

I frown as I take in the destruction around me. Somehow, I feel better now. In his own twisted way, Frank managed to cheer me up.

THERE IS A LIGHT THAT NEVER GOES OUT

Alana

"Oh. I wanted to be there when you woke up," Thom said as he came in.

The coffee machine's light clicked on. "Be glad that you weren't. I had the worst headache." I served two cups of hot steaming coffee.

The hickeys on his neck made my heart drop twelve stories. There for all the world to see. *Oh, hell.*

He added two spoonfuls of sugar to his mug and stirred, not meeting my gaze. "What happened last night?"

"I drank. A lot."

"Why?"

He gave me time to find the words.

"I wanted a night off from my life," I answered honestly.

"And how are you feeling?"

He was really asking: do you regret what happened?

I did regret it, and at the same time, I didn't. Years wouldn't be enough to untangle that knot.

A knock on the door bought me time.

Thom's eyebrows knitted together. We never had visitors. He

grabbed a gun from the kitchen drawer and motioned for me to check the windows as he aimed the barrel at the door.

I crouched and peeked outside. "It's a man with a book in his hands. I think it's the Bible."

Thom lowered his gun. "Damn door to door preachers."

I walked to the door.

His hand twined with mine, pulling me away. "Don't answer unless you want a lecture on the safety of your soul."

"Right."

"So..."

"Yeah." No matter how foolhardy my actions had been, they only made more sense in the light of day. Thom was the right choice.

I stood on the tip of my toes, traced the back of his neck and met his eyes.

He gulped, and his stare fell to my lips.

My heart flipped upside-down.

The sound of broken glass ripped through the air. A yellowish dust rose from a grenade-shaped device at Thom's feet and formed a cloud of smog around us. I clamped my hand over my mouth and nose. A forceful fit of coughs barreled through my chest, and I spat a thick overflow of saliva.

Thom's eyes rolled inward before he crashed to the ground, and I emptied my stomach on the floor, the air thick with a toxic taste. The black spots pulsated, and I blinked.

The front door was opened. A dark silhouette obscured it, a gas mask covering the man's lower face. He was wearing a Roman collar and the traditional black garbs of a catholic priest.

Hazy, I leaned to retrieve my dagger but froze as he pointed a peculiar gun at my face.

"Keep your hands in the air."

I obeyed.

The yellow cloud lifted, and I could breathe again. "Who are you?"

The intruder ripped the mask from his face. He was old. Deep lines pruned his patchy skin, and his lips were thin and flaky. "Who I am is not important. What I came for is." His voice was rough and quiet like each word caused him immense pain.

"And what did you come for?" I almost expected him to say he'd come for me.

"Retribution, child."

He stepped over Thom's limp body and grabbed his gun.

"What did you do to him?"

"I made him sleep, but it didn't work on you. Satan touched you." He inched towards me.

I raised my dagger. "Don't come any closer."

"I don't have to. I'm not sure this would work on you, but it'll work on him." He pointed the gun to Thom's head. "Drop your knife and sit." He pointed at a kitchen chair.

I did as he asked.

"Now, put these on." The weird knots he kicked towards me were made of white ropes.

I hesitated, but he aimed at Thom's head once again, so I slipped my wrists into them. They glowed, ensnared my skin, and shrunk until they were digging deep into my flesh. I cried out.

He scratched his chin with the barrel and glanced at the clock. "We have time. Hours before the demon comes back. Let's wait for him, shall we?"

The crazy old man had prepared his visit well. After he strapped my feet to the heavy chair, he tied up Thom, too, and retrieved a few crates from outside. He unpacked a baton, pliers of different sizes, a hammer, and a blue and white whip that branched into nine different strands. My throat bobbed.

The preacher was thin and frail, and my eyes widened as he picked up heavy bags of a powdered product marked with Fe in a square and set them at equal intervals around the room.

My mind went back to chemistry class and the abominable periodic table. Fe. Iron.

Liam would walk back into a carefully laid trap.

About ten minutes later, Thom regained consciousness. He shot me a concerned look, and I nodded to signal I was okay.

I chatted up our uninvited guest to distract him. "What's your name?"

"Irrelevant."

"What did Liam do?" I asked.

Thom squeezed his hand out of his ropes. Unlike mine, they weren't supernatural.

"He did as devils do. Killed without remorse," the preacher said.

Thom almost had both hands out.

Our aggressor whipped around, snatched the baton from the table, and swung it hard at Thom's right leg. The cracking sound brought bile to my mouth.

Thom groaned in pain and bent over his injured leg.

Father Unhinged kneeled. Chin propped over his laced fingers, he prayed, his lips moving without sound. I wondered what God would have to say about him.

Hours passed.

By the end of the afternoon, Thom's right leg had swollen up to about twice its usual size.

I'd been trying to reach Liam via our mental link since the beginning of the attack, the connection stale. When I felt my broadcast reach something other than nothingness, I tensed up.

"Liam?" My hail found footing, and adrenaline shot through my veins.

Agonizing seconds passed as I wondered if he'd heard me.

"Yes." The answer reeked of contempt. *What the hell? "Don't come in. It's a trap. He's got crates of iron and—"*

"Who?" He said, alarmed.

"It's an old man. He's insane."

"Is he alone?"

"Yes."

"Does he have a gun?"

"A gun plus crates of iron plus a torture kit and weird glowing ropes."

"Who is he?"

"He said he's here for revenge. I'm tied to a kitchen chair, and Thom's on the floor next to the fridge. He's hurt. Broken leg."

"And you?"

The contentious undertone from before had morphed into something resembling pain. *"I'm fine. What about you?"*

The preacher pointed his gun to Thom's head. "I know you're here, demon. Come in at once."

Liam opened the front door and walked in at human speed.

"Liam Walker." The old man shook with emotion, like he could barely believe it. "Took me nine years to find you."

Liam smirked. "Must not have been looking hard enough. I'm on Facebook."

The man bared his teeth. "You're the devil."

"I've been called worse."

What was he doing? What did he hope to achieve by egging on the psychotic man that had come equipped with a torture arsenal?

"You think this is all a joke? Do you know who I am?"

Liam shrugged. "Not really."

"You killed my daughters."

My gaze flew to Liam's face.

Shame flickered in his eyes as he briefly glanced at the floor. "It's possible."

"And my wife."

A nasty shiver went up my spine.

Liam's teeth gritted together. "Now that you mention it, I do remember. You're Reverend Fitzpatrick."

"Yes. You covered your tracks well, but God showed me the way. He said, 'His name is Liam Walker, and he's the devil. You'll kill him for me.'"

A snicker twisted Liam's face. "If you hope to kill me, you shouldn't have come alone."

Fitzpatrick raised both hands to the sky like he was receiving God's grace. "I'm not alone."

My eyebrows created a perfect line, and I gasped.

Five tall figures flickered into existence, creating a circle around us. All male, they wore black satin suits and matching ties over black shirts. Their medium-length, chestnut curls made them look like young boys, but their bodies were all men. They looked so beautiful I thought they might be vandellas, but they didn't exude sex. Peace, not lust, rushed over me when I looked at them, and their aura wasn't gold but white, like a halo, particularly noticeable around the head.

Angels.

Fitzpatrick drew a circle with his arm to showcase his backup. "I thought they added a nice touch."

Liam's dumbstruck expression told me all I needed to know.

We were in deep trouble.

A set of silver ropes landed in Liam's hands.

"Put them on and sit down."

Liam moved slowly, the coils of his brain turning. "You have me. Let them go."

"Maybe later. You need to know how I felt when I found my daughters exsanguinated in their beds." He plucked the whip from the table.

Liam's face became white as a ghost. "Where did you find that?"

"The demon that helped me find you said you'd recognize it."

The demon that... Frank. I groaned. Of course, Frank had to be involved in this. But why wasn't he here? He wouldn't miss the chance to kill Liam himself, would he?

The old man sliced my restraints off. "Stand up." He motioned for me to stand between him and Liam. "Turn around and kneel."

Thom shouted, "No! You asshole! She's innocent in all this. She's as innocent as your daughters were. Use me!"

Fitzpatrick waved the whip around. "You'll get your turn."

My eyes locked with Liam's.

"Do as he says." His inner voice boiled with rage and grief.

"You have a plan?"

He shifted his neck a hair to the floor to nod in the affirmative. Whatever that plan entailed, it wouldn't spare me the flogging. Cold sweat ran down my back. I anchored myself to the glimmer of hope in his eyes and inhaled. I knew the whip was coming when he looked away.

Each of the tails lacerated my skin, the knots slashing deep. The air was sucked out of my lungs, and I gagged on a scream. The whip hit again.

You can't suffer quietly through that kind of pain. I shrieked and fell on all fours. I couldn't have imagined the agony burning, stinging, palpitating across my back. I shook, expecting a third lash, but it never came.

A high-pitched noise morphed into a fanfare of howls as the angels broke the circle and closed in on me, their fangs deforming their cherubic faces.

Fitzpatrick screamed, "What's happening? Stop! You work for me."

Liam's blood sprayed everywhere as he tore his ropes off and lunged at the confused preacher.

I jumped to my feet.

One of the angels glided towards me.

It was tall. Taller than the others. The leader. I blinked, certain I was imagining the black wings shimmering at his back. His face wasn't distorted but smooth, and his eyes were so, so blue I thought I might have been staring up at the sky. He was perfect. Boyish cheeks. Chiseled jaw. Warm smile. Straight white teeth.

How had I not noticed him before? I couldn't breathe, totally absorbed by the way he moved. He wrapped his wings around me and cupped my cheek. "I'm so sorry luv, we didn't know how precious you were." His accent was pronounced but atypical. Irish, probably, but with a hint of something else. Something ancient.

He brushed my hair away from my neck and kissed my pulse point.

Fangs dug into the tender flesh. The room spun, and the pain...

The pain was exquisite.

I arched my back and hummed. Nothing hurt anymore, and I floated on cottony clouds, high in the sky.

Another pair of fangs bit into my arm.

No wonder they were called angels. This was the only heavenly way to die.

No fear. No doubt.

Just peace.

Liam ripped my favorite away from my neck, but another just teleported into its place. They did that for a while, teleporting back and forth from the fight, taking turns. My legs gave out, but my favorite was back, and he held me up. He was stronger, more hypnotic than the others.

"You're the best I've ever had," he murmured against my skin.

I chuckled in delight.

"Fight him." Liam's thought-speech tasted absolutely wretched, and the disturbance made me frown. The thought of fighting my angels was ludicrous.

Feathery wings caressed my back, the world beyond them blurry and cold.

The angel on my right wrist grunted, a hand sticking out of his stomach. He crumpled to the floor, and I met Liam's stare. Black as night, it lingered on the blood dripping from my arm before flying up to meet my angel's blue stare.

Liam bared his teeth and growled. "She's mine." He lunged at us but was caught in mid-air by two others and flung into the wall with such force that he fell on his stomach. My eyes were wide as the angels flickered in and out of existence. One of them loomed over Liam, holding a long sword. He raised it into the air, ready to cut Liam's head right off.

Gunshots thundered into his chest, buying my demon enough time to roll away.

My vision was obscured once again by black translucent feathers. My head was heavy on my shoulders. "Tired, so tired."

My angel whispered against my ear, "We shall meet again, beautiful girl." He kissed my jaw before vanishing.

There was still one feeding on my arm, but things weren't so peaceful anymore. The thrall dimmed. My wrists throbbed, lacerated deep. I cried out in pain as I fisted the silky curls of the one who was still drinking. That place behind my skull soared, and I clung to it with all my fear, hate, and disgust.

A surge of power passed through my fingers. The remaining angel shrieked, and his eyes widened in horror as his skin shriveled. Pieces of flesh exploded into the air before turning to dust, and I slumped to the floor, hitting my head hard.

The ceiling danced before my eyes until Liam hovered above me. "God, Lana."

He'd never called me that.

Something snared around both my arms to slow the bleeding. "Heal yourself!"

I was too busy dying to do anything else.

He cradled the sides of my face. "Fuck, fuck, fuck." He raised me up to him and applied pressure on my neck, his tight jaw angled away from the gash. His shadows wrapped me up.

Thom shouted in the background, but I couldn't hear anything.

I existed beyond panic, beyond fear, beyond life.

I'd always known I'd die in his arms.

21

BLEED IT OUT

Liam

Too much blood. Too much temptation.

Deep tremors shoot up and down my spine as Alana's scent drills against my rational mind. I'm slipping. She's curled up against my frame. All I've got to do is lean in to taste her. She's dying. Might be my last chance. I crush her to my chest, and the sight of her lacerated back makes me pause.

"Step away, Liam!" Thom shouts at my back.

My shaky legs catapult me headfirst into the cupboards. Wood splinters shred my fingers as they dig into the hardwood floor. I look back to her body and the puddle of perfect, delectable blood.

Thom meets my hungry stare and drags himself to my side with all the speed he can muster on his injured leg. Both of his hands clasp around my shoulders, and he searches my gaze, his ashen face telegraphing exactly how dire the situation is. "Leave! Now!"

He pushes me toward the back door, and I bolt. I crash in the grass outside, crouched on all fours, and I howl at the moon like the beast that I am.

Sirens and lights alert me to the ambulance's arrival. I make a fist as I hide both myself and the mayhem from them. Thom and Alana are whisked away, and I'm left behind with nothing but my shame to keep me company. Not only has my past gotten them into trouble, but my arrogance almost sealed their fates. I shouldn't have assumed this man came unprepared.

My damn ego almost got us all killed. I was so sure I could handle anything. So sure of my superiority. So full of myself, I thought a mere human could never be more than an ant under my foot.

Fresh air moves in and out of my lungs for what seems like forever until I can pick myself off the ground and inch toward the house. My knees buckle in the doorway, and I hold the frame to keep from crumbling, tearing the moldings apart. Back covered in sweat, hands shaking, and heart beating in agony, I stare at the stale, half-coagulated leftovers. My fists clench tighter and tighter until my nails rake deep into my palms.

I thought all this Alana nonsense had at least helped me with my addiction. I was foolish enough to think I was better, but I want to get on my knees and lap her blood off the floor. I want to rub my disgusting face into it. I want to chase after that ambulance and tear her limb from limb.

You'll never be normal. You'll never be cured. You're a monster, and that's all you'll ever be.

All my disappointment and rage are distilled into concentrated acid liquefying my guts.

I punch the wall hard enough to break my bones and find solace in the pain until they rearrange and mend themselves.

My attention turns back to the man I killed earlier. I recognize Fitzpatrick all right. It's not every day you get to bleed identical twins.

Damn him for reminding me of who I used to be. Damn him for reminding me I haven't changed. Damn him for reminding me I *can't* change.

I kick his head. It flies to the opposite wall, his dead eyes witness to my lamentation.

The Collective is swimming through my mind, the voices so frantic I can barely make one out of the storm.

"Such a waste," the voices seethe at the red pool, its appeal evaporating as slowly as its magical properties. In a minute, it'll be unusable. I can bear a minute.

Fucking angels. I hate them. I can't believe they tasted my girl. I knew they'd lose their shit when she'd bled. Counted on it. Counted on the commotion to break free and kill that fucker. I still loathe that I had to share her. The tall one was more powerful than the others. The most powerful of his kind I've ever encountered.

He touched her. He kissed her. He wants seconds.

Over. My. Dead. Body.

She's mine.

For fuck's sakes, she's not yours.

I get into arguments with myself about that a lot. My brain says she doesn't belong to anyone. My heart cries that she'll never belong to me. My blood yells that she's mine and mine alone. It screams that saying otherwise is the biggest fucking lie that ever was. It howls so loudly that sometimes it swallows all the other voices.

Now is one of those times.

I both hate and love the clarity I get whenever my beast takes over. It's got a simple mind, and it's not happy with the carnage. The floor is missing three sets of entrails, six mangled arms and feet. It's missing three dead angels. They should never have got away. I'm off my game.

My tongue presses against the roof of my mouth in silent outrage. The anger does me good. I'm no longer thinking about the blood I crave. I'm thinking about how my girl's out there without me. Those angels are already plotting to steal her away, and I'll tear their hearts out of their chests one by one.

My phone vibrates in my pocket. Thom.

"How is she?" I croak. She's not dead. I know it like I know the sun will rise in the morning. If she'd died, my soul would have wept.

"She lost a lot of blood. They're transfusing her right now. Listen. You need to come. The police are here."

A visit to the hospital is not what I need. I tap my forehead and groan. "I'll be there."

"Are you able?"

"Yes." I say it with confidence to make it so. I don't need to ask which hospital because she's true north, so I run.

Her scent lingers like a drop of sin on my tongue.

Two policemen stand outside her door.

I glamor myself as an FBI agent and deal with their questions. I confirm that Thom works for the Bureau, too. It's easy but annoying, and I'm relieved when it's done.

The hospital room is bleak and depressing. The dull rhythmic beeps of the machines hooked up to her grate my eardrums. She doesn't belong in this bed, in this hospital. A few hours ago, I thought I could never hate her more. Now, I'm fucked because I'd do anything to make her smile.

The loss of blood makes her skin so white it's almost translucent. Her hair's been cleaned, but a few flakes of dry blood remain. I brace myself for her scent but find it tepid and uninteresting. A blood bag hanging from a pole reminds me why. It's not the first one she received, and I realize with both relief and a hint of regret that her essence has been washed down by the odious, human red cells.

Thom's holding her right hand tightly in both of his.

I clear my throat. "I took care of the police."

"Good." He shoots me his classic I'm-concerned-but-I'm-playing-cool look, the one that reminds me I'm not human. "You okay?"

"Yes."

"You were in bad shape earlier."

I rub the arch of my brow. "I'm an addict with homicidal tendencies. What else did you expect?"

He clicks his tongue. "Don't do that."

"What?"

"Pull this I'm-allowed-to-act-psychotic-because-I'm-not-human crap."

"It's a valid argument."

"It's bullshit, and we both know it. Self-derogatory humor is your defense mechanism."

He's absolutely right. It pisses me off. "You're playing psychologist—"

"—am not playing psychologist—"

"—totally playing psychologist." My lips quirk. "You nag me."

"You nag me more."

I pat his back. "Good talk, Junior."

He sighs in aggravation, but I know this spat soothed him. It allows us to pretend I didn't almost kill his girlfriend. I swat the thought away with a quick shake of the head.

"I'll let them tend to this." He points to his injured leg. "The makeshift external brace they put together to keep the broken bones in place has to be replaced by a proper cast."

"I'll watch her."

"Don't eat her."

"Ha. Ha. Very funny."

He gives me a look.

My shoulders hitch. "I won't."

He nods and scratches his neck. "The angel that almost... I know him."

My eyes widen. "Who is he? I got a feeling he's going to come back."

"He's pretty old. Old enough to turn humans. He tried to recruit me a few years ago."

I raise a hand in the air, shock slithering up my spine. "Slow down. An angel tried to *recruit* you?"

"It was right after Dad's death. During my rebellious phase. He said I had 'the look.'"

I am flabbergasted, my jaw slack, my mind reeling. Thom went through a rough patch after our parents died, but I never imagined...

"We'll talk later. I'm pretty sure he won't be back today." Thom calls for the nurse.

"Finally," the middle-age woman says as she enters the room, thrilled her difficult patient finally consents to treatment. She rolls him out, and I sit in the chair in the corner of the room.

Useless. Paralyzed.

I hate hospitals. I hate the sight of her in this too white and too clean room that reeks of industrial disinfectant. I hate that she's hurt. I hate that she can die. And easily, too. Unlike me.

A male nurse enters and approaches me. I'm still wearing my FBI glamor for the hospital staff.

There's a bouquet of flowers in his hands. "These were delivered for you, sir."

I yank open the card.

Humpty Dumpty sat on a wall,
Humpty Dumpty had a great fall;
All the king's horses and all the king's men
Couldn't put Humpty together again.

Frank. The bastard sent me flowers.

My knuckles are balled so tight they hurt.

It's my fault. I let him through my walls, and he saw our location. The message is meant to taunt me, but it also gives me unparalleled insight into Frank's plans. Whatever he hopes to achieve, he's still too nervous to come close, and I bet it has to do with Alana. Frank knows something about her. Something I'm blind to. Something like why she's able to disintegrate demons.

If only she stopped lying to me, we might have a shot of getting out of this unscathed.

2 2

JEALOUS

Alana

*N*ightmares aren't real until they are. My mind was full of feathers and voices promising eternal peace. Death bloomed like a rose, blood red and seductive, its hot petals splashing down on my hungry tongue. When dreams fizzle out and reality bleeds into shadows, how can you tell if you're awake?

I drifted for a long time. Sirens. Needles. Hurried voices. Scissors. Nurses. Thom's hands clasping mine. When I conjured enough strength to keep my eyes open for more than a moment, Liam was sitting in the corner of the room. We exchanged a solemn look. I lifted my head up, but my vision blurred, so I sank back against the pillow.

"Where's Thom?" I asked, worried not to see him.

"He's getting his leg fixed."

The roof of my mouth stuck like wet paper. "Water?"

"I have coffee."

"Even better." Anything to erase the stale metallic taste in my mouth.

"I'm not sure—"

"Oh, it won't kill me. I won't throw up I swear."

He walked over to me and held a Styrofoam cup to my lips.

I took three large gulps of lukewarm coffee and sighed in relief as the bloody taste receded.

Liam raised the cup out of reach. "Take it easy. You lost a lot of blood." His jaw clenched. "They keep whispering between themselves that you shouldn't have made it."

Our gazes met, and he brushed a strand of hair behind my ear. The gentle touch betrayed how shaken he was. On Liam's scale, this simple caress equated to tears. I shifted in the bed. Machines beeped from my left and right, and there were catheters in both my arms, though one was disconnected.

Liam called a nurse who called a doctor who explained about blood loss, transfusions, and how close it'd been. I'd lost almost 50% of my blood volume but, against all odds, I was going to live. They asked me to rate my pain from 1 to 10. Too much drug would have knocked me out, so I said 4. The nurse pushed a syringe into my IV.

Liam's stare would have heated up my cheeks if I'd had any blood to spare. His super-sight created ripples of goosebumps wherever he looked for too long. The bandages on my arms, the sprinkles of blood in my hair, the gauze covering my neck.

He sat next to me as the doctor left and whispered, "Fucking angels."

The words brought sweat to my palms. The death they offered was the most perverse death there is. A death you welcome with open arms. A death that robs you from the will to live. A death you long for after they're gone.

"They made it so I wanted to die," I murmured in shame.

"Fucking angels," Liam repeated, sliding his hand over mine.

I angled my face away, and my lids screwed shut for a moment. "I didn't fight."

"You did."

I shook my head. "Not fast enough."

He still hadn't let go of my hand. The sight of our entwined fingers was outrageous. My eyes darted around the room so I wouldn't stare at them. There was a fist-sized hole smack in the middle of the wall behind him. "What's that?"

He didn't have to look to know what I was pointing to. "A hole."

"You punched a hole in the hospital's cement wall?"

"Yes."

I would never understand all that testosterone business. "It's a pretty stupid thing to do."

He raised a brow. "After all I did, this is where you draw the line?"

I chuckled and squeezed his hand tightly. "Shut up." Clearly, the pain meds worked like a charm.

He grew somber again. "You killed that last angel with your bare touch."

"Yes."

"You'd done it before." His eyes pleaded with me not to leave him high and dry again.

My voice trembled. "Yes."

"That night at Frank's. You killed Caleb. That's why Frank left."

I bowed my head in silent admission.

As if in slow motion, his hand left mine, his jaw twitched, and he sprung to his feet. His voice sounded hollow as he asked, "Does Thom know?"

"What?"

"Does he know about Caleb?"

"Don't yell. My head hurts." I straightened my back against the pillows and grabbed my forehead. What difference did it make if Thom knew? We should have been concentrating on getting me out of this hospital, not arguing about whether or not I'd told Thom about killing Caleb. My thoughts staggered over the name. It was the first time Liam had mentioned it, reminding me I'd killed someone he knew. I propped my legs over the edge of the bed and stood up, but my knees buckled.

Liam caught me in his arms. "Thom knows. Otherwise you'd already have said no." He was furious, but in that rage, there was something I'd thought I'd never see again. Vulnerability. Our noses were almost touching. I wet my lips, and his eyes flickered to them.

All of the sudden, he dropped me, and I fell flat on my ass.

"Ow." My body exploded with pain, and I patted my bruised butt-cheek. "What the hell?" Too dizzy to stand up, I straightened out my IV line.

Liam towered above me, his aura dark and gloomy. He mumbled under his breath before offering me his hand, which I took only because I was buck naked under that damn hospital gown and the floor was cold.

He held me up, his hands solid around my waist. The roughness of his touch unnerved me, so I pushed against his chest with weak arms to create some distance.

He pulled me closer. "Tell me about New Orleans."

"It's a beautiful city."

A dry snicker passed through his lips. "Be careful, princess. If you're putting us all in danger, I'll have to put a stop to it. Freedom has a price."

I finally met his stare. "You wouldn't dare."

We both knew it was a lie.

He wouldn't think twice about bringing me back to Virginia by the hair, kicking and screaming. I was surprised he hadn't done it already.

I tucked my chin up. "You're the one who's putting us in danger. What did you do to Frank? This vendetta is going to get us all killed."

Teeth gritting together, he dumped me back on the bed. "We're not having this conversation."

"You yell at me for lying, I yell at you."

He paced the room. "I'm not lying. I'm telling you this is none of your damn business."

"Then my trips to New Orleans are none of yours."

His hand sliced the air. "Everything about you is my business. You keep forgetting, but I'm the only reason you're alive."

"You're the only reason I'm a walking bruise, you mean."

Thom chose this moment to appear at the door, battling with crutches. Joy and concern flickered over his features as he saw I was conscious. "Are you okay?"

I blew air through my nose and nodded.

Liam's voice was very quiet when he asked, "Did you know Alana could disintegrate people with her bare hands?"

Thom gave him a confused glare. "What?" The verve of the answer told Liam all he needed to know.

Liam's rage went from flaming Armageddon to smoldering ashes. "You didn't know."

"It only happened once before today," I defended myself.

"On Caleb," Liam clarified.

Thom shot me a disbelieving glare. "You said he disappeared."

"I freaked out. I wasn't sure what happened."

Liam cleared his throat loudly. "Frank knows we're here. He sent us flowers." He motioned to the trash can.

My jaw dropped, and I fisted my frizzy curls. Why hadn't he mentioned that before? "How do you know it was him?"

Liam's eyes were dark. "There was a card."

Thom sighed. "Of course there was."

"We should leave before he sends another surprise," Liam said with a grunt.

Thom's brow furrowed. "Now? She might need another transfusion."

"The doctor said she needed rest and an IV. We can bring saline bags with us." He turned to me. "I guess it's up to you."

"I want to leave." I looked down at my naked legs. "Err—clothes, maybe?"

Liam vanished in a blur and reappeared thirty seconds later with clothes in his hands. "That's all I could find." He passed me faded, blue scrubs.

"That's fine." Better than a hospital gown, anyway.

Thom picked up his crutches. "We'll wait for you."

The simple task of changing clothes sent jolts of pain down my body. After battling with the IV line and the large scrubs, I joined Liam in the hallway, bag of fluid in hand. Thom was nowhere to be found.

Liam was explaining our departure to the nurse.

"We're transferring her for her safety. We have our crew waiting outside in an ambulance." I had no clue what Liam made her see, but she nodded in agreement.

I wet my lips, my mouth dry again. "Where's Thom?"

"I sent him ahead. He's not exactly fast on his feet."

"Neither am I."

He looked me up and down and sighed. "That's why I spend half my life carrying you around, princess."

"You do not spend—" A quick overview of the times he'd carried me made me pause. There was the night we met, the Cerberus incident, the sprained ankle, not to mention my drunken performance barely hours ago. "Okay, that's fair."

He handed me two extra bags of saline and picked me up. The embrace was carefully considered and gentle. There was no hurry in his movements, and he handled me as though I might break, with softness and care.

Not like a bag of potatoes you tote around, and that made all the difference. The discomfort from my wounds barely registered. Feeling dauntless, I draped an arm around his neck and let my fingers wander his hairline.

The heat of his body quickened my breath. My nipples hardened, threatening to show through the thin, horrendous hospital fabric. I shifted in his arm. He adjusted his hold under my thighs to put less pressure on my back, probably thinking I was in pain. In this position, his hand rested dangerously close to my ass. Deeply aware I was not wearing underwear, I swallowed hard.

I had to find a quick distraction. "You know what?"

No answer.

"I think you like carrying me. Makes you feel like a hero."

His arms tensed. "I'm no fucking hero."

"I was just teasing. God. You're so serious."

"Excuse me if I'm not cracking jokes the night you almost died." His words were dripping with sarcasm, but the hurt in them spelled out how terrified he'd been to lose me. I cowered into his heat and rested my head in the crook of his neck. A slight stagger interrupted his steady pace when I pressed my lips to his skin, but he didn't say anything. The hospital was huge, and I didn't mind how long it took to get outside.

THE MOON GLOWED BRIGHT in the sky as we joined Thom on the curb. We walked up to a woman who was parking her car nearby. Thom stole her keys right from her purse, and just like that, we had a ride. We drove for about five minutes when Liam pulled up in front of a house.

"We can decide what to do here. Nobody's home."

Liam plucked me from the driveway and transported me inside. A languid ache had taken hold of my body.

Thom beelined for the fridge. "I'm starving."

I hadn't eaten in 24 hours, but I wasn't hungry.

Liam's thumb grazed the nape of my neck. "You want to eat or lie down?"

"I'm beat."

We found the master bedroom on the first try.

The darkness beckoned, the fatigue claiming me whole. Liam pulled down the covers and set me on the big bed. I should have felt guilty for invading these peoples' home, but I was way too tired to care.

He hung the bag of saline on the headboard and checked that the line was working. "Rest, and you can try to heal when you wake up."

I nodded and rolled onto my stomach.

A sharp breath escaped his throat. "Fuck. Your back's bleeding." He got a bowl of cold water and a bunch of hand towels. Sitting next to me, he ripped the scrubs off my back.

"Hey!" I protested.

His hands carefully pried away my knotty hair. "You can change into a shirt later. The fabric's itchy anyway."

Had to agree with that. Didn't change the fact that I was practically naked.

Liam placed a fresh towel against my cuts. The cold water felt amazing against my inflamed skin, and I melted into the sheets. "Feels so good."

"I can't believe you're letting me do this. I almost ate you earlier." His voice trembled over the last part.

"But you didn't. And you won't now."

He leaned in closer to my ear. "I'm not so sure. You smell delicious."

I smiled into the pillow. "You give the weirdest compliments. I thought you weren't in the mood to crack jokes?"

"Sleep, Lana." He continued his ministrations. With my eyes closed and my breathing even, I clung to consciousness, enjoying the quiet intimacy of the moment. His lips pressed against my shoulder blade before he walked out.

I WOKE up to him changing the towels for fresh ones. I wanted to wait until he was done to let him know I was awake, but pee was close to bursting out of my bladder. Damn fluids.

My shoulders tensed. "I need to get up."

He held me gently in place. "Easy."

"Get out of my way. I need to pee."

I hugged the shredded scrubs to my chest, grabbed the fluids, and inched to the adjoining bathroom, dizzy. The last thing I wanted was to drop to the floor, pee myself, and have Liam deal with it. I made it to the bowl and sighed in relief.

When I got back, Liam tossed me a big shirt and turned around. I pulled it over my head and sat on the edge of the bed.

"Where's Thom?"

"Passed out on the couch." He ran a hand down my arm. "Time to heal yourself."

Pressing my fingers against my wound, I concentrated hard. No result. "It's not working."

His expression darkened. "Well it better. Those lacerations will leave a mark, and I'll be damned if you will keep a scar from that disgusting whip. Give it time."

"It's no use. It either works, or it doesn't."

There was a big hole in his shirt underneath his arm pit, and I grabbed the torn fabric. "You're hurt."

"That's nothing."

I grazed the white, new flesh, and he drew back under the guise of grabbing a new shirt from the dresser. I bit my lips at the sight of his naked back, and my tattoos seemed to heat up. The fact that we were in a barely lit bedroom didn't help my imagination to stay in check, so I concentrated on the healing again.

I'd seen how his wounds mended themselves by creating new tissue and skin, but I didn't know how it worked exactly. "Is it hard to heal yourself in a combat situation?"

"No. Unlike yours, my healing ability is passive. I can be unconscious, and it's still going to work."

"That's a nice trick."

"There are some perks to being me." He sat so we were shoulder to shoulder.

The heat of his body radiated in my direction, and I was dying to scoot closer. "Do you think I'll ever figure my powers out?"

"Sure you will."

I shook my head. "Can't find that damn trigger."

"Your trigger..." Liam breathed the word like it struck a chord. "Talk me through this. What happens when it does work?"

"I can barely remember anything before I healed my father. He fell from the roof, and my mind went into full-blown panic mode. I remember his blood pooling against the asphalt and his broken arm and how quickly the life drained from his face."

Liam's knuckles whitened against the edge of the mattress. "And when you healed me?"

My breathing hitched. If I hadn't almost bled to death, or if my back hadn't been in shreds, or if the room had been less dark, I don't think he would have asked. Any mention of my incursion into his brain left him bitter and angry, so I knew how rare of an opportunity this was. The fragile moment pulsed in my hands, and I willed myself not to shatter it.

"I didn't know if I could do it. I remember thinking I was the crap-piest witch ever. Then I realized I couldn't fail, because I cared way too much about you to let you die." Shit. That sounded way more intimate than I intended.

The silence was too heavy to bear. "I thought at first that I could only heal in life-or-death situations, but..." I couldn't tell him I'd healed myself at Adeline's, so I said, "but I don't think that's it."

Kneeling on the carpet in front of me, he reached into his jeans, pulled out his pocket knife, and placed my right palm to the ceiling. "Don't move."

The bed wasn't very high, so we were at eye-level, and my mouth dried up. "What are you doing?"

"Testing a theory." He sliced his wrist and let the blood pour into my hand.

I crunched my nose at the thought that it sort of smelled good. Blood loss had done a number on me.

He looked straight into my eyes. "When you healed me, you had blood on your hands. A lot of it. I knew a demon once who had to be drenched in blood for her powers to work. Maybe it's the case with some witches, too." There was a hint of doubt in his voice. "Try again." He ripped the bandages off my neck and guided my hand, smeared with his hot blood, to the worst bite mark.

I closed my eyes. The world faded away, and the maze of strings appeared. *Yes!*

Liam's hand over mine acted as an anchor, and I waited for his mind to join the swirl of memories, knowing instinctively it would. I couldn't care less about reliving random moments of my life, so I concentrated on him.

I saw a girl. About sixteen years old. She was beautiful. A younger Frank laughed at her side.

A breadcrumb of a memory that Liam had accidentally dropped in the ether, so fleeting and incomplete that he never noticed I'd seen it.

Frank had said he'd only ever loved two people. Was she the second? Had Liam killed her? Stolen her away? The more I thought of Frank, the more agitated I got.

The inside of my mind darkened, black clouds hovering above the surface of the long mirrors flanking the labyrinth of yarn-like strings. My reflection disappeared into the storm for a moment before it stepped out again.

The other Alana wore a white lace dress streaked with blood, the fabric in pieces like a wild animal had clawed it off her back. She shrugged off the shredded gown and stood naked without a single mark on her body, munching on a piece of raw meat. Her smile was more animal than human. With red teeth, she raised her arm to offer me a bite. Her snack was a beating heart, blood rushing out of the severed arteries with each contraction.

The jarring image nullified my hold on the tide of memories, and I got sucked into a whirlwind that didn't make much sense.

The present seeped back into place.

A thousand times lighter and more energized, I snapped my eyes open. Saliva filled my mouth, and I flexed and stretched my muscles, pleased to find them pliant and painless.

"So easy! Blood is my trigger. Brilliant!" Elated, I grabbed both sides of Liam's face and pecked him on the lips before ripping out my IV line and bouncing off the bed. "I'm feeling phenomenal." The energy sizzling in my veins was crisp and thrilling. "You know what this means? We can actually rely on this damn magic from now on."

Liam's eyes narrowed.

"What?" I asked.

"You're moving really fast."

"I'm excited." I would have thrown a party for the whole world.

I ran to the living room to find Thom.

Liam caught me in his arms. "Wait. Maybe you should give yourself time to recharge. After you healed me, you were pretty weak."

I pushed him off with a smile. "I feel great."

"That worries me."

I ignored his warning and walked to Thom. The second my hands connected with his broken leg, I got swallowed into his mind in no time, confirming my hunch that we'd indeed found my trigger.

It always had to be blood, and this was no exception.

The process took me to the heart of Thom's mind. I gritted my teeth together not to influence the flow of memories, but the more I tried not to think about myself, the more I did. It's the Murphy's law of psychic healing powers.

Suddenly, I was inside Thom's body in a crystal-clear memory.

We were walking alongside Liam in front of my old apartment in Amherst. Liam was mad at us for insisting we go to Alana's birthday party instead of watching it unfold from the shadows.

"You told her you would call her back," Liam growled.

"I didn't want to be rude."

Liam shook his head. "You meant it."

"No." We scratched the back of our neck under Liam's scrutiny. "Okay, maybe I thought about it for a second. But I know I can't."

"You can."

"What?"

"Call her back. Take her on a date."

"It's too dangerous."

Liam paused. "Not if you quit."

We frowned. "What are you talking about?"

"Thom, we've been doing this for six years. It's been tough on me, but it's been tougher on you. You didn't get to go to college or have a normal relationship."

"You haven't either."

"I'm different. You're not. You can have all those things. We're ghosts everywhere we go. We can't form attachments."

"I know, but you're wrong. I'm not normal. What if I stay? What if I fall in love? We buy a house and get married. What then? If we're lucky enough to have kids, I'll be petrified to have a boy. I'll either have to lie to my wife for the rest of my life or tell her our sons might become demons. Or my grandsons. There's is no clean slate for me either."

I braced myself for the next wave of images, trying hard not to pick and choose which one I wanted to bring to the forefront.

Over French fries and burgers, we finally managed to broach the delicate subject again. "It got awkward this morning because I don't know how to act around you anymore."

"Why?" Past-Alana winced and grabbed her forehead, but we could see she was genuinely confused.

She didn't know. How could she not know?

We almost said it right then, but we didn't.

What good would it do? She didn't feel the same way. Maybe it was better that she had no clue and believed that only our pride was hurt. We took the easy way out.

When she said, "I wish it would go back to the way it used to be," we froze. "I don't know if I can do that. Maybe..." Could we do that to ourselves? To her? Was it fair to either of us? What had happened to our resolve to distance ourselves?

"But you see, it would be a waste of a great snuggle buddy." With a cute tilt of the head, she sealed our fate.

Of course, she had to make the perfect joke. "Great? I'd say you're adequate."

Being with him in his personal recollection of a moment we'd share together took my breath away. Perspective is everything. Feeling the burn of the walls I'd erected between us from his point of view slammed some much-needed perspective into me. Thom was in love with me. And I'd had no idea. I used to be an open book to him, but lately he couldn't tell where my head was. He'd made resolutions to keep his distance and move on because every time I pushed him away it broke his heart a little.

How had I been so blind? The healing had tangled up our minds and love simply gushed out of me as I re-entered my body. I planted a sweet kiss on his lips and wrapped my arms around his neck. "I'm sorry." I kissed him again.

"For what? You healed me. I'm grateful."

"I can't believe how stupid I've been. I didn't mean—"

He patted my back with a shaky hand. "Hey, I'm fine. We'll talk about it later." He shot his brother a glance, and I remembered where we were.

The grim curve of Liam's mouth drove me mad. That hypocrite

had rejected me twice. All he had to offer was an uneven temper and stolen kisses while he thought I was unconscious.

Looking anywhere but at us, he said, "Frank's in New York. We should get back to Virginia before he decides to come himself or sends any more crap our way."

"I'm not leaving before Rachel's birthday," I said.

Thom hesitated. "You're sure he's in New York?"

"He was this morning. God knows where he is now. I'm leaving. Maybe I can catch his trail."

I wanted to object, but Thom beat me to the punch. "No." He disentangled himself from me and stood up. "You're not going alone on another crazy hunt. We finish this Rachel thing. Then, we'll make a plan. All of us. Stop trying to fix everything by yourself."

"It's my mess."

"It's *our* mess. And it's only a week." Thom motioned to his leg. "Can you?"

Liam ripped the cast apart. "If I agree, she has to stop gallivanting on her own."

I crossed my arms. "You do not get to set the rules."

"See how she is? How can we work as a team if she conceals important facts?"

"Your attitude is not helping," Thom said.

Liam's eyes widened. "My—"

Thom interrupted him, "We do the opposite of what we usually do. There are a few hotels where the 65 meets Dauphin Street. We rent a big suite on the highest floor."

Liam scratched his neck, considering the idea. "Okay. I'll clean up the scene at the house tomorrow morning and grab what we can't replace. It'd be a good time to switch burner phones, too."

And just like that, the Walker brothers were in full business-mode again.

23

LAST TO KNOW

Alana

The hotel suite was on two levels and fully furnished. This time, I took the master. Having a bathroom to myself would be a treat, if only for a week. The bath was enormous, and I filled it to the brim. The gunk had to go.

I must have spent an hour in that bath, thinking over what I'd seen in Thom's mind.

From his point of view, it was utterly obvious. Thom wouldn't jeopardize a great friendship with someone he lived with on a whim or for a chance to get laid. He'd kept his distance at first because I couldn't leave and he didn't want to make me uncomfortable, but his interest in me had never been casual. Why else would he trust me so much?

He'd been patient and optimistic until we first kissed. After I'd rejected him, he'd felt confused and disappointed. After our talk, he'd decided he'd be okay with being just friends. My drunken attack had rekindled his romantic hopes big time.

I tapped my forehead against the ceramic at the thought that I'd basically issued myself an ultimatum. With deep wrinkles on my skin,

I got out of the tub and wrapped a big, fluffy towel around my wet body.

Thom was the least of my problems.

Frank had to be dealt with. We were always on the defensive, always the ones being hunted. That had to change.

No matter how hard Thom insisted, Liam would hunt Frank alone. He'd never let Thom or me within ten miles of Frank, and it was utter macho crap. Liam and Frank were linked by more than history. They lived inside each other's heads. Frank expected Liam to go after him and waste months on his trail as he'd be one step ahead. To catch him, we'd have to blindside him. Completely. That meant taking Liam by surprise, too.

Getting the upper hand meant getting more power. I dialed Faye's number from the hotel phone, and she answered on the second ring but didn't utter a word.

"Faye?"

She clicked her tongue. "You're beyond late. Where are you calling from?"

Shit. I was supposed to meet with her yesterday. I'd completely forgotten. "A hotel. We were attacked."

"By who?"

"Long story short: Frank sent someone to kill us. I'm fine, but I'm done waiting for the other shoe to drop." I gritted my teeth together. "I want to kill him."

"That can be done." She didn't pester me with questions. You had to commend Faye for her pragmatism.

"How do we find him?"

She took a second to think about it. "We need something of his. Something meaningful. And a picture would speed things up."

"I can get that."

"And we need a weapon."

"We have one." I didn't mention *I* was the weapon.

"What's the time frame on this?"

I nibbled on my cuticles. "I'm not sure. A few days max." If I wanted this plan to work, I'd have to act fast.

"Text me when you get your hands on what we need, and I'll drive up."

"Okay. I'll pick up a new cell and text you a frog emoji so you know it's my new number."

"Take care, kid."

"You too."

Beyond exhausted and now famished, I tied a robe around my frame and ventured back downstairs. The sun was rising above the horizon. Thom was on the phone with Lilah, telling her about our misadventure and warning her to grab a new phone, too.

Liam was gone.

He came back 10 minutes later with big bags from the drugstore. Toothbrushes, toothpaste, a hairbrush, clothes, and snacks piled in the center of the table. I threw myself at a brownie.

Liam was on edge, the air around him alive with shadows. Definitely thinking about going after Frank. "I'll go back for our things while you guys sleep."

"You need rest, too," Thom said.

"I can't sleep now."

Thom searched his brother's eyes. "Swear to me you won't bolt."

Liam nodded. "I swear. I'll get our stuff then check on Rachel until she's done with class. We'll switch places when you're rested."

"What about me?" I asked.

"Stay here, and don't do anything stupid."

I smacked his shoulder on my way back to my room.

My DREAMS WERE INTERRUPTED by black feathery wings and sultry Irish accents. I woke up in a sweat and shivered all the way to the shower. When I returned, my purple duffle bag lay at the foot of the bed, crammed full of clothes, shoes, the book I'd been reading, and basically anything of mine that laid around the house. My dagger was in there. My red katana was nowhere to be found.

I hurried downstairs.

Liam was inventorying his weapons on the kitchen table.

"Where's my katana?"

"Here."

I sighed in relief as he handed it to me and eyed the stack of weapons. Knives, daggers and other pointy, sharp objects littered the table. My fingers ran over the shiny wood of the spear that had almost killed Liam, and my pulse quickened when I spotted a wavy-bladed, gold-plated dagger. But Liam's name was written across the hilt, so it wasn't the one I needed.

"Why did Frank send that man?" I asked.

He pressed his lips together, and for a moment I thought he'd brush me off, but his arms fell at his sides, and he exhaled. "Fitzpatrick had two daughters. Twins. After I killed them, I spiraled. Frank and two others had to sequester me." He squeezed his eyes shut. "But I'm not sorry. The mayhem I left in my wake helped my father find me. I figure Frank knew Fitzpatrick was looking for me and saw an opportunity."

Most of Fitzpatrick's gear lay around the room with one exception.

My shoulder pressed against Liam's as I considered the loot. "What did you do with the whip?"

His mouth tensed. "I burned it."

I skimmed his lower arm and almost twined our fingers before chickening out and letting my hand fall at my side. "It was the one Marcus used on you, wasn't it?"

He stopped his movements and tilted his head to the side. His eyes drilled holes into me. "You know about that?"

"Yes," I breathed, aware of what I'd just admitted to. *Shit.*

His voice was real quiet again, his eyes pulsing with grievances. "You didn't see that in my mind. I made sure you didn't."

My lips quivered.

"Thom told you," he snarled as he backed away. "What else do you guys talk about behind my back?"

"Don't be like that." I reached for his arm.

He recoiled, disgust rolling off his tongue. "You lie in bed talking about what Marcus did to me?"

"Of course not."

With a high voice, he said, "Poor Liam had a difficult childhood. That's why he's so messed up. We better not upset him."

I opened my mouth, but before I could argue, he stormed out, slamming the door behind him.

Thom arrived 20 minutes later wearing a worried grimace. "What did you say to him? He barely spoke a word to me besides, 'go home to your girlfriend.'"

"I slipped and asked if the whip was Marcus's. He realized you and I talked about the torture thing and freaked out."

"Well, fuck. He's already a flight risk. I swear, if he goes after Frank alone, I'll kill him."

A sad smile quirked my lips. "I'll be here if you need help."

My attempt to lift his mood fell flat, and his shoulders tensed. "I found the seer." He looked torn, like it was actually bad news. "It's Margery."

"Margery? As in Rachel's friend?" *Designated-driver Margery?*

"Yes," he whispered.

My jaw dropped. "Wow. Are you sure?"

"I got to thinking: why haven't we picked up a trail by now? Our surveillance is pretty tight. I figured it might be because the seer was above suspicion. The only person who we know talks to Rachel every day is her best friend."

I frowned. "That's hardly a smoking gun."

"Then, I looked through her file. Margery Bennett went to high school with Rachel, but she moved away for college. Then, three months ago, she transferred back. She must have been handpicked for the job since she knew her."

"Still…"

"I needed hard proof, so I stole her laptop." He handed me his phone.

It was a screen capture from Gmail. The email read:

We're not the only ones whiffing around her. I've got two players here. A young red-headed woman and a drop-dead-gorgeous, dark-haired demon. I need a raise if you expect me to stick around.

Well that settled it. "Okay. She's the seer. Did you tell Liam?"

"No. He didn't exactly give me the opportunity, and I prefer taking care of it myself. He's in a mood... Do you want to come with me? We've got to hurry before she misses her computer."

The starkness in his eyes contrasted with the urgent words. We had to hurry, and yet he looked ready to crawl under the covers, his forehead creased.

My heart panged as I realized he knew he had to kill her. "I'll go with you."

This wasn't any different from killing the gorgon with Faye. This girl sought to profit from Rachel's death. Still, doubt crawled. "But what if she has no idea why she's paid to do this? She's pretty young."

Thom nodded like he'd been thinking the same thing. "We can ask her."

He didn't say it sarcastically. Thom respected my opinion, and we were both looking for the best in people. A big plus in his column.

He drove to Margery's apartment. I was curious to see how he operated. He had no special powers, but he was confident he could do this without back-up because he'd done it before. "Her car's not here yet," he said as he parked across the street. He made sure his gun and silencer were ready before tying the holster up around his waist.

We walked to the back of the apartment complex.

"I left a window open." He jumped to the balcony and offered me his hands. "Stand up on that patio chair and grab on."

I did as he asked, and he supported my weight so I could climb over the ledge. Our bodies grazed as I straightened up, and a shiver derailed my thoughts. God. It'd be so much easier if I could stop being attracted to one of them, but I was pretty sure it'd never happen.

For the next two balconies, he boosted me up instead, and I was amazed by his stealth and speed. If I'd had any fears Thom couldn't take care of himself, they were extinguished on the third balcony as he jumped in to join me, not fazed by all the climbing.

We waited about an hour for Margery in her living room. She came home alone, exactly as Thom had predicted.

"Shit," she said as she spotted us, reaching into her bag.

"Stop. Hands on your head." Thom's voice and aim were mightily intimidating, so she took the warning seriously. He waved her inside, and I closed the door behind her.

She shifted from foot to foot, her eyes wide. How could a girl like her, so young, do this for a living? Didn't she know she was ruining innocent lives?

An unexpected wave of disgust awakened my temper. "How much are you getting paid?"

Her gaze latched onto mine. "Why? Do you want to hire me?"

"Maybe." I played along, knowing I was more likely to get the truth this way.

"This is a jealousy thing, right? I mean, you're clearly the demon's favorite since he marked you, but lately he's only had eyes for Rachel." The tension in her body evaporated, and she cocked one hip to the side. "I couldn't believe it when you showed up at the party. Gave me a good laugh with that fake cousin story. Must sting like hell to see him with her. You need someone else to get rid of her so he doesn't suspect anything. I get it. Tell you what, you give me $100,000, and I'll solve your problem."

So much for giving her the benefit of the doubt. "Don't you have a boss?"

She shrugged. "For the right price, I'm a free agent."

Thom called it before I had to and shot her in the head. I forced myself not to look away. Here we were, acting as judge, jury, and executioner. I didn't know if it was right, but I truly believed it was needed. We could either hope that she would one day become a better person and let her live or take the gamble she wouldn't and learn to live with ourselves.

The sad curve of Thom's mouth told me exactly how he felt.

I knelt next to the body, a boulder in my throat.

A warm hand grazed the hair at the base of my neck, and I put two fingers over the hole in her head and dusted her with a sigh. No need to leave evidence behind us.

Thom looked taken aback. "Wow. That's useful."

"Yeah," I choked up. Useful and incredibly sad. "She saw lives as dollar signs. Business. I'll never get it. Even now, I feel so guilty I could cry. Does it get any easier?"

Tears glistened in his eyes. "Do you want me to lie?"

I gulped. "Yes, please."

"Then yeah. It gets easier."

I stood on the tip of my toes and kissed him because I could not bear not to. It wasn't passionate or chaste, but full of love.

That kiss cleared any doubt I had on the path I had to take. I couldn't go about my life sampling the two men I liked until I made up my mind with no regards for Thom's feelings. He loved me. I loved him. So simple, and yet I'd made it out to be rocket science.

But, back in our hotel room, when Thom pulled me into his arms, I tensed up. It was like my body was physically rejecting my brain's decision.

He winced. "Lana, you can't let what you saw in my mind change the way you act around me. First of all, it's not fair. Second, it's not any of your concern. I didn't tell you for a reason. You're not responsible for my heart. I can recognize a heat-of-the-moment kiss. It's no big deal."

"But I've hurt you."

"I don't care about that. I have enough of Liam who tries to fix everything himself to spare me. I don't need you walking on eggshells. I'm fine with how things are."

"I'm not. I—"

As long as we were into painful territory, I realized it was time. Enough was enough.

"I've been lying to you. To Liam." I combed my fingers through my hair. If Faye and I were to succeed in killing Frank our way, we'd need Thom's help. "I've been struggling with it for weeks, but you have to promise it'll stay between us."

He grazed my arm. "Promise."

We sat down on the stiff hotel couch. The old clock above the suite's kitchen sink clicked loudly as he waited for me to speak. I shifted in my seat, unsure where to start, and wet my lips. "I found my biological aunt. She's a witch too. She was adamant I couldn't tell you about her, and I had to go along with it."

A blend of worry and curiosity lit his face. "Wow. That's huge. Can you trust her?"

"Yes." I smiled. "She freaked out at first because of the demon marks, but we're getting to know one another. She's pretty great, actually. She's teaching me spells and stuff. That's why I keep disappearing on you."

Suspicion twisted his features. "Does she want something in return?"

"She wants me to join her coven."

He raised his brows.

"I won't." Not if it meant disavowing Thom and Liam.

He scratched his neck. "Can I meet her?"

"Maybe." I tucked a curl behind my ear. "I'll have to convince her, though. She kind of hates you."

His jaw slacked. "She hates me? We never met."

"She has a Walker family tree that dates back to the 1600s. Her coven is on a warpath against Shadow Walkers, and you're the next generation."

He frowned. "She told you this?"

"I'm filling in the blanks, but it makes sense. They're afraid Shadow Walkers will turn to covens to replenish their blood supply. They've been spying on them for centuries. My biological Mom was a spy. She died." I let my hair fall around my face.

Thom's knee bumped against mine as he scooted closer and grabbed my hand.

His warmth unknotted my tongue.

I told him about Adeline. About potions. About demon compasses. He appeared utterly fascinated, his eyes bright and his mood light even though I'd lied to him for weeks. Every word was like a weight being lifted off my shoulders.

The story was coming to an end. I'd told him every detail about Faye down to the last joke we'd shared. I could have stopped there, but the last few days had left my heart all disheveled.

I lived with two drastically different but insanely similar men. One loved me, the other didn't. One was human, the other wasn't. A no-brainer decision, but I kept dipping my feet in the devil's water. I couldn't snap my fingers and untangle the conflicting threads of my heart in an instant, but as long as I was coming clean, I had to start fresh. Our world was full of magic, truth serums, and maniacal enemies that couldn't wait to fuck up our lives. Thom deserved to have all the variables.

I hadn't rehearsed this conversation. There are some moments in life when you've got to jump in with both feet and pray you'll find water and not cement at the bottom. Heart hammering in my chest, heat spreading to my chest, I leaped. "That's not all. There's something else. Something worse."

Thom breathed deep, and lines appeared on his forehead like he was bracing himself for impact.

"We flirted for months, then I pushed you away because—I've been acting weird—it's—damn it, it's hard to say. It's horrible, really, and it makes no frickin' sense, I know, but I'm attracted to Liam, too. We kissed, and I felt weird after, and I kept hoping for whatever that feeling was to go away, but it hasn't and now—it's a mess. I made a mess." I didn't look at him as I said the words.

He stood up and paced to the kitchen and back.

I peeked from behind my lashes.

Eyes closed, he rubbed the arch of his brow. "I'm not going to lie and say it's a total surprise. I've seen you guys fight."

"Please don't hate me." I grabbed my forehead, embarrassed by my total lack of eloquence.

His posture was beyond rigid as he breathed, "Why didn't you tell me you were into each other? I would have backed off."

I shook my head. "It's not like that."

"No?" The higher note he gave the word made it a loaded question.

"We don't even get along. He hates me."

Thom groaned and pressed on his lids. "Liam doesn't hate you."

"After today, he will."

"Yeah, well..." He slumped into the chair across from me.

"I'm sorry I jumped you the other night."

"You were drunk." He said the exculpatory words, but I could tell he was mad anyway.

"Yeah, but I insisted. God, Thom. Please don't think I did any of this on purpose. I don't want to feel this way. Things would be so much easier if I didn't. I'm so confused."

"Confused. Yeah, me too," he said with a dark chuckle.

"You're angry."

"Of course I'm angry—" he quieted down before continuing, "Yes, I'm angry. But I'm most angry at him." He swiped his palms over his jeans and stood up.

I reached for his wrist. "Wait. There's one last thing. I have a favor to ask."

His blank expression telegraphed exactly how disinclined he was to grant me a favor.

"Faye knows a way to kill Frank, but she needs something we have."

Interest sparked over his haunted features. "What does she need?"

"Frank's dagger, the one we kept after he kidnapped me."

He thought about it for a second. "Liam left it in the vault in Virginia so Frank wouldn't use it to locate us."

"We need it."

His eyes narrowed. "What is she going to do with it?"

"She'll summon and kill him." I brushed over how I had appointed myself as the weapon of the operation. "Liam can't know anything, or Frank might learn what we're planning."

He sighed. "Okay."

"Really?" Our eyes locked. I'd thought it would bug him more to keep Liam in the dark. Maybe I'd given him the best reason not to feel guilty.

"I'm pissed, not dumb. We need Frank dead, and it's better if Liam's not involved. I'll fly out in the morning and be back before nightfall."

"Okay. Thank you. This could work."

He nodded. "You'll need to cover for me."

"I will. What about the picture?"

"Can't help you there. I don't keep pictures of Frank around," his said, his voice sharp and hollow.

I stood and gripped his shirt. "Thom, I'm so sorry."

His angry lips fused with mine, and I gasped in surprise, his tongue taking advantage and diving deep inside my mouth. It wasn't an "I forgive you" kiss. It was a "how could you" one. He fisted my hair and held me to him, desperate.

As I was about to wrap my hands around his neck, he pushed me away, leaving me breathless. My heart was beating in my throat as he disappeared from view.

24

THINK TWICE

Liam

*A*fter Rachel is safely tucked in bed, I return to the hotel and park my car a few blocks away, out of view. I haven't eaten since this morning. Haven't got an appetite.

Thom accosts me on my way to the fridge. "I want to spar. There's space on the roof. Come."

I'm not in the mood. I shouldn't blame him for this Marcus thing, but I do. The thought that he shares secrets with her that I barely admitted to him makes me sick. I guess every topic is fair game when you're in bed with the girl you love.

I wouldn't know.

"I was going to grab a bite—"

"Now." The zeal in his tone will not be denied.

I can't get out of it without delving further into my petty grievances, but I put up a fight. "Isn't it a little late for training?"

"Yes. I have some pent-up aggression I need to work through."

Join the club.

His body's rigid and jerky as we climb the flight of stairs leading to the rooftop. There's no pool or any real amenities up here. The view isn't all that either, so I suspect it's mainly used by smokers.

I duck as he takes a swing at my head. *Whoa. Eager much.* "So human speed? Half and half?"

"Give me all you got."

"Really?"

"Yes."

The last time he brought so much angst to training was in the aftermath of Alana's kidnapping. He gets like this whenever she's in danger.

Frank shouldn't be afraid of me. Thom's wrath is way scarier.

I cringe as he lands a few nasty blows. He's relishing the violence way more than usual.

When he steps forward and aims a mean right hook at my cheek, I twist his arm and immobilize him.

There's more going on here than an impromptu sparring session. The vibe rolling off him is way too raw. Just as I'm about to bring it up, he elbows me right in the eye with his free arm. Luckily I have healing powers, or I wouldn't see through this eye for days.

I grab my head and stagger. "Wow. That hurt."

"Good."

The way he says the word makes me pause. "What's going on here?"

"You tell me."

I play it safe. "Spit it out, Junior."

"I asked you point blank if anything was going on between the two of you, and you said no."

Damn right I said no! "Because nothing is."

Jaw clenched, he slices both hands through the air between us. "Bullshit. It sucks that we're both into the same girl, but you lying about it made it worse."

There's no denial left in me, and my arms fall at my sides. "She told you." The bitter tang of blood floods my mouth as I bite the insides of my cheeks. "She wasn't supposed to."

"*You* should have." The hushed words ripple through my selfish heart. They chomp down on it and shake it around.

Damn her. Damn her for kissing me back instead of slapping me back to reality. Damn her for being the reason my brother is looking at me like I'm a stranger. Damn her for having the courage I lacked to come clean.

That's the true tragedy. I should have gotten in front of this. I could have spun it right, but I was too damn cowardly. As long as he didn't know, it wasn't real, and I didn't have to face it.

My lungs wheeze, the wind knocked out of me. "I fucked up."

Thom's fury melts in the face of my quiet admission. He passes a tired hand over his face. "Do you love her?"

I huff. "Don't be an idiot."

"Don't be a jerk." The warning in his voice is thick.

I take a deep breath. "She likes *you*. Always did. That kiss didn't count."

"Now who's the idiot?"

He wasn't going to let me off the hook short of me baring my soul. "I'm attracted to her, okay. Because of the blood thing." I point to my head. "There's a stupid fanfare of pissed off demons in here who won't let me forget that, and I slipped up. Once. That's all. It won't happen again. You guys belong together."

His shoulders sagged. "How can you be so sure of that when I'm not?"

"I just am."

"You're wrong. She likes you more than you think, and you like her more than you want to admit. That's why Frank's after her. I was right all along, wasn't I?

I press my tongue against the roof of my mouth. "Yes."

"You denied it for *months*."

"I know. I'm sorry."

"I had to hear it from her. It sucked, okay? Honesty, Liam, is all we owe each other." He motions between the two of us.

I switch my weight from one foot to the other and scratch the back of my neck. "You're right." I wince. *What should I do? Fuck.* "Okay, I kissed her twice."

"You jerk." I let him hit me square in the face.

My nose breaks, and the bones mend while he shakes his hand from the pain. "When?"

"I don't see the point of—"

"When."

"Things got really weird when she healed me. That one doesn't count."

"Agreed." He raises a brow that says, if I have to ask you again, I'll bury you.

"New Years, but it wasn't..." I don't know how to finish this sentence. It wasn't a *Happy New Year* kiss. I should have kept my mouth shut.

Thom's chest falls, and his face creases. "But—what happened?"

I raise a hand in front of me. "If you're fishing for a play-by-play, I'm afraid it's beyond me."

I know my brother. He's running a diagnosis on his relationship with her as we speak. He's weighing the magnitude of her betrayal. I don't know how they left things.

I'm not going to ask. Even if they broke up, it changes nothing. I don't understand why she told him. She lies about everything else. Couldn't we have one secret to share together?

Thom's shoulders hitched. "I'm just trying to understand."

I sink my nails into my palms. "Understand this: it's never going to happen again."

He shakes his head. "I won't fall on my sword on this, but I won't let you fall on yours. If we both have feelings for her, then so be it. She's a big girl, she'll figure it out, and we'll just have to move past this."

I snort and stare out to the dark sky. "I'm not an option."

His brows create a perfect line. "Are you pulling the no-commitment card again? Because it's getting old."

I envy his ability to distance himself from a problem to find a solution while I tear everything apart and deal with the mess after. *Go with the blood. It always works.* Even better if he compares notes with her after. "It's not that. If I spend any more time with her than I already do, I'll rip her open out of sheer blood lust."

His eyes are wide. "You still struggle?"

"Every *fucking* day." It's true enough. It doesn't stop me from wanting to slam her against the wall and erase that damn pout of hers with a bruising kiss.

"Why didn't you say anything?"

I shrug. "I'm a proud idiot."

"You never had this issue with Lilah."

"Alana's different."

"Turning-people-to-dust different or want-to-fuck-her-into-oblivion different?"

My eyes widen at the crude words. Maybe we're not so genetically different, after all. "The first one."

He squints at me. He's running a diagnosis on me, too.

I place my palms face-up in surrender. "Honest." If anything, the prospect of having sex with her helped me resist the urge to kill her.

I'm a piece of work.

Thom's relief at my answer is quickly replaced by fear. "What happens if Frank runs his mouth about her powers?"

A witch is valuable. A witch that can kill a demon with a bare touch is too dangerous to be left alive. Period.

"If he talks, she's in serious danger," I say.

His jaw clenches. "Then we need to find him. Quickly."

"I couldn't agree more. But he's not just quiet since New York. He's not even on the radar."

Bottom lip tucked between his teeth, he looks like he's pondering something of grave importance. "Then we'll have to find another way to get to him."

I nod and wipe the blood that started to dry on my face.

He palms his knee and winces. "My leg still hurts. I think I'll stop by the hospital in the morning to have it looked at."

I gulp. "Shit."

"It's not you. It's been hurting all day."

"You fought me on a bad leg?"

"I was too pissed to care," he snarls as he glares at me sideways. "I still want to rip your guts out."

I nod solemnly. "Good."

25

SET FIRE TO THE RAIN

Alana

The morning after my big admission to Thom, I woke up to an empty hotel room. Checking my phone, I saw he'd texted me from the airport at 7 am. Our plan was on track, and Liam was probably shadowing Rachel. There were only a couple of days left before she turned 20, so the chances of her powers manifesting were multiplying by the hour until they'd drop to zero at midnight on her birthday.

As long as Liam was focused on her, he might not realize what we were plotting. If I could find a picture of Frank, we'd be in great shape and ready to kill the bastard.

The thick curtains were drawn inside Liam's room, so I turned on the switch. Liam packed all his stuff in matching gym bags. Black ones, of course. The first one was full of gear. Probably the weapons he'd inventoried yesterday. I patted down the clothes in the next one, running my fingers over fabric until they tensed around a smaller leather pouch tucked safely inside a side pocket. I unzipped it.

A watch. Money. A beautiful rosary. A stack of pictures. I flipped through them quickly. His parents. Thom. Thom and Liam. The four of them together.

Vicky and Liam on a sailing boat. My nose creased.

And… Yes! A Polaroid of Frank and Liam looking young and silly. I slid the picture in my back pocket.

As I straightened the rest to put them back minus the one I needed, I paused. Amongst the ones I hadn't looked at, I'd caught a glimpse of Lilah's colorful Christmas picture.

I fanned the last few on the nightstand to look at them quickly. Me with a huge grin as I pointed to the reindeer antlers on my head. Another Christmas picture of Lilah, Thom, and Liam from before I came along. A picture of his dad and him fishing.

The last one was a card. The paper was soft and creased like it'd been crumpled and unbent multiple times.

I unfolded it. *Shit. How on earth?*

Blood rushed to my chest.

The surveillance camera footage montage displayed 4 stills total. All of them of Liam and I lip-locked in Frank's hallway. A heart had been drawn around us with the caption, *Merry Christmas, Thom.* The wink emoji made me flinch in revulsion.

Frank had mailed that for Christmas? How? Liam must have intercepted it, but he'd kept it… Nerves shook my hands, and I dropped a few pictures to the floor. I bent down to retrieve them, squared the mass, and put them back as if they were poisoned.

A loud bang alerted me to Liam's return.

Fuck. Me.

I hurriedly put the pouch back into the bag and walked to the door, but Liam was already there. A snarl curled his upper lip. "What now? You're stealing from me?"

Shake it off, girl. He can't know what you're up to.

His eyes moved quickly around the room. "What were you looking for?"

"Nothing." I switched gears to calm his suspicions. "I was waiting for you. We need to talk. I told Thom that we kissed." Nothing made Liam flee like the threat of a serious, heart-baring conversation.

His teeth clenched. "How high school of you."

"I needed to come clean."

A quick smirk twisted his lips before the scowl reappeared. "Nothing clean about your lies, princess."

"I have to lie. You're not alone in there." I pointed to his head. He was a liability. Frank couldn't know what we were planning, but I hoped Liam would read between the lines and back off.

He choked on a vicious snort. "I'm the one who's untrustworthy. Great. That's not how this works. They can only see what's happening when they're inside my head. At the moment, they're not. It's just you and me." He closed in on me, each muscle rippling underneath his shirt. "Now. One last time. What's in New Orleans?"

I held his stare. "Who's the 16-year-old blond girl Frank loved?"

Blood drained from his face. "I can't believe you went through my mind while I helped you focus your healing powers."

"I didn't mean to."

"Bullshit. If I raped your brain the way you constantly rape mine, you'd never forgive me."

My jaw about fell to the floor. "I didn't *rape* your brain."

"Yes, you did. We both know you control it now. You did it to me. You did it to Thom. But that's your MO."

My temper flared. "What does that mean?"

"Exactly what you think it means."

My throat constricted. "I'm not doing any of it on purpose."

"Then figure out what you want!"

My eyes widened. Did he mean— was he saying I had to choose? Between them. The subtext in his words floored me. "I didn't know you were an option."

He cringed at his mistake. "I'm not."

The world-class backpedaling didn't fool me. He'd implied he was an option.

I tilted my head to one side then the other, trying to make eye contact. "You can't even look at me."

He clicked his tongue before meeting my gaze, his eyes hard as diamonds.

"Before, we were friends," I said.

"We were never *friends*." The word *friend* bled with disdain, like the idea of being my friend was either repulsive or ridiculous or both.

Rage heated my face. I fisted his shirt and pulled him closer, our lips only inches apart. Our chests rose and fell, each new breath shallower than the last. A wave of liquid fire crashed in my belly.

A sinister warning emerged from his mouth, his voice so quiet I barely heard it, "Alana, get the hell out of my room." He wrapped his hand in my hair as he spoke, the soft touch contrasting with the harsh words. "Better yet, get the hell out of my life."

Tingles tickled my spine. My gaze fell to his lips and jumped back up again.

He cocked an eyebrow that said, your move.

My hands hiked from his collar to his neck as I planted my ferocious lips on his.

He kissed me back. Hard. Hard enough to bruise me, and I retaliated with every bit as much abandon.

A terrible clarity came over me. Liam was the wrong choice, but there was no choice to make. His touch thrilled me. His kisses charred me. His hands emboldened me to pull, tug, and yank him closer. My head put up a fight, my heart stumbled, but my body knew its own mind. It didn't care about resolutions and issued no apology.

I was addicted to the rush, and I wanted to see where it'd lead, no matter the consequences.

Liam vanished in a blur during my epiphany.

When my eyes found him again, he was standing against the wall on the opposite side of the room, his edges blurry. I growled. I wanted him to make good on all the promises his hungry gaze had made and headed straight to him.

His fists balled, curled and flexed. "Walk away, Alana."

"What if I don't?" I taunted him.

He circled around me so I wouldn't reach him. "Leave. NOW."

"No." That jerk was going to reject me again, and my pride couldn't stand it. "Your blood lust excuse; it's bullshit. You're not afraid to break me. You're—for heaven's sake stop moving around!" Quaking in exasperation, I dug my heels into the carpet. "Is Frank in your head again? Tell him to fuck off."

"You know about—"

"Yes. I heard him the other day. He's a pig. Don't let *him* ruin your life."

His arms sliced the air between us. "Frank has *nothing* to do with this."

I puffed my chest. "Then what? Why do you keep pushing me—"

"—you can shove your questions up—"

"—you freak out every time we kiss—"

"—something is seriously wrong with you—"

"—you never let me in unless one of us is dying—"

"—you lie to me—"

"—why, why, why—"

He fisted his hair and roared, "You're fucking my brother! You kiss me, but you come home to HIM. And I can't STAND it!"

Oh.

"He looked at me like I'm a disgusting traitor, and he's right. Do you have any idea what he means to me? Can't you wrap your brain around the fact that I can't afford to think beyond that? It's not a game."

"It's no game to me either."

"Then stop playing," he breathed the words, cupped my cheeks and pressed his lips on mine. A bitter and firm farewell kiss.

I watched him as he turned to go, and my heart ran away from me. "Thom and I aren't—not really—we've never—" The half-finished explanation hung in the air. I hadn't cleared up Liam's misconceptions out of fear and cowardice, but this admission felt too self-serving.

A hand clenched on the door frame, his back to me, he asked, "Never what?"

He jerked a glance over his shoulder when I didn't answer.

I exhaled. *What else?*

In a blur, he was back in front of me. He tugged on my hair and angled my face so I'd look straight into his eyes. "Don't lie to me. Not about this."

I hiccupped. "I'm not."

"Never?" His eyes were clear.

A tremor shook my breath. "Never."

The most awestruck look of wonderment rendered his face totally unrecognizable. He claimed my mouth again and kissed me slowly and thoroughly until my knees buckled. His forehead rested against mine as he stood demon-still, not even breathing.

Nestled against his broad frame, I was fragile and yet strong. His thumb caressed the small of my back, and the gentle graze turned my legs to jelly.

Unlike our previous make-out sessions, our kisses were slow and totally disarming.

It felt like...more, and I sank against him.

More than gravity. More than lust. More than a guilty stolen moment.

His arms caged me in. I snaked a hand under his shirt and ran my nails across his abs. He trembled under my touch, and an incredible sense of power invaded me knowing I had this effect on him.

Me.

I hummed. His tongue tasted the sensitive skin of my neck like he was committing every nip to memory. Strong hands stroked my waist underneath my thin cotton top and caressed my back up to my shoulders.

There went another delicious shiver.

I curled one leg up around his thigh and rested my head against the wall as he traced my spine and lowered his hand under my jeans, beneath my underwear, and followed my curves down to the space between my thighs.

Yes. This is what I need.

I fisted the waist of his jeans and fumbled with the button for less than half a second.

Next thing I knew, my ass landed on the mattress of the double bed. He shackled my wrists with his hands and stretched my arms over my head.

Eyes dark, he poured his body over mine, filling the space

between us like he was made of liquid instead of flesh, heat dripping into every crevasse. His kisses were hungry and possessive. He tugged my shirt down to reveal the swell of my breasts and bit his mark. It was hot as hell, and the sight stripped me from my last inhibitions.

I dug my nails into his shoulders and sucked in air when he unbuttoned the top of my jeans. His hand spread the zipper open as it glided beneath the elastic of my underwear, and my legs parted of their own accord. A deep shudder quaked me. I was soaked, and now he knew how much I longed for him.

A hoarse, strained noise rumbled at the back of his throat.

Our eyes locked.

All the scenarios playing in his mind flickered over his face.

Heat surged through my entire body as he buried two fingers inside me. My hips buckled, and I cried out a moan that made me blush all shades of red. We had such a strong physical connection that I could only imagine the rush of being sprawled beneath him while he entered me.

He seemed to read my thoughts, too. "Fuck. You're so wet." He licked the sensitive skin at the edge of my jaw. "Swear that you're not lying."

"I swear."

His fingers caressed me from within, my eyes fluttering at the sensation. Lust, need, and pleasure coiled in my belly. He nicked my earlobe. "I'm going to make you come so hard you'll never be able to look my brother in the eyes again."

I forgot to breathe for a second as his mouth kissed me stupid. His hand left the confines of my jeans, and I grieved the loss before he cupped my ass over my pants and ground his erection against my center.

I purred.

There was a long, eerie pause.

A dry chortle heated my neck. "Liar, liar..."

He pinched my ass before shoving his hand into my back pocket and retrieving the stolen picture.

I gaped at the proof of my deception. I'd forgotten all about it. "It's not—"

In one fluid motion, he rolled off me. "What I think? You're so full of shit I can't believe a single word that comes out of your damn mouth." He bounced from one foot to the other so fast the air around him vibrated until he finally balled the picture and threw it at me.

Acting on instinct, I caught it in mid-air.

"You got what you came for." The starkness in his eyes tore me open as he raised his arm and pointed to the door. "Get. Out."

The stiff angle of his jaw crushed me, and I wished I'd never found that damn picture. I wanted to throw it to the floor and stomp on it on my way to him, but before I could move, he vanished.

"Liam," I called after him. No response.

I used thought-speech for the second try. Not only did my plea get no footing, it bounced back over a solidly sealed door and bit the dust. My legs wobbled as I stood. The imprints our bodies had made over the covers taunted me as I re-buttoned my jeans and straightened my top.

I'd made this bed a long time ago with sheets of lies, pillows stuffed with denial, and covers stitched in pride. I'd made this bed, and I would lie in it. Alone.

2 6

JAR OF HEARTS

Alana

$\mathcal{T}$hom returned from the airport late in the afternoon, and I showed him the photograph of Liam and Frank that had cost me so much.

"No offense, but I don't know this Faye yet, and I'd prefer not to give her Liam's picture," he said as he took scissors to it.

He handed me the Frank half of the photograph, and I returned it to my purse. "Where's the dagger?"

"In my room." He avoided my eyes. He didn't want me to have it, yet. Did he fear I would cut him out of the plan? "So, what's next?" he asked.

"Faye told me to call her when we had everything."

He looked at me expectantly, so I dialed Faye's number.

She answered right away. "Hey, kid. What's up?"

"I have Frank's dagger and the picture." Impatience scorched my blood. After killing Frank, I'd explain everything to Liam and convince him to forgive me. "When can we summon him?"

"I'll explain everything tomorrow. I'll be at my apartment by the middle of the afternoon."

I gulped. "Tomorrow?"

"Yes. I need something I can't get to until tomorrow."

"I'll meet you there." My heart fluttered at the notion that soon we'd put an end to this fear-based life, at least in part. Frank was not the only menace out there, but he was the only one obsessed with bringing us pain.

After relaying the succinct conversation to Thom, I asked, "Want to go for a run?" I needed to purge the anxiety out of my system.

He smacked his lips and sized me up like he couldn't believe how normal I was acting. After all, I'd imploded on him yesterday with the weight of all my secrets. He seemed about to refuse, but he just chuckled and shook his head. "Sure. Why not?"

We jogged first to warm ourselves up and find a good stride. I let the wind soothe my heavy heart and concentrated on the rhythm of my running shoes hitting the asphalt. After a few minutes at full speed, Thom struggled to keep up, so I slowed down.

He fought to catch his breath. "You're fast. Faster than me."

I combed my hair back with my fingers. "Really? You're not just tired?"

"No. It's unbelievable." His eyes narrowed. "Care to explain?"

"I have no clue. Promise."

He grumbled something that sounded a lot like "fucking magic."

Liam had mentioned the other night that I was moving faster than usual. Was it another witchy power rearing its head?

I made a mental note to ask Faye if true born witches had any superior physical abilities, but I had an inkling the answer would be no. That potion had worn off a few hours after the demon hunt, so it couldn't be that, and the adrenaline from the attack couldn't still be in my system after a few days. This new development fell under the "weird unexplained shit like seeing auras" column. Speaking of seeing auras, I really had to ask Faye about it again.

In the elevator, Thom's brows created a perfect line as he checked his phone for the millionth time in an hour. "Liam refused all my offers to switch places with him. Any idea why?"

I wet my lips. "He caught me rummaging through his bags, and I couldn't explain why. He's furious."

The soles of my sneakers squeaked against the tile leading up to our room. Thom reached into his back pocket for the electronic key. "He doesn't get to judge anyone." The shroud darkening his features made his current feelings about his brother perfectly clear. "If we tell him what we're planning, we might as well tell Frank."

We walked into the suite. "You're right, but I feel like crap."

"It'll be fine."

I kicked my shoes off. "Thanks for coming with me. I needed the company."

"I almost didn't." He paused. "There's a lot going on, and frankly, my mind's still spinning."

"I'm sorry I sprung all this on you."

He grabbed both sides of my face, and his eyes bore deep into mine with a graveness that was uncharacteristic. "I can trust you, right?"

"Always." I was going to be 100% honest with him from now on. Lies ruined everything.

He stroked my arms and twined our fingers. I shrunk away when his eyes flickered to my lips.

Before I could say anything else, Liam erupted from Thom's room into the common area. He had Frank's dagger in his hand and dangled it for us to see.

His scorching stare zeroed in on our joined hands before settling on Thom. "Explain to me why you went home to get this. You told me you'd gone to the hospital because your leg still hurt. I thought honesty was all we owed each other."

Thom's fingers clenched around mine, and he didn't move an inch, like he wanted Liam to see. "You searched my room?"

"I knew Alana was lying her ass off. I wanted to believe you weren't in on it." The venom glazing my name was so thick it made my heart sprint.

Thom made a calming motion with his hand. "We can explain."

He really shouldn't have said *we*.

Liam's jaw tightened, knuckles flexing and extending. "It's pretty clear. The dagger and the damn picture. You want to summon him."

No, no, no. He couldn't figure it out. I shook my head in denial. "No, it's—"

Liam's index raised in my direction. "You. Not a word."

Thom stepped forward. "She went through your stuff. It's not the end of the world."

The darkness around Liam swelled. One corner of his mouth dropped while the other curved, forming a hollow smirk. "Oh, she was very dedicated in her search. Went to great lengths to get away with it, too."

I stepped towards the demon and threw my arms in the air. "If I'd wanted to get away with it, I would have left your room when you screamed at me to do so!"

He tucked his chin up and walked even closer. "Then why didn't you?"

"Right now, I can't remember!"

Liam's mouth opened and closed. A big frown appeared on his face, erasing the snide smile, and he said, "Summoning rituals require at least five." The lines around his eyes deepened. "New Orleans. You found a coven."

My pulse spiked. "I found someone willing to help us kill Frank."

Liam shook his head as though he couldn't wrap his mind around the depths of my foolishness. "At what price?"

"She's my aunt. She wants to help."

"Your aunt. Right. In a country of 325 million people, you happened to stumble upon your aunt. Get real, Alana. She's lying to you." He stepped forward, and so did I.

"She's not lying, and I didn't *stumble* upon her. I looked for her." I yelled, aware I'd lost all control over this conversation.

"You've known her for what? Five minutes? How can you be so naïve?"

"You just can't imagine that everyone isn't as cynical and self-serving as you. She's a good person. She's taught me a great deal about potions and spells. She even took me demon-hunting."

Liam's heated demeanor transformed into a brush-off iciness. "Wow. She taught you all that... I'm impressed." Liam turned to Thom. "And of course, this is no surprise to you." He studied the dagger in his hands like it fascinated him.

"We need it. Please give it back." I held my hand out.

Liam swatted it away. "It's always about what you want. Whatever Alana says in Alana-land. I'm done risking our skins for you."

Thom put himself between us. "Hey! You're not responsible for me. I agreed with her plan."

The demon waved dismissively. "You don't think straight when it comes to her."

"Oh, and you do?"

Perfect silence rose from the ashes of the testy question. Thom and Liam locked eyes in a staring contest, having a silent conversation I wasn't privy to.

A muscle twitched in Liam's jaw. "Are you doing this to get back at me?"

"No." The words sounded true, but Thom's gaze flew to the corner of the room and stayed there way too long for his answer not to register as a lie.

Liam's chest deflated. "Here." He bowed his head. "Keep the *damn thing*. It's all yours." He threw the dagger in a blur, and it dug into the wall next to my head with a sharp thump before Liam stormed out yet again.

The routine was getting old and exhausting. Both Thom and I stared at the door for a minute.

He rubbed the side of his nose. "I'm sorry he's such an ass."

"Don't apologize for him."

"I feel like I have to." His eyes were closed, his face ashen.

I cleared my throat. "Are you? Doing this to get back at him?" Had his leniency towards me only solidified his anger for his brother?

"No. I want Frank dead as much as you."

"Good." I nodded, relieved. "Then why did you make him think that?"

Thom shrugged. "Because he'll sulk over this fight instead of thinking about the ritual."

"Are you serious?"

"I know him. Sometimes, I think I know him better than he knows himself. He's never lashed out at anyone the way he does with you."

I snorted. "So what? I'm lucky?"

"I'm saying it means something." He shoved his hands into his hoodie's pockets and dragged his feet to his room.

THAT NIGHT, I had another nightmare.

A low voice called out from the shadows. Husky, seductive. Ancient. My bones chanted for me to obey that voice at all cost. I scurried out of bed and opened my window. It wasn't one I'd seen before, but the type of guillotine window that slid all the way up instead of opening to the side.

My angel waited on the other side, his chestnut curls flowing in the windy night. He bounced off the roof and into my dark room. His wings were nowhere to be found, but his upper body was covered in red tattoos. Feathers, I realized.

"I missed you, beautiful girl." He licked his lips, looking me up and down.

I brushed aside my hair so my neck was bare to him.

The bells of his voice rang as he chuckled. "So eager." He kissed my pulse point. His lips were like silk, his tongue hot on my cold skin, and I whimpered. He untied my robe and slipped it from my shoulders before sinking his teeth deep into my neck.

After quenching his thirst, he gave my ear a soft bite. "Tell me want you want."

"I want…" I nibbled his neck, and he laughed.

His razor-sharp nail traced a red line on his own neck, and my mouth watered. Pulsing in anticipation, I licked his offering, and the rush turned my legs to foam. He gathered me in his arm and kissed my lips. The taste of my blood on his tongue was totally erotic.

"You were waiting for me, weren't you?" His large hand traveled from my back to my side, and he grazed my nipple with his thumb.

My back arched in desire. "I ached for you, Master."

I looked down to my breast. Where Liam's snake had once been, there was only a red feather.

I GASPED as I woke up, fingers grasping at my neck for traces of blood. Finding none, I patted my body down to make sure I was wearing my pajamas. The haze lifted.

What. The. Hell. Am I losing my mind?

Sure, the vivid dreams scarcely came to pass, but this one won the prize for being the most fucked up. I would have preferred the cave/Liam sex dream a hundred times over this new, insidious presence. I did not want to lust after yet another creature of the night.

I yanked the curtains away from the windows, and the morning sunshine assaulted my retinas. I squinted and checked for the windows' opening mechanism, but there wasn't one. Comforted in the knowledge that my dream had not actually come to pass, I checked my phone.

It's already late. Eleven o'clock, and I had a busy day.

I packed everything I owned neatly, knowing our time in Mobile was coming to an end, and texted Rachel to invite her for lunch. If she didn't turn, it might be my last chance to chat with her. She refused, saying she had to go to the library, so I decided to meet her there.

I didn't cross paths with Thom, so I figured Liam had seen me coming and left.

Rachel was sitting in the back of the library, typing on her computer. She didn't look my way when I slumped into the chair in front of her.

"Hi," I said.

Her lips were tight. "I texted you a few times. You didn't answer."

I hadn't seen any of those texts because I'd thrown away my old phone, but I couldn't say that. "Had a rough week."

She didn't ask why.

I fumbled for an explanation that would appease her. "Had to go to court, for the restraining order thing."

Her manicured nails paused over the keyboard, and she spared me a glance. "Oh."

I didn't want to elaborate on that real/fake stalker story, so I swiftly changed the subject. "Can I copy your notes from stats?"

She nodded and pushed one of the notepads in my direction. I opened my own and started transcribing.

"What are you doing tomorrow?" I wondered what she had planned for her birthday. There had to be a party in the works. Rachel wouldn't let her twentieth birthday go unnoticed.

"It's my birthday tomorrow."

"Cool. Are you doing anything special?" If she had something planned, I would consider texting Liam to tell him.

A bright smile lighted her face. "Actually, I have a date. Mike's taking me out."

Well, I won the price for foolish endeavor. Liam had his night lined up like a pro.

She wet her lips. "I know you said he's not into relationships, but he's making a hell of an effort. He planned something special. It's a surprise."

A surprise. Yeah, right. Like "oh, surprise, you're a witch" or "oh, surprise, you'll never see me again."

She snickered. "I don't think we'll make it through dinner though. He's not a very patient lover."

The pencil broke on the line I was copying, and my fingers turned cold. "Ugh?"

"I expected him to be cocky and rough, but he's actually kind of sweet."

Salt, meet wound. I suspected Liam had gone back to Rachel the night I drank myself silly, but dreading something and hearing about it actually happening is not the same. I swallowed hard, jealousy and disgust competing for the honor of tearing up my heart.

It's not like he'd cheated on me, but how come my hands were shaking? I was suddenly very glad he'd found that picture. If we'd had sex yesterday...

Either Rachel interpreted my silence as interest, or she wanted to brag because she went on. "I swear the first time I thought he wasn't that much into it, but then he became really intense."

The *first* time? The implication of the word liquefied my brain.

"Yesterday, he all but abducted me from class, and we had sex in his car. It was a first for me."

Yesterday. Was she telling me he'd gone to her after we'd almost... Nausea chomped on my stomach and gave it a good shove. He'd gone to her for a quick fuck to get rid of his hard-on? What kind of man did that?

Rachel wrinkled her nose. "We spent the night together, and something weird happened. Last night, as he came, he called me Lana." I lost a heartbeat, and she added, "Give it to me straight. Is that his ex?"

"No."

"Who is she?"

"No clue." I fisted my notepad back inside my purse and let my hair fall around my face. "Excuse me. I forgot—I have to go."

"Nina, wait!"

I ran out as fast as humanly possible. I didn't care what she thought. I didn't care how confused she'd be or that she might figure things out from my reaction. The only thing I cared about was getting out of there.

She ran after me, but she was wearing heels, and I was fast.

Casual sex might not be my cup of tea, but this was nothing but casual. I knew her, and she still might turn. It was twisted and sick, and I couldn't stomach it.

Leaning against the brick exterior wall of the library, hidden from view by the stairs, I squeezed my eyes shut tight and broke out into a mighty fit of ugly crying.

I was in pieces. Angry tears, sad erratic breaths, and a disenchanted mind stacked on top of a sore heart. I hadn't followed through with any of my sensible resolutions. Who was to blame for that?

Fool me twice... shame on my pathetic ass.

I hugged my knees to lessen the bite of loneliness.

Why did his presence blur my ability to see things as they were instead of how I wished them to be? I couldn't reconcile this Liam with the one who had tended to my injured back or the one who had kissed me with such tenderness when he'd learned I hadn't slept with Thom, but my rose-colored glasses had to be destroyed once and for all. He wasn't harboring a secret love for me, but pure, blood-driven lust. Lust could be satiated in many ways, and Rachel was clearly less complicated than I was.

I had to get it through my head that he had nothing else to offer.

Stifling the sniffles with my sleeve, I texted Thom that I needed to meet Faye early and called a taxi. I rummaged through my bag for sunglasses and tousled my hair to hide the red patches on my face before heading for the curb.

FAYE'S snarky greeting caught in her throat when she opened the door to her apartment. I guess I didn't look so good. "What's wrong? Are you hurt?" Worried eyes screened me up and down for signs of an injury, and finding none, she squeezed my shoulders. "Alana, speak."

I hid my face in my hands, my resolve to act as though nothing happened evaporating. "He had sex with her."

"Oh boy." A gentle hand guided me inside, and she closed the door behind me.

"You were right. He doesn't give a damn about me."

I'd never explored the depths of my feelings for Liam. Never dared to.

Turns out they were pretty fucking deep.

2 7

HOW IT ENDS

Alana

Sitting in Faye's living room, I finally told her about Rachel
and what we were doing to save her from a destiny that
might not come knocking. I spared her no details about my lousy day
and admitted out loud that I had a serious crush on Liam. Caught in
the storm of emotions, I might even have used another word. They
say the first step to solving a problem is acknowledging there is one.
She listened even though the drama with Liam made her head
explode.

After tears, indignation, hugs, and ice cream, my blotchy face
returned to a somewhat normal state, and my eyes stopped burning.

"No more waterworks?" Faye teased as I threw the used tissues in
the trash.

My cheeks heated up. I was more than embarrassed by my melt-
down. I wanted Faye to think of me as a strong, independent woman,
but that ship had sailed somewhere between the "how could he" and
the "I'm such a fool." I cocked my head to the side. "I'm better. I have
the dagger in my purse."

"Let's see it."

She whistled loudly as I deposited the gold, wavy blade on the coffee table and leaned in to examine it. "That's not just a dagger; it's his personal, sacrificial knife." Her fingers ran over the hilt. "The cuts dealt to its owner do not heal supernaturally, though it's not quite enough to kill. Nice work, kid."

"Thom flew to Virginia to get it."

Her forehead creased. "How did you manage that?"

I picked on my cuticles, knowing she wouldn't approve. "I told him everything."

She dug her fingers into my arm. "You told Thomas Walker about me?"

"Thom." Thomas made him sound so serious and old. "And yes, I told him. It was time."

Faye pouted. "What about the weapon?"

I twirled a curl around my finger. "Don't be mad."

She rolled her eyes and groaned. "You're the weapon."

"Yes."

"I'd given it 5:1 odds."

"Really?" I thought she had no idea.

"You're pretty transparent, kid."

My voice raised in excitement. "But it'll work?"

"Well—don't be mad," she gave me a sheepish grin, "but we need help. I need four other witches to summon him."

When Liam had said we needed at least five, I'd hoped he was misinformed.

Faye gnawed on her thumb. "There's the other thing."

"What other thing?"

She loosely waved in the direction of my chest. "The demon marks have to go."

I narrowed my eyes. "I said no."

"Yeah, but I thought maybe by now you'd have realized it's no big deal."

I looked down at my breast. The sheer thought of Liam enraged me but getting rid of the tattoos was a big decision, and I didn't think I was in any shape to make such a decision. "It's complicated."

"Come on. You said it yourself: he doesn't care. It's a benign ritual, and I'll teach you how to protect yourself from possession."

Maybe it'd be best to get rid of them, but I still hated the idea.

"I could bring you to headquarters and show you everything."

Headquarters? She was making a great case.

"I—I don't know. I'll sleep on it, okay?"

"Okay, but if you're serious about being involved in this summoning thing—"

"I said I'll think about it."

She bounced to her feet. "I'm hungry. I'll order something. Do you like Chinese food?"

"Sure." My darkened thoughts knotted together. There didn't seem to be a way to both kill Frank and keep the tattoos.

Faye disappeared into the bathroom. When I heard the water running, I texted Thom to warn him I'd be spending the night here.

The delivery man arrived with the steaming fried rice, and we sat in the kitchen. My phone rang while we ate, but I muted it without answering. It was selfish and irrational, but I couldn't deal. I never wanted to go back to that hotel again. Whatever it was, it wasn't home. It wasn't safe.

Faye had a towel wrapped around her hair, and I noticed a dark shape at the base of her neck.

"You have a tattoo, too?"

She gave me a better view. "It's the coven brand."

"What does it do?"

"Nothing. It's a calling card for when I meet new witches, so they know they can trust me."

I swallowed a mouthful of chicken. "You don't know everyone that's in your coven?"

She chuckled like it was a ridiculous misconception. "Hardly."

"How come?"

"One more thing I could explain in detail if you agreed to come with me. You could do good with us, Laney."

I scratched my right brow. My innate curiosity begged for me to accept her terms while my cautious side poked my chest from the inside. "I thought helping randoms was my calling. I'm not so sure anymore."

"You should have told me about this Rachel. I could have helped you."

I scoffed. "You told me numerous times you didn't care about randoms."

"I vowed never to share our customs with outsiders, and my days are full, but I get why you do it. It's an insanely inefficient way to save lives, but your heart is in the right place." She stroked my hair as she spoke, and the ache inside my chest eased up. We'd met barely a month ago, but she was already family. And it wasn't about blood or genes. Everything about her resonated deep in my soul. We were kindred spirits.

I dipped my head and looked at her from beneath my lashes. "Do you like me because I make you think of her?"

A warm but sad smile stretched her lips. "Kid, I like you because you make me think of me."

"You?" I raised my eyebrows.

She shrugged. "I was young and idealistic, once."

"Hard to imagine. You being young, I mean."

She cracked up. "Get some rest, smarty pants. We have a big day tomorrow." She turned off the lights on her way to her room, and I laid on the couch under a large blanket.

In the dark, the heartache resurfaced. I tossed and turned for about an hour before giving up. Frustrated, I yanked the covers away and walked to the fridge. Warm milk was one childhood indulgence I'd never been able to curb.

A large truck pummeled through the street, it's lights casting shadows on the wall. I poured a full a glass and heated it up in the microwave. As I took a tentative sip, testing the temperature, I pivoted back to face the living room. The curtains on either side of the window blew in the wind, the breeze spiraling up my thighs, and my heart leaped.

This window had been closed a moment ago.

Liam loomed in the darkness, standing in the middle of the room, immobile and rigid, the darkness around him thick like he was merely an apparition. The glass shattered into pieces at my feet, and warm milk splashed on my legs.

No. I needed time to collect myself and melt all this pain into indifference.

His scowl dragged down my body. Frizzy hair, black camisole, black boy-shorts, naked legs. "You're not dead. Good. Why the fuck aren't you answering your phone?"

"I texted Thom."

"He was afraid you weren't the one texting."

Everything about him was the same, from his leather jacket to his unruly hair, including the gloomy curve of his mouth and the beckoning silver of his eyes, but he felt like a stranger.

I bit down hard on my bottom lip.

He'd been my roommate, my savior, my sparring partner, both in words and blows. Now, he was nothing but a guy I couldn't stand to look at.

"What happened to you?" His head tilted to the side.

Faye's bedroom door cracked open. She had her hand wrapped around a grenade, but as she threw it, Liam's curved dagger flew directly into the crystal and shattered it.

He shot her a dark glare. "Next time, I'll aim for your hand."

Faye puffed her chest. "How did you track her through my wards?"

While she spoke, Liam placed himself between Faye and I, like she was the one I needed protection from. Rage engulfed me, a snarl twisting my mouth. I marched forward and shoved his back with both hands. He stumbled in surprise and whipped his head around.

"Get out, Liam."

His hand wrapped around my shoulder. "You're coming with me."

My muscles tensed under his touch. "No."

Faye walked over to us and dug her nails into the arm that was holding me in place. "You heard her. She's staying."

Liam's attention returned to Faye, and he appraised her like he did every enemy. "So... you're that supposed aunt."

Faye's knuckles turned white, but she held his gaze. "And you're the devil scumbag who beats her."

Liam's defensive stance wavered like she'd sucker punched him in the stomach. I'd never seen such horror in his eyes.

My jaw clenched.

His thumb grazed my skin before he let go. "I want to speak with you alone. Then I'll go."

I crossed my arms. "Fine."

Faye shook her head. "I'm not leaving you with him for a second."

"Faye, please," I begged.

She cursed but returned to her room.

The corner of Liam's mouth twitched in satisfaction.

I didn't want to say a word, but all of the sudden I couldn't live through another second without yelling at him. The fury pumping in my veins was blinding, and I riddled his chest with punches. "I'll kill you, Liam Walker. You get on your high horse about lies and make me feel like a whore for kissing you, and it turns out you're full of shit."

"I never said you were—"

"You implied it, but I guess it takes one to know one." My fists balled at my sides.

He looked lost.

"You. Rachel. Leather seats. Ring a bell?" I cried out, masking my sadness with disdain and sarcasm.

"Alana, calm down."

I saw red, my voice bordering on shrill. "Don't tell me to fucking calm down. You're sleeping with her, you bastard, using her as your personal plaything even though she might turn. You disgust me."

"I'm not *sleeping* with Rachel. I'm—"

"Fucking her? Playing games?"

"I'm not playing games." He wanted me to listen, but I'd never listen to him again. He grabbed my arm to keep me from stomping away.

I gave him a good kick in the shins and punched his stomach as hard as I could. After a few strikes, he finally caught both my wrists and immobilized me.

"Don't touch me." He made my skin crawl and not in a good way.

He let me go.

I snickered. "And last night you slipped," I punctuated the word with air quotes. "—you slipped and called her Lana."

"Alana—"

"We both know you don't slip. It's one thing to fuck her, but don't fuck with me at the same time. You let me think—"

He grabbed my face and forced me to look at him. "ALANA! I did not see Rachel last night. I never called her anything. I was furious yesterday and drove for hours to calm down."

I fought against his hold. "I don't believe you."

The door to the bathroom opened. "He's telling the truth."

"No, he's not. If he's telling the truth, then Rachel's crazy or—"

Oh.

My.

God.

I dialed Rachel, my fingers shaking so hard I struggled to hold the phone to my ear.

Her voice sent my heart into a frenzy, "What do you want?" She asked. Venom dripped from every syllable.

"Rachel, where are you?"

"Home."

"You have to meet me at the coffee house. Now."

She clicked her tongue. "Listen girl, you have to start taking your meds."

My throat tightened. "What?"

"The jig is up. I know why you're really in Mobile. You need to let Mike help you."

I heard a voice behind her. A deep, masculine voice. "Yes *Nina*, you have to let me help you." The voice was Liam's, but the oily words were all Frank.

My eyes shot up to meet Liam's, and I mouthed, "Hurry."

Liam vanished in a blur.

My lids fluttered as I prepared to play the stalling game. "Frank."

"Lana."

Teeth gritting together, I whispered, "What do you want?"

"Right now, I have everything I need." He hung up.

"What just happened?" Faye asked.

My eyes fluttered shut. "It wasn't Liam with Rachel, it was Frank."

"Frank Hale is with this Rachel girl? Now?"

My whole body shook. "Yes. I've been so wrapped up in my anger I didn't even think—"

Faye grabbed her purse, probably packed full of grenades, and threw a pair of pants at me. I clawed them on, dug my feet into my sneakers, and ran after her down the stairs.

She followed my directions to the letter, but it took a good 15 minutes before Rachel's house came into view.

My mind was buzzing as we ran inside. When I reached the top of the stairs, Liam exited Rachel's room, his shoulders stiff and his face unreadable. He grabbed my waist. "Don't go in there."

"Let me go." I stumbled as he released me.

Rachel came into view. She was naked on her bed, and her open, lifeless eyes knocked the wind out of me. My hand flew out to my mouth to catch a silent scream.

Rose petals had been sprinkled over her body, and there was a folded piece of paper on her belly. Liam grabbed it before I could.

"Let me see."

His lips pressed together. "Don't bother with that."

I held my hand out. "Let me see."

> *Three blind mice, three blind mice,*
> *See how they run, see how they run,*
> *They all ran after the farmer's wife,*
> *Who cut off their tails with a carving knife,*
> *Did you ever see such a thing in your life,*
> *As three blind mice?*

"It was our job to protect her." Shock stilled my legs, and I held onto the foot of the bed for balance. "I should have known. If I'd connected the dots this afternoon..."

"Then he would have killed her this afternoon. Come on, let's go outside." He pulled me towards the door, but I violently shook him off. Where had Frank hurried off to? "We have to warn Thom."

"Thom is a male Walker of reproductive age. He's off limits. If Frank were to kill him, he'd declare war on the whole clan. We can't have kids, but the lineage needs to survive. As my brother, Thom is untouchable."

A nervous laughter grated my throat. "Because Frank loves to play by the rules."

"If Frank could mess with Thom, he wouldn't have bothered with her."

I swallowed hard.

Liam rubbed the back of his neck. "Go back to the witch's apartment and wait for us there. I'll call Thom and take care of this."

Take care of this? There was nothing left to take care of. "How?"

"I'll wait for her parents to come home, pick a fight, pack a bag, and make it seem as though she caught a bus to New York. We can bury her in Virginia."

I shook my head. "No."

Liam raised his hands to the ceiling. "No? We inserted ourselves into her life, and Frank has done hell knows what wearing my face. I don't want my picture on national television."

"How can you think of yourself in a moment like this? Rachel's dead, Liam."

"Really? I thought she was taking a nap."

The sarcasm cut, sharp as a knife. If he'd said something else, I might not have put oil to the fire. We'd had a shitty day, and I didn't imagine things could get worse. "You're heartless."

"I'm pragmatic. We can't all afford to throw a fit and expect others to take care of the mess. If we hadn't invaded her life—"

I shoved his chest again. "If you hadn't flirted with her so much, he would have left her alone." Somehow, this conversation had taken a drastic and wrongful turn. "You did this. You shouldn't be thinking about covering your tracks. You should be hunting Frank. Do you even want him dead? Because you're doing a very poor job."

"If you think it's so easy, then, by all means, do it!"

"Fine. I will!" Spinning around, I hooked my arm around Faye's and dragged her outside. Once Liam was out of earshot, I said, "I don't want to wait until tomorrow. If we do this, we do this now."

Faye was pale, and her lips cracked as she said, "Kid, if we do this now, you'll have to agree to the coven's terms—"

"Yes. It's fine." Killing Frank trumped all the rest. It wouldn't make anything right, but at least it would prevent him from killing again. Rachel didn't deserve to die on our watch, and I had to do something. Now. Before I talked myself out of it. Liam and I, we were responsible for this mess. An innocent life had been taken while we postured and fought over meaningless stuff. If nothing else, it proved how wrong we were together, and we certainly didn't deserve to get out of this unscathed.

I thought Faye would throw a parade, but she shot me an ambivalent smile.

BAD MOON RISING

Alana

Faye drove us down to the coven's headquarters, her foot heavy on the pedal. She chatted for half an hour with her assistant, Fiona, barking orders about the ritual and asking her to find Kathryn ASAP. I was baffled that Faye had an assistant.

My abdomen was banded so tightly that I wasn't sure I'd ever feel normal again. I was beyond tears, in a place where discouragement met resignation. We'd failed at the only important goal: saving an innocent girl. If we hadn't come to Mobile, she might have never turned and lived a long, happy life. Best intentions, hellish outcome.

All because death shadowed us everywhere, in the form of one goal-oriented, imaginative, and diabolical demon.

The ache inside my heart turned to fire and determination. I'd never felt such an unadulterated, unapologetic, and all-consuming need to take the offensive and kill.

When we got to Louisiana, Faye handed me a black scarf. "I need to blindfold you."

I tied it around my head, covering my eyes. Another half-hour passed. When the car stopped, sweat poured out from everywhere.

My head was swarming with butterflies, the remnants of dinner tickling my stomach. I blew air out through my mouth to calm down.

Faye removed the scarf and passed me a big sweatshirt before stepping out of the car. "Kathryn is waiting for us. I trust her. She's the only one I told about the demon marks, and it should stay that way. The others might not understand."

My irises adjusted painfully to the bright floodlight shining through the cavernous interior garage. There were at least 30 other cars parked along the concrete walls, but Faye's parking spot was right next to the elevator. "You don't trust your own friends?"

Faye's army-style boots clanked against the cement. "Most of them are not my friends. They're my coworkers. You don't realize the scale. We are the biggest and most organized coven in North America. All in all, we have 1,260 witches to look after."

"1,260?" I was shocked. I didn't know there were that many witches in the world.

Faye pushed the elevator button. "There are 40 different families with 33 different surnames." We entered the metal cage, and my eyes widened at the numbers depicted on the side. This building had 10 floors.

Faye swiped a card into a magnetic slot and pushed the button for the last floor. "The coven is divided in castes. Hierarchy is very important when you're dealing with so many people. Most members have never been to headquarters and never will. The lowest ranking caste, or level 1, are witches with no inherent power. They can cast easy spells and brew simple potions, but that's it. That's the bulk of our numbers. We are responsible for their well-being. They live normal lives, have normal jobs, and only communicate with us when they're in trouble or when their child is ready for initiation."

She wet her lips. "The level 2 witches have some sort of mild ability, like telepathy, and are eligible to work here or at one of our satellite offices. Taking calls, planning initiations, making sure the building runs smoothly.

"Level 3 is low management. They make sure everyone is doing their jobs. Level 4 is upper-management, and they make decisions on the day-to-day running of this place. They all have what it takes to be Level 5 but lack either common sense or social skills, or they prefer to live quieter lives."

The door dinged and spit us out into a white hallway, and we glided down trendy, laminate floors. We crossed sleek, glass offices furnished with desks, laptops, and top-of-the line phones. Nothing like I'd imagined a coven's headquarter would look like, though my vision was shaped by TV and movies. This was a well-oiled corporate machine.

Faye pointed to one of the doors. Faye Garret. Head of security. "Level 5 lives on the tenth floor. We're the active operatives. Spies, hunters, whoever has sanction to work in the field. We also have tactical teams dispersed all over the territory."

"Ophelia's the boss. She green-lights the operations, promotions, and mutations and oversees everything that goes on here. She also acts as force of law in every conflict. That's a lot for one person, so she keeps an entourage. We meet once a week or more depending on how many emergencies come up."

So much information. My brain was about to explode with the implications, the scale, the possibilities. "Wow."

"You could be one of us, after I catch you up on witchcraft and office politics. It'd take a couple years, but you have the potential. This is your rightful place." She nodded to herself. "We need to get rid of the marks first, but we have to hurry if we want to summon Frank while the moon's still up."

"Causing mayhem again, Fifi." A woman about Faye's age with long straight black hair accosted us at a fork in the corridors. Her smooth, ebony legs were showcased by her pencil skirt, her traits open and eyes beaming as she looked me up and down before turning to Faye. "You were right. She's a ringer for Jane." She extended her hand. "Nice to meet you. I'm Kathryn. I'm the closest thing Faye has to a best friend."

"Alana."

"Welcome. Things move fast here. Since we had to scrap the sched-ule, I had to make last minute arrangements. Follow me." She turned on her heels and headed to what I approximated to be the center of the building. "We have to hurry before someone else sees her." She showed us into a large room. A huge skylight pierced the darkness, the moonlight cooling the red pentagram painted on the floor.

They walked me over to the very back of the room away from the pentagram and next to a small circular pool. Kathryn pushed a button on the wall and another skylight opened above us. The surface of the water undulated under the silver rays.

Faye clicked open a secret pantry, and I glimpsed over her shoulder before she said, "Strip down."

I grimaced. "Everything? Can I keep my underwear?"

"Not if you don't want it melting into your skin."

I groaned.

Kathryn chuckled. "It's nothing we haven't seen before."

They prepared things while I peeled off my clothes. Once naked, I crossed my arm over my chest and bounced from foot to foot. The black tiles were cold against my bare feet. Goosebumps tickled my neck, and I shivered. Under the light of the moon, the tattoos on my breast and hand were phosphorescent, and I stroked the one aligned with my heart with trembling fingers. A shaky breath popped out of my lungs.

I'm doing the right thing.

I needed to explore my connection with these people with a clean slate. Maybe distance would do us all good. The path I'd chosen was clearly not working out.

Faye motioned for me to go down the steps heading to the water. I hesitated as the freakishly clear liquid licked my feet. It felt different from regular water. It was heavier, softer, like a velvet blanket grazing my skin, and the substance hugged my ankles in a way that defied gravity.

Faye shot me a soothing glance. "It's called the devil's water. It makes the ritual quick and painless. It's perfectly safe."

I let the warm substance envelop me up to my shoulders, shielding my body. "How does it work, exactly?"

"When I give you the signal, you'll take a deep breath and go underwater. Surrender to it and don't freak out whatever happens. You can't drown in devil's water," Faye explained.

I nodded.

She stood on one side while Kathryn went to the other. They held their palms up to the sky. The chant they sang was so quiet and yet beautiful that it took my breath away. Their voice joined into one, crystal clear pitch that got louder with each second.

Faye gave me a sharp nod.

I submerged. The liquid pushed its way inside my mouth, ears, and nostrils, but it didn't feel like drowning. My skin tingled, like a thousand tiny teeth were biting down on me at the same time, but the sensation was painless if a little unpleasant. A powerful pulse echoed through every single one of my cells, and my back arched of its own volition, arms spread on both sides. Everything turned black.

I GASPED AS I EMERGED.

Dark ink swirled around me and formed a thick, tar-like substance. I didn't know how much time had passed, but I was wiped out. My muscles were strained and my breathing ragged.

The devil's water stayed in the pool as I climbed out. My body— even my hair—was completely dry.

Faye smiled. "It's done. Congrats, kid."

My tongue strained against the roof of my mouth, dry as sand. Faye handed me a glass of water, which I hurriedly gulped down, moans of satisfaction scratching my throat. I grazed the breast where Liam's mark had once been, expecting for something to remain. A scar, a faded blotch of ink or anything that proved the snake had been there.

There was nothing. The skin was smooth and soft with no trace of the tattoo. My breath flirted with the edge of a sad sigh. I already missed it.

Then, I reminded myself why I couldn't belong to him anymore in any way, shape, or form. It was just skin anyway. With the marks, I'd never get to know my mother's world.

Faye gave me back my underwear and handed me a tailored, midnight-blue jumpsuit identical to the one she was now wearing. It had a plunging V-neck with satin lapels and an adjustable belt, very chic, and not at all the sort of uniform I expected. She zipped it up my back. "They'll probably whine that you're wearing this uniform, but your clothes smell of him, and this is the only thing we have here."

I fluffed my hair. "Now, we summon Frank?"

"Don't freak out, but when you passed out, we had to improvise. Kathryn ran interference, but she had to move ahead with the ritual without us. They summoned him while we were in here."

My jaw dropped, and I yelped, "What?"

She put an arm around my shoulders. "We have him. It's fine."

I staggered. "It worked?"

"Of course."

They had him. Frank was no longer running free, and it seemed too good to be true. "What now?"

"We have a bloodhound in the coven. She can tell exactly who you are with one drop of blood. She'll confirm your identity without any spell needed. They still won't trust you after, but you'll be untouchable. Any Garrett is welcomed in the coven. Your mother was almost high priestess, and I don't like to brag, but I'm the best demon hunter they got."

"I believe that." As long as Faye had my back, it would go well. Eyes closed and heart hammering inside my chest, I breathed through my nose.

Fay guided me through the large building again. "They'll argue a bit over what to do, but ultimately they'll put you in my care." She opened the door to a large conference room with about ten people on each side, mostly women.

Kathryn was nearest to us on the left, and Faye went to sit next to her. Everyone was wearing blue except the woman standing at the other end of the long table. The high priestess, I figured, was wearing white. She was in her forties with short blond hair and defined cheekbones. She exuded confidence and towered above the rest in black heels, all business-like. "Welcome, Alana." Her voice commanded attention and obedience, and I wondered if she'd been chosen because she was a born leader or if she'd learned as she went.

"Err—hi."

Most of them had curious but reserved expressions on their faces. A few were smiling. A couple were frowning. The one sitting on Ophelia's right glared like my presence repulsed her.

Ophelia put her hands on the table. "Welcome. We were distraught to learn of your ordeals. Be sure that, if we'd known you existed, you would have been protected from that beast. You'll be happy to learn he's in our custody."

The solemn atmosphere kept me tongue-tied, and the rows of strangers whispered to one another.

Ophelia shushed them. "We will do the initiation as is customary, but I don't think anyone here doubts her lineage."

The sullen woman on her right scowled but remained silent.

One of three men leaned forward and shot me a gut-wrenching look. "When Ophelia told me Jane had given birth to a child, I didn't believe it and campaigned against your presence here today. I'm deeply sorry. I feel in my bones that you are her daughter."

I bit my lips, unsure if he literally felt it by some power or if he just believed it now.

Ophelia put her hand on the shoulder of the oldest woman present. "Heidi, will you do the honors?"

Heidi bowed her head, and I mirrored her polite smile as she came up to me. She pricked her finger before she handed me the needle, encouraging me to do the same. Good thing I wasn't queasy about blood anymore.

Once red drops glistened on both our indexes, her hand rose to meet mine. I almost chuckled and whispered, "Phone Home." It was silly and awkward, especially with an audience of riveted viewers.

After the blood on the tip of our fingers mixed, she put the blood in her mouth to taste it. Her face changed, the lines around her mouth and eyes getting deeper, and she spat on the ground. Everyone's brows arched in surprise. They exchanged worried looks.

Heidi's knees shook. "She's Jane's daughter, but she is not one of us."

Everyone rose to their feet in a cacophony of gliding chairs. The only one who remained in her seat was Faye, her face white as a sheet.

"She is *Njóla-barn*."

What the hell did that mean?

They all froze and ogled me in disbelief, fear visible in their eyes. All except the mean-eyed woman by Ophelia's side. She smiled.

Faye looked shell-shocked.

I cleared my throat. "What?"

"Like you don't know, *bikkja*," Heidi hissed, and I didn't need a translator to know she'd called me a whore.

They started arguing among themselves loudly, the voices blurring together, and anxiousness scorched me from limb to limb.

"Faye, can you hear me?" I asked through thought-speech. I'd never tried this with anyone but Liam before.

"Yes." The simple acknowledgment was laced with misery.

"I don't understand what they're saying."

Tears glazed her eyes before she hid her face in her hands. *"They're saying you're an abomination."*

SAIL

Liam

$\mathcal{A}$rms braced on my knees, hands rubbing my face, I sit on the hood of my car.

My life is a farce considering how many hours I devoted to helping a girl that's now dead in my trunk. All that time to end up here, alone, with my brother mad at me and nothing to show for it besides a dull ache.

I'm fucking tired.

Everything I build breaks apart faster than I can say, *Whoops*. Alana's crazy plan to kill Frank might work, but I hate to rely on the honesty of strangers when my own team can't be straight with me.

Finding that picture in her back pocket left me empty. My fingers were inside her, for God's sake, and she was still lying to me. I left in a blaze of fury and regretted it every fucking second afterward. If we'd had sex, she would have realized Frank had seduced Rachel. If Rachel was alive, Alana wouldn't have blamed me for her death, and I wouldn't have dared her to hunt him down. If I'd stayed, she would be here, with me.

I lost her.

She didn't go back to the witch's apartment. She ran away, and now, I can't *feel* her. My demon senses say she's not anywhere, and that has *never* happened before, not since I marked her.

I'll find her. I *need* to find her.

Jesus, she shoved me away like I disgust her.

All I've ever done when it comes to her is walk the line. The line between what I should do and what I want. The line between the promises I made to myself and the desire rumbling in my veins. I'm done being reasonable. My demon has his own mind on what we should do with her, and I'm tempted to agree. The second we have her in our reach...

"Any change?" Thom treks from the hotel with his packed bags and checks his phone again.

I bounce to my feet. "Nothing."

He hesitates as he puts his stuff in the back. "Should we stay? In case she shows?"

"She won't come back here." I don't know how I know, but it's a certainty. "The witch's apartment, maybe, but not here."

"Let's go there. We can find out more about her aunt from the landlord and track her down."

I pause, hand on the car's handle. Maybe I've been going about this all wrong. Maybe I'm not supposed to find her. Maybe that's what she wants. "Should we?"

Junior casts me a dark glance over the roof. "What do you mean?"

"She left of her own free will."

His shoulders stiffen the way they do when we're about to fight. "So?"

"Maybe that's it." I thought the only solution to our problem was for me to leave, but maybe this is better.

He crosses his arms. "You want to give up?"

"Not *give up*. Thom, if this woman's saying the truth, maybe she's better off with her coven."

He sighs. I hit a nerve. "But she didn't say goodbye. They were supposed to summon Frank. What if they ran off to do that and something happened? We can leave once we've made sure she's okay."

I sense Frank before I see him, the way one senses a familiar tornado tapping on his shoulder. My dagger is in my hands in less than a second, and I motion for Thom to turn around.

Hands in his pockets, Frank prances up to us like we're buddies leaving on a road trip. "Your girlfriend's missing. Gosh."

Fear grips me at the thought that Frank took her again. Why else would he show his face? I need to find out where she is before I attack.

Frank greets Thom with a wave. "Hello Junior. Long time no see."

Thom shoots at Frank's head, but the bullet finds nothing but air. I slip my leather jacket from my shoulders knowing it won't be long before this turns to a brawl. "Where is she?" My voice is sharp and impatient, but I secretly shudder with the scenarios that come to mind. She got away last time because he was taken by surprise. Frank won't let that happen twice.

He ignores my question. "So... Lana's in the wind. Maybe she found a third bloke to satiate the needs that the two of you don't satisfy. Maybe smooching with both of you made her realize she needs a real man."

Thom's icy but knowing glare tells Frank he's too late on spilling the secret.

Frank snickers. "You already know. Well, phew. That would have been awkward. I thought of a solution for you, a schedule. You can get Lana Monday through Thursday and Liam gets her on the weekends. Or maybe you alternate weekends and do Monday-Tuesday against Wednesday-Thursday. Would every other day work best? Wow, it's complicated. You should cut to the chase, embrace your emotions, and go for a threesome. She'd love that."

"He's my brother, you sicko," Thom growls.

"So? You're both oiling your junk at the same pit stop."

Thom hisses and shoots again. He needs to keep some bullets for later. Frank's in glib-mode. If he speaks too much, we might learn where she is.

Franks motions to his crotch. "You're both fucking the same girl. Well, I'm not sure Liam closed the deal yet with all his newfound

275

ethics, but you certainly have and believe me it won't be long until she spreads her legs for him too. Tell me, Thom, is she worth the trouble? Would you say she's the best you ever had? Don't spare me the details."

My brother pauses for too long before saying, "Fuck off," confirming Alana's claim.

Sweat gathers on my palms. I'd believed it for a second in that room, but it was so improbable. So inconceivable. And yet...

Frank claps in rhythm with his vicious words. "Shut the front door. You haven't had sex in all these months? If I know Liam, and I think I do, that's all he needed to know. He'll swoop her up and never let you touch her again. Wow. I can't believe it. You two should talk more. Did you hear that Liam? All this guilt eating you alive over nothing." His voice becomes low and conspiratorial. "He hasn't fucked her yet." With a groan, he bites his lips. "Boy, it makes me want to be the first. Shall we make a bet? Whoever beds her first wins. She'll look so good with her red lips wrapped around my—"

He always prompts me to attack first, and it always seals my fate. I keep falling for it, over and over and over again. He manages to knock the blade from my hand, and I roll away from his grasp with a snarl. "Where is she? If you touched one hair on her—"

He tucks his chin up and throws the dagger out of play. "You'll kill me? I'm dying for you to try, brother."

Punches and kicks blur into one another. He's stronger, but barely. I'm faster, but by a hair. We've always been evenly matched.

Finally, I manage to punch his throat, and he staggers backwards. Thom shoots him in the chest. I use the diversion to knee his head, fling him to the ground, and tackle him in place. He writhes against my hold, unable to build enough kinetic energy to break free. Inertia is a bitch.

I press on his spine. "Where is she?"

He laughs, blood spurting out of his big mouth. "Wouldn't you like to know?"

I smile, then, because Frank is a lot of things, but he sucks at bluffing, which is why we seldom played poker. Grating his face against the asphalt, I say, "Shouldn't have gone all in, man."

He doesn't have her, which means I can kill him. Thom fumbles around in the trunk, probably looking for that demon-killing spear. Good thinking.

A sizzling energy builds inside my chest at the thought that the moment has finally come. Consequences be damned. The voices in my head swell in alert, warning me not to do this, whispering that I won't get away with breaking the rules again.

My tattoo heats up, and I frown as the sensation morphs from a small nick to a raging inferno. My vision blurs. The sight of Thom heading towards us melts into modern art. Blotches of colors are all I can see, and my skin starts itching like crazy. I shut my eyes and see a pool. It's filled with hot sand, white freckled skin, and torrents of red hair.

The quiet light of the moon burns bright. I clasp Frank tighter. "What are you doing?" I ask, my strength gone in an instant.

"It's not me," Frank gloats as he shoves me off.

My entire body is ablaze, and I can see again, but what I see worries the shit out of me. The runes branded beneath my dermis swirl to life and shimmer. Crashing on my back, I meet Thom's gaze and yell, "Stay back."

Frank kneels next to me. "She disowns you. What a bitch! After everything she put you through… Your precious Lana found a coven. She's in the big leagues now. Do you think she has any idea what it's going to do to you?"

My teeth clank together, the fire spreading to my chest. "I'll survive."

"The piece she'll carve out will make you vulnerable. Something nasty is bound to cram itself into the gash. Good luck digging yourself out of that sink hole."

When a red pentagram materializes beneath Frank's feet, it's almost enough to cast away the pain. "I'm—not—the only—one in trouble."

Frank's eyes go wide. "Well, shit."

"You're being summoned, Francis. And it's not our side making the call." I'd laugh if my flesh didn't hurt like someone's peeling my skin off.

"Oh, you've got to be fucking kid—" he disappears in a flash of light.

Thom drops the gun and the spear and takes a step closer. "What's going on?"

I try to stand but end up on my side. "Alana's exorcising me from her body."

"What? How?"

"The witches convinced her to do it."

Thom shakes his head. "Or they're forcing her."

Blood fills my mouth. "I don't think so."

"What can I do?"

"Nothing. You can't stop it. Listen." I scream in pain, and it takes me a minute to find my thoughts again. "It's going to fuck me up like nothing you've ever seen. Don't—"

He speaks, but I can't hear. My head is filled with sand. It itches. It burns. I try to shake it out, but it sticks.

It swallows everything.

And I feel it.

The void.

It throbs.

I hear its voice, clear and intense.

It sings.

Throbbing-robbing-popping. It's a fat lady dressed in pink with a falsetto that makes me want to tear my ears off.

It's dark and cold and violent.

It bites.

It tears.

It gnaws.

I am undone.

Until I'm not.

I think. I breathe. I have a will.

But who am I?

I have always shared a brain with demons but never wondered if I had one. Now, I wonder.

I had a name.

I have ears.

"Liam? Liam, can you hear me?"

That's it. Liam. It used to be my name, but now I'm not so sure. I am less than "Liam", but do I also have to surrender the name?

I have eyes. I see him. He's important.

I think of a word.

Brother.

Thom.

I have a tongue. "Thom."

"Thank God. You haven't spoken a word or moved an inch in an hour. I thought you we gone."

Gone.

Erased.

"Dead."

"What?" Thom asks.

I search for the right words. "You thought. Dead."

"Yeah. I was scared that you might die. I'm still scared. You don't look so hot."

A shiver swells the already potent nausea. "Cold."

Thom puts a brown thing over my shoulders. It itches and reminds me of the sand.

I have legs. I stand. "Why? Cold."

"The witches did this to you."

"Witches?" The word is familiar. It rhymes with hate and desire and tastes like blood.

I hear them. The demons. They're confused. They skedaddle around the darkness, scared of being swallowed. They fear it, but they're hopeful. They think it might work in their favor. They observe. They bide their time.

Thom helps keep me steady. "They exorcised a piece of your soul."

"Soul?"

"The one Alana had inside her."

This word is blinding.

It echoes.

It swallows all the other words.

I'm no longer gone.

I know my name. And Thom's.

I know all the words.

I remember everything.

But the memories aren't enough to stitch my seams together and make me what I was.

The hole slithers, hisses and swells.

I am broken.

I am empty.

I am void.

30

SMOTHER

Alana

"I believe you didn't know what you were before now, but we can't take any chances," Ophelia said as she and four other witches escorted me to what I could only describe as a tomb. Faye had been taken away by two men back in the conference room, and my mind was spinning.

We crossed an iron door clearly designed to short circuit any demonic powers and descended into the coven's prison. My eyes widened as we passed four animal-like creatures. Their bodies were gray and smooth like roman statues, their muzzles long with prominent teeth. Complete with horns, they looked like small devils and didn't move an inch, but their stony gaze followed me as I passed, so they were definitely alive, guarding the place.

The witches forced me into the cell directly across from the entrance and locked it up tight. The little squared space was barren but clean, the walls made of some fancy plastic. My questions and pleas went unanswered.

I passed my hands over my hot face, reining in the urge to scream. The ropes of my life were slipping through my hands one by one no matter how tight I clenched them. Nothing ever worked out. All my plans ended in disaster, the bite of one wrong call erased only by the burn of the next.

A ruffle of fabric on my left, coming from another cell, startled me. "Aren't you in a pickle."

I groaned as I recognized Frank's voice, and my eyes darted to the darkened cell across the way. My retinas were slowly adjusting to the obscurity, and I could almost see his form. At least they hadn't lied about summoning him. I wet my lips. "Said the kettle to the pot."

He shrugged. "They'll release me."

Disbelief cracked my voice. "Yeah, right."

"It's true. Prisoner exchange. Me for two witches we've held captive for a decade. I offered the deal the minute they had me, and they'll say yes." The confidence in his tone screeched through the dark prison.

No. They wouldn't. They *couldn't.*

All my witty comebacks got stuck in my throat.

Frank being Frank, he didn't care for silence. "Lana, have I told you how I admire your acting skills? I mean last time you totally got me with the tears and the 'is it over?' Bravo. I get his fascination with you, I really do. I wish I could get you out."

He'd talk, whatever I said or didn't say, so I figured I might as well get answers from him. I'd been curious for some time now about the mysterious Jonathan Hale. A man neither Thom or Liam had heard about. "Who's Jonathan Hale?"

Frank's face creased. "My uncle. Why?"

"I think he killed my mother." Faye was certainly convinced he had, and that was enough to consider him the prime suspect.

Frank smiled at the news. "Really? Nice." He paced his cage in excitement. "It's like we're meant to be enemies. You're no longer that girl that I tried to kill to piss off Liam, and I'm no longer your sort-of boyfriend's ex-best friend. We share history on our own." He wasn't mocking me. He looked genuinely thrilled to learn that.

"You're insane."

"Princess, crazies have more fun. All this right and wrong bullshit gets old. Even on my end, they expect me to obey all these rules and show up for work on time. I'm about to defect, too. Would be nice to get the same freedom Liam has enjoyed these last few years."

Frank had a job? "You work nine to five?"

"I wish. I work on *assignments*. Wherever and whenever they want me, I'm there."

I pursed my lips. "You're a hitman, you mean."

"Mostly, but they can really make me do whatever. I once had to babysit an actual baby for three weeks. Let that sink in."

"They?"

Frank clicked his tongue. "Liam never explained our hierarchy? Figures. We answer to a Council if you must know."

"And they sent you after us?"

"Are you insane? They love Liam over there. Could build him a fucking shrine. And they don't know shit about you." He paused before adding, his voice back to a slow, dirty drawl, "Nah... I used my vacation days to pursue you, Lana."

The big door creaked opened.

Faye. *Thank God.*

Her face was guarded like it had been when we'd first met. Her white knuckles clutched the bars of my cell. "Did you know that you were demon-born?"

Frank whistled. "The plot thickens."

I shot him a nasty glare and turned back to Faye.

She was losing patience. "Did you know?"

"No," I answered on a troubled breath.

A low growl rose between her teeth. "That's not the whole truth."

"I can see auras and nobody else is able to, so I figured something was wrong with me. I didn't know demon-born was a thing. Never heard of it. Never read about it." She had to understand I hadn't expected any of this to happen. Seeing auras worried me, but Liam had tasted my blood, and Adeline had done a spell to learn my identity and never had any of them hinted that I was *demon-born*. What did the word even mean? "Is my biological father a demon?" I asked, wide-eyed.

God, does it mean I'm not human?

Faye shook her head. "You would think, but that's impossible. Demons can't breed with witches."

"But Loki fathered the first Shadow Walker, at least according to legends and every damn reference I've ever read on them."

"Demons like Loki haven't walked the Earth in a millennium," she said like she was flabbergasted by my ignorance.

"Then what?"

She tugged on her hair, clearly overwhelmed. "I don't know. Demon-born witches aren't supposed to exist."

I grunted. If I'd learned one thing about the supernatural, it was that the rules were blurry at best. "Let me out." I thought I'd done a pretty good job at staying rational through all this, so the squeaky edge of my voice surprised me.

She bit her lips and averted her gaze. "I can't. I would, but they've got familiars out front because of him."

"Those devils out front? They're called familiars?"

"Yes, and they're pretty powerful." She hesitated, her thumb flying to her mouth before she added, "I'll do my best to convince them to keep you prisoner."

"Prisoner!?"

"It's the best-case scenario for now."

My heart skipped a beat. "Are you saying the alternative is…"

Tears glistened on her cheeks as she whispered, "They want to have a vote on whether or not to kill you."

"Faye." There was no hiding the panic clawing up my spine. I searched her eyes, but they wouldn't meet mine. She couldn't be serious. Was she saying she'd let them? Her slippery stare seemed to indicate so, and it knocked the wind out of me. "Faye, I had no idea."

"I—I'll figure something out. If it comes to it," she quieted down, "I'll stop them. I promise."

Frank hurried to his feet. "Stop them how?"

Faye ignored him completely.

I grimaced. "He says he's getting out."

She snarled, "He might. Believe me, I'm seething. It's not like they'll let the hostages live anyway. They've been gone for 11 years."

The fact that they would kill their own prisoners after release put my situation in perspective. Big time.

Faye sighed. "They never told me about them. I'm the damn head of security, and they never said a word about missing witches. They knew I'd want to save them…" Her body was shaking with barely contained rage.

"Call Liam. Please," I begged, thinking it was time to call for back-up.

Blood drained from Faye's cheeks.

Frank laughed. "Oh-oh. Someone hasn't realized the consequences of her decision."

My teeth gritted together. "He might not be my biggest fan, but I doubt he'll let me die."

Frank turned to Faye, smiling ear-to-ear. "Tell her. Tell her what you did." He sounded absolutely gleeful.

My throat tightened. "What is he talking about?"

"Your demon—"

"Liam," I corrected her.

"Liam." The name vexed her tongue. "He's not in a state to come and help you."

My pulse quickened. "You said the ritual was like ripping off a band-aid. *Benign* is the word you used."

Frank snickered. "Benign like being split down the middle."

My mind went blank. I'd gotten so comfortable with Faye the last few weeks, I'd forgotten that, even though I couldn't lie to her… "You lied to me?" My voice was quiet with betrayal. One I hadn't expected, and, frankly, one I kind of had coming. Liam's incessant warnings flooded back into my mind.

She paced around the room and waved her hand dismissively. "He's alive."

"Alive? What the hell does that mean?"

"The ritual left him incomplete."

"Incomplete how?" I was so done with mysterious magic terms.

Frank was more than happy to enlighten me. "When I left him, he was screaming in agony, cursing your name."

Kathryn put her head through the door. "Hurry. Everyone's back and ready to debate."

With one last, saddened glance, Faye marched out.

I pressed my nails hard inside my palms, wondering how true Frank's words were, and if Liam was really in danger and in pain out there, without me. I had to get out of here fast and help him. I had to make things right.

FRANK BABBLED AWAY HALF my sanity before long. "Imagine my surprise to learn you haven't done the naughty with Thom yet. I mean—his face was haunted. It's like he knew he'd missed his chance."

I bashed my head in rhythmic thuds against the wall at my back. "Do you ever tire of hearing yourself talk?"

"Never. So then I thought that maybe you're still a virgin, and that's why you're holding out on them. Are you?" The wolfish smile on his lips made me shudder.

I debated whether or not to answer, but I didn't want him to fantasize about taking my non-existent virginity. "No."

"Then why would you wait so long? Do you hate sex? Because that'd be a major bummer. I always imagined you'd be great in the sheets. Ravenous. Responsive."

"Are you fishing for references?" I barked.

He chuckled. "I love your temper. So, really, why'd you wait?"

"Does everything have to be about sex?"

"Everything that matters does."

I pursed my lips in disgust. "I'm sure you think so."

He missed a beat in the conversation. "I have a theory. I think you're holding on to the boring, traditional, and archaic notion of happily ever after. You always figured you'd meet a nice man, buy a house, have kids, and never deal with the base, ugly, and delicious reality of falling in love."

I combed my hair away from my face. "And you're one of these *love is pain* peeps."

"Love isn't brains. It's scary, and it's raw. You hold on to your childish ideals, and neither of my boys fit into the box. Thom fits best, but he doesn't make your blood boil, and deep down you're terrified to choose wrong. Liam's too volatile, and he can't contemplate the idea of being happy. I appreciate the dilemma, but you got it all wrong."

I didn't ask, "how so?" because I didn't have to.

Frank continued, "There is no forever. There is only here and now. And now, you're spending the night with *me*."

He was right. My choices had led me to this moment. "Do you have a therapist fetish or what?"

"If this helps you at all with your decision, Liam asked me that exact same question once."

I huffed. "He did not."

"Did too."

I saw it then, the similarities between them. Frank always ranted about how Liam and he were *the same*, but until now, it'd been easy to forget they'd been best friends for years.

I traced a random pattern on the wall next to me. "How was he when you met him?"

"Shocked. Scared." His lips curled into a smile. "A lot like earlier when he realized you'd betrayed him."

"I did not—" Why bother? I shouldn't have asked at all, but once again my damn curiosity had gotten the best of me.

A few minutes passed in silence, and I peeked his way. He was standing, his hands braced over the horizontal bars that ran every few feet, his back arched forward, staring at the floor. Not the devil-may-care I'm-sure-I'm-getting-out attitude.

His silver eyes rose to mine. "I'm pumped that he's suffering, obviously, but what will be left of him in a few months? If he forgets me before I kill him, I'll be pissed. And I'm not sure what I'll do after he dies. You'll try to fix him, of course, if you survive. I'm sure these witches have a spell or two up their sleeves that might reverse the damage. But at what cost? And how much of him will be left if you succeed? One thing's for sure: forgiveness isn't in his DNA."

I squeezed my eyes shut at his honesty before the sound of the main door opening forced me to my feet. The woman who'd looked at me with murder in her eyes back in the conference room stood in front of me. The same one who'd smiled at my demise.

"Who are you?" I asked, puffing out my chest like Faye would have.

She ignored my question and wet her lips. "You've been tried and sentenced, and you'll be killed at sunrise. I'm here for your last confession."

I wrapped the fear shooting up my spine with a healthy dose of sarcasm. "You held a trial in half an hour and without asking any questions? The standard of proof is as high as a middle-age witch-hunt here."

Her smile melted into a sneer. "You have no respect for our ways."

"Absolutely zero. Killing me after a farce of a trial is not justice; it's a lynching."

"You are guilty, which makes it just."

"Guilty of what?"

She spat on the ground. "You are a child of darkness."

"So, my crime was to be born? Forget lynching. It's genocide."

She raised her chin, fury deforming her traits. "You're a traitor, and you'll hang. Like mother, like daughter."

I frowned. "My mother wasn't demon-born."

"No, but she was every bit as much a whore."

The ramifications of her claim sizzled inside my brain. My mother was a traitor? I'd never asked about Jane Garrett's murder, steering away from details that were sure to haunt me, but now it seemed like a huge oversight.

"What about me?" Frank asks.

"You got lucky, demon. You in exchange for them. Nothing else. Tell your people the switch will happen tomorrow at dusk at a place of our choosing." She turned on her heels and glided out of the prison.

The tension in Frank's shoulders evaporated, and he flashed me a wicked smile. "Don't you just love supernatural politics?"

HERO

Alana

"They wouldn't let me see you again, but Kathryn distracted the guards. They sentenced you to die. I'm trying to push the execution to a later date, but they won't listen. There's a weird undercurrent of urgency, like you're a bomb about to explode," Faye explained when she returned a few minutes after the horrible woman had left.

"I am about to explode. Faye, a witch came to see me. She said I deserved to die like my mother," I said.

Her head whipped back a few inches. "What?"

"I think my mother was killed by the coven."

Her head shook from side to side. "Impossible."

I wet my lips, trying to recall the exact words. "She said, 'you're a traitor, and you'll hang. Like mother, like daughter.'"

Faye gnawed on her thumb. "Who? What did she look like?"

"Brown hair. Tall. Tan. Oh, and she had a weird ring."

"A demon snare," Frank clarified.

"That's Kim, Ophelia's sister." Faye's face lost all color, and she leaned against the bars for support. "Kim said Janey was hanged for treason?"

I nodded emphatically. "Yes."

"But that's impossible." The more she repeated the word *impossible*, the more it seemed to lose its power. "They wouldn't have... they couldn't have." Her lips were white, and her fists clenched.

She paced the corridor between the cells back and forth, back and forth.

"What are you thinking?" I asked.

"Give me a minute." Finally, she dug her heels into the ground and met my gaze. "I'll be back. I'm getting answers whether they're inclined to give them or not."

She didn't have to go far because this Kim woman thundered into the prison as if on cue. "You can't be here, Faye. I strictly forbade it."

Faye smirked. "I outrank you."

"Not for long, and not on this. Come with me now, or I'll be forced to call the guards in."

Before Kim could say anything else, Faye had her in a rear choke-hold, a knife flirting against the neck of the smug witch.

Kim's eyes were big. "You'll hang for this, Faye."

"You mean like my sister?" Faye's eyes were dark, darker than I'd ever seen them.

Kim bit her lips.

Faye's blade drew blood as her arms tensed around Kim's neck. "How come I never knew?"

"You Garrets think you're so special. You always break the rules. Your sister betrayed the clan, and for that, she died."

"No one in this coven can be sentenced to die without the accord of the high priestess. That's a sacred rule."

"Rina was soft for your sister. Something had to be done."

"And it's a coincidence that your sister happened to take Jane's place? Who else knew? Adeline? Kathryn? Margot?"

"They all knew," Kim whispered with a gratified smile.

Faye's ashen skin became green. "You're lying."

"They didn't know then, but they know now. All but Kathryn.

After Rina died, Ophelia held a trial, and the sentence was confirmed as good."

"Even Adeline?"

Kim snickered. "Adeline was the one who insisted not to tell you. You were 16 and angry. She was afraid you'd do something stupid."

"Now, I'm 32 and pissed, and I *will* do something stupid." Faye got a vial from her jacket and poured it over the bloody line on Kim's neck. Her body slumped to the floor.

Frank sighed loudly. "Too bad, I liked the idea that we were part of this big family feud." He peeled himself off the floor and walked as close to Faye as he could. "I can break her out of here, but I want the thing they refused to give me as part of the deal for my release."

I expected Faye to shut him down, but she turned her head and listened. She really had no good plan up her sleeve if she was willing to entertain the idea of teaming up with Frank. "How am I supposed to get to that?"

"What is he talking about?" I asked.

He waved dismissively. "A witchy trinket I've wanted for years." His eyes were solely focused on Faye. "I save her. You give me what I want. No muss, no fuss."

"Okay," Faye said through tight lips.

Frank smiled. "I'll need proof of payment before we leave."

"I'm not sure I can get to it now."

He shrugged. "That's really not my problem."

Faye hurried out and returned shortly. She showed Frank a small, black vial. The twisted joy on his face made me flinch. Whatever that vial was, it was probably meant to bring someone eternal pain.

Faye paused as she was about to unlock my cell and turned back to face Frank. "I have an additional demand. You can't kill any witches on your way out."

His jaw clenched. "That wasn't part of the deal."

She dangled the vial in front of him. "You want this. I'm not stupid. If Alana says you killed even one witch, I'll break it before you can lay hands on it."

Faye opened my cell and passed me a knife.

"You're positive there is no other way?" I asked, not naïve enough to think Frank would keep his word.

"I hate this more than you do, believe me. Give me 10 minutes to clear out of here. Head north until you cross Lapalco Boulevard then follow it to the north-west. I'll be waiting on the right side of the road half a mile before it meets the US-90."

We hugged. "Good luck," she whispered, affection and pain mingling on her breath.

"You, too."

She gave me Frank's electronic cell key and left. I played with the blade, piercing the tip of my finger discreetly. I didn't want Frank to know about my trigger, but I'd make him go boom if needed.

Exchanging quips when we were separated by two sets of solid iron bars was one thing. Setting him free was another. It cost me every ounce of self-preservation I possessed to slide the key into the slot. A loud beep resonated about the room as his cell opened.

Frank pranced over to me in full Liam glamor, and a boulder of sorrow splattered my heart. I pinched the bridge of my nose. "This trick of yours is getting old. Besides, I can see through it."

He leaned closer. "But you're choosing not to. Isn't that interesting?" The low timbre of Liam's voice made me shiver.

How did he know that? The glamor calmed me. Teaming up with Frank repulsed me, but it was easier to go through with this horrible half-hatched plan without having to see his face.

Frank snaked Liam's body around mine, picking me up in his arms. I put both hands on his chest and pushed with all my might, but he just chuckled and angled my chin to him.

"You know, if we made out now, it would only even the score," he said, his voice thick with lust.

I gave him a blank stare, my body screaming for me to get away.

He pressed me closer. "Come on. Aren't you curious about what happened between Liam and Rachel?"

"No." My chest tightened, the wound fresh, gushing with guilt. I didn't take the bait and ask why he'd said that. He was trying to mess with my head.

Liam's form melted into Rachel's. The sight of her blue eyes full of life was absolute torture, but I was too shaken to see beyond the illusion.

Faux-Rachel cocked her hip to the side. "I always suspected you were into him. That's why I asked if you were actually cousins. You were supposed to be my friend, but you bolted like a bat out of hell once I told you. If you'd stayed, I'd still be alive."

I pressed my palm to the illusion's neck. "Don't remind me why you should die. I can kill you remember?"

Frank reappeared. "You wouldn't. You want to live far more badly than you want me to die. I understand, and Liam will, too. We both are far too selfish to give our lives to kill one another, and yet, we spend 99% of our time fantasizing about doing so."

"Why do you hate him so much? Did he kill your girlfriend, your dog, what?"

"Ah!"

"You love to blabber about him. We have seven minutes. I'm listening."

He licked his lips. "In seven minutes, we can do loads. Kiss me, and I'll tell you."

"I'll pass."

"Come on. Rachel couldn't tell the difference."

"I can."

He kissed me anyway, but I fought hard to break free.

"Oh," he raised his index finger to his ear. "Liam says hi." Frank sobered up. "There's one thing I don't get. If he was so infuriated by your lies, why didn't he get answers?"

"He tried."

A loud snicker made my shoulders hitch. "There is no trying. Yoda said it best, baby. He could have gotten the truth out of you on day one. Those marks of his weren't harmless. Why would someone like me bother if it didn't involve some perks? He could have gone inside your head and forced it out of you."

"He wouldn't do that. He's not like you."

Frank's deviant smile widened. "Or you."

And then it hit me. I HAD raped Liam's mind. Maybe the first few times had been accidental but not anymore.

"He could have known everything weeks ago, and you wouldn't be here with me," Frank said mockingly. "Now, I think that's enough chit-chat. I need every ounce of power you have. You remember the drill?"

I groaned and motioned to Kim's body. "Why can't you use her blood instead?"

"I could. I'd need to drain it from her body first and inject it into my bloodstream. It'd take time, and I wouldn't be half as powerful," he explained.

I froze. "I don't understand."

"Cutting yourself without being forced makes this more than feeding. It makes it a spell. You surrendering your essence and power is different than me taking it against your will."

"I thought consent was rhetorical?" I grimaced as I fed him the line he'd once fed me.

He chuckled. "That was sex. This is magic. With magic, consent is everything."

I sliced my palm open and passed him the knife.

Frank bounced up and down like a kid on Christmas, his eyes aglow.

The second our cuts touched, my knees buckled. My strength rushed out of me and poured into him. I hadn't understood how it worked the first time. I'd thought the adrenaline and fear had washed me out, but it was really Liam taking everything I had.

Frank clapped his hands together and leapt into the air in excitement. "Yeah! Let's do this!"

THE FIGHT to the outside was a blur. Frank made good on his promise not to kill any witches, at least not on purpose. He did break some arms and legs, though, and one probably had a bad concussion. He simply tore through the beasts guarding the door. Still, I felt he'd upheld his end of the bargain.

For now.

Before we left the premises, he wrapped my hands in a torn piece of fabric from one of the witch's jumpers and tied my wrists behind my back. "You might not have enough juice left to make me go boom, but I'm not willing to take the chance," he said into my ear before picking me up again.

I'd been thinking about killing him the second I was out of danger.

He ran through the woods with me slung over his shoulder.

"How come you're not all black-eyed and dying to eat me whole?" I asked, surprised to see him unaffected by the amount of power he'd stolen from me.

"Do you drink?" he asked.

"Yes."

"Are you an alcoholic?"

"No."

"Same for me. I can hold my liquor. Though if you were a bottle, you'd be a pretty great one," he said, his nails sinking in my ass for a moment. His simple answer shed a different light on what I always assumed was a species-wide addiction to witch blood.

My heart panged.

The woods cleared, and we followed Faye's instructions until her car came into view.

She was about 30 feet away when Frank arms wrapped around my neck. "Show me the flask, and hold both your hands up."

My hopes of her throwing a grenade at Frank died in my chest. Faye shot me a questioning glance, and I nodded, confirming Frank hadn't killed anyone.

He deposited me on my feet and swatted a piece of flesh away from my clothes. "Here. As per our agreement. One witch, good as new. You, start walking, and you," he motioned to Faye, "throw me the flask."

Faye threw it as far as she could, and I ran next to her. Frank squealed when he caught it in his hands.

A grenade followed the mysterious artifact pretty quickly, but Frank was too fast to fall for that.

I was stumped when he started walking away. "You're really going to leave us alone?"

He nodded and faced us, walking backwards. "I don't need you anymore. I have this." He pocketed his treasure.

"What is it?" I asked.

Frank's lips were deformed by his most vicious smile yet. The wicked glint in his eyes burst with pride. "They cut him out of you. They had to put him somewhere."

Liquid ice poured through my veins, slithered into my stomach, my heart, my brain. "No." I lurched forward on weak legs, but for each breathless step, Frank moved back two-fold. Faye yelled for me to stop, but I ignored her.

"Yes! You get to live, and I walk away with something I've only ever dreamed of possessing. A piece of Liam's soul."

"Give it back. I'll do whatever you want."

He raised an interested brow, undressing me with his eyes.

I shuddered in disgust but held his leer. "Yes, even that."

"I'm tempted, but this is the holy grail. I'm keeping it."

He curtsied like he was the star of the theater. "It's been a pleasure to work with you both. Let's do it again sometime."

As his silhouette disappeared into the night, I fell to my knees and roared.

God, Lana. What the fuck have you done?

The sunrise had never held less peace.

We drove straight north to lose the coven's agents that were bound to search for us.

I was both pissed and incredibly grateful I'd survived the night. "I'm calling Thom," I announced.

Faye groaned. "Laney, forget them."

I sank my nails into her arm. "Let's get one thing crystal clear. If you're not willing to help me undo whatever we did to Liam, we should go our separate ways now." I meant every word.

She huffed. "Don't be ridiculous. You're stuck with me now, kid."

"Then it's not a request. Give me your phone and start heading east soon."

"East? What's east?"

"Virginia."

She arched a curious brow. "And what's in Virginia?"

My throat pulsed. "Home."

WATCHING AS I FALL

Alana

*W*hen we pulled up in front of the Walker's mansion, my legs were so jittery I had to hold them down. Liam's Vanquish was parked out front, and my heart leaped. I had to see him. I had to see how bad he was so I could start thinking of a solution.

Faye had explained during the drive that he would not be the same as before though she did not know exactly how. "Less coherent and unstable," she'd said.

I knocked even though I didn't have to. I still had a key.

Thom looked 10 years older as he yanked open the door. "Oh. It's you." He crossed his arms over his chest, his broad frame guarding the door to his home.

"Where is he? Is he okay?"

His jaw tensed, and his eyes jeered to the side. "Liam's not here."

Shock paralyzed me. "You let him leave? He's not well."

"No kidding." The biting sarcasm dripping from his mouth was like a slap in the face. "And I did not *let* him do anything. After he writhed for hours in the passenger's seat, he managed to form one coherent thought. He said that he wanted to cut the sniveling bitch in half. I'm pretty sure he meant you, and he was *not* kidding. He jumped out of the car a few miles back, and by the time I stopped, he was gone."

"Where do you think he went?" I asked, trying hard not to cry.

"Let's hope for your sake that he didn't stick around these woods."

I tugged on my hair and groaned. "I wanted to kill Frank."

"How did that go?"

My chest deflated, and I wished the earth would swallow me whole. "I know. I fucked up."

His eyes brimmed with disappointment. "That's all everyone seems to say. You said she'd help you find Frank. You used me to get what you wanted, then turned around and stabbed us in the back."

"She didn't know," Faye said in my defense.

Thom pointed his index finger at her. "You stay out of this."

"I didn't lie, Thom. I genuinely thought—I never meant to—" I didn't know what else to say. I'd make a huge mistake.

He grabbed the bridge of his nose. "You can come in, but not her." He stood sideways to allow me inside.

I hiccupped. "Are you kidding?"

"You're right." His hand disappeared at his back for a second before he pointed a gun at Faye and motioned for her to step inside. "I'll put her in the basement until she reverses the spell."

Faye smacked her lips. "It's not possible."

Thom raised his gun to her head. The vindication in his eyes left me no doubt he'd pull the trigger. "Better rethink your answer."

"Not without the part of the soul we cut out," she clarified.

He lowered his gun. "My brother has already been through hell more times than I can count. You'll fix him if that's the last thing you do. Where is it?"

"In a flask, but we don't have it." I hid my face in my hands. "Frank stole it."

Thom shook his head in disbelief, passed a hand over his face, and punched the wall. "Fucking hell."

AUTHOR'S NOTE

Curious to know how Liam and Frank met? The free short-story prequel Lost Boys is available through my newsletter.

Click here: http://bit.ly/anyaslair

Okay... that cliffhanger was rough, but there was nowhere else to end this book. The next one is the last in the trilogy, though spin-offs are in the works. Sneak Peek below.

Buy here: *http://bit.ly/readcursedsouls*

Did you know that reviews really help authors to promote their books? Please take the time to review on the Amazon page.

Xoxo, Anya.

Facebook: https://www.facebook.com/AnyaJCosgrove/